A PART OF YOU

A NOVEL BY
LYNDEN M. RENWICK

First paperback edition, November 2018

Cover design, editing and interior by Ebook Launch

ISBN 978-1-7326899-0-9 (paperback)
ISBN 978-1-7326899-1-6 (ebook)

Self-Published by Lynden M. Renwick

This novel is dedicated to the woman who taught me to love, and who gave my heart the means to write this story.

To my wife, Katrina, for giving me the right words.

PART ONE

CHAPTER 1

DIAGNOSIS

Ashleigh clenched her husband's hand tightly as they waited for the news. After weeks of repeated visits to different doctors, of tests, probing, and more tests, the results were in. Dr. Schwartz sighed as he removed his glasses, and with a pained expression, looked at the couple seated in front of him.

"Infertile." The doctor's words fell brutally flat against the walls of his office.

Ashleigh released Desmond's hand and burst into tears, pressing her head into her husband's chest for comfort. It was the news they had quietly feared for weeks. Desmond put his arm around his wife, and pulled her tightly toward him to comfort her. Her sobs shook his body. For a time, the only sounds in the room were of the traffic passing outside the nearby window, and Ashleigh's muffled sobs.

"Perhaps you'd like a moment alone to adjust to the news?" Dr. Schwartz asked as he half-rose from his chair.

"How could I be infertile?" Ashleigh barked at the doctor. She leaned away from Desmond's chest with bloodshot eyes. "Just a few weeks ago, you told me I had a high egg count!"

The doctor fell heavily back into his chair and put his glasses back on. He began going into technical details about his diagnosis. He rotated one of the computer monitors on his desk so Ashleigh could see, and used his pen to point at the diagrams and test results displayed on the screen. He detailed something about Ashleigh's uterus being unable to carry a child to full term, or even through a single trimester—something about the walls lacking stability.

Desmond didn't hear the details. His mind was blank as he tried to adjust to the diagnosis. His eyes glazed over as he glanced around the room. The drawn blinds let only a few strands of sunlight pass between them, leaving them all in modest darkness. The room itself was void of any real personality or taste—a well-maintained potted plant sat in the corner, dual computer monitors rested on the large wooden desk, and the doctor's credentials were duly framed and hung upon the wall. He wondered why there were no pictures of the family, as he knew the doctor was married, and had children.

Fitting, Desmond thought to himself, *that we receive news about infertility in a room so... sterile.* He looked at his wife, now barely seated to his right. She was half-raised out of her seat, pointing at the computer screen and asking more questions. Her left hand clenched the arm of her chair, her tight fist whitening the skin over her knuckles. His gaze rose to examine Ashleigh's profile. There was something hard in her face—defiant. It seemed she was trying to argue with the doctor, as if asking the right question would change his diagnosis. She rose farther out of her chair and became more animated, her knuckles whitening even more. She was desperate for a child.

Desmond examined his right hand. It was still a little stiff from Ashleigh's grip in the moments before they'd received the diagnosis. As the passing of clouds outside the window cut the thin streams of light being cast into the room, Desmond's mind wandered. Although the news received from the doctor was bad, at least it brought certainty. The mystery surrounding their inability to conceive had been solved. He and Ashleigh had decided a few years ago to start trying for a baby. He was in his mid-thirties then, and the couple didn't want to put off their first child too much longer.

Ashleigh was younger than Desmond—not so young that strangers would stare or comment, but enough that they'd notice when the two walked together. He remembered the youthful flame that trying for a baby had reignited in their bedroom. Having unprotected sex was something new for both of them, and it immediately brought playfulness and laughter into what had been a slowly declining sex life.

However, as months passed without a positive reading on the many pregnancy tests that followed, that playfulness subsided. Before long, the playfulness was replaced with strict scheduling. Ashleigh had set up calendars and alarms to remind her when she was ovulating. The sex became something cold and clinical, devoid of any real emotion. As months passed without result, the laughter also left the bedroom; despair took its place.

Ashleigh became increasingly frustrated with every negative pregnancy test. Desmond recalled the day he was sitting at home in his study, and had heard a crash from the bathroom. He had risen quickly and run to Ashleigh, calling after her to see if she was okay. She had opened the bathroom door in front of him and, with a tear-streaked face, confessed that she'd punched the bathroom mirror in frustration. Blood trickled from a cut in her hand, covering the indicator she held from yet another negative pregnancy test. It was then that he suggested that they both consult their doctors to see if anything was wrong.

A year had passed since then. It had been the most testing year of their marriage. Now in his late-thirties, Desmond's dark-brown hair was showing streaks of gray at its edges, and his blue eyes showed deep smile lines around them. In another year, Ashleigh would turn thirty. As that day loomed closer, she became more determined than ever to get pregnant. She had expedited tests and doctor visits by every means tenable, including hounding doctors and their receptionists on the phone until they advanced their appointment, or agreed to see the couple outside of normal operating hours. At home, Ashleigh had become obsessed. Her time was consumed by the countless books and articles she read as she searched desperately for tips on how to increase their chances of conceiving. She devoured literature on every topic, from fertility boosting to sexual positions most likely to result in conception. Desmond drew the line when she surprised him at work for a "quick tryst" when she was ovulating. She had made him sleep in their guest room for almost a week as punishment for declining her too frequent advances.

Desmond's mind snapped back to the present. He looked again at his wife. She was now leaning forward, both arms outstretched on the doctor's desk, as if pleading for a different diagnosis. He noticed the white scars left from the broken mirror on her outstretched right hand.

"What are our options?" Desmond broke into the conversation between the doctor and his wife. They'd begun talking in circles.

"Well," began the doctor, "not much more than the traditional options available for...infertile couples." Ashleigh tensed at the mention of the diagnosis. Desmond took her hand in his once more. "You could adopt," the doctor continued stoically. "There are always plenty of children awaiting adoption, but the evaluation process can take some time and can be rather invasive."

Dr. Schwartz, who had always been rather patient with them, was beginning to sound rehearsed, as though he was going through the motions after having been asked this same question time and again. "Desmond," he continued in the same flat tone, "your sperm are fine, so you could use a surrogate. However, to my knowledge, there is not a single medical practice in the country engaging in the procedure at present. You may be aware that there is a notorious wrongful birth lawsuit going on against an IVF clinic by a former patient. The litigation has scared most practitioners and insurers out of the practice for fear of attracting further liability—including me."

Desmond broke eye contact with the doctor and fidgeted with his lip. He knew the case the doctor was referring to. A mother was suing her doctors for implanting several fertilized eggs during an artificial insemination procedure, which had resulted in multiple births. Implanting several fertilized eggs was normal practice, with the hope of ensuring that at least one egg would survive the costly procedure. However, after giving birth to quadruplets, this mother alleged that the doctors simply implanted "too many" eggs. Although the case was still being litigated, it was expected that if this woman won her case, hundreds of former IVF and surrogate mothers would also sue their doctors.

Ashleigh cursed this woman under her breath, the curse attracting a look from the doctor.

"The costs and risks aside," Doctor Schwartz continued, a note of contempt now in his voice, "there are no guarantees of conception."

Ashleigh cut in. "What about fertility boosting? Natural remedies? Homeopathy? Naturopathy? Surgery for the uterine walls? Anything?" She was near the point of shouting, and the doctor moved back in his chair reflexively.

"I'm afraid not, Ashleigh. The uterine walls aren't the only problem. As I showed you on the computer, your eggs are also incapable of supporting a child to term. In fact, given the quality of your eggs, I doubt you could conceive in the first place. Even then…" He let the sentence trail off.

"So, I can't even donate my eggs to a surrogate?" Ashleigh queried, quickly shrinking into her seat in defeat.

"No." The doctor's response fell into the room with finality. "Ashleigh," Dr. Schwartz continued, his tone warming slightly, "you and Desmond have spent the past year in and out of doctors' offices, and at no small expense, mind you. Perhaps you could take a moment to consider another option? You could focus on other life goals besides having children...Perhaps concentrate more on your career—"

"I'm a kindergarten teacher," Ashleigh interrupted sharply.

The doctor opened his mouth and breathed in, as though he were about to respond, but he stopped short, and sat forward silently once more. He'd been trained in medical school never to apologize, as the recipient could interpret an apology in unintended ways. They might mistake it for an admission of liability, or a shortcoming on the part of the doctor. After more than a decade of running his practice, he had never apologized to a single patient. The doctor sighed heavily, and met the defeated and pleading gaze of the young woman in front of him. He placed his hands on his desk, his palms facing upward. "I'm afraid there simply are no other options, Ashleigh. You're infertile." He paused. "I'm so sorry."

Desmond thanked the doctor as he escorted his wife out of the office and closed the door behind them. Ashleigh strained to keep herself together until they reached a private place, but failed. As she walked through the waiting room filled with expectant mothers in different stages of their own pregnancies, she burst into tears and hugged tightly at Desmond's jacket, burying her face into his shoulder.

• • •

As the couple left his office for what would likely be the last time, Dr. Schwartz stood up from his chair and opened the drawn blinds. Light flooded the near-empty room. He saw the couple cross the street behind the office and watched Desmond kiss Ashleigh's cheek as he helped her into their car. The doctor forced himself to look away as Ashleigh buried her tear-streaked face in her cupped hands. As the sound of their car ignition filtered into his office, the doctor returned to his desk, and pulled framed photographs of his wife and three daughters from the top drawer. He placed the photos back in their usual places on the desk and walls, and for a time, quietly sat, just looking at his girls.

CHAPTER 2

THE MORNING AFTER

Ashleigh lay awake in bed, unable to sleep. Through bleary, bloodshot eyes and the gloom of the still-dark bedroom, she peered at the clock on the bedside table. It was still early morning. She had spent most of the night stifling her sobs in an effort not to wake Desmond, who was sleeping next to her. She was physically and emotionally exhausted. A few hours later, Ashleigh was still awake to hear the quiet tick that Desmond's alarm made right before going off. He shut off its shrill beeping more quickly than usual, and Ashleigh wondered if he had been awake, like her. He rolled over and looked into her eyes.

Even through the gloom and her forced smile, Ashleigh was sure Desmond could see that she had been crying. "I'm going to call out from work today," he said quietly, "I'm sure they'll understand."

"Don't," Ashleigh whispered almost immediately. The breaking morning light was beginning to brighten the bedroom, and Ashleigh could see the confusion on his face. Since receiving the news of her infertility, Desmond had stayed by her side. While she appreciated that her husband was trying to comfort her, she felt unable to grieve in full while he was there, and the effort she expended in trying not to fall apart in front of him was exhausting her beyond her limits. "I just don't want anyone to know just yet about what the doctor said," Ashleigh lied. "But you should go to work."

Desmond began to protest, "But I think that you need—"

"I want you to go to work."

Ashleigh laid in bed, in silence, as Desmond quickly readied for work. She followed him through their house to see him off at the front door.

Before leaving, Desmond turned and placed his briefcase on the floor. He kissed Ashleigh on the forehead, and with lips still held against her skin whispered, "I love you." He grabbed his briefcase once more and closed the door behind him. Ashleigh silently stood where Desmond had left her, and listened to the sounds of his car starting, and being driven down their street. Now in a safe place, her emotional walls came crashing down, and she fell to her knees. With shaking hands held over her heart and mouth, she cried out, her half-wail, half-scream revealing her anguish in full.

• • •

A few days later, Ashleigh heard the chinking of keys followed by the sound of the front door to the house opening and closing. Desmond was returning home from work. She glanced at the clock next to the bed, and was surprised to see it was already late in the afternoon. Her eyes closed again. She knew that any second now, her husband would find her, still lying in bed. She hadn't moved all day, and her constant crying and lack of sleep left her feeling drained.

Desmond came into the room and smiled weakly. He crossed the room to the bed and leaned in to kiss her on the cheek. Ashleigh stared blankly at the ceiling, barely registering the soft kiss that touched her skin. Desmond's words were little more than white noise to her as he began to take off his suit, and tell her about his day.

Her eyes remained fixed on the ceiling, where she watched images of a life she'd never get to live play out in front of her.

She pictured herself holding a newborn, making sure to cradle the neck. The image shifted, and she watched herself waking up in the middle of the night to breastfeed a hungry baby. A tear straddled itself on the rim of her eyelid as she imagined her child calling her "mom" for the first time. She rolled over, facing away from Desmond, and closed her eyes to remove the images from her sight. A tear broke free in the process, wetting the pillow under her cheek.

Desmond pulled on a T-shirt, and turned to see his wife lying on her side, facing away from him. Ashleigh telling him to leave that first morning had taught him that his words couldn't heal her wounds. He approached the bed once more, and slowly lowered himself to lie behind his wife. Ashleigh tightened her face as she tried to hold back the tears. However, she was too exhausted to put her emotional walls back up, and as Desmond wrapped his warm arms around her and closed the gap between their bodies, her features broke, and she again surrendered to silent, shaking sobs.

CHAPTER 3

THE WOMAN IN RED

C amera bulbs flashed, punctuating the evening gloom with bursts of light that bounced off of long, golden curls. The crowd of photographers and media representatives pressed against the barrier and strained their eyes against the spotlights as they tried to reach their subject. Those who could peer through the mass of bodies could only glimpse the lone woman standing on the red carpet.

Although there were no signs or labels to identify the cause of the crowd, no one could mistake the golden curls, brilliant white smile, fragile body, and elegant poise of Hannah Lenore. Hannah forced a continued grin as strangers photographed and called out to her. With her hands on her hips, she maintained her practiced pose and made it look natural, even though she thought it was ridiculously contorted.

Men's pulses quickened as their eyes enveloped her and focused on the lines of her body, tantalizingly visible under her clinging red dress. Her hands rested confidently on her hips, accentuating a narrow waist. Heads turned, and eyes followed Hannah down the red carpet as she was led away by her handler, and whisked off to a pre-show interview. As she disappeared behind the expansive dance-theater entrance, the media throng turned silent and gave little notice to the other guests still walking the red carpet. The new silence was broken only by wistful sighs, and a long, low whistle of appreciation.

Standing in a corridor just short of the theater hall, Hannah shook her head violently as she tried to unstiffen her usually wild hair. *I don't know why they insist on using so much hair spray*, she thought to herself. Settling a few curls back into place, Hannah rubbed her jaw, now sore from forcing a smile for too long, and tried to ignore the uncomfortable tightness of her scalp. She took a deep breath, reset her forced grin, and stepped into the theater vestibule for the quick interview.

"Is this being recorded?" Hannah asked inquisitively.

"Um, yes, of course. See the cameras and microphones everywhere?" answered Jack Katan, a well-known journalist and dance critic. "That's not what I meant," Hannah shot back, briefly forgetting her celebrity smile. "I mean, is this live, or is it getting edited before airing later on *E! News* or some other show?"

Katan sighed impatiently. "Edited and shown later, Ms. Lenore. Are you ready?"

"Yes!" Hannah answered, perking up again. At the gestured reminder from her handler standing behind the camera, she managed to restore her smile. Hannah tried not to squint from the overbearing spotlights as she listened to Katan rattle off an introduction to the interview.

"I'm here with the illustrious Hannah Lenore, celebrated dancer, choreographer, and all-round beauty. Hannah, your unique fusion of ballet, contemporary dance, and stage play have single-handedly revived modern dance and brought the traditionally aristocratic entertainment to the attention, if not the demand, of the general population. Now that it's all coming to a close, what's next for you?"

Hannah's brow furrowed a little in confusion. "What do you mean? Why is it all coming to a close?" Katan gave a cheesy, forced chuckle for the benefit of the camera filming a few short feet from them.

"Hannah, we're standing at the entrance, only moments before the final show of your final tour—"

"Wait," Hannah interrupted, shaking her head a little. "What do you mean 'final' tour?" Katan again gave a forced laugh through an over-the-top smile to cover his clear annoyance at being interrupted. "Well, isn't this good-bye for you, Hannah? All of this is a celebration and send-off at the close of your career."

"Well, that's news to me, *Jack*," Hannah responded with thinly veiled enthusiasm, which did little to hide her annoyance. "This is the last show of my most *recent* tour, not my 'last' tour. Why would anyone suspect that this is my last show, that I'm retiring, or that—"

"Well," Jack interrupted, bringing his microphone closer to himself, "you're nearing forty, you haven't danced in one of your shows in years—which isn't surprising given your age and the physical demands of ballet—and it's simply hard to believe that there's anything new for you to bring to the stage. You've mentioned that your personal experiences influence your work, and it seems you've covered everything. After more than fifteen years of success, what's left for you if not 'retirement', as you put it?"

Hannah had dealt with rude and chauvinistic media personalities before, but she was still surprised that Katan managed to fit so much offense into one breath. If there was a downside to having had such a long and successful career, it was that she was forced to continue working with Jack Katan. Katan had closely followed and commented on Hannah's career and personal life since her breakout success nearly twenty years earlier, when she had become the youngest choreographer and playwright to debut on Broadway in New York City.

Hannah paused, and glared at Katan with contemptuous steel-blue eyes. She pierced his gaze in silence long enough to cause him to shift his balance awkwardly. Relaxing her delicate features, Hannah drew a deep breath and attempted to respond with pointed grace. "I haven't covered everything yet, Jack. It's is a big, wide, and beautiful world, and it's always ripe for new experiences. If all else fails, you know I haven't written an interpersonally inspired show. Even if there's nothing left to write about, there is still love—and there is plenty to write about love."

Katan grinned. "Ah yes, relationships."

Hannah suddenly felt uncomfortable. There was something in Katan's tone and manner that suggested that this was rehearsed, like he'd practiced this line of questioning and its delivery in front of a mirror. She looked behind the camera, her eyes peering through bright spotlights as she scanned the room and searched for her handler.

Katan noticed Hannah's discomfort and tried to contain his excitement as he pressed on. "You're somewhat infamous for your reclusive personal life...Few romantic partners over the years, and never really being seen with the same man for more than a few weeks. Most of the time—like tonight—you walk the red carpet alone."

"Is there a question here?" Hannah cut in, still glancing around for her handler.

"Of course," Katan continued. "It seems you don't have any ideas left for another show, except perhaps 'love.' After so much failure in that aspect of your life, do you really expect to suddenly find it, and save your career? What makes you think this isn't the end for Hannah Lenore?"

Hannah's face turned hard as she threw off her practiced smile and lofty stance. She locked eyes with Katan and raised a pointed finger as she leaned toward him and spoke. "Listen here, Jack. First, my career isn't over, and it doesn't need 'saving.' I have danced and choreographed shows all over the world, and if I died tonight, I would die damned proud of my career and those with whom I have shared it. Second, there are many kinds of love—as many kinds of love as there are kinds of happiness. Love doesn't entail just romantic love. There can be love for your family and friends, love for a child, a city, or even a memory. Just because I haven't found a love that inspired a show doesn't mean that I haven't had a lot of love in my life, and although I haven't found love with a man, it doesn't mean that I won't, or that I even want to!"

Jack had intended to break Hannah's composure, and his face showed his delight in his success. "Those are all beautiful words and sentiments Hannah, but nothing more. What if, after all of this," he said, sweeping his hand and gesturing at the large theater hall and media representatives amassing nearby, "all you have left is the memory of a career forgotten in the wake of someone else who is newer, younger, and more exciting? What if you never find this love you claim is out there?"

Hannah paused. It was not the first time she'd considered this possibility. In truth, she secretly harbored a fear that she might never find love. Although she had spoken of love and its different forms, she truly doubted that she had ever felt love for anything, or anyone. Despite her fame and success, she knew that she had never truly experienced any kind of love, and the thought that this "universal" concept might elude her forever secretly terrified her. She had never written a show about love because she suspected that, having never experienced it, she could not convincingly portray it; that everyone would be able to tell that love was something she had only ever imagined, but never felt. Katan had just publicly given life to her greatest fear. Still in a deep state of introspection, and without looking up, Hannah breathed only the words, "Then I'll pursue it forever."

"Excuse me?" Katan leaned in closer, and brought his microphone inappropriately close to Hannah's lips.

The intrusive microphone in her face penetrated Hannah's consciousness, and brought her back to reality. She steeled herself, and grabbed the microphone out of Katan's out-stretched hand. "Beautiful things never last. Fall leaves turn, snow melts, and no matter how passionately or brightly it burns, fire burns out. Despite this, I am content to live constantly in the pursuit of the perfect love without its realization, happily deluded by the false promise of its beauty. Because while beautiful things never last, I can make the pursuit of them last forever. Now, if you're done trying to humiliate me and find a headline for yourself, this interview is over."

Hannah shoved the microphone into Katan's chest and stormed off, her eyes downcast to avoid being blinded by the flashing cameras now bursting with light as photographers attempted to steal pictures of her in a rare state of discompo- sure. She entered the large dance theater, and the room fell quickly into a hushed silence. Hannah gave a brief glance over the crowd as all eyes fell upon her. She carried herself with hurried steps to the far side of the theater, toward a door leading to the dancers' preparation suites, her heels echoing off the acoustically prepared walls. She rushed the final few steps to the door and quickly closed it behind her. Relieved to find herself in an empty corridor, she leaned back and pressed herself against the back of the door.

Struggling for breath, Hannah hunched over as far as her tight dress would permit, supporting herself on her shaking legs. She straightened up again, pressed both hands to the door behind her, and gasped for breath. Her heart was racing, and her lungs refused to fill with air. She was having a panic attack. Some of her dancers entered the corridor from one of the doors ahead of her.

Recognizing Hannah immediately and spotting her silent gasps, a few hurried over to her. Two dancers took her hands and attempted to run through the meditative exercises Hannah often practiced with them. "Focus on following our breathing," one of the girls said as they placed her hands on their chests. The dancers began taking slow, deep breaths, and soon, Hannah could feel her pulse slowing as her lungs unlocked, and filled with air.

The dancers released her hands as Hannah recovered. "Your handler came into the dressing room looking for you. His phone is blowing up with messages and calls asking whether this is your swan song."

A few of the girls in the back exchanged worried glances. "We're so sorry Ms. Lenore. Everyone knows Jack Katan is an ass."

"It's fine, girls. If you've finished getting ready, you should get into place and begin stretching. The show should start soon," Hannah spoke without emotion.

"But what about—"

"Go!" Hannah ordered, as she pointed to a door at the far end of the corridor. One of the dancers opened her mouth, seemingly about to protest, but quickly turned and followed the other girls out of the corridor. Hannah pushed herself off of the door and pulled her dress down to flatten out the creases that had developed over her stomach. She stood erect on legs that were no longer shaky.

The girls don't understand, she thought. Hannah didn't care that Katan had brought up her personal life, or her failed relationships. She didn't care that he'd unknowingly forced her to confront her fear of never truly experiencing love, or that he'd suggested she was old and irrelevant. What had caused her panic was the suggestion that this was her last show.

Since the start of her career, Hannah had always thought about, and begun preparing for her next show before the current tour closed. She frequently found herself impatiently waiting for one tour to finish so that she could start training her dancers on the choreography for her next project. In fact, she was often so impatient and inspired by her next creation that she'd announce the next tour before the current one had even closed.

What caused her to panic was Katan recognizing and announcing to the world that Hannah was out of ideas. For the first time in her life, she was without a story, without any inspiration, and without any clue about where to find it. She looked to the door at the opposite end of the corridor. Above the doorframe hung an exit sign, its soft light creating a red halo over the otherwise darkened doorway.

She turned on the spot, and once again leaned against the door leading to the theater hall. She peered through the small window and watched as the mass of guests began taking their seats, ready for her ballet to start. The men in the crowd, dressed in a variety of black-and-white suits, looked like penguins as they sidled along the seat rows and avoided the legs of guests who were already seated. The lights twice dimmed and brightened in quick sequence, signaling that the entrance doors would soon be locked, and the ballet would begin.

"This isn't my last show," Hannah said aloud to herself as she pulled away from the window. She turned and faced the exit. Graceful once again in her movements, she strode with purpose down the corridor. The lights overhead dimmed and brightened again in quick succession: the final seating call.

"I wouldn't miss my last show…" Hannah pushed the exit door open forcefully and saw that it was raining. The smell of the rain made her smile. She tousled her hair to loosen the last of the hairspray still fighting to keep her wild blonde locks in check. She took off her heels and held them on her fingers as she stepped outside, cool rain falling softly upon her exposed skin. She looked left and right to gain her bearings. She was standing several feet away from the theater entrance. With her shoes in hand, she took off down the street at a slow run to avoid the attention of a few photographers setting up to photograph the guests after the show. Hannah had turned a corner and was in a cab before anyone noticed anything more than a rain-soaked woman running barefoot down a New York street in a red dress. On any other day, no one would have mistaken the golden curls, white smile, fragile body, and elegant poise of Hannah Lenore. However, no one recognized her like this.

CHAPTER 4

FOCUS ON THE POSITIVES

Two weeks had passed since receiving the diagnosis from Dr. Schwartz. Since then, Ashleigh had fallen into a deep state of apathy. The days that passed followed the same routine. Desmond would wake each morning and make breakfast, leaving a tray of food beside the bed for Ashleigh. Each evening, he would return home to find her still in bed and would clear away the same tray of untouched food.

Each time he'd tried to talk to her about her infertility, she'd given a quick and sharp, "I'm not ready," abruptly ending the conversation.

At the close of the second week, Ashleigh's school colleague called the house. "Desmond, it's Maha. Is Ashleigh planning on coming back to teach her classes? We understand her absence over the past two weeks, but she has used up all of her leave, and we can't continue to use substitutes without some indication that Ashleigh is returning soon. A number of the students' parents have already started complaining."

Desmond had answered the call in the hallway outside of their bedroom, and he paced the hall as he spoke. "I understand. It's just a little difficult given the circumstances. Ashleigh hasn't been herself since we received the news, and I can't imagine she's ready to be in a room full of young kids just yet."

Ashleigh listened to the conversation from the bedroom; she could hear her colleague's voice through the receiver.

"Thank you, Desmond. We're trying to be patient. It's just that we haven't mentioned the infertility or given any explanation for Ashleigh's absence to her students' parents, and so their patience is being tested. Kindergarten is a critical and formative time, and many of these parents chose our school because of our kindergarten program. They're not taking the extensive use of substitute teachers very well."

Desmond looked at the open door leading to their bedroom and lowered his voice. "I'll let Ashleigh know, and try to speak with her about it. How much more time can you give us?"

The line was silent for a moment before Maha's voice came through once more. "One more week is the absolute most we can offer. If she's not back by next Monday, we'll have to take steps to replace her on a long-term basis. We really hope it doesn't come to that. We're all heartbroken for you both."

"Thank you, Maha. We appreciate it." Desmond ended the call and entered the bedroom. He was surprised to find Ashleigh sitting up in the bed, and he stopped in his tracks when he realized she was glaring at him in wide-eyed fury.

"How *dare* you!" Ashleigh hissed at her husband with a scowl. "You told them I'm infertile?"

"I needed to explain—" Desmond started.

"You had no right!" Ashleigh yelled. She stood on the bed, so she towered over him, the blankets falling around her legs. "This is *my* body, and anything about it is *my* business and *my* problem."

"This is *both* of our business!" Desmond yelled, his voice rising to match Ashleigh's, his eyes locking with hers. "Do you think the news hasn't affected me? That it didn't break my heart too? You know what my childhood was like and what having a family means to me! I've been hurting too Ashleigh, but I haven't even been able to talk about it—" Desmond was cut off as he ducked to avoid a pillow thrown at his head.

"Don't you dare!" Ashleigh cried, her misery-filled, glaring eyes sending silent tears down her angry face. She made a less-impassioned effort at throwing another pillow at Desmond before collapsing onto her knees into a sullen pile on the bed. She raised her hand and pointed accusingly at him. "Don't you dare compare your pain or disappointment to mine." Her outstretched hand returned, and she pointed at her heart as she referenced herself.

Ashleigh's face was marked with dark, tear-streaked lines from running makeup. Desmond didn't know she'd put on mascara. He crossed the room to try and console his wife, but she shied away from him to avoid his touch. Her eyes met his and showed betrayal.

"*Don't* touch me." Ashleigh's eyes followed Desmond's as he took a step back from the bed.

"I don't know what you want from me, Ash. I don't know what I'm supposed to do here." Desmond gestured wildly with his hands as he yelled. "There is nothing I wouldn't do to fix this, but I don't have any answers. I don't even know what you want me to do!"

"You don't need to *do* anything!" Ashleigh's voice lashed again, and she straightened up from her crouched slouch. "I just want to be left alone to process this, and not have everyone know that…that I can't have a baby!" Her voice quivered as she finished her sentence. It was the first time she'd said those words aloud, and her stomach twisted as the words left her lips. "You couldn't understand! You don't know what it means to know and feel that your body can't do what it's meant to do— what I've *dreamed* of it doing my whole life! You don't know what it's like to lay here in bed, wondering if I'm even still a woman if I can't get pregnant; to be jealous of all those teen moms out there who fall pregnant *so* easily and by accident. I have spent my whole life expecting that one day I'd find my calling in being a mother, and for the past two years, I enjoyed the excitement of knowing that I'm finally there, that I'm *finally* at that point in my life where I'm going to have a baby. And now, after all of this time, after all of this hope and excitement, it's all just been ripped from me! You see, Desmond? I spent my whole life expecting that one day I'd be a mother—"

"Maybe you're just not meant to be a mother!" Desmond blurted out. Ashleigh leaned back, away from his hurtful words. Her eyes misted in an instant, and her lips curled at his betraying comment.

"You don't mean that," she scoffed. Ashleigh shook her head as silent tears continued to fall. "I know I'm supposed to be a mother." Her hands unconsciously cupped her lower abdomen, "God made me feel incomplete if I'm only one, not part of two…" Her voice trailed off, and the room fell silent.

"You are a part of two, Ashleigh. You still have me. We still have *us!*" Desmond's voice was low and sincere. Ashleigh's angry tears continued to fall and hit the bed with low thuds, carried by the full weight of her mixed emotions. "I don't need you to fix this, Desmond. I just need time to be alone. Call Maha and tell her I'll be back at work next Monday, and then make yourself comfortable in the guest room."

Desmond remained where he stood for a moment, and silently questioned whether he should obey. It was the first time he and Ashleigh had really talked since their visit to Dr. Schwartz's office, and he felt he hadn't finished everything he'd wanted to say. However, as Ashleigh rolled onto her side and showed her back to him, he knew the conversation was over, and he turned to leave the room. "I love you," he called softly over his shoulder as he paused in the doorway. A pang of guilt hit his stomach when Ashleigh didn't answer him, and he closed the door softly behind him.

A similar pang of guilt struck Ashleigh as she heard the door latch click close behind her.

• • •

The next morning, Desmond quietly stepped into the bedroom where Ashleigh slept. He left the now-familiar tray of breakfast he'd prepared in the space next to Ashleigh's side of the bed. As he placed it down, he grabbed the tray that he'd been unable to remove the previous evening and saw that the food had once again been left untouched. He returned the untouched tray to the kitchen and discarded the stale contents.

He stood alone in the kitchen, arms propped up on the kitchen counter as he thought about the state of his wife. He grabbed his briefcase and reentered the bedroom to say good-bye. However, when he saw her features relaxed in sleep, he thought better than to wake her. Sleep rarely visited her these days, and it seemed her only escape from her waking nightmare. He scribbled a quick note on a piece of paper, and left it on his pillow for her to find when she awoke. He left the house quietly, unaware that the sound of the closing front door would wake her.

Ashleigh awoke with a start. She sat up numbly, squinting through the light coming in through the bedroom window. Her back ached from staying in bed for too long, and typically being an early riser, she was annoyed at herself for forming a habit of waking so late. She noticed Desmond's note on the pillow next to her and the food beside the bed. She brought the note before her eyes and read aloud, "Focus on the positives." Ashleigh knew her husband was just trying to be nice, but the message irritated her. *I'm not choosing to be unhappy*, she thought, as she tossed the note back onto Desmond's pillow.

Ashleigh glanced again at the food next to her. Even though she was hungry, she wasn't in the mood to eat. She forced herself to get out of the bed and walked stiffly into the bathroom. Knowing she was home alone, she didn't care to close the door behind her. She stripped off her shirt and bed shorts, each sticking to her skin a little after several days of wear, and stepped into the shower. She kept her mind from wandering by focusing intently on what she was doing—shampooing her hair, shaving her legs, washing her body, and moisturizing.

The room filled with steam, and she relaxed a little as she stood under the warm water, soothed by the scent of the shower oils. After nearly an hour, she stepped out of the shower and toweled off. Returning her towel to its hook, she wiped the mirror clear of condensation and noticed a row of pre-pregnancy supplements on the counter in front of her.

Focus on the positives, she thought to herself as she let out a shaky sigh. She stretched, and examined her naked reflection in the mirror, her head slightly tilted to one side. "Focus on the positives," she repeated to herself aloud. "We're healthy," she began. Ashleigh's body was toned, her chestnut-brown hair was healthy, and her skin glowed—the product of frequent exercise and pre-pregnancy supplements as she had vainly prepared for motherhood. She was pleased to see that her body had not lost the benefits of her pre-pregnancy preparations.

Desmond was also fit. To ensure his sperm remained healthy, Ashleigh had placed Desmond on a controlled diet, and she made sure he exercised regularly. Desmond may have been close to forty, but his physique and masculine bulk matched that of athletic men almost half his age. The mothers of her students had noticed this the few times he'd visited her at work.

She sighed as she realized that the prenatal preparations had been in vain, and quickly shook her head to banish the thoughts of pregnancy that battered their way into her mind. She tried again. "I'm young ... ish," she said to herself, not entirely convinced. She shook her head violently once again as thoughts of pregnancy and her biological clock invaded her mind. She sighed in frustration.

This isn't working, she thought, as she placed both hands on the counter and met her reflected gaze in the mirror. Every positive thing she tried to think about somehow led back to thoughts of pregnancy and children. She broke her mirrored gaze and turned her head to see the breakfast next to the bed and the note left by Desmond, discarded on the pillow. She thought about how Desmond had cared for her over the past few weeks, how he'd listened to her during the few times she'd spoken without trying to provide answers or heal her confusion, and how he'd hidden his own pain from her.

Ashleigh smiled to herself in the mirror—her first smile in weeks. "My marriage…" she said, her smile broadening. "I have a wonderful marriage."

CHAPTER 5

PROGRESS

Desmond leaned into his office desk as he sat with his face all but buried in hands held against his forehead. He peered through his fingers and gazed at the framed photo of Ashleigh and himself that stood next to his computer monitor. The photo was taken a few years ago at a kindergarten fundraising event, and showed the two of them laughing as Ashleigh tried to paint his face. Desmond smiled.

His mind turned to the different ways their marriage had changed since they began trying to have a baby. From the very moment that he had awkwardly carried Ashleigh over the threshold of their home after returning from their honeymoon, they had shared in the jubilation customary to newlyweds. They'd lain together into the wee hours of the morning, talking about all of the events leading up to their first meeting. They'd laughed together in the kitchen as each tried to adapt to the other's culinary pallet, and fallen into the other's passionate embrace as they explored marital bliss.

After roughly a year of marriage, their googly-eyes gave way to what so many would call "the small death." Certainly, their lovemaking began to lack the youthful frenzy that followed their marriage, and they would find themselves capable of thinking of more than just their desire to be in their spouse's company, but this change was in no way a small death. Both Desmond and Ashleigh entered a stage of what he could only think to describe as the comfort of the familiar.

If their first year of marriage could be defined by the frenzy and fury of their passion for one another, this "comfortable" stage could be defined by the way that everything seemed to slow down amid a quiet appreciation for all that had accumulated between them. He and Ashleigh had found themselves capable of experiencing the pure joy that came from simply being in the other's presence. Desmond's mind turned to a particular spring morning when Ashleigh had sat at the high table in the corner of their kitchen, reading the morning news from her tablet while he busied himself in the kitchen fixing breakfast for the two of them. His "bed hair" flared in odd directions, and his white shirt was stained under the chin from coffee spilled during a mid-sip yawn. He'd patted the stain with his free hand only to look up at find Ashleigh, smiling adoringly at him.

"What?" he'd asked her, unable to help but break into an embarrassed smile.

"Nothing," she replied lovingly. "I'm just taking this in. In a few years, we probably won't be able to have simple mornings like this. We'll have kids screaming in the other room or under our feet, and my hair will look as crazy as yours."

His mind now back in the present, Desmond smiled to himself as he recounted the memory and the slow, intimate lovemaking that had followed. He realized for the first time that Ashleigh's words on that occasion had led to their first discussion about having children.

As their marriage progressed, their conversations about children became more frequent, and Desmond and Ashleigh explored the many questions familiar to young couples. Across many months, they languished over whether they had saved enough money or traveled enough, and had real arguments about how they'd raise their hypothetical children when it came to certain issues.

When they had finally decided that it was time to start trying for kids, they grew giddy talking back and forth about whether they would prefer a boy or girl first, and reveled in the excitement of suggesting baby names. Again, Desmond's thoughts turned back time as he recalled the occasion he and Ashleigh had explored which baby names were off limits.

"Absolutely not," Desmond had said after his wife suggested yet another awful name for a girl.

"Oh, please," she'd implored, "I *loved* the movie when I was a little girl and always wanted to have a girl by that name."

Desmond chuckled in disbelief. "No! We are not naming our daughter Pollyanna!"

"Ugh," Ashleigh uttered in forfeit as she lay lazily on their bed. "Well, I don't have any other ideas for girls' names. I always counted on having a husband who loved me enough to let me name my future daughter Pollyanna." She shot him a wry grin.

"Don't even try that!" Desmond had said with a smile of his own. "I love you with every piece of me, Ash, but I still won't let you do that to my little girl."

Ashleigh's smile broadened lovingly as her husband talked affectionately about children that didn't even yet exist. She gazed absently at the ceiling of their bedroom as she pondered more names. "What about Hannah?" Still looking at the ceiling, she hadn't noticed the change in Desmond's expression or the stiffening of his repose. "My favorite playwright is named Hannah, and so was your grandmother. I think it's such a pretty name."

Desmond shook his head dismissively. "Nah, we can't do that. You know I had a big crush on a girl named Hannah before we met. Besides, we already agreed that the names of exes are out of the question, and I figure this one has to fall into that category. I don't want to think about another woman every time I say my daughter's name."

They had finished that conversation unable to agree on any names. As the many months passed without a positive pregnancy test, the mood around the subject of children darkened, and the name-swapping game lost its appeal.

Coming out of his reverie once again, Desmond lifted himself from his desk and began packing his briefcase as he prepared to leave the office and head home. As he put his reading glasses in their protective case, he gazed at the framed photo of Ashleigh once again. He compared the version of his wife in the picture to the one likely still lying in bed at home. *I wonder if she'll ever be the same after this*, he thought. *I wonder if we'll ever be the same.*

He grabbed his briefcase and left his office, still wondering whether he and Ashleigh would ever again be as happy as the couple smiling in the photograph he left behind on his desk.

Desmond took a deep breath on his front doorstep before unlocking the door and stepping inside of his home. A fragrant scent wafted through the house, and he could hear the sizzle of cooking oil coming from the kitchen. Curiosity got the better of him, and without hanging up his jacket or putting his briefcase down, he walked further into the house and peeked around the corner that led to their kitchen.

Ashleigh had heard the front door open and shut, and knew Desmond was home. She watched as his head poked around the corner and she smiled briefly at his playfulness.

"What's all thi—" Desmond said as he stepped into full view. Ashleigh held up a wooden spoon as a finger to stop Desmond speaking.

"No," she said, matter-of-factly, returning her gaze to the meal she was preparing on the stove. "We're not making a big deal about this. I love you, but please just get changed out of your work clothes and help me set the table. We can talk over dinner."

Happy to see his wife out of bed and talking to him, Desmond obeyed without another word, and hurried up the stairs to their bedroom.

Desmond poured a glass of wine for each of them before seating himself at the table. Ashleigh soon followed into the dining room wearing a striking black and blue dress. Her long, chestnut hair hung loftily around her shoulders. She smiled at Desmond as she noticed him staring at her, and her smiling eyes curved into half crescents.

Desmond tilted his head in curiosity, and Ashleigh could tell he'd noticed she wasn't wearing a bra or shoes. "Baby steps," she whispered to him quietly, as she kissed him on the cheek and took her seat.

To his surprise, it was Ashleigh who spoke first. "I don't know how much I'm ready to talk about any of this."

Desmond nodded his understanding, his mouth half-open as he prepared to place his first forkful of food in his mouth.

Without touching her dining utensils or raising her eyes from her plate, Ashleigh continued, "I'm sorry that in all of my wallowing I never gave you time to grieve or talk about how you felt about all of this. I know you've always wanted a family of your own, and the thought that I can't give that to you makes me feel guilty. I've felt so much grief, anger, guilt, and confusion lately, and I was just so overwhelmed by the weight of it all. And in all of my pain, I never considered that you might be silently going through the same thing."

Desmond gestured for Ashleigh to start eating, put down his fork, and leaned back to respond. "I have been hurting, sweetheart, and I've dealt with it in my own way…bit by bit." He picked up his knife and fork and continued eating. "But I never suffered the overwhelming weight of feeling everything all at once like you did. It was wrong of me to compare my feelings to yours, and I'm sorry."

Ashleigh smiled. Her eyes briefly met her husband's, and her heart fluttered a little at his understanding. *He's always had a way with words*, she thought. "Do you want to talk about how you feel?" she asked.

Desmond smiled and looked away introspectively as he answered. "No. For now, I'm happy to just focus on us for a while." He raised his glass of wine in a toast, and Ashleigh followed suit.

Smiling shyly and feeling self-conscious, she joined in her husband's quiet toast, "To us."

Ashleigh rose at the end of the meal and began to clear the table. Desmond rose to help her, and she gestured for him to sit back down. "You kept this house in order for the past few weeks on your own. The least I can do is take care of things tonight."

She emptied the bottle of wine into Desmond's glass as she cleared the table and ventured into the kitchen. Calling over her shoulder as she focused on rinsing dishes in their sink, she raised her voice to overcome the sound of the rushing tap water. "I decided something today." She waited a moment to confirm Desmond was listening.

He appeared in the doorway, his glass of wine in hand, and she continued. "I've done enough wallowing. I'm not over this, and truth be told I can't imagine that I ever will be, but things aren't going to get better just by lying in bed every day. I'm going to stay busy, focusing on one thing at a time—like this meal, these dishes—and see where that leads me. I've told Maha I'll be back at work on Monday, and in the meantime, I'm going to try and do some things I've put off for so long. I'm going to see some girls I haven't seen in years, and I'm going to see that ballet up in New York I keep telling you about. Couples are forever complaining about all the things that they can't do when they have kids. We've been missing these things too, and we don't even have kids. Now I want us to do them all.

Like Dr. Schwartz said, we've spent the past year focusing on nothing but kids, and I guess it's time for us to start living life again."

Desmond had finished his glass of wine and set it down on a kitchen bench. He stepped behind Ashleigh, so their bodies touched. He reached around his wife, grabbed a plate from her hands and placed it at the bottom of the sink before switching off the tap.

Ashleigh felt moisture seep through her dress and touch her skin as Desmond's wet hands wrapped around her waist. He turned her around to face him, and she couldn't help but return his adoring smile. Embarrassed, she shied away from him, but couldn't overcome his embrace. "I'm gross, and you're making me all wet!" she exclaimed with a giggle.

"Stop talking," Desmond commanded as he kissed her deeply and hoisted her onto his hips. He continued to kiss her as carried her up the stairs and into their bedroom, using his foot to shut the door behind them. For the first time in years, he and Ashleigh made real, passionate love without the pressure of making a baby impregnating their thoughts.

CHAPTER 6

VALUES & VINO

*M*ilitant forces continue to push back American troops, frustrating efforts to maintain peacekeeping activities in the region. Frontline forces suffered higher than expected casualties in yesterday's melee, with twenty-six American soldiers confirmed killed-in-action. The President is receiving criticism from Congress as he will neither commit additional combat reinforcements, nor order a retreat from the region.

Ashleigh continued to watch the news program on the television in the living room as she sipped on her breakfast smoothie. *My gosh,* she thought, *would we really have wanted to bring a child into this world?* She quickly grabbed the remote and switched the television off, annoyed that something so unrelated could still prompt her mind to wander to the subject of children. She shook her head to banish the thoughts, and returned to the good mood she'd been enjoying that morning. She had awoken early for the past few days and gone for a dawn jog to try to return to her usual routine.

A yawning Desmond entered the room in his bed shorts. "Good morning, beautiful!" he called to Ashleigh, while stretching. "What have you got on for today?"

"I'm going back to work tomorrow, and so I'm seeing some of the girls in DC today," she said excitedly, turning around in her sofa seat to face Desmond. "What about you?"

"I have to go into the office today," he said, slumping over in exaggerated resignation. "One of the partners is briefing me on a big new case the firm just picked up, and I want to be familiar with the materials before I meet with him."

"Ooo!" Ashleigh cooed excitedly. She turned the rest of her body and crouched on her seat, so she could sit in a reversed position. "Do you think they'll make you partner if this one goes well?" Desmond had been a senior associate at one of Baltimore's larger law firms for the past eight years, and had been pursuing a promotion to partner for most of that time.

"Honestly? I have no idea. I don't know anything about the case just yet, but I'm hopeful!" Desmond wasn't too optimistic about the prospect, but he found Ashleigh's excitement contagious.

Ashleigh stood up from the couch and coyly glanced at the clock behind Desmond. "How long do you have before you have to leave for work?"

Desmond turned to look at the clock on the wall behind him. "Not for another hour or..." his voice trailed off as he turned back and discovered Ashleigh stripping off her clothes in front of him.

"Only an hour?" she teased as her shirt fell to the floor. "Better call and tell them you'll be late."

• • •

Ashleigh had spent hours getting ready to meet her friends. She'd deep conditioned and curled her hair, finished a face mask, moisturized her skin, trimmed, buffed, and painted her fingernails, and tastefully applied makeup, including her favorite dark red lipstick. She hadn't seen some of these friends in years, and she wanted to look her best. The weather was forecast to be fair, and so she'd picked out a bright sundress that still clung to her skin in the right places to show off her toned figure. She grabbed a cute clutch purse to match her outfit and threw on some flats. She already had her favorite heels in the car and would change into them just before her lunch.

Ashleigh's arrival at the upscale eatery was anything but subdued. Pedestrians passing by the DC street cafe were startled by a woman's piercing scream. Many turned and relaxed when they saw that the scream had come from a young, blonde woman wearing oversized sunglasses who was merely excited to see a friend. Ashleigh ran up to her squealing friend, and the two embraced. The other women sitting at the cafe table with the blonde friend were looking around and telling her to stop screaming. "People are staring, Heather!"

Ashleigh took a seat next to Heather, under the umbrella of the outdoor café, and immediately removed her heels. She and Heather giggled as Heather pointed under the table to show Ashleigh that she'd also removed her shoes.

"I don't think I've seen you once since your wedding. That's too long. Bad Ashleigh," Heather mockingly chastised her friend. They had all been bridesmaids at Ashleigh's and Desmond's wedding, and most of them had been her friends since high school. She'd been so preoccupied with trying to get pregnant that she hadn't made time to see them, often completely ignoring their invitations to catch up.

"It feels like forever since we last saw you!" Danielle exclaimed. "Where have you been? What have you been doing?"

Ashleigh quickly ordered a drink from the passing waiter and tried not to turn red at the question. She didn't want to have to talk about her infertility. She wasn't yet ready to deal with the words of sympathy and condolences she knew would immediately follow from her friends.

"Oh, you know…Desmond and I just let time get away from us. What's new with you girls?" she said, as she tried to avoid Danielle's inquiry.

All the girls began talking at once.

"I got married!" Heather yelled, again too loudly, and full of excitement.

"I got divorced," Emily said matter-of-factly, a sense of self-satisfaction evident in her tone.

"This menu is really unhealthy," Danielle contributed, her face buried in the cafe's food offerings, and not listening to the conversation.

"I got married, then got divorced!" Heather yelled again.

"Seriously. Where are the vegan options on this menu?" Danielle came in once more. She looked up from her menu and saw a dumbstruck smile across Ashleigh's face; she was clearly overwhelmed at the huge news being thrown at her all at once.

Danielle quickly registered the dialogue which had preceded Ashleigh's shocked look, and as she put the menu aside, decided to add her own piece. "Oh, and I'm pregnant."

Ashleigh's smile vanished.

• • •

Desmond stood in the rising elevator of his office building and pulled on the tail of his tie so that the knot tightened and fell flush against his collar. He felt uncomfortable wearing a full suit on hot days, so he made a habit of putting on his tie and jacket at the last possible moment before reaching his firm's foyer. He had planned to arrive at his office at least an hour before his meeting with the partner so he could review the case files in advance, but his morning romp with Ashleigh gave him a mere fifteen minutes to get settled in the conference room.

Well worth it, he thought, exiting the elevator between parting steel doors. He stood briefly in the foyer, and looked at the golden names hanging on the wall next to the elevators.

"Rennick, Spectre & Co.," a voice sounded from behind him. "All in due course, my boy."

Desmond turned on the spot, and his gaze was met by Hayden Rennick, the founding partner with whom he was due to meet.

"How many times have we said that to you, Desmond? Always 'in due course.'" Rennick came to stand by his side, and both men faced the golden letters on the wall. Most of Rennick's hair was missing, and the tufts of what little hair was left blended with his white beard, giving the impression that he was completely bald. His skin was dotted with brown spots, and blue veins were visible beneath pale, loose skin that hung below gray, discerning eyes. Despite his aged appearance and the heat of the day, Rennick stood erect and authoritative in a full, finely tailored three-piece suit. His pocket watch ticked faintly through the silence that surrounded the two men, alone in the foyer.

"When Graham Spectre and I started our firm, we never expected it to become the size that it did. Sure, we always strived for success, but the money and growth that came with it were always just bonuses. As we grew, Spectre and I expected that one day our children would inherit the firm, or at the very least, have a role in it. Sadly, Spectre's son died when he was a boy, and he and his wife Robin never had another child."

"And what about your kids?" Desmond asked, remembering the large family portrait hanging in Rennick's office that showed a son and daughter.

Rennick chuckled. "My daughter," he began slowly, his words even and considerate, "preferred medicine to the law, and has a residency at Johns Hopkins. And my son, well, he's an imbecile." He chuckled again and looked at Desmond. "Follow me."

The two men began to stroll around the offices. Desmond could hear the clicking of keyboard strokes coming from the open-office bullpen—a number of the junior attorneys were usually in the office on the weekend, each trying to get the upper hand on their peers and earn a coveted closed office space. Rennick and Desmond continued to walk toward the glass-walled offices of the senior partners. Rennick's erect posture never waned as they wandered through the office and past the conference room. Desmond noticed that the conference room was empty and looked at Rennick inquisitively.

"All in due course, my boy," Rennick repeated wryly. The two men rounded a corner and began walking between the senior partner offices. "Stop here," Rennick commanded. "Desmond, what do you notice here?" Desmond looked down the corridor straddled on both sides by glass offices.

"They're all empty. The lights are off."

Rennick nodded somberly. "And what can you hear?"

Desmond lowered his head and allowed his eyes to glaze over as he focused on his hearing. Again, he noticed the sound of typing coming from the junior bullpen. "The juniors are here," Desmond answered flatly as he returned his focus to Rennick.

The old partner nodded again, smiling slightly. "That's right! Poor bastards, working on a Sunday." He chuckled again and gestured for Desmond to continue walking with him. They arrived at Rennick's office, and Desmond took a seat on the small leather lounge in the large room. Rennick remained standing next to the window of his corner office, and looked over Baltimore's harbor expanding below him.

Still looking out the window, he continued, "Somewhere between the bullpen and senior partnership, our attorneys stop caring about their cases and their clients, and they start focusing on themselves, on *their* money, and *their* advancement. This creates something of a dilemma for Spectre and me. We want the man or woman who succeeds us as managing partner to hold the same philosophy as we do: that the clients and their cases come first, and the growth and money are just bonuses!" He finished his sentence with a light thump of his fist on the window, leaving a slight blemish visible on the glass. Rennick turned on the spot to face Desmond. He stood behind his chair and leaned on the headrest to support his aching knees.

"You've been something of an anomaly to us, Desmond. Your presence here late at night and on weekends has not gone unnoticed. Your habit of intentionally under-billing your needy clients, and not recording billable hours has also captured our attention."

Desmond became alarmed. He had under-recorded his time and under-billed his clients every year he had spent with the firm. This potentially represented hundreds of thousands of dollars in lost billings and revenue. He had always made up his time by working late, and coming in on weekends so that he still met his billing quotas, but he thought that no one had noticed. He turned red, and tried to calm himself as he recalled the empty conference room and stories of senior attorneys being fired outside of regular business hours to avoid interoffice disruptions.

Rennick pushed himself off the chair and began to move slowly to the front of the chair. "Finally, Desmond," Rennick continued, "you have not spoken up, acted out, demanded a promotion, or so much as Googled another job, even when we promoted other less-deserving attorneys to partner." Rennick lowered himself slowly into his chair, a low groan escaping on his breath as he fell heavily onto the chair cushion. He wheeled himself slowly toward the low coffee table, which sat between him and the lounge upon which Desmond sat.

He noticed Desmond's anxiety and dismissed it with a wave of his hand. "My boy, I didn't ask you here to fire you. Relax."

Desmond relaxed a little, but continued to lean forward, sitting on the edge of his seat. He still felt uncomfortable under Rennick's discerning gaze.

"Your altruism, while noble, is also the reason Spectre and I have been unable to promote you to partner. Because you under-bill, your billings are not impressive enough for us to get a sufficient number of partner votes on a motion to make you partner. However, Spectre and I consider that if you have a big win, this would likely be enough to secure the vote. Once you are a partner, the bylaws provide that Spectre and I can name you the presumptive managing partner, and begin grooming you to inherit the firm from us." Desmond nodded slowly, his mind racing. His heart was pounding, and he was sweating beneath his suit. It took no small effort for him to maintain his composure. He had spent years working toward becoming a partner of the firm without success, and now the role of managing partner was within his grasp, if he could win just one more case.

"What's the big case you have in mind?" Desmond asked.

Rennick chuckled again and shook an appreciative finger at Desmond's intuitiveness. "You're a very talented attorney, Desmond—probably one of our best medical negligence attorneys." He stood and walked over to a filing cabinet next to his large desk and removed a manila folder. "As you know, big medical negligence cases are hard to come by, especially as they are typically settled and hushed long before the public or medical industry gets word of them. However, Spectre and I worked to acquire this case because it already has so much notoriety attached to it, and because there is likely zero chance of it settling." Rennick returned to his chair and held up the folder. "Even with your talents Desmond, this case will be no easy win. That is why, *if* you win, we expect that the partners will vote for your promotion."

Rennick threw the manila folder onto the coffee table and watched for Desmond's reaction as it slid in front of him. Desmond picked up the folder, and his heart sank as he read the case name and description from the cover: *Poe v. Maryland IVF Clinic - Multiple Wrongful IVF Births.*

• • •

Ashleigh sipped on her second glass of red wine as Heather finished regaling the story of how she had spontaneously married and divorced an Italian tattoo artist in Las Vegas. "… and so, now Leonardo says it's really hard for him to meet girls because his wedding band was a tattoo on his ring finger!" Ashleigh laughed along with the girls at the story. However, behind her laughter, Danielle's pregnancy news continued to gnaw at her.

As the conversation had naturally ventured in other directions, neither Ashleigh nor the other girls had discussed Danielle's pregnancy since she'd first mentioned it. Ashleigh's eyes passed over Danielle and appraised her body. Having been a vegan for several years and an accomplished long-distance runner, Danielle was always a physically slight woman. However, there was no discernible baby bump or other indication that Danielle was pregnant. The fact that Danielle sat with fresh fruit juice instead of wine was also of little consequence as she rarely drank alcohol.

Ashleigh couldn't contain her curiosity any longer, almost bursting from holding in the question. "Danielle, how far along are you?"

Danielle sat the fruit juice on the table and smiled. "Six months."

"Six months!" Ashleigh exclaimed, looking at Danielle's frail figure. "But you're so small!"

Ashleigh's friends looked at each other and burst out laughing. Ashleigh looked about, wondering what joke she had missed. Still insecure about her infertility, she was a little worried that they might be laughing at her, and she unconsciously gripped the napkin in her lap tightly.

"*She's* not pregnant," laughed Emily.

Ashleigh looked about again in confusion, and then back to Danielle. "But you said—"

Danielle finished laughing and wiped a tear from her eye. "I'm sorry, Ashleigh. *I'm* not pregnant, but my surrogate is pregnant with my and George's baby. I said that I was pregnant because the doctors say that talking about the pregnancy in the first person is good for bonding and psychologically preparing myself for when the baby arrives."

"A surrogate?" Ashleigh questioned inquisitively.

"My sister," Danielle answered preemptively. "Because of my veganism and running, the doctors said I'd have a tough time carrying a healthy baby. Because George and I both want kids, we began exploring other options. When we found out that IVF and surgical surrogacy services were no longer being practiced, my sister offered to carry the baby, and we managed the insemination on our own."

"Ew!" Heather exclaimed, and then burst out laughing when the other girls gave her a look.

"Grow up, Heather," Danielle berated her friend through her own laughter.

Emily finished her glass of wine and signaled for the waiter to bring them another bottle. Impatient with the waiter's slow pouring, she took the new bottle from him and shooed him away with her free hand. Danielle covered the top of her glass to make sure Emily didn't sneak some wine into her juice as she began pouring wine for her friends. "Why aren't the clinics and hospitals doing IVF and surgical surrogacy services anymore?" Emily asked, as she finished pouring and placed the bottle in the center of the table.

"You don't know?" Danielle asked. "It's been all over the news around the whole country!"

Emily shrugged her shoulders to show her ignorance and huddled herself around the wine glass clasped between her hands.

"Oooh," Danielle cooed excitedly, and she sat forward as she began the story. "So, this woman from Maryland—Poe I think is her last name—she went to an IVF clinic and wanted them to inseminate her eggs pre-fertilized with her husband's sperm—"

"Ugh, I *hate* the word 'inseminate'!" Heather interjected.

"Heather!" Emily chastised, and returned her attention to Danielle. Heather giggled and returned to sipping on her own newly-filled glass of wine.

"So, they *inseminated* her with four or five fertilized eggs," Danielle continued with a pointed glance at Heather, "which is normal in IVF procedures because usually only one or two of the eggs will be viable. However, they *all* took, and she ended up having quadruplets or something, and so now she's suing the clinic because she says they implanted too many eggs. It's a serious case too, and now no clinic in America is willing to implant *any* eggs in anyone until the case goes through the courts and they're told how many fertilized eggs are 'too many' to implant."

Ashleigh slumped in her chair. She'd heard this story a hundred times before and followed the development of the case closely through the news. She hated the unknown woman in the case. Hated her because she had four healthy babies while Ashleigh couldn't have any. Hated her because her lawsuit prevented Ashleigh from being able to use a clinic to find a surrogate of her own. Hated her because just talking about her made her heart pound painfully in her chest, and because she was thinking about babies again.

"That's not all," Danielle added, snapping Ashleigh out of her reverie. "Apparently, the woman in the case just fired her attorney, and the case has been picked up by one of the firms in Baltimore. There aren't a lot of details coming out of the switch, but I read online this morning that her previous attorney was citing 'irreconcilable philosophical differences' with the woman. It's all very interesting."

Ashleigh continued to seethe for the remainder of the luncheon. She returned to her car after saying good-bye to her friends. Alone once again, she tore off her fake smile and the semi-interested mask she'd worn as her friends talked about anything other than pregnancy. As she pulled out from the curb, she allowed her jealousy to wash over her as she thought about Danielle, her pregnancy, her ability to find a surrogate, and the IVF lawsuit that stopped Ashleigh from finding her own surrogate. She clenched the steering wheel tightly. *If ever I meet someone associated with that damned lawsuit...* She left the thought unfinished as she began the long drive back home.

CHAPTER 7

I'M FINE

A shleigh sat in front of the vanity mirror. The lights surrounding the glass surface lit her eyes with an amber hue as she held the gaze of her reflected twin. Nerves rattled by the prospect of returning to her kindergarten class that day had left her struggling to fall asleep the night before.

"I'm fine." She maintained her forced smile in the mirror and practiced the phrase she expected she'd have to repeat all day. She continued to practice until the muscles in her face felt sore. Dropping her smile, she leaned closer to the mirror and said, "I'm fine," one last time—not entirely sure whether she was still just practicing, or trying to convince herself.

A cacophony of children's voices could be heard from the playground as Ashleigh parked her car in the faculty parking lot. She had intentionally arrived shortly before the morning bell to ensure that her workmates would have little time to make a fuss about her return when she passed through the faculty lounge. Entering the lounge, she noticed the familiar smell of cheap coffee from the machine in the corner filling the room. She felt eyes fall upon her, and she heard one of the other teachers whisper, "She's here," to a colleague. Ashleigh avoided the empathetic faces watching her, and noticed that the walls had been painted in her absence. The walls were now a dull gray, and they clashed harshly against the faded green carpet below her feet. Maha spotted Ashleigh from the other end of the room, and walked over to her.

"Hey, Ash! How're you doing, sweetheart?" Sympathy painted her face.

She gave her best-practiced smile, and it came to her naturally, which surprised her.

"I'm fine."

"Mmkay, hon," Maha consoled. "Just so you know, Megan will be in the classroom with you today, just in case you find it's too much." Megan was the substitute the school used when regular teachers were on leave. She had been teaching Ashleigh's class in her absence. Only a year out of college, she still had a naive perkiness to her, and this, coupled with her southern upbringing, gave her a glowing positivity that charmed young students and their parents.

"I don't think that's necessary," Ashleigh began. "Really, I'm fine."

The school bell rang overhead with a shrill buzz, and an audible groan echoed through the room. The teachers picked themselves up and began marching to their respective classrooms to start the day, a few of them glancing awkwardly at Ashleigh, or muttering, "Welcome back," as they passed.

"It's just a precaution, just in case in you need it," Maha said to Ashleigh, and she left to grab her mug of coffee from the counter at the other end of the room.

The day continued as usual, and soon after the lunch break, Ashleigh approached Megan as the children in her class were busy coloring in a picture. "Thanks for holding down the fort while I was gone Megan, and for being here today, just in case. I appreciate it."

"Oh, it was nothin', Miss Ashleigh." Megan smiled warmly and touched Ashleigh's arm. "You doin' okay?"

"I'm fine," Ashleigh repeated with a smile. "I love kids, and the past few weeks have taught me to appreciate what little miracles these children are, even if they're not my miracles."

The brief respite of the two young women was broken by a crash as one of the young girls in the class tripped and fell into one of the low tables.

"Mommy!" The little girl sat up on the floor and started crying, her sobs little more than high-pitched, intermittent squeaks. "I want my mommy!"

Ashleigh smiled once more and touched Megan's arm. "It's fine. I've got this." Ashleigh walked across the room and crouched down next to the crying girl. She scooped the little body and hugged her. Tiny arms wrapped around her neck, and a wet, pale face buried into her shoulder. "It's okay, sweetie," Ashleigh consoled, as she held the girl and rubbed her back through thin strands of blonde hair.

Megan looked on and watched as Ashleigh held and consoled the girl, seeing the ease and peace with which Ashleigh looked after the child. A lump formed in her throat as she was reminded that Ashleigh would never be able to have a child of her own, and she turned away. It didn't feel right to watch Ashleigh hold onto something that she'd never call her own.

• • •

At the end of the working week, Ashleigh lay against her husband on the couch as they each enjoyed a glass of wine— their usual Friday night routine. Still feeling the gnaw of Danielle's surrogate-pregnancy at the back of her mind, she ran her finger around the edge of her wine glass and asked nervously, "Des, do we know anyone who could be our surrogate?"

Desmond, who had his glass halfway to his lips, lowered the glass without taking a sip. "I thought we were going to focus on us for a while?"

Ashleigh sat up so the two could face each other. "I know, and I'm trying to stay busy and keep my mind off of kids, but it's hard. I work all day long with young children. I found out Danielle is pregnant while at lunch with the girls, and I look at you," Ashleigh paused as she looked into her husband's eyes and placed her free hand against Desmond's whiskered cheek, "and I just see you aging out of fatherhood."

Ashleigh could see the deep lines carved into Desmond's face. His eyes showed the crow's-feet of a man who smiled too often and refused to use a facial moisturizer, and his forehead was creased after years of holding a furrowed brow for hours while he studied and researched for his cases. His dark-brown hair was showing increased signs of graying, and his stubble was peppered with silver specs.

Desmond smiled, and the wrinkles next to his eyes deepened. "I'm not that old, Ash." His free hand came up gently to stroke his wife's soft cheek before taking her free hand into his own and intertwining their fingers.

Ashleigh frowned, and her head tilted to one side as she carefully considered her words. "Well, you're not that young either, Des. You're closer to forty than thirty, and the quality of your sperm declines with every passing day. The longer we wait, the more complications we'll face if we ever find a way to have kids in the future, and we can't just wait for that IVF lawsuit to finish."

Desmond choked on his latest sip of wine. "You know about that lawsuit?" He coughed as he began dabbing his mouth with his sleeve.

Ashleigh shrugged. "Of course. It's been all over the news."

Desmond had yet to inform Ashleigh that the IVF case had fallen under his portfolio. He had intended to tell her once the time was right, and she had adjusted to returning to work and being around children once more. He always believed that omission was as much a form of deception as outright lying, but he didn't think she was ready for the news.

"Des?" Ashleigh asked, snapping Desmond out of his introspection.

"Sorry?" he asked, returning his attention to her.

"I asked what you think of the case. You're a lawyer, a medical negligence one too. You'd understand the case better than anyone."

He breathed in heavily and blew out a long breath. "You really want to talk about this Ash?"

"Yes. I want to know your opinion of it," Ashleigh said as she leaned back and took another sip of her wine.

Desmond looked upward pensively. "Which opinion do you want?"

Every lawyer formulates at least two opinions of any case: the personal, and the professional. The professional opinion was black and white, void of emotion, like the law itself, such as believing that a *factually* guilty client should be acquitted for lack of *legal* guilt—an inability to prove a matter beyond reasonable doubt. The personal opinion, however, was entirely emotional and captured the essence of their moral bearing, such as hoping that the factually guilty client, even though acquitted, still burned in hell.

The problem with this dichotomy was that the two opinions rarely reconciled. People were messy. They were naturally imperfect and emotional, and the law—emotionless and absolute—made no allowances for that. A lawyer's professional opinion was black and white, and their personal opinion existed in the gray shades in between.

In asking for his opinion, Ashleigh was asking for a black-and-white answer to a matter that was cloaked in those shades of gray.

"What do I think about the IVF case?" he repeated, as he looked into the whirlpool of red wine he created by swirling the glass in his hand. "Personally, I'm angry that the case has affected our ability to explore surrogacy through clinics, but I

51

know it's not all about us. I can appreciate the woman's desire—if not her desperation—to have kids. I can understand that. She must have known that the doctors were going to implant multiple fertilized eggs in her uterus, so she should have accepted the outcome, however unexpected.

"However, maybe she was told that it was unlikely that all of the eggs would be viable. Maybe the clinic didn't elaborate on what they meant by 'multiple' eggs. Perhaps she was misinformed? There are a lot of things about this case I don't know yet." He caught himself after his last sentence. He hadn't received all the case briefs yet, and he was afraid that by saying "yet," Ashleigh might realize that he was expecting more information. He quickly continued talking to distract her from the implication he'd unwittingly made. "Professionally, however, I think she has a case. There's no guidance or rules on how many fertilized eggs clinics should implant to ensure a viable pregnancy. The outcome of this case won't just help the woman look after those babies, it will help refine the law and pave the way for better and more responsible treatment in the future for other mothers. Professionally, I think it's a good case, and I'm intrigued by the legal issues it raises." Desmond trailed off as he noticed Ashleigh's discomfort with his answer.

She said looking at him with disappointed eyes. "You realize we can't have a baby because of her?"

Desmond shook his head sympathetically and tightened his lips. "That's not true. There's no way this woman could have known that the IVF clinics would shut their doors until her case is resolved. That was the decision of the clinics to avoid further potential liability, not hers."

Ashleigh's disappointment turned to annoyance. "You sound like you're on her side," she said coldly.

Desmond shrugged uncomfortably without breaking his wife's challenging gaze. "You asked for my opinion. I gave it to you."

Ashleigh's face showed she was unimpressed with his candor. She came to her feet and stood over him. "Tell me something, Des. Would you represent her? Would you represent this woman, whose selfishness has not only robbed women all around the country from experiencing the joy of motherhood, but also has visited so much grief on us, to your *wife?*"

Desmond sighed. This was precisely why he hated when friends and family asked his opinion on controversial cases. Most people couldn't divorce their personal sentiments from objective reality, or the law attached to the case. Moreover, they judged him harshly for being able to do so. He looked at his wife sternly and gave his answer. "Everyone ... *everyone* Ashleigh, is entitled to vigorous representation, given at the best of the abilities of the attorney of their choosing. I have given an oath to represent people who choose me to represent them to the best of *my* abilities, no matter what my personal feelings are toward them, or their case. If she asked me, then yes, I would represent her."

Ashleigh's face twisted under glaring eyes, and her mouth hung slightly open in disbelief. She leaned forward over Desmond and slapped him across the face with her free hand, her glass spilling dregs of red wine down the other.

"Ashleigh!" Desmond yelled in surprise.

Ashleigh swung her free hand toward Desmond's face once more, and he caught her wrist with his hand. She dropped her glass of wine to free her other hand and slapped him again across his other cheek, the sound of the glass shattering on the ground muffled by the crack of her powerful strike. Impassioned with fury, Ashleigh pulled her wrist free from Desmond's grip and stormed out of the room, leaving him to sit alone in a patch of red wetness.

• • •

Allied forces suffered further casualties on the front lines this week, among them were another sixteen American soldiers killed, and many more wounded. Congress today continued to criticize the President's delay in acting on their repeated calls for reinforcements or the implementation of a retreat and extraction plan.

Desmond was listening to the television as he scrubbed the carpet and couch to remove the quickly setting red stains. Ashleigh remained locked in their bedroom.

In other news, Baltimore firm Rennick, Spectre & Co., after being appointed as the new attorneys in the notorious Poe IVF case, are seeking to turn the case into a class action. They are urging women across the country who may have experienced unwanted births from IVF treatment to—

Desmond quickly reached for the remote and turned off the television. He listened in silence to discern whether Ashleigh might have heard the broadcast from their bedroom upstairs. There didn't seem to be any noise. He wanted to tell her about him having acquired the case, but her reaction to his mere willingness to represent Poe showed that she was not ready to hear the news. *If she got this upset from just a hypothetical...* He left the thought unfinished.

Two hours later, Ashleigh came downstairs and found Desmond reading on the wine-stained couch. He'd managed to get the wine out of the carpet, but by the time he got to the sofa, the stains had set in. He had tried to speak to Ashleigh through the door an hour earlier, but she had told him to go away. She sat down next to her husband, and he lowered his book to give her his undivided attention.

Ashleigh sighed. She knew she'd overreacted. It was just such a damned touchy subject for her. She rubbed the wine stain on the couch with a pawing finger and tightened her lips in self-directed annoyance. Too embarrassed to look up at him, she uttered, "I'm sorry." She paused, struggling to find her next words. "I asked for your opinion, and you gave it to me. It wasn't fair of me to react like that just because your opinion is different to mine." She felt Desmond place an understanding hand on top of her own, and she looked up to find his reassuring half smile. "It's just been so hard," she continued. "I try to focus on other things, but it's really hard. I work all day with young kids, Danielle's pregnant through a surrogate, and with this IVF case..." she sighed as she let her sentence trail off. "There's just so many reminders *all the time*! And then I hear you talk like you're on this woman's side. I just cracked."

"Just try to focus on the positives," Desmond intoned.

Ashleigh gave a smile. "That's *so* annoying," she said. "But I know you're trying." Desmond put his book to one side and pulled Ashleigh in towards him. She moved closer, and she pulled his arm around her, so they sat huddled together on the couch.

Desmond kissed the top of Ashleigh's head warmly and kept his lips pressed against her as he spoke, "I tried looking into things that might take your mind off having kids for a while."

"Like what?" she asked, looking up without displacing the lips still touching her scalp.

"I looked into that ballet up in New York you told me about," he offered. "I was trying to buy tickets, so we could make the trip and see it together."

Ashleigh gave a short laugh. She knew Desmond would hate the ballet, and she would have preferred to see it alone, so she could enjoy it without worrying about him.

"It's finished." She sighed.

"That explains why I couldn't find any tickets," said Desmond. "Well, we can always try for the next one."

Ashleigh sighed and shook her head slightly. "They're saying she's retired now, so there won't be any 'next one' to go and see either." She sat up and kissed him on the cheek in a votive of thanks.

Desmond leaned back, a quizzical look painted across his face. "Who retired?"

Ashleigh raised an eyebrow, surprised her husband didn't know who she was talking about. "The choreographer? The famous playwright? The woman I follow on Instagram that I keep telling you about?"

Desmond shrugged.

Ashleigh laughed. "You're serious? You've never heard of this woman? You've never heard of Hannah Lenore?"

Desmond sat up from the couch, his quizzical expression morphing into stunned confusion. "Hannah Lenore? *That's* who you've been talking about!?"

Ashleigh leaned back and looked at him with an equally confused expression. "Yeah. Why?"

"Hannah Lenore," Desmond repeated as he looked away in disbelief before returning his gaze to his wife. "I know her."

CHAPTER 8

OLD FRIENDS

Hannah changed into her workout clothes in front of her apartment's living room window. The rain pattering against the opaque glass obstructed the view. Her high-rise directly overlooked Central Park, and only one other apartment building was close and high enough to see into her window. She didn't worry if the occupant of that apartment had seen her undress. Even if he had seen her, it wouldn't have been anything she hadn't already shown him.

The dull gray light that filtered through the window matched the white and light gray tones of her home and the *New York Times* web page displayed on the tablet lying on her kitchen counter. Her publicist had called her earlier that morning to let her know that Jack Katan had published an article following their interview. She expected the piece would anger her, and not caring about the rain falling outside, she'd planned to use it as motivation for a hard morning run.

She took a deep breath as she tied her unruly blonde hair in a ponytail and clicked through the *Times* to find Katan's article. She rolled her eyes as she read the title: *Beautiful Things Never Last.* She braced her arms on the countertop and stooped over the tablet as her eyes continued to skim the article, key phrases popping out to her. *Left alone to face the cold winter of retirement ... no one knows for certain who Hannah Lenore is in private ... the envy of every woman and desire of every man ... no one ever said she was happy.*

She straightened her posture and leaned back. "He even writes like an ass," she muttered. She looked down to continue reading, but her attention was redirected as her cell phone rang on the counter behind her.

Her outstretched hand paused briefly as she wondered whether she should answer the call. Few people had her personal contact number, and the timing seemed suspicious in light of Katan's article. However, not wanting to let Katan get to her, she cast aside her trepidation, and picked up the phone. "Hello?"

"Hannah, it's Desmond. It's been a while."

Hannah smiled. "Desmond? I'm sorry sir, you'll have to be more specific. I only know one Desmond, and we haven't spoken in a *very* long time." She could hear a choked silence as her teasing caught Desmond off guard. "Des," she said through a playful smile, "it's good to hear from you. It has been a while. What has prompted a big-shot attorney to call me so early on a Saturday morning?"

Desmond laughed aloud at Hannah's mockery. "My wife, actually. She's a huge fan of your work, and she missed your last show by a couple of days."

Hannah's smile disappeared, and she turned on the spot to lean against the marble counter beside her. "That wasn't my last show, Des."

"Oh," Desmond replied, "I didn't mean last-last show. I meant most recent. Trust me, I don't believe any of the stories about your retirement. I was just telling Ashleigh that you won't stop writing and choreographing your dances until it kills you."

Hannah smirked slightly at his understanding, and waited in silence for her old friend to continue.

"Listen, I was hoping that if Ash and I couldn't come up to New York to see one of your shows, perhaps we could come up just to have dinner with you and catch up? Ashleigh would love to meet you and talk about your work. I know you always have a busy schedule, but…"

Hannah stopped listening as she turned to look at her wall calendar. For years, events, meetings, rehearsals, and shows had been penciled in every second of every day. However, since her last show, the boxes on the calendar remained hauntingly empty, acting as daily reminders that she still had no ideas for a new show. She spoke over Desmond's voice, cutting him off. "No, I'm free. I'd love to catch up, and meet your wife." She looked over at the still-open *New York Times* web page on her counter and remembered Katan's scathing commentary on her life. "Plus," she continued into the phone, "I could use the distraction. Text me when you're coming up, and I'll make sure I'm free."

As the call ended, Hannah grabbed her cell phone, headphones, and a hooded sweatshirt, and took the stairs to the bottom floor to begin her run in the rain. The scent of the wet trees in the park across from her rushed to greet her, and she pressed play on her phone. Music filled her ears. She briefly stretched limber muscles under the canopy to her building's entrance, and pulled the hood of her sweatshirt over her head. She placed her first step against the wet concrete in the city that never slept, and smiled to herself as she began her jog in the rain, completely forgetting the half-read article in her apartment, several stories above her.

• • •

Ashleigh could hardly contain her excitement. She had brought two suitcases with her to New York, one of them carrying nothing but outfit options for their dinner with Hannah.

"I don't understand," Desmond had said while pinching the bridge of his nose. "It's one night—one dinner. Why do you need to pack six outfits?"

"Eight," Ashleigh corrected without looking up, as she struggled to zip her bursting suitcase.

"Eight! Why do you need to pack eight outfits for one night?" Desmond finished, perplexed.

"Whew!" Ashleigh stood up proudly after finally getting the suitcase to close. "It's simple. I don't know what I'm going to want to wear on the night."

Desmond sat down on the edge of the bed, certain he was losing his mind. "I still don't understand. Why don't you decide what you want to wear now and just pack *that* outfit? Then your decision is made for you."

Ashleigh laughed. "That's silly." Sensing her husband's confusion, she elaborated, "It's simple: I won't *know* what I want to wear until just before we leave for the dinner. I don't know how I'm going to feel or what I think I'm going to feel comfortable in."

"Then just pack whatever is comfortable! Those tall heels I saw you pack aren't comfortable. You complain every time you wear them, and I wind up carrying them." Desmond's brow furrowed, deepening the creases in his forehead.

Ashleigh laughed again. "I don't mean that kind of comfortable! I mean I don't know how I'm going to feel about how I look—my makeup, my hair, my body. It could all change between now and when we leave for dinner, so I need to pack alternatives and make sure I have something I'll *feel* comfortable wearing. Does that make sense?"

Desmond was sure it didn't. He stared blankly at the chest of drawers opposite him and tried to comprehend what Ashleigh was telling him because he clearly didn't understand.

Ashleigh walked over to her husband, sat on his lap, and draped her arms around his neck. "You don't need to understand," she said playfully. "You just need to let me do this," she leaned in closer to Desmond's ear and whispered, "and then pack all of these heavy bags in the car for me."

She bit his earlobe lightly, and mocking him lovingly, laughed as she stood up from his lap. "And don't frown, love. You'll ruin your good looks!" She winked at him as she turned to finish packing her other suitcase.

Desmond smiled, and he watched his wife's hips swing as she walked away from him. Snapping out of his reverie, he stood up from the bed, and began carrying Ashleigh's impossibly heavy suitcase to their car in preparation for their road trip to New York.

• • •

"I don't like my outfit," Ashleigh said flatly as the two stood, side by side, in the elevator in Hannah's apartment building.

"What?" Desmond's head turned sharply to face his wife.

Ashleigh repeated. "I don't like my outfit; I don't feel comfortable in it."

"Ngh. Well, it's too late now!" Desmond blurted in disbelief. He and Ashleigh had planned to spend the day visiting the sights, and having lunch before returning to their New York hotel to get ready for their dinner with Hannah. These plans were canceled, as Ashleigh spent the entire day deciding what to wear and pampering herself before the dinner. Their hotel room was left in disarray—littered with clothes, makeup, shoes, and hair accessories. The news that his wife was somehow unhappy with the result after so much time and deliberation was too absurd for Desmond to comprehend.

"You're not helping, Des," she responded sharply, as her eyes rose to look at the changing lights above the elevator doors. The numbers illuminated as they passed each floor on the way to Hannah's penthouse—forty-two...forty-three...forty-four.

"I just need you to tell me I look good."

Desmond's mouth hung open; he was left without words. He was saved from the need to respond by a ding from the elevator, heralding their arrival at the top floor.

The steel elevator doors parted, opening directly into Hannah's living room. Ashleigh stepped first into the lavish living space, mouth agape. All thoughts of her outfit and their conversation were forgotten. Desmond hung back in the elevator, unsure of whether he was supposed to wait to be invited inside. The elevator began to beep due to the doors being unable to close, and he stepped out awkwardly.

Ashleigh beckoned for him to join her. "She knows we're here. She already buzzed us up!"

Soft music wafted through the space, which was dimly lit by an overhead chandelier that cast soft, shadowy overtones in the monochromatic room. The light gray walls complemented the soft white carpet, creating a crafted contrast to the small, ivory-colored wooden dining table accompanied by a single chair, over by a far wall. The bar at the opposite end of the room was well stocked with various wines and liquors, and the star-filled night sky watched from outside the large living room window.

"Desmond!" Ashleigh whispered, "It looks like an Instagram photo!" She quickly took off her heels, and placed them by the closed elevator doors to avoid staining the lush carpet. They were also hurting her feet. As she placed bare feet against the plush carpet fibers, she had to suppress a murmured coo. The carpet felt luxuriously soft, and massaged her skin as she walked. *I want to lie down on this*, she thought.

She continued to walk quietly around the room, impressed with the simplicity and elegance of the design. "My goodness, Desmond, just look at that view!" she said, now standing by the large window overlooking the park. "And all of this space! It makes the room look so spacious and inviting!"

"I'm glad you think so!" Hannah stepped into the room from her bedroom. "Most people tell me it looks like I'm still moving in, but I like having all the space. I don't like to feel weighed down by things, and having too many things everywhere would just make me feel—"

"Cluttered!" Ashleigh finished.

"Exactly!" Hannah enthused. "Plus, it gives me the room to dance and stretch. You must be Ashleigh."

Ashleigh was awestruck by Hannah. Her smile was genuine and featured the flash of brilliant white teeth. Her skin was softly tanned, yet still glistened with a pearlescent glow, and even though she was roughly the same age as Desmond, her happy face lacked the harried lines that characterized his. Hannah's untamed blonde locks hung loftily over one shoulder that was exposed through the cut-out of a gray T-shirt, emblazoned with the name of a small local band. She walked towards Ashleigh with a soft grace, and with each step, her hips swayed slightly beneath tight blue jeans. Ashleigh couldn't tell if Hannah was wearing makeup, and she wondered how a woman could look so naturally beautiful. None of the photos she had ever seen of Hannah seemed to do justice to her effortless, striking beauty.

Ashleigh took Hannah's outstretched hand in her own. "Ms. Lenore, it is so wonderful to meet you."

Hannah laughed. "Oh please, Ashleigh, call me Hannah."

Ashleigh returned a blushing smile. Hannah turned to greet Desmond, gently tugging her hand free from Ashleigh's grip—she was still unconsciously shaking her hand and staring. Ashleigh looked down at her own black dress and could almost feel the weight of the makeup on her face. Already feeling uncomfortable, she felt downright shabby next to Hannah.

Standing back from Desmond, Hannah appraised the couple in front of her. "My goodness, you both look so handsome!"

Desmond, you're certainly punching above your weight. Ashleigh, you look amazing. You both make me feel so underdressed!"

Ashleigh looked at her feet to avoid the undeserved compliment. Desmond simply smiled.

Hannah suddenly clasped her soft hands over her mouth before continuing, "Oh gosh! I hope I mentioned we'd be dining-in! I don't often eat out as it can be a little awkward eating alone, and I tend to prefer the privacy."

"Thank goodness!" Desmond said, smiling. He took off his suit jacket and untied his tie. "Is there somewhere I can leave these?"

A short time later, Hannah was pouring red wine for the three of them. "I hope you both like Chinese. There's a place downtown I'm quite fond of, and I've ordered various items from their menu that we can just sample. I know red wine doesn't really 'go' with Chinese food, but I like red wine, and I like Chinese food."

Ashleigh and Desmond smiled appreciatively and nodded as they took their first sips of wine. Ashleigh licked a single droplet of red liquid from her pink lips. "My gosh, Hannah, this wine is beautiful! What's the label?"

Hannah shrugged and looked back at the bar, trying to read the label. "Honestly, I have no idea. I can't tell the difference between a five-dollar bottle of wine from the corner liquor store and expensive bottles I occasionally receive as gifts."

Desmond recognized the label from dinners he occasionally had to have with some of the firm's wealthier clients, but declined to mention the incredulous expense of the now-open bottle.

An hour later, Desmond's shoes had joined his wife's by the elevator door. The distant sounds of New York traffic filtered up through the dark night to the softly lit room, and a soft-gray ottoman that matched the color of the walls sat nearby, holding their now discarded Chinese takeout boxes.

The dining table had been designed to seat only one person—Hannah usually ate alone and rarely entertained guests at home—and so the three of them sat with fresh drinks in hand on the soft carpet by the window.

The libations had made Ashleigh a little more relaxed, and the easy flow of Hannah's conversation made her more comfortable. "So, I'm curious. How do you and Des know each other? I didn't even know the two of you were acquainted until recently."

Hannah exaggerated mock indignation, and lightly slapped Desmond's forearm. "You never told her about me?"

Desmond chuckled, shrugged, and took another sip of wine. "I told her *about* you, I just never mentioned that you were...*you*."

Hannah feigned a gasp and turned back to Ashleigh. "We were in the same poetry class in college. I was a sophomore and Des was a senior. I was doing poetry as part of my playwriting and dance study, and Des...well, he *said* he was taking the course to improve his writing skills, but I think he just had a soft spot for poetry."

The two women looked at Desmond. He smiled and shrugged again, refusing to indicate which version was the truth.

"Anyway," Hannah continued, now wearing a smile of her own, "after that class we kind of just stuck as friends. Even after he graduated, we'd still get together from time to time. Then I finished college, and I didn't have a clue what I wanted to do next. So, I came to Desmond for some advice, and the next thing you know, I broke up with my boyfriend, packed a bag, and jumped on a plane overseas on my first big adventure."

Ashleigh looked back at her husband in shock and asked Hannah, "What kind of advice did he give you!?"

Hannah giggled. "I don't quite remember what he said, but it was the best decision I've ever made. I really found myself

65

while I was traveling abroad for those first few years, and the journey gave me the inspiration to write the show that launched my career. A few years later, I was back in New York and managing the show when my dad passed away. I went to Desmond again, and sure enough, by daybreak the next morning I was already on a plane. After that, it kind of became a tradition. Each time I was about to leave in pursuit of inspiration or the next big adventure, I'd come to see him."

Ashleigh looked at Desmond quizzically before calling back to Hannah, "That's weird. You never stopped by in all the years I've known Desmond."

Hannah's eyes found Desmond's, and her lips pursed slightly. "I guess that's because it's been a while since I found the time to go on another adventure—or found one worth pursuing."

Her mind once again turned to her lack of inspiration for her next show, and she sighed. In her brief reverie, she allowed her glass of wine to slip from her fingers, and its crimson contents spilled onto the carpet. "Ugh! This *always* happens!" she said, annoyed at herself. "I'm forever spilling things. It's a curse!"

She rose quickly and grabbed a paper towel from the bar. She said to Ashleigh as she knelt on the carpet and began dabbing at the spill, "So you've heard how Des and I met, but what about you? How did the two of you meet?"

Desmond and Ashleigh's eyes met, and he smiled. "I, um, I represented Ash's father in a case—one of my first cases at the firm, actually."

Ashleigh leaned back as she listened to the familiar story.

"Her dad had been in the construction business and spent a lot of time tearing down old buildings to make room for new ones. In the process, he was exposed to a lot of asbestos. He contracted mesothelioma—lung cancer—and I fought to make sure he was looked after."

"He did more than that," Ashleigh cut in. "None of the other firms would help my dad because he didn't have money, and when Des overheard a lawyer in his office rejecting the case, he stepped in and took the case pro bono." She grabbed and squeezed her husband's hand as she continued. "Dad deteriorated really quickly, and soon he couldn't leave the house. I had been away at college for most of Dad's case, and so even though Des was making house calls by that stage, I still hadn't seen him. Of course, Mom had told me all about the strapping young attorney who was helping Dad. Anyway, I was home from college for one summer, and Dad started coughing. And I mean he was *really* coughing like he couldn't breathe. I hadn't heard Dad coughing like that before, and so I rushed into the study where he was meeting Desmond."

Desmond squeezed Ashleigh's hand again, and Hannah retook her seat next to Ashleigh after finishing with the spill. "I don't know what I thought I was going to do, but while I was hysterical in the corner, crying and yelling for Dad to breathe, Des was just next to him, helping hold his oxygen mask in place and rubbing his back, telling him everything was going to be okay. That's how Des and I met. I'm pretty sure I started falling for him that day. It's hard not to fall for a guy who stays so calm in a crisis like that."

Hannah broke in softly. "So how did you start *dating*? I imagine there must have been some transition from being the family lawyer to part of the family?"

Ashleigh continued, "Well, eventually Des negotiated a settlement with the construction company. We knew that a trial was a long way away, and Dad didn't think he had much time left. Des negotiated for the company to put Dad into one of the best care facilities in the city, plus a small payout to cover his lost earning capacity. This paid off Dad's house and my college tuition, which Dad was always so worried about. Even after he finished with Dad's case though, Des continued to visit Dad.

He walked in one day when I was sitting with Dad at the care facility—"

Desmond cleared his throat. "I wasn't just there to visit. At least, not that time. That time it was business. Her dad had asked me to draw up his will, and I was there to have him sign it. I walked into the ward and Ashleigh was sitting by his bed, still wearing her University of Maryland Terrapins T-shirt, mind you." Desmond gave his wife a wry smile.

"Ash's dad asked her to leave, and I sat down and started going through what I had put together to make sure it reflected his wishes. After signing the will, he gestured to the door with his thumb and said, 'That's my only daughter. I've been too sick for too long, and I never really got to show her what a good man looks like. I want you to promise me you'll ask her on a date.' Of course, I'd wanted to ask Ash out on a date for years, but always thought it would be inappropriate because of the age difference," Desmond said.

"About a week later Ash and I went on our first date. A little less than a year later, we were engaged, and six months after that we got married. For years, Ash's dad kept telling me he was hanging on just long enough to walk Ashleigh down the aisle, and at our wedding, he scolded me for making him wait so long."

Ashleigh laughed nostalgically and held back the tears welling in her eyes.

Desmond's faced turned sullen as he finished the story. "Sadly, it seemed he wasn't kidding. We attended his funeral just a week after returning from our honeymoon."

"Geez, Desmond," Hannah cut in, as she grabbed a tissue being offered by Ashleigh, "You really know how to bring the room down!" She laughed halfheartedly as the story called to her mind memories of her own father that she'd also lost to cancer a few years prior.

The hour turned late, and the mood grew lighter with each empty wine bottle added to the regimen accumulating on the bar. The conversation turned to Hannah, and her work.

"I saw one of your shows on Broadway many years ago," Ashleigh said. "I was in college and still hadn't selected a major. I felt lost because I had no idea what I wanted to do with my life. I watched your show, and one of the acts just spoke to me, gave me a sort of clarity or perspective I didn't even know I was looking for. It led to me becoming a kindergarten teacher. I don't know if I would have found that calling if not for you. Your work is incredible, Hannah."

Hannah smiled and raised a pointed finger at Ashleigh. "That right there, that's why I write and choreograph these shows."

Ashleigh turned her head curiously. "What do you mean?"

"You know that feeling you get when you hear the lyrics of a song, or read a line in a book that just resonates with you? When you feel a connection with the words, and you think, 'That there! *That* was written for me!' Where you feel a connection with the author and know *exactly* what they felt when they wrote those words? That's the feeling I love, and what I try to give to people through my work. All the shows, the press, the money, or the modest fame—none of that means anything if my work doesn't touch the audience. Music, art, literature, and dance are the only things that can touch us without our permission, and I try to capture this axiom in my work. I aim to touch the audience and help them feel something within themselves, as I share my stories and experiences."

Ashleigh's heart was beating faster as she was captured and enamored by the beautiful woman's passion. "Oh gosh!" she chagrined. "Now I really hate that I missed your latest show." Desmond had reminded her not to describe the missed show as Hannah's last.

Hannah drank the final sip of her wine and put her glass on the ottoman before turning to Ashleigh. "Oh, you didn't get to see it? Come by my studio, and I'll have the dancers perform a private show for you. Of course, there won't be any of the props or lighting you'd expect at the theater, but I vainly like to think that people come for the dancing," she said wryly and with a smirk. "My dancers need the practice anyway to keep in form. You can even come with me tomorrow since you're already in town."

Ashleigh was delighted. She accepted enthusiastically, and before long, she and Desmond were readying to leave Hannah's apartment, each a little unsteady on wine-afflicted feet. When their cab arrived to take them to their hotel, they each said goodnight to Hannah and entered the elevator.

Hannah watched as Desmond put his arm around his wife before the cold elevator doors closed and removed the couple from view, leaving her alone once more in the vast, empty apartment.

CHAPTER 9

NEW FRIENDS

T he next morning, Desmond sat numbly in an airplane seat. He squinted as he fought against the light pounding behind his forehead and tried to focus on the brief materials on his tablet. He had awoken early that morning to catch a flight back to Baltimore to continue working on the Poe case while Ashleigh spent the extra day in New York with Hannah. The flight attendant invited him to put his tablet away during takeoff, and he obliged thankfully. It was a much-needed excuse to put away his work and rest his weary eyes. He closed his eyes and began reflecting on the previous evening as he sank into the uncomfortable economy seat. He recalled Hannah telling Ashleigh about how she would come to visit him before embarking on her adventures. When *was* the last time she'd visited him? For that matter, when was the last time they had spoken?

His mind turned to that first time she'd visited him before leaving for several years, and he watched the memory play out like a movie on the back of his eyelids. He was living in a crappy little apartment he could barely afford on his junior attorney salary.

"I just don't know what to do!" twenty-four-year-old Hannah exclaimed. Her blonde hair was wild even then, and it hung toward the floor as she lay across an old, one-seater lounge chair. Her feet dangled over the other end of the seat.

"Martin keeps telling me I need to get a job...'Any job' he says. But where does that lead? Working forty to fifty hours a week in a job I don't care for with people I don't even like, looking forward to weekends just so I can't sit in a dirty little apartment and relish the fact that I don't have to work that day?"

She looked up at Desmond and found him looking at her from behind his desk, one eyebrow raised as if to say, *seriously?* "Oops" she laughed back halfheartedly. "You know what I mean though, Des." She returned her gaze to the ceiling above her. "You always seem to get me, even when I can't think of the right words to say what I mean."

Desmond ignored the work splayed out on the desk in front of him, and examined the lines of her body as she stretched out in front of him. There was something special about Hannah. The other men in her life would fawn over her for her body or her beauty, but that wasn't what drew him to her. Certainly, he noticed those things—how could he not? But it was her spirit that made him always find time for her whenever she called or came knocking.

"I just wonder," she continued ponderously, "why am I different? Or am I even different? Maybe everyone feels like this, but just resign themselves to the daily grind, as if there is no alternative? But then, if they felt like this, how *could* they resign themselves? But I won't, so I guess I am different. Right?" Hannah sat up in the chair with proper posture. Her hands gripped the edge of the seat, and she leaned forward, her loose T-shirt falling open.

Desmond struggled to keep his eyes on hers as he answered, "I love—" he cleared his throat. "I love that you're different, Han. The way you stand out everywhere you go, the way your eyes are always somewhere else." He smiled to himself as he noticed her eyes drift away from his as she continued to gaze around the room. "Don't change. If you feel that taking any old job isn't for you, then don't. You're still young, Han.

You've got no debts, no job to worry about, no career you're dying to work on, no kids to worry about. You're free—free to not care, to be who you want to be. Free to make mistakes, to get lost, to be lonely. Free to just…stop. The only thing you have keeping you here is your boyfriend—"

"And you!" she said sweetly, with a wistful smile. She paused, and her smile faded naturally. "How would you feel if I just disappeared tomorrow? Just, I don't know, jumped on a plane and was…gone?"

I'd be devastated, he thought. "I'd be fine," he said. "I'll still be here plugging away at my caseload when you get back. But what about your boyfriend?" he asked, trying to bring the conversation full circle. "Is it serious?"

Hannah smiled at him as she came to her feet. "I guess not," she answered. "Not anymore."

Hannah had broken up with her boyfriend, and left the country on a plane the next day. Desmond had no idea where she'd gone.

Turbulence in the plane jolted Desmond's eyes open, and the light coming in from the adjacent window reminded him of his hangover. He closed his eyes again and tried to remember the last time he and Hannah had met. He recalled Hannah mentioning the night before that she had come to visit him after her father had passed away, and again the memory was projected against the back of his eyelids.

"Look at you, mister fancy attorney, with his very own office!"

Desmond had looked up to find Hannah standing in the doorway. She was wearing an all-black ensemble that clashed harshly with the white, fluorescent office lights. A few years had passed since the last time he had seen her. He was now working out of a New York law firm—the one he'd worked at before joining Rennick, Spectre & Co.—and was just shy of thirty. "Hannah! How did you—"

"Google," Hannah answered presumptively. He invited her to sit as he rose to shut the office door behind her. "What— Why— How have you been?" Desmond asked, not sure where to start after not having seen her for several years. He took his seat behind his desk once more. "I've been well, for the most part," Hannah began. "I'm famous now. Well, not famous. What do you call it when a person isn't universally famous, but they're reasonably well-known within their field of work?"

"Renowned?" Desmond asked, his inflection making it clear he wasn't entirely sure of his answer.

"Yes! That's it! I am renowned." Hannah gave an exaggerated bow from her seat. Desmond laughed.

"But...ah," Hannah continued, her voice failing her a little, "I'm not okay now. Dad died, Des. I buried my dad today." She looked at the ceiling as she tried to cage the tears welling in her ocean eyes.

"And I...um, I don't know what to do. All I could think about after the funeral was that the last time I felt this lost, you had the answers. Plus, I remember what you told me about your dad, and it got me thinking, if you learned how to live without your father, maybe you could teach me how to do it? Because right now I'm breaking, and I just want someone to help me feel whole again." Her tears broke, and Desmond rose from his seat to give her a hug.

She pushed her arms out and shied away from him, "No, I don't want to be hugged right now. I just ... I don't know, Des. I always figured that by the time this happened I'd have someone to comfort me, you know? Someone who would help me not feel so broken. I thought I'd have someone like you. Someone good and dependable. Someone strong who could just let me be weak for a minute. Someone who loves me enough to tell me 'don't go' when I feel like running off like I did last time, like I feel like doing now. My dad was that guy."

She looked up at Desmond, her mascara unashamedly streaking down her perfect face.

A long silence hung between them before he answered.

"Hannah," he began, "I don't know why you came to me. I ... could be a lot of those things to you. But no man is ever going to replace the hole in your life left by your father, and I'm never going to be the guy who tells you to stay when your heart says it's time to leave. If you're here to say that you're back from your adventuring and you want to give *this*," he gestured back and forth between them, "a shot, then I'd be lying if I told you I hadn't been hoping for that for years."

He paused briefly to see if Hannah gave any kind of reaction to his confession. She gave none, so he continued. "But if you're here to ask me to just ... temporarily fill the void, then I'm not your guy."

Hannah's frozen features melted to reveal a mixture of disgust and disbelief. She came to stand in front of his desk. "You think I'm here to ask you to have sex with me? Or to start some grand romance? Desmond," she whispered, "my dad just *died!* I'm here to just ... I just wanted you to say the words that would have me leaving your presence feeling like I did the last time we met. I used to think you understood me! You've changed. You used to be one of the good guys." Her eyes scanned over him as though she were looking at a stranger. "I think I should leave."

The next morning, Hannah had flown out of the United States. Desmond didn't know where she had gone. In the years that followed, maturity gave perspective to that encounter, although he didn't try to reach out to her to explain that he had misrepresented himself, or to apologize. What would be the point? He had been sure that he would never see her again. He would never know where she'd disappeared to, and what reason could she have for seeking him out again? He continued his practice, and moved to Baltimore after joining Rennick, Spectre & Co. as a senior associate.

Desmond smiled to himself as he remembered that it was there that he had last seen Hannah. The film playing in his memory shifted, and he recalled their last encounter. He was working in his office late one night when she appeared in his doorway.

"I didn't know you'd moved," she called, causing him to look up abruptly from his desk.

He looked much older now. His early-thirties had treated him much less kindly than her. His tie was loosened around his open collar, and his suit jacket was thrown over the chair sitting in front of his desk. He sat up in his chair quickly, and she could tell by the easing of the wrinkles around his eyes and forehead that he was surprised to see her.

"I'm sorry," Desmond answered.

Hannah cleared her throat and spoke a little more loudly. "I said, 'I didn't know you'd moved.'"

Desmond smiled. "I heard you. It's just that I promised myself that if I ever saw you again, the first thing I'd do is apologize."

Hannah smiled and waved the apology away with her hand. "Ah, forget about it. I was emotional, and it wasn't really all that fair for me to just surprise you in your office like that." Desmond raised an eyebrow, and she laughed at him. "Hey now, I didn't say it was fair this time either. Do you have a second for an old friend?"

Desmond smiled. "Come on, Hannah; I always have time for you."

She entered his glass-walled office and closed the door behind her. "Moving up in the world I see," she teased him. She removed her tan coat and placed it on the back of the chair to join Desmond's discarded jacket. Beneath her coat, she wore a striking, knee-length red dress.

He glanced down the length of her profile, and his eyes paused on the flats she wore beneath the dress. Hannah sat on the lounge at the opposite end of Desmond's office, and crossed her feet to hide one foot behind the other. "Don't stare. It's hard for me to wear heels these days."

Desmond returned his eyes to hers, and he smiled. "I was just thinking that you look as beautiful as ever." She smiled back at him. Desmond sighed, "If you're here, then I guess you're leaving again. Did you really fly all the way down here just to say good-bye?"

Hannah smiled, but it was a genuinely shy smile. It carried with it a quality she'd never shared with him before. "Actually, Des, I just got back. I just completed another tour of the last show you helped me find. Do you realize that every time I leave you, I come back with inspiration for my next show?" She spoke without ever taking her eyes away from his.

"It hadn't occurred to me," Desmond answered with an appreciative grin. "But I don't understand. If you're not leaving, then why did you come all the way here?"

Nerves forced Hannah out of her seat, and she stood to face the glass wall to Desmond's office, avoiding his gaze. She looked down. "I've been thinking about what you said the last time we met—before I left again—and I think I'm ready."

"Ready for what?" Desmond asked to her back.

Hannah turned to face him, her expression a mixture of fear and excitement. "I'm ready for this." She gestured back and forth between them, mimicking the gesture he'd made all those years ago. "I'm ready for this adventure. You and me."

Desmond abruptly came to his feet. "Hannah … I … I can't. I've met someone."

Her hopeful smile vanished, and she nodded slowly, somberly, as the words sank in. "Is it serious?" she whispered quietly.

Desmond nodded slowly, almost painfully, and he braced himself against the need to say his next words. "It's serious enough that I think you should leave."

Hannah bit her lip softly. She kept her eyes on his large, apologetic eyes, and tried desperately not to let herself fall deeper into them. Her lips parted and pursed several times, as she searched for words to speak. Finding none, she grabbed her coat from the back of the chair between them, and turned to leave the office.

"Hannah!" Desmond called, as she opened the door to leave. She stopped and glanced over her shoulder, not completely looking at him. "Hannah, I'm sorry. I'm sorry I'm still not the man who tells you to stay."

Hidden from Desmond's view was the first tear Hannah had ever shed for him. It crept silently down her cheek, and fell to the floor. "She's a lucky woman, Desmond. I hope she realizes that." Hannah straightened up and walked quickly out of his office, bundling her arms and her coat around her.

She left Desmond standing behind his desk, and as he watched the woman in red walk out of his life, his cell phone lit up with an incoming call from his girlfriend, Ashleigh.

Desmond would never know it, but Hannah had headed straight for the international airport, once again escaping to her next adventure.

Desmond was abruptly brought back to the here and now as his plane to Baltimore landed with a thud on the tarmac. He opened his eyes and strained to see as he looked through the window. After remembering that his most recent encounter with Hannah was in his Baltimore office, he suddenly felt no desire to return there.

• • •

Back in New York, Ashleigh caught a cab to Hannah's studio. The studio building was an ugly, brown, and run-down structure with barred windows. The concrete footpath outside the entrance was cracked and uneven, graffiti polluted the sides of adjacent buildings, pungent smoke rose up from a nearby street grate, and a small square of dirt was all that was left of a dead grass patch.

Ashleigh would have thought that she'd been brought to the wrong address were it not a small golden sign next to the front door that said *H.L. Studios - Second Floor*. Not trusting the integrity of the rickety elevator she found inside, Ashleigh took the stairs to the second floor.

She found herself as taken aback by the studio as she had been with Hannah's apartment. The interior was as clean and lavish as the exterior was dilapidated. The rear windows were great arches that carried brilliant white light onto the polished hardwood floors, and an expanse of mirrors reflected the pale walls, bouncing natural light to every corner of the wide-open space. A few dancers were spotted working against the barre affixed to another wall, and others engaged in whispered conversation by the door to the lobby.

The stairwell door closed behind Ashleigh with a loud crash as the strike plate scraped against the bolt and found its hole. The noise was exaggerated by the acoustics of the open studio, and each dancer, startled by the loud interruption, looked in Ashleigh's direction. Her face burned brightly in awkward discomfort, and she stood rooted to the spot until Hannah revealed herself from among the whispering dancers now dispersing onto the studio floor.

"You made it!" Hannah said with a sweet smile, as she opened her arms to hug Ashleigh. "Newbies often get lost looking for the building. It doesn't exactly look like a studio from the outside, does it?" Hannah wore a beautiful and tight dress, though its business-like look and her use of makeup made her appear professional and commanding. She pulled her face into a kind of apologetic contortion. "Listen, Ash, some of my dancers are accepting other roles while I'm in between shows, and so I don't have everyone I need to show you the performance you missed a few weeks ago. Would it be okay if we presented my second show to you instead? My dancers haven't performed this routine in quite a while, and they may be a bit rusty, but—"

"Oh, my gosh—of course!" Ashleigh answered enthusiastically. She wasn't about to pass up an opportunity for a private show from Hannah's dancers, no matter which routine they performed.

A tall, slim, young woman about Ashleigh's age with incredibly straight posture approached them. She spoke in a thick French accent asking, "Madame Lenore?"

"Yes, Jacqui?"

"Le dancers are en position, et ready to begin pe'forming."

"Thank you, Jacqui."

Jacqui spun on the spot in a lofty twirl and raised her arms as she walked to the center of the studio en pointe to join a number of dancers already crouched in position. Hannah gestured for Ashleigh to follow her upstairs to a loft area where a viewing studio accompanied the sound and lighting controls.

● ● ●

Ashleigh dabbed tears from her eyes with yet another tissue as the dancers completed the final act of the private show. They had danced with as much vigor and passion as could be expected on Broadway stages. This may have been their final performance of this particular Lenore ballet, and it closed with thunderous applause and a standing ovation from their sole audience member in the overhead loft studio.

The dancers waited in their final poses until Hannah came back down the stairs and thanked them for their performance. The ballerinas dispersed to grab drinks from the side of the studio, and to stretch sore muscles.

"That will be all for today. Thank you, everyone!" Hannah called out, loudly enough for everyone to hear. "That was a wonderful performance; I'm still so proud of all of you. Jacqui, I'm going to leave with my friend now. Please lock up once everyone has left the building."

"Oui, Madame," Jacqui's panting voice echoed over the sounds of the bustling dancers.

Hannah turned to Ashleigh. "I'd love to hear what you think. Let's go to lunch. I'm starving!"

Ashleigh and Hannah walked side by side as they left the studio, and waited outside for a cab. The sparkling condition of Hannah's studio and the softness of her ballet contrasted harshly with the dilapidated condition of the street they endured outside.

"Hannah, why is your studio in the middle of the Bronx, in Port Morris? Why not set up closer to the theater district?" Ashleigh asked as she looked around at burned-out car shells on the side of the road.

"A couple of reasons, I guess," Hannah began. "For one, I don't get recognized in these areas like I do near Broadway, so I can walk around without being bothered by strangers or photographers. Don't get me wrong—I always appreciate it when a fan tells me what they took away from my work, or if they ask for an autograph, but it can be distracting when I'm trying to think, focus on work, or just spend time with a friend."

Ashleigh smiled.

"Another reason is that the rent is so much cheaper in this part of town. My apartment is really the only thing I ever felt comfortable spending money on. For everything else, I'm quite content using whatever will do, rather than upscale to some outrageous substitute that, in the end, fulfills the same function."

Ashleigh continued to pepper Hannah with questions until they arrived at a cafe near Hannah's apartment.

"So, what did the show mean to you?" Hannah asked as she sat across from Ashleigh at the outdoor cafe. The sun was shining down upon them, and Hannah's face was shielded by large-rimmed sunglasses, partly to cope with the bright sunlight and partly to obscure her identity. The inconsistent noise of hundreds of passersby and traffic made it difficult to regulate appropriate conversation volume, and so guests at other tables were all conversing in somewhat raised voices.

Ashleigh drew a breath to respond and nearly coughed. The traffic fumes that hung in the air painted the back of her throat like old, bitter coffee. She wasn't used to the city's air pollution. She took a sip of the cold water that sat on the table in front of her and held the chilled glass against her wrist to slightly cool herself. "Well, it seemed to be about a father and daughter, and it made me think about my dad. There was a scene at the beginning where the male lead was carrying the female lead around the stage—like a child—but at the end, she was carrying him and leading him around like he couldn't walk. I thought this showed a father caring for his daughter when she was younger, and then she caring for him when he was older."

"Spot on!" Hannah exclaimed, and she high-fived the air above her head in a small celebration. "I started writing that ballet several years ago, after my father died. I was in Norway, and I'd lost track of the date. Next thing I knew, there were families out everywhere celebrating—all ages, all generations— it was Father's Day. I found myself just missing my dad, missing that impermeable male presence in my life, and the show sort of evolved from there, leaving out the part where I was bawling my eyes out walking down the street, of course!" Hannah laughed at herself. "Most of the critics thought it was about marriage and that the leads were a couple taking turns carrying each other through the ups and downs of their lives.

I generally let the audience believe the show is about whatever it makes them feel it's about. Every experience with my work should be unique and personal, but very few people seem to identify the true inspiration behind my stories. I've found that everyone will interpret my work in their own way as it unearths and brings consciousness to their struggles, their hidden emotions, or what they're unconsciously avoiding, but it gives me no small amount of pleasure when someone connects with or senses what I felt as I wrote the piece!" Hannah picked up the hot tea in front of her and leaned back in her chair to take a sip, reveling in the delight Ashleigh's understanding brought her.

"Where do you find the inspiration for these stories?" Ashleigh asked, intrigued that she had connected with Hannah through the loss of their fathers.

Hannah paused. Ashleigh had just reminded her that she still had no inspiration for her next show, and the fact gnawed at her once more. "Normally, everywhere," Hannah responded, gesturing around them while still holding her teacup by the handle. "I often find it in my own experiences, so I am always looking for the next adventure."

She leaned forward and sat on the edge of her seat. "The show you just saw found its genesis in coping with the loss of my father. Another show, the one you missed, that was inspired by the heartache I confronted on my last adventure after losing a close friend. For my other show, I drew from my experiences when I backpacked on my own across Europe in my mid-twenties."

Hannah began gesturing animatedly with her hands, and tea spilled out of her teacup as she spoke enthusiastically, "I gorged myself on life—hiking mountains, canyoning down rivers, crawling through historic pubs—and pushed my body to its limits in an orgy of nature, alcohol, and one-night stands.

I wrote most of the *Free* tour on that trip as I collected new experiences, day after day."

Ashleigh gasped. "That's the show I saw in college! That's the one that helped me discover myself and find some direction for my life!"

Hannah giggled excitedly. "And it's just as well it did that! That entire show was about a young woman's journey of self-discovery—again, not that the critics recognized it. After I finished that show, I realized that life is something that needs to be pursued. New experiences aren't just going to find us, Ashleigh. We need to go out there and find them! That's why I'm always looking for a new adventure. New adventures mean new experiences, and new experiences lead to fresh inspiration." Hannah sighed, collapsing into the back of her chair once more, simultaneously impassioned and exhausted as she mentally relived the highs of her past.

Ashleigh's thoughts turned to her husband, and how she had married Desmond not long out of college. She wondered if she'd ever given herself permission or the opportunity to pursue life in the way Hannah had described. She had Desmond, but perhaps not as much experience as Hannah; yet Hannah had experiences, but no Desmond of her own.

"Did you ever find someone you thought you could have a future with?" Ashleigh asked pointedly. She wasn't sure if it was appropriate to ask such intimate questions so bluntly, but she didn't feel uncomfortable in asking.

Hannah seemed to have no issue with the question as she gently placed her now half-empty teacup on the white linen of the cafe table. "No," she answered honestly. "Don't get me wrong, there were times when I thought I'd fallen in love, but I know now that I've never fully loved anyone. I always had at least one foot on the ground, so no one was ever really able to sweep me off my feet, so to speak. Plus, the men I dated were always so controlling, always asking me to stop doing this or that. Or, they'd give me this feeling that I couldn't trust them, so I always had my guard up. None of them ever really stood a chance. But, in protecting my heart fully, I didn't spend it on the wrong man, and it gave me space to lose it in other things—music, art, dance, travel. My heart being free gave it the opportunity to get lost in the pursuit of its own desires, instead of someone else's, or someone else."

Ashleigh sat listening, in awe of the woman in front of her. There were only a few years between them in age, and yet Hannah seemed to possess a self-awareness and emotional wisdom that Ashleigh could only consider otherworldly. Hannah smiled and shook her head slightly. "Gosh, so much about me! You asked a personal question, so I'm going to take the liberty of asking my own."

"Of course!" Ashleigh smiled, leaning comfortably back in her seat.

"Ashleigh, what's wrong?" Hannah asked pointedly.

Taken aback in blunt surprise, Ashleigh reflexively tried to lean back farther in her seat, through the rear of her chair. "What do you mean? Nothing's wrong! I'm having a great time!"

Hannah smiled empathetically. "I'm sorry. I was unclear. I mean what's wrong *here.*" She pointed to her heart. "Desmond may think you're okay—I can't really speak to that—but I just get the sense that something is hurting you…that you're making a conscious effort to ignore it, and I'm wondering if it's me, or something else."

Ashleigh glanced around, suddenly feeling uncomfortably transparent and as though her seat was suddenly far too large for her. Her gaze returned to Hannah's soft, but appraising look. "How can you tell?"

Hannah shrugged, leaned in, and spoke quietly, but with a smile, "I think women just know women."

Ashleigh placed clasped hands in her lap and stared at the tips of her thumbs as she tried to find simple words. "I … um … recently found out that I can't have kids, and I've always wanted kids. I'm infertile."

Hannah placed one hand over her open mouth, and her other hand outstretched on the table in sympathy. "Oh, I'm sorry I asked, Ash."

Ashleigh shook her head, surprisingly unmoved by her own confession. "No, it's fine. Or it will be fine. It's just kind of always on my mind. Everywhere I look, I see kids or something that makes me think about kids. I'm a kindergarten teacher, and my friend is pregnant using a surrogate, and then there's that big Poe IVF case, which doesn't help."

Hannah nodded in understanding. News of the Poe case was nationwide, and was a hot topic even in New York. "Are there any alternatives you can explore?" Hannah inquired, unsure whether Ashleigh was comfortable continuing the conversation topic.

Ashleigh actually found herself becoming lighter in talking to Hannah about her infertility. It was too much for her to talk to Desmond, her friends, or her colleagues about what she'd been feeling, but in Hannah she found a level of empathy and neutrality that made her feel comfortable and safe.

"My eggs aren't viable, so I wouldn't be able to donate them to anyone, but I still want Desmond's baby. When my friend told me that she was using a private surrogate, I thought quite a lot about finding my own. But she and her husband managed the insemination of their surrogate on their own, and the whole thing just seems so … cold. I want a baby to be born of love, intimacy, and warmth, not from the end of a cold syringe! Plus, I couldn't think of anyone who we could ask. My friend's sister is acting as her surrogate, but to manage this privately… I just don't think we could afford, let alone trust, a stranger. The costs of using a private surrogate are very high under normal circumstances, but with this IVF lawsuit nonsense, the costs are just insane!"

Hannah sat and nodded as she listened intently. A few years ago, as she approached her mid-thirties as a single woman, she'd quietly resigned herself to the idea that she would probably never have children of her own. Having already accepted that prospect, Hannah could empathize with Ashleigh a little. However, she had never been one of those women who had always intended to be a mother, and so she understood that biological infertility might affect Ashleigh more than her own circumstantial childlessness had affected her.

Ashleigh continued. "But it's more than just that. It's the guilt. It's one thing to have to deal with my own disappointed expectations of motherhood, but to have to deal with Desmond's as well?"

Hannah nodded, and her eyes glazed over. "Hmm, he always did want children of his own after what happened with his father." Her eyes came into focus again as Ashleigh leaned back in surprise once again.

Ashleigh leaned across the table, closer to Hannah, and lowered her voice to something just louder than a whisper. "He told you about that!? He's always refused to tell me about what happened to him! I've only ever managed to get a few details out of him here and there. The only thing he ever told me outright was that his father was abusive, and that he didn't like to talk about it."

Hannah shrugged. "I don't know what to tell you. We were very young when he told me—still in college, in fact. A lot of the poetry he wrote for that class was very dark. I asked him about it when we were out having drinks one night, and I guess the alcohol just loosened his tongue a little bit."

Ashleigh looked around the cafe to see whether anyone might overhear their secret exchange. She looked back at Hannah and asked in a low voice, "What did he tell you?"

Hannah looked uncomfortable. "I don't know that this is really my story to tell," she said awkwardly. "And I don't think Desmond would appreciate me talking about this."

"Oh please," Ashleigh begged, "I've pieced together that his dad would beat his mother when he was little, and that after he tried to stand up to him to protect her, his father started beating him instead. But whenever I try to get more details out of him, all he ever says is that he doesn't want to talk about it and that he 'never wants to be a victim again.' But you know details?"

Hannah nodded somberly. "The details aren't pretty, Ash. It's really not my place to share them. If you want to know, you really should talk to him about it."

Ashleigh sat back in her chair feeling a little dejected. She understood why Hannah wouldn't speak further about what Desmond had told her, but knowing that her husband had shared information with another woman that he'd withheld from her made her uncomfortable. Ashleigh cast aside her discomfort for the moment and brought her attention back to the conversation with Hannah. She began to think out loud more than talk to the woman sitting across from her. "I think that's why he's always trying to protect people," Ashleigh ruminated. "With the law, I mean. And why he never talks about his parents. And why he stays in good shape. And why he's really good with kids. I mean, *really* good. That's a big reason why the infertility is hard, you know? I know he's always wanted kids, and I know he'd be such a great dad, but my body just can't give that to him."

Hannah smiled, and the smile banished the gloom that the subject had brought with it. "I hope you don't tell him all of these nice things! He'll get such a big head!"

Ashleigh laughed.

"He's not so perfect, you know." Hannah smiled knowingly behind her large tea cup. "That poetry he wrote when we were younger ... *awful!*"

The two women laughed together, and their conversation turned lighter.

As lunch finished and the day cooled, the girls parted ways. Ashleigh caught a cab alone back to her hotel as Hannah opted to walk to her apartment through Central Park. Hannah removed her flats, so she could walk barefoot in the tall, cool grass alongside the gravel path. Despite her delicate features elsewhere, her mangled toes and calloused feet bore testament to her years of dancing, and she relished the feel of the soft earth beneath feet that always ached. Her hair sailed behind her in the soft breeze that began to blow, and tall lamps flickered on nearby as dusk descended.

Her apartment building grew larger in front of her as she continued through the park and reflected on her conversation with Ashleigh. She enjoyed the younger woman's company and genuinely meant it when she'd told Ashleigh that she hoped to catch up again soon as they said good-bye.

Her thoughts turned to Ashleigh's infertility, and for the first time in years, her mind turned to thoughts of her own biological clock. Hannah still got her period regularly and had never experienced symptoms of perimenopause, so her clock hadn't stopped ticking just yet. She crossed the last bridge at the end of the park and passed a young couple walking a baby in a stroller. The young infant pawed at some ornaments dangling in front of him from the stroller's crossbeam. Hannah smiled as she walked past the young family, exited the park, and strode up the stairs to the entrance of her building. In the privacy of the closed elevator, she cupped her hands in front of her flat stomach, and briefly imagined a baby of her own growing inside of her.

CHAPTER 10

THE PROPOSITION

The sky outside of Desmond's office window was clear, save for some bladelike clouds carving white gashes through the otherwise unpunctuated blue. The sun shone softly upon Baltimore's skyline, and its reflected rays bounced along building windows until it settled to create an annoying glare on his computer monitor. Desmond threw a futile glance over his shoulder as he tried to gauge for how much longer the glare would continue to distract him from his work on the Poe case.

He caught a glimpse of the photos on his desk and stiffened slightly at the thought that he'd still failed to tell Ashleigh that the case had fallen into his hands. He'd found himself in a rather unlikeable position. He didn't want to tell Ashleigh about his involvement in the case, when she was still sensitive to their recent infertility diagnosis, for fear of throwing her into an even deeper state of despair. But now, as his wife increasingly returned to her usual self, he was perhaps even more reluctant to tell her the truth for fear of throwing her *back* into despair. Desmond turned to face his computer monitor and sighed in annoyance, partly at himself, but mostly at the persistent yellow stain the sun streaked across his screen. He stretched idly in his seat, and forfeiting his fight against the glare, he grabbed his cell phone from his desk and called Hannah.

Hannah and Ashleigh had continued to spend some time with each other after their lunch date in New York. Although they had little in common with one another—besides Desmond—each of the women had found a convenient distraction in the other. Ashleigh rarely thought about her infertility during the time she spent with Hannah, and Hannah rarely thought about her next, unknown show during the time she spent with Ashleigh. Although their relationship could hardly be described as close, each found they could be entirely at ease with the other to discuss and confide things without fear of judgment or unwanted sympathy.

"Desmond?" Hannah asked as she answered the phone. "Two calls in the same year? I'm flattered!" she teased.

"Ha-ha, very funny," Desmond said with a sarcastic laugh.

"I'm kidding. I'm glad you called, actually. I arrived in Baltimore today for my date with Ashleigh tomorrow, and have nothing to do! I'd hoped to see Ashleigh tonight as well, but she has parent-teacher meetings tonight. Would you fancy meeting me for tea or coffee?"

Desmond grabbed reflexively at the half-drank mug of coffee on his desk. He took a sip of the now lukewarm brew. The bitter taste made him screw up his face at his slowly clearing computer screen. "I can't right now," he said, returning the mug to his desk. "I'm a bit swamped at work. Listen though, the reason I called was just to say thank you. Ashleigh has been more herself since she spent the day with you in New York. I really appreciate that you're spending this time with her."

"Well," Hannah began, levity returning to her tone, "if you want to thank me, how about joining me for dinner?"

• • •

Hannah sat at the bar in a Baltimore sushi restaurant as she waited for Desmond. Jacqui had recommended the restaurant to her, and it was, if anything, disappointing. The low-hanging lights did little to illuminate the room darkened by black walls and red accents. The wait staff looked bored, and it was empty for the most part.

Hannah tried her best to wear her, "I'm just not interested" face in between sips of Moscato, but it didn't stop the few men in the restaurant from trying to flirt with her. She wasn't really in the mood to drink, but she was unexpectedly a little nervous as she waited for Desmond. Apart from the brief conversations they'd shared after she'd shown up unannounced on his doorstep, this was the first time she and Desmond had spent any real time together in over a decade.

She checked the time on her phone for the sixth time in as many minutes, and glanced over her shoulder again at the restaurant's entrance. Desmond arrived shortly after. The bartender offered Hannah his cell number as she grabbed her purse and rose to join her friend. Hannah rolled her eyes impatiently and left the bar to join Desmond at the entrance, abandoning the dejected bartender with his arm outstretched, and the piece of paper still in his hand.

Hannah and Desmond were silent as they walked together toward a table. The silence continued as a waitress introduced herself and ran through the day's specials. They continued to say nothing to each other, and the silence was allowed to drag on further. Each held the menus in front of their faces to shield themselves from the silence that quickly evolved from normal to awkward, and then to weird.

"Is this weird?" Desmond asked, lowering the menu to reveal his face.

"*So* weird!" Hannah answered, likewise lowering her own menu.

Despite their exchange, silence once again prevailed. Hannah and Desmond sat quietly, looking at each other from behind their menus. After several long seconds of staring, they both spoke at the same time, their words tumbling together:

"You look—"

"Good," said Desmond.

"Old," finished Hannah.

The awkward silence finally died as Hannah let out a sweet, embarrassed laugh. Desmond smiled as she covered her blushing face with her menu. "I'm sorry!" Hannah squealed through her laugh. She lowered her menu once more, again meeting Desmond's eyes. "You look quite good, actually. I just meant that you don't look like I remember." She gestured toward him with her menu. "It's the hair. Bits of gray here and there. It suits you though. Also, your eyes... Your eyes look didn't look this sad before."

"Well," Desmond answered, still smiling. "I don't know what gray hair you're talking about. I'm clearly in denial, but that's my story, and I'm sticking to it! You look as good as ever."

Hannah made a face, as though she'd just tasted something unpalatable, and dismissed the compliment. She placed the menu on the table in front of her and stretched her back, reaching her long arms toward the ceiling. "I don't *feel* good though," Hannah said on a breath. "I feel old. Like everything is slowly breaking down."

Their waitress returned to their table. "Any drinks?" she asked, in a somewhat unenthused tone after taking their food orders. Hannah and Desmond exchanged glances and shook their heads a little. The waitress left without removing the empty glasses from the table.

"Not in the mood?" Hannah asked Desmond.

"Not right now. Ashleigh didn't want me drinking while we were trying. It affects the quality of my ... boys," he finished euphemistically. "What about you?"

Hannah picked up her empty glass of Moscato and gestured toward the bar, where the bartender was still watching her. "I just don't want another drink from that bartender." Hannah dismissed Desmond's raised eyebrow with a wave of her hand.

"So," she began cautiously, "you're still not drinking even after the whole infertility thing? You're still ... hoping ... for kids?"

Desmond leaned back in a stretch of his own. He seemed smaller in his seat by the end of it. His brow creased into a parade of lines, and he rubbed at his forehead absently. "I don't know. I just ... yeah. I don't know. Do I still *hope* for kids? Honestly? I've kind of just stopped hoping for anything."

"What do you mean?"

Desmond looked up from his hand, his face a pensive ball. "Hope isn't bright and lofty. It's not the happy or noble thing that everyone makes it out to be. Hope is heavy. It's a burden. Hope is carrying around a belief that something will happen even when everything around you says that it won't. I've hoped for a lot of things in my life, and what did it get me? I hoped that I'd be a partner at a firm by now. I hoped that my dad would tell me that he was sorry and that he loved me before he died. I hoped that I'd get a chance to be the kind of dad I always wanted. And I hoped that—" he stopped himself short as his eyes caught Hannah's.

She sat listening, her eyes wide and attentive.

Desmond's tone shifted. "Suffice to say that I never got anything I ever hoped for."

"But you're still not drinking," Hannah observed with a nod. "So, you must still be hoping for something?"

Desmond smiled to himself as he tilted the empty glass in front of him to peer through its clear glass bottom. "I guess," he began softly, almost to himself, "I guess it's because I know Ashleigh still has hope ... somehow. Even if I don't hope myself, I can still help to hold hers."

Hannah's lips curved into a smile. She held a hand over her heart. "Aw," she cooed, "that's so sweet." She lifted her own empty glass in front of her and gestured toward Desmond's in a mock toast. "Well, if nothing else, we can all have hope that you'll continue to be a good husband."

• • •

Desmond arrived home just as twilight was handing ownership of the sky to the night. A warm breeze blew across his face as he made his way toward the front door to his home, carrying with it the scent of freshly mowed grass. Ashleigh smiled at him as he found her in their bedroom and kissed her lips. She had strewn all of her workout clothes over their bed and was comparing the different pieces of clothing.

"It's for tomorrow," she replied in answer to her husband's raised eyebrow. "For my day-date with Hannah. She said we're going to a bar, but she also said to bring workout clothes. It didn't make much sense to me but, oh well." She shrugged and smiled.

"She mentioned you two were going out tomorrow," Desmond began, eliciting a similarly raised eyebrow from his wife. He threw a thumb over his shoulder. "I just came from dinner with her," he said in answer. "How'd the parent-teacher meetings go?"

Ashleigh's smile survived, but her eyes narrowed slightly. "You went to dinner with Hannah?"

"Yeah, just now. She's in town early for your date tomorrow. Said she was hoping to spend the evening with you, but you had your meetings," Desmond answered casually.

Ashleigh scratched the back of her head.

"Everything okay?" asked Desmond. "Something happen at your meetings?"

Ashleigh smiled genuinely at her husband's ignorance. "No," she said. "You know, I think this is the first time you've gone out with another woman since we met. Makes me a little jealous, is all."

Desmond's eyes shot open, "Oh! I didn't even think of that! Honestly, it was just two friends catching up."

Ashleigh smiled and waved a hand at him as she continued to compare her active wear. "Don't worry. I know I can trust you. I'm not the least bit worried. How was it?"

Desmond shrugged. "Fine, I guess. A little awkward at first. We haven't seen each other in so long, apart from when you and I went up to New York. We just caught up, really. Talked about work, what's happened since we last saw each other, talked about you—"

"Did you talk about your parents at all?" Ashleigh asked, with her back turned to him.

Desmond paused. "It came up, kind of."

Ashleigh turned around, still clutching an "Under Armor" shirt in her hands. "You two were pretty close, weren't you?" she asked, squinting slightly.

"What makes you think so?"

"A couple of things. You never really told me about her. I mean, yes, you told me that you were hung up on a girl named Hannah for a long while, but you never told me that she was a famous playwright, that she's model-level beautiful, or that she used to visit you up until we started dating. But most of all, because you've talked to her about your parents."

"And?" asked Desmond.

"And?" Ashleigh answered incredulously, annoyance quickly rising within her. "And you won't talk to *me* about it. *That's* the 'and.' Des, it's not really right that you'll talk to another woman about that part of you, but not your wife."

Desmond shook his head, and his mood became sullen. "I don't talk to her about it. I don't talk to anyone about it."

"Anyone … but her," Ashleigh cut in pointedly. She could see Desmond was becoming increasingly uncomfortable and agitated, the way he always did when the topic of his parents arose. He opened his mouth to speak, but Ashleigh headed him off. "Don't get annoyed and try to turn this around! Des, this is important to me. I understood before when you said you didn't want to talk about it, but it's gnawed at me knowing that you *have* talked about it to someone else, that that someone else is another woman, and that you *still* talk about it with her!" She could see the muscles across her husband's jaw tightening as he clenched his teeth unconsciously.

"I don't want to talk about it, Ashleigh. You don't know what you're asking. I'm done talking about this," Desmond answered, making a clear effort to maintain his composure. "And if I seem annoyed, it's because I don't like what you're doing!"

"Me? What am *I* doing?"

Desmond's voice rose with his annoyance. "You're insinuating that I'm being inappropriate with Hannah by mentioning my parents to her, or that I've *been* inappropriate because I didn't tell you more about her in the past, all to make me feel guilty. And you're trying to use that guilt to compel me to talk about my parents. I don't want to talk about it, Ash. I don't *ever* want to talk about it. Not with you, not with her, not with anyone. I'm done with this topic."

"Well, I'm not!" Ashleigh answered hotly. "It's not ri—"

Desmond's voice boomed angrily over hers as he exploded in a way she'd never experienced before. "What do you want me to say, Ash? You want to know more about how my father *beat* me? That I remember the look in his eyes as he broke my arm with his *bare hands*? That I remember what it felt like when the bone cracked? How about the fact that he put

97

cigarettes out in my back? That I had to wear sweaters in the middle of summer, so the other kids couldn't see the holes he'd burned into my shirts? You want to talk about how every time I think of my mother I can still hear her sobbing to the cadence of his kicks?"

Ashleigh shook and hid behind the shirt she had raised to her face. Her eyes welled. "I'm sorry," she whispered, as her heart broke for her husband.

Desmond stepped toward her and closed the distance between their bodies. She could see the glimmer of the tears he held back in his own eyes as he leaned toward her. "How about the fact that I loved him? Even while he beat me with everything he had, I *loved* him, Ashleigh. Desperately and unrequitedly."

Ashleigh lowered the shirt still clutched in her shaking hand. Her upper lip was trembling, and her eyes were wide with pity. She stood just looking at her husband, slightly afraid of the edge quickly evaporating from his eyes.

Desmond's heavy breathing was calming as he looked back at his wife. "Please stop looking at me like that. Hannah looked at me that way after I told her, and she never looked at me the same way again. After I told her, all I ever was to her was something that needed fixing—something broken, fragile. I'm not. I told you before, after what my dad did to me, I never want to be a victim again—not to him, not to the memory of what he did to me, and especially not in the eyes of other people!" Desmond's face softened from anger to sadness, and he made his way toward the bedroom door.

He paused for a moment, and turned back to face Ashleigh. "I'm sorry I went out with Hannah without telling you. Before tonight, I hadn't seen her in nearly a decade, so I don't expect I'll be spending much more time with her. Even so, if I'm ever going to be alone with another woman, I'll be sure to let you know in advance." He turned and left the room.

Both Ashleigh and Desmond spent much of that night unable to sleep, each prodded by their guilty consciences— Desmond, for raising his voice, and Ashleigh, for forcing her husband to relive his abusive past in order to satisfy her jealous curiosity.

• • •

"I don't understand," Ashleigh confessed, as she walked down a street in Baltimore beside Hannah. Ashleigh shifted her grip on her gym bag so that the zipper stopped catching on her shirt.

"It's hard to explain," Hannah replied. She adjusted her grip on her own gym bag, and threw a small towel over her shoulder. "Barre uses small, but controlled movements—think squeezing, pulsating, and repetition—to tone and build muscle. You use a combination of postures inspired by ballet, yoga, Pilates, and other disciplines, and perform high reps of really small-range movements."

"And there's a bar in the studio?" Ashleigh asked, still confused.

Hannah laughed. "No, not that kind of bar. It's barre with another 'r' and an 'e' on the end, like a ballet barre."

"And what's that for?" Ashleigh asked as they rounded a corner and came up to the barre studio.

"You use the barre to help with balance when performing exercises that focus on contracting a specific set of muscles. It sounds bizarre, but it's fun, and you'll be surprised just how good a workout you can get from such small movements."

The two women headed inside the barre studio. It was unlike anything Ashleigh had ever seen. The wood flooring of the studio was polished, just like in Hannah's New York studio, and a ballet barre was installed on a mirrored wall. The brightly lit crystal chandeliers hanging over the studio would normally have seemed out of place in a room designed for exercise, but the refinery of the floor, mirrored walls, tastefully exposed brick, and clear windows made them feel cohesive to the surroundings in a strange, but pleasant way.

Ashleigh followed Hannah to the far side of the studio, where women were removing their shoes and leaving their gym bags. Hannah sat in the lone available seat and placed her gym bag and towel in a pile at her feet. Ashleigh was still looking around the busy studio when Hannah looked up at her.

"You'll want to lose your sneakers," she said, carefully untying the laces of her own shoes. "We do this barefoot." Hannah quickly replaced her shoes with a pair of traction-pad sockettes and stood to allow Ashleigh to take the seat.

Ashleigh took the seat and leaned forward to begin removing her own shoes, and Hannah began stretching in front of her. Ashleigh watched her absentmindedly. It was clear she had a dancer's body. Her limber muscles stretched leisurely as she leaned over her knees and placed both palms on the ground with ease. Her taut and supple skin moved with her as she twisted her body into shapes impossible for the average woman, only to resume its natural form when she'd finished stretching.

Hannah tied her wavy blonde locks into a bun behind her head, and removed the light jacket she wore over her workout clothes. Ashleigh's mouth hung open as Hannah peeled away the light over-garment. Ashleigh herself was a fit woman. She exercised regularly and intentionally; she ate right, and was by any measure young, athletic, and in the prime of her life. Even with that, however, she couldn't help but gape at Hannah as she revealed nothing but a sports bra beneath her jacket. Her stomach was otherworldly flat, her ribs peeked out from beneath toned muscle and an even skin tone, and her breasts looked full and shapely even when compressed by the sports bra.

Ashleigh caught herself staring and hurried to remove her shoes and socks, placing her belongings besides Hannah's.

She stood to take her place by Hannah, and began performing her own stretches before the instructor stepped out and began marshaling the class over to the barre on the other side of the studio.

As the two women made their way over to the barre with the rest of the class, Hannah leaned into Ashleigh and whispered, "Don't worry if you can't perform some of the movements. I've been practicing barre for years, and I've been dancing my whole life, so don't feel intimidated if you can't keep up."

Ashleigh looked sideways at Hannah a little indignantly. She removed her shirt to reveal her own sports bra and flat stomach and threw her shirt to join her discarded gym bag. "Don't worry," she answered with a smile, "I'm not intimidated by you."

An hour later Hannah and Ashleigh stepped into the sauna at the other end of the barre studio building. Hannah was still panting from the barre class. "I ... have never ... been pushed ... so hard!"

Ashleigh was also panting. Her face was still slightly red and tightened in self-directed annoyance. She had done her best to keep pace with Hannah and the other advanced-level members of the class, but had been forced to abandon the pace near the very end of the class, as the poses and maneuvers escalated into something she could barely comprehend, let alone perform.

Ashleigh's efforts, and the silent competition it caused between the two women, had resulted in an extreme workout for each of them, and both were eager to continue the sweat session in the sauna. Hannah led the way as she opened the door to the empty, wooden sauna. She sidled her towel down to her waist and took a seat on the bottom row of the bench. Ashleigh mentally rolled her eyes as she spotted Hannah's hip bones peeking above her towel as shyly as the ribs beneath her sweating skin. Allowing the door to swing closed behind her, she sidled her own towel to her waist. She caught Hannah appraising her naked body as she moved to take a seat next to her. The two women sat in enjoyable silence as the room filled with hot air. Wisps of steam rose from the hot rocks in the corner of the room and filtered through the space around them.

After the passage of half an hour in relaxing silence, Ashleigh's racing heart had calmed, and she opened her eyes. She looked around the room—at the sweating wooden walls, the steaming rocks, and the blonde beauty beside her—she noticed that Hannah was still wearing sockettes on her feet. "Why do you wear those?" Ashleigh asked curiously. Hannah opened her eyes at the question. "The socks, I mean," Ashleigh clarified. "I noticed you wore them during the barre class as well, even though you told me that everyone did it barefoot. And you're wearing them now too, even though you're wearing nothing else but a towel."

Hannah crossed her smooth legs and flexed her foot about playfully. "These?" she asked, now looking down at her feet. She shrugged her shoulders up to her ears shyly, and her breasts rose with her shoulders. "I'm very self-conscious about my feet. After nearly three decades of dance, they're a mess. I've had countless broken toes, painful bunions, disfigured and lost nails, and blisters so bad they left scars. My feet are ugly, and they make me feel ugly. So, I cover them up, even when I'm at home by myself. Once they're covered up, I don't feel so ugly."

Ashleigh laughed, and it only made Hannah feel all the more insecure. "Are you serious?" Ashleigh began. "*You* feel ugly? C'mon Hannah. *Look* at you!"

Hannah gave an uncomfortable smile, and her shoulders found their normal resting place. "Look at me!? Look at *you*, Ashleigh! I felt intimidated even when you had your shirt on." She sat forward and gestured at Ashleigh with her chin, "And look at you now. I mean, good for Desmond—good for *you*!

You've got the long and beautiful brown hair, your skin is beautiful, your boobs are nice. You don't just look young, you look damned good. I've spent the past thirty minutes wondering whether I should pull my towel up to cover the rest of me, like my feet!"

Ashleigh tried to hide her blushing smile. She never took compliments well, even when they came from other women. She mumbled a quick and quiet thank you. Seeking quickly to change the subject from herself, Ashleigh leaned back and asked a question. "Speaking of your dancing, what's going on with work?"

"Ugh!" Hannah covered her hands with her face and leaned back as far as the bench seat would allow. She shook her head beneath her hands and groaned again. "Not good," she said before lowering her hands and placing them beside her on the bench. "I'm losing my dancers. I can't blame them, I suppose. I can't expect them to just hang around the studio doing nothing when there are other opportunities for them to keep performing. I've lost most of them, actually. That, plus the fact that I'm no closer to writing my next show than I was weeks ago means I'll probably have to let the studio go altogether. My agent has been pestering me with calls, trying to get me to agree to trigger the early termination buyout in the lease. It's just hard, you know? I could justify holding onto the studio if only I had an idea of what my next show would be. I wouldn't even need to have it written, or even know what it's about. I just need some *inspiration*! I could convince myself to keep the studio if there was something that made me *feel* something. Anything!" Hannah stared sullenly through the wall in front of them.

Ashleigh cut in. "Why don't you leave again? On another adventure, I mean. That's where you've found inspiration for your shows in the past, so why not go away again?"

Hannah's features tightened in contemplation. Her eyes squinted in the kind of way women's eyes do when they consider something they already know they're not going to agree with. Hannah's features relaxed once more. "Something's different this time around. There's nothing in me that's saying that the answer is somewhere out *there*. It's like I'm being told that the answer is somewhere in here." Hannah clutched heavily at her flat gut with her hands. "But here I am talking about where to find an answer, and I don't even know what the question is! *That's* the measure of how far I am from my next show, and why I'll probably have to get rid of my studio."

The clouds of steam were displaced by clean, cool air as the door to the sauna opened. Another woman stepped in. She looked up at Hannah and Ashleigh's toned and topless bodies, turned on the spot, and walked out, pulling her own towel higher to cover her body. Hannah and Ashleigh looked at one another and giggled, each a little embarrassed. Hannah poured more water on the sauna stones to replace the steam lost in their brief encounter with the third woman. Hot steam rose up from the sizzling stones, and their sweat session continued.

"What were we talking about?" Hannah asked, as she took her seat next to Ashleigh again. "It doesn't matter. Anyway, what about you? What's next for you and Desmond?"

Ashleigh bit her lip nervously. It was a question she had silently and relentlessly asked of herself since her infertility diagnosis. She rubbed the nape of her neck, which was wet with steam and sweat. "I still want a family," she said before shaking her head violently. "No, not a family. I have a family. Desmond is my family. What I mean is that I still want a baby. I can't explain why. I have always wanted kids. Even when I was a little girl I wouldn't just play with dolls—I'd *mother* them. I'd undress them and pretend to change their diapers, I'd soothe them while pretending they were crying, and I'd feed them all with a plastic bottle that came with one of my other dolls.

And when I was given my cousin's hand-me-down Betsy Wetsy doll? You wouldn't believe that a little girl could get so excited about a doll that pees itself! I just always wanted to be a mom. It's who I am, who I've always wanted to be. In some ways, it's even what I do for a living. I want a baby. It's as simple and as difficult as that. And ever since I was told I can't have them— that I *won't* have them—it's like my spirit stopped moving. Like I don't feel like myself anymore. I want to feel like myself again. I want to be the woman I always dreamed of being. I want to be a mom. I want a baby. I haven't talked to Desmond about it, but I hope that what's next for us is finding a surrogate."

Hannah nodded, trying to understand as best she could. "Why haven't you talked to him about it?" she asked.

Ashleigh drew a deep, slow breath of warm, steamy air. "Mostly because I'm afraid he'll just say no and close the door on my dreams for good. I can't be a mom if he won't be a dad. Don't get me wrong, we've talked about having kids *a lot,* and for a long time before we found out about my infertility, but ever since then, it's like he's given up."

"Desmond never struck me as the kind of man that gives up on anything," Hannah interjected.

Ashleigh shook her head again. "I don't mean it like that. I think he still wants to be a parent. It's just that the infertility was such a shock to both of us, and it took a toll. I think Desmond wants to be a dad, but he's afraid of being disappointed like that again, and of seeing me break if it happens again."

"So, what are you going to do? How do you even find a surrogate?" Hannah asked.

Ashleigh's face tightened in contemplation. "Normally there's a registry of available surrogates at most IVF clinics, but they've all closed down because of that lawsuit. So, we have to find someone privately. That's difficult enough in itself, but it's made almost impossible when we consider all of the criteria I have for a surrogate. I need to find a woman who we know and trust, who wouldn't need to be paid for the surrogacy, who has no health issues, is healthy, who's willing to use her own eggs, and who'd be willing to have sex with Desmond."

Hannah, who had been nodding as Ashleigh rattled off her list, shot Ashleigh an alarmed and confused look. "What!? Why on earth would she have to sleep with Desmond? When you talked about using a surrogate, I always just assumed that you meant that you'd manage it manually ... *privately!*"

Ashleigh's set her eyes downcast, and her lips pursed with a quiet, pained expression. She shook her head softly, so slightly that even with Hannah watching her, she didn't notice that she shook her head at all.

Hannah remained motionless as she watched Ashleigh, knowing that she was slowly processing not just her next words, but another million things all at once, as only a woman could.

After several moments, Ashleigh turned to look at Hannah. "Do you remember when I told you that I wanted my baby to be born of love and intimacy? That the idea of a baby born from the end of a syringe was just too cold for me?"

"Of course," Hannah replied.

"That's just it. As much as I love kids and the idea of one day having my own, I don't know that I could bring myself to create a life so ... artificially. I know that the children those procedures create are just as human as you and me, but the idea to *me*—it just doesn't sit right. That's why I want a non-surgical surrogate. The woman would have to sleep with Desmond."

Hannah tried her best not to judge Ashleigh. She had plenty of experience controlling the muscles in her face so that her expression did not reflect her true feelings, but even with that experience, she was failing. Ashleigh's suggestion was simply too strange for her to empathize with, or understand.

She managed to remove the alarm from her expression, but the disbelief and confusion remained. "Ashleigh, how could you be okay with that? He's your *husband*!"

"I know!" Ashleigh answered, avoiding Hannah's eyes. Shame oozed out of her pores on every droplet of sweat she secreted. Ashleigh stared at the floor of the sauna as she continued. "I'm not *okay* with the idea of Desmond sleeping with someone else. The very thought of it breaks my heart." She fidgeted with her dangling feet absentmindedly. "The only reason I feel even the slightest bit okay with the idea is because of you."

"*What?*" Hannah repeated, alarm once again returning to her face. Another woman entered the sauna only to be quickly told to get out by Hannah. She obliged, her indignant mutterings barely audible through the sauna door as it closed behind her. "How did I make you okay with the idea of another woman having sex with your husband!?"

Ashleigh sighed, and a slight smile crept across her pink lips. At some level, she enjoyed the fact that Hannah had unknowingly comforted her on the idea of a non-surgical surrogacy. "I only discovered that your latest tour ended after I read an article Jack Katan wrote about you."

Hannah rolled her eyes as she recalled the article Katan had written about her "retirement."

Ashleigh continued, "He quoted you saying something about there being different kinds of love. I found the video on YouTube, and I loved what you said."

Hannah racked her brain trying to remember what she had said during the interview. She could only remember feeling overwhelmed and irritated by Katan's manipulative and contrived conversation, and she shook her head, unable to recall her words.

Ashleigh finally looked up from the floor and found Hannah's eyes. "You said that there were many different kinds of love—for friends, family, places, memories—and it got me thinking about how I'd feel about a baby born of a different kind of love than the love Des and I share. The more I thought about it, the more comfortable I became with the idea of a non-surgical surrogate. I know it's not the same as having a baby of my own, but I know that the love required for a woman to volunteer her body and her baby like that, and the love it'd take for Desmond to agree to do something like this ... well, it's a lot warmer than the cold end of a turkey baster."

Hannah listened as Ashleigh confided the accidental impact her impromptu words had had on her ideas of love, intimacy, and children. She was unsure of how to feel about the weight her words had carried. If anything, she felt a little guilty. This isn't what she had meant when she had said those words.

The two women sat in mute silence as each contemplated their role in a complex weave of happenstance. Hannah rolled Ashleigh's suggestion around in her mind like food on her tongue. No matter how she twisted the idea, no matter what seasoning she tried to place on the suggestion, it tasted terrible. Her expression turned painful, and she turned to Ashleigh, who once again sat with her face cast toward the ground.

Ashleigh had pulled her towel up higher to cover her body, partly because the room was cooling, but mostly because she felt the need to hide behind something.

Hannah parted her lips to speak and summoned her most sympathetic tone. "Ashleigh, I understand you want a baby, but don't you think that this is a little ... extreme? If you want a baby so badly, couldn't you compromise on some of these ... requirements?"

Ashleigh turned to face Hannah. The sympathy in her expression and tone annoyed her. She was tired of people pitying and feeling sorry for her. "No," she answered a little defiantly. "How far would you be willing to go to get what you want?

ART OF YOU

What would you be willing to do to find the inspiration you keep talking about and searching for?"

Hannah looked down at feet. The sockettes she still wore hid the mutilated testament to just how far she was willing to go to satisfy her dream of being a dancer, to satisfy the deep, burning craving to *keep* dancing, long after her feet begged her to stop.

Ashleigh followed Hannah's eyes and answered her own question. "Look at your feet, Hannah. *That's* how far I'm willing to go. I don't think anybody who truly understands my desire to be a mother would call *that* extreme.

• • •

Hannah sat at the small writing desk by her hotel bed the following morning. The hotel's air conditioning had failed early that morning, and the air in the room was heavy and matted with humidity. She leaned back in her chair, a pen clenched between her teeth and her eyes closed. She had been trying to write something for a new show—a piece of music, a narrative for a story, anything—but nothing came to her. The warmth of the room was distracting, and she found it hard to focus. The sheer robe she wore was light and open, but it gave little respite from the warmth of the room. She tried to blame her lack of focus on the heat and humidity, but even without it, she'd have been equally unproductive.

In fact, her mind had been less occupied by the uncomfortable warmth than it was by her conversation with Ashleigh the day before. They had parted ways after their discussion in the sauna, each feeling uncomfortable with the other. There was nothing that either of them had specifically said or done to make the other feel uneasy—each had simply shared more than they had intended.

Yesterday's conversation had shattered the illusion that their relationship could be enjoyed free of the vulnerability and judgment they had expected—and avoided—from others. Seeing her relationship with Ashleigh free of any illusion immediately brought questions to Hannah's mind. Why was she even spending time with Ashleigh? Wasn't she just the wife of a friend she had hardly seen in almost two decades? What was she even doing in Maryland when she needed to focus on her work, her dancers, and her studio back in New York? And why was Ashleigh spending this time with her, and confiding all of these personal things to her, a complete stranger? Neither of the women had much to say after Ashleigh compared Hannah's attitude toward her feet with Ashleigh's desire Desmond to have sex with another woman, if it meant she'd have a child of her own. They'd both left the sauna soon thereafter, each absorbed in the complex web of thoughts now brought out into the open.

Another question had plagued Hannah that morning, and although she had tried to banish it from her mind, it had forced its way in, determined to be confronted: *Could I be Ashleigh and Desmond's surrogate?* The question finally breached her consciousness, and a chill swept through her despite the warmth in the room as she began to fully explore the darkness of the question. *It's just sex*, she thought to herself, as she took the pen from her clenched teeth and placed it on a page in her workbook. The page was blank, except for a series of question marks she'd absentmindedly doodled in the corner of the page. *We'd do the deed, and once I'm pregnant, it'd be done.*

She looked down at her body through the half-open sheer robe, and briefly imagined undressing in front of Desmond. Her stomach twisted, and she stood and walked away from her seat, uncomfortable and guilty at the mere thought of being with another woman's husband. She unconsciously tied the front of the robe in an unsuccessful effort to cover her otherwise bare body. *Husband ... that's somebody's HUSBAND*, she thought to herself, becoming increasingly uncomfortable with the thought of acting as Ashleigh's non-surgical surrogate. It wasn't just *anybody's* husband, it was *Desmond*. She briefly wondered whether Ashleigh had given real thought to what she had suggested, and whether she'd considered the impact it could have on her marriage. *What would it do to my relationship with Desmond?* she pondered rhetorically.

Hannah had spent most of the night unable to sleep, and between her overnight ruminations on Ashleigh's stance, and the conclusions she'd come to in the solitude of that morning, she decided that she was not concerned with the sexual element of a non-surgical surrogacy. One of the benefits of not being puritanical or sanctimonious about sex was not having to feel guilty about having it, or not having it. But sex with Desmond? That was an entirely different matter.

Like most women, Hannah had her fair share of regrets about the men she'd shared a bed with, but she'd never let those experiences scare her from enjoying her sexuality. To her, sex was sex. But could she separate emotion from any intimate acts with Desmond, just as many of her previous partners seemed to be able to divorce emotion from sex with her? Her mind turned briefly to past boyfriends and flirts who had disappeared, abruptly ending contact shortly after bedding her. If she could share her bed with regrets, one-night stands, and other jerk ex-boyfriends, why couldn't she share it a few times with Desmond, the older version of the sweet boy she knew in college? Hannah once more thought about sharing her bed with Desmond, and was slightly more comfortable with the idea. *No, not more comfortable*, she thought, *just less uncomfortable.*

Even if she could overcome her own discomfort with the idea of sleeping with Desmond, it would solve only half of the issue. Ashleigh and Hannah might be able to tolerate a temporary arrangement with Desmond in order for her to get pregnant, but how would *he* feel about it?

Hannah spied a clock on the far side of the hotel room. It was just after noon, and she realized she'd spent hours contemplating a role in Ashleigh's proposal. She turned and saw the still-blank page on the writing desk, taunting her from across the room. She sighed in frustration. "Why is this so difficult?" she said. She walked over to the writing desk once more and stared at the empty page. In years past, page after page would be filled with compositions, choreographic diagrams, and notes on half-finished ideas to be finished and incorporated later. She'd lose track of time, forget to eat and sleep, and lose herself in whatever inspiration affixed itself to her heart.

She was suddenly hit by a shot of clarity. It occurred to her that previous inspiration had always come to her unbidden, either out of spontaneity or circumstances outside of her control. Of those within her control, she had rarely dwelled on any decisions long enough to experience hesitation, and she usually let her heart and her confidence in her own abilities lead her to adventure. Indeed, she'd left her boyfriend and backpacked across Europe after a mere conversation with Desmond and less than a day's thought. She'd joined volunteer mission work in Norway the day after she buried her father, and she disappeared on a silent, three-month trek in the mountains of South America after embarrassing herself in Desmond's office several years earlier. She realized that she had never given an adventure so much thought as she had the idea of having Desmond's baby.

Hannah's head snapped up, struck by a moment of clarity. "I may not be comfortable sleeping with Desmond," she processed aloud, "but an adventure isn't an adventure until you leave comfort behind!" She nodded, self-affirming her newfound sense of resolve. She was ready for an adventure, and

A Part of You

whether Ashleigh and Desmond were prepared for that adventure, or comfortable with her being their surrogate—surgically or naturally—was a matter for them.

Hannah strode intently into the hotel bedroom and toward the landline on the bedside table, seeking to act before hesitation and doubt had a chance to creep in. With trembling fingers, she dialed Ashleigh's number and closed her eyes. Sweat trickled down her neck and fell between her breasts, no longer solely from the heat of the room. She listened intently to the ringing on the other end of the line to deafen the doubts clamoring in her mind.

"Hello?" Ashleigh asked, not recognizing the hotel's number on her caller ID.

Hannah's eyes shot open. She hadn't thought of what she'd say! Her focus was broken, and her mind instantly flooded with unanswered questions, with doubts and hesitation. The heavy pounding of her drumming heartbeat deafened her ears. She knew that if she gave Ashleigh the green light now, she wouldn't have the heart to change her mind down the line. *Am I ready? What's going to happen to the baby? What's going to happen to me? Ashleigh doesn't know it's me calling. I can just hang up and forget about the whole thing.*

"Hello?" Ashleigh's voice came through the line once more.

Hannah spied the blank page on the writing desk by the bed a few feet away from her. Afternoon sunlight poured onto the desk through the window above it and married the light of the desk lamp to illuminate the bleached whiteness of the blank page. Hannah had money she neither used nor needed, fame she didn't care for, friends that didn't care for her. She had no boyfriend or husband, no prospects who might soon fill these roles, and no family. She had rarely given these matters much thought, and that which she had given them had never bothered her. She had always felt fulfilled by the satisfaction that her work brought her. However, her studio now stood empty, save for Jacqui and a few loyal dancers who hadn't sought roles with different playwrights and choreographers. Jack Katan had the entire industry believing she'd retired. Her work, her source of fulfillment, was no longer there to distract her from the other, less fulfilling, aspects of her life. The glowing white page sat starkly on the hotel desk, reminding her that her heart and soul were empty and that without some great inspiration or adventure to fill her, they would remain that way. Hannah's features hardened, and her blue eyes narrowed. The deafening pounding of her heart stilled, and the clamor of her doubts and hesitations quieted. She sucked in a deep breath, hot with the humid air, and spoke a few short words into the phone's receiver:

"Ashleigh, it's Hannah. I'll do it. I'll be your surrogate."

PART TWO

CHAPTER 11

FORSAKING ALL OTHERS

A rough hand began creeping softly up Hannah's ankles beneath a thin white bedsheet. The delicate touch tickled her soft and sensitive skin, and she let out a sigh as the touch crested over her knees and continued slowly up her thighs. The tracing of gentle fingers was replaced by soft, wet kisses that punctuated steps along her inner thigh, and she felt her nightgown gently peel open and fall behind her shoulders. The kisses continued higher, and her heart began to race in her chest. Her pulse quickened with excitement, and she grew hotter still despite the already warm room.

She looked down at the man moving his way up toward her, but his face was shielded beneath the white sheet. She pressed her hips closer to the lips gently kissing the inside of her thigh to invite the kisses ever so slightly higher. Each kiss, now accompanied by a subtle tongue, continued to tease her, and she began to writhe with pleasure on her hotel bed. Impatient for the excitement to continue, she reached at the bedsheet to uncover her lover. She threw back the sheet to reveal Desmond between her legs, smiling seductively, hungrily.

Suddenly, Hannah was awakened from her dream by a loud, pounding knock on her hotel door. Still excited by her dream, she breathed heavily and tried to calm her racing heart. She sighed, still on the edge of satisfaction. She had decided to lie down after her short call to Ashleigh, and at some point, she'd fallen asleep, and the contemplation of her undertaking had segued into a dream. The loud, impatient pounding came at the door once more, and Hannah looked out the window—night had fallen, and it was drizzling rain. She gathered her robe closely around her, and realized she was cold. The air conditioning had restarted while she slept, and the thermostat remained unadjusted at fifty-five degrees. She had set it low when the system first started failing. The cold kept her nipples hard, even though the excitement from her dream was dissipating.

Hannah quickly stepped out of the bedroom and over to the hotel door. She peered through the peephole and was surprised to see Desmond, dripping wet, standing in the hallway. She opened the door. "Desmond?"

He burst inside without an invitation. Hannah closed the door behind him and quickly gathered her revealing sleepwear around her. She tightened the robe and crossed her arms over her chest to conceal her breasts. She turned to face Desmond and was shocked to meet a finger pointing accusingly at her. Desmond's face was contorted with anger.

He drew a deep, shaking breath, and his raised voice bellowed through the dark hotel room. "What the hell were you thinking?"

• • •

Four hours earlier …

"Absolutely not!" Desmond stood defiantly before Ashleigh.

Ashleigh had hung up the phone after Hannah's brief call, sat on the breakfast bench in their kitchen, and waited for Desmond to finish his post-workout shower. She used this brief time to consider how she'd approach the proposal with her husband, and to explore her own mixed feelings.

Desmond had appeared wearing a thin gray T-shirt and Chinos. The gray shirt clung closely to his large biceps and barreling chest, still swollen after his workout. The dampness of his hair made it look darker than normal, hiding his grays and wiping years from his appearance. He stood behind her, and leaned over her shoulder to kiss her on the cheek.

With his lips still pressed against her skin, she blurted out, "I want you to sleep with Hannah."

Desmond jolted back. "What?!"

Ashleigh spun in her chair and locked eyes with his, her face a stone mask of seriousness. "I want you to sleep with Hannah. She offered to be my surrogate, and I want you to sleep with her."

Desmond shook his head slowly in disbelief. "Is that what you two have been doing together all of this time? Planning a surrogacy? I thought you were just enjoying yourselves. Just having fun as … friends! I thought that's what you wanted—to do all the things you'd been missing out on?"

Ashleigh was on her feet. "No!" she shot back. "That's what *you* wanted. *You* wanted me to 'focus on the positives,' and I went out, and I tried to do that. I kept myself distracted so that *you* didn't have to keep carrying me. But no matter how much I distract myself, the topic of children keeps coming back to me—my friends, that IVF lawsuit, with Hannah. This time it's different! This time I don't have to pretend it doesn't hurt, to hide from you when I cry about it all. This time we can do something about it! We don't need IVF. We don't need to worry about that lawsuit, or doctors, or paying for a surrogate. This time we have a solution. We can have a *baby,* Desmond!"

"You're assuming I'm okay with this Ashleigh, and I'm not. Even if I were, I don't need to have sex with Hannah for us to have a baby! You could both manage the insemination manually and on your own!"

Ashleigh's hopeful eyes narrowed, and she shot back, "What do you mean you're not okay with this? Are you saying you don't want to have kids?"

"Of course I do, Ashleigh. It's just that I've just been adjusting to the idea that we might never have kids, and I've been coping with that idea. Now you surprise me not just with the opposite fact, but also with instructions to go and have sex with another woman! What if I'm not willing to have her as a surrogate at all, let alone have sex with her?"

Ashleigh's voice rose in exasperation. "Why wouldn't we choose her as a surrogate? She's fit and healthy. It would have taken months and a huge expense for us to get any other woman to that level of health before I'd have been ready for her to carry our baby. And she's not just healthy, Desmond, she's *beautiful*. Why wouldn't we choose her?"

"Because she's nothing like you!" Desmond shouted, and his voice bounced off the kitchen walls and bellowed through the house. "You told me before that you didn't want to adopt because you wanted *my* baby. Did it ever occur to you that maybe I'd want yours? That I want a little Ashleigh in my arms? That I'd want *your* brains, *your* beautiful brown eyes and hair, *your* compassion, your *every* quality in *our* baby?"

Ashleigh drew a breath as though she was going to say something, but nothing came out.

Desmond continued, his voice now quieter, almost sympathetic. "Ash, I don't think you've thought this through. I don't know if Hannah has thought this through either. She's always leaped before she looked. How much have you talked about this with her? How are you going to feel knowing I'm in bed with another woman?" Ashleigh shrank in her seat as Desmond continued. "Would you want to join us? Would Hannah let you? Does Hannah want to help raise the child? Be a part of its life? Who would the child call 'Mom'? What would this do to you? To me? To our marriage? I don't know if you and Hannah have answers to these questions, or if you've even discussed them. These are the questions that come to my mind less than five minutes after starting to talk about this. There'll be thousands more, and you still haven't explained why I'd need to have sex with her!"

Ashleigh looked away from Desmond. "I don't want a test-tube baby," she answered sullenly. "I want a baby to be born of love, and there are many different forms of love."

"That's it?" Desmond asked.

Ashleigh glared at him. "That's it? *That's it?*" she repeated angrily. "Do not belittle me, Desmond! You don't know what it's like—what it's *been* like—finding out that I can't bear a child! You don't know what it's like at school, where my good days now would have been my worst days six months ago. You don't understand what it does to a woman to be unable to have a baby…To wonder if I'm even still a woman; to not be able to give that to *you*.

"We've talked for years about having children. Do you think I've forgotten all the times you told me you can't wait to have kids? How excited you'd get when we'd talk about it? How happy you were when we first started trying? I've seen you play with little kids, and I see how much you love it. Don't belittle how I want us to conceive, or why I want to do it that way when part of the reason I want to do it so desperately is because I want it for you too!"

Desmond paused and looked at his wife. She'd placed her hands on her hips, let out a little sigh, and tightened her face. He knew her well enough to know she was trying to hold back the angry tears that had formed in her eyes. Everything that she had said was true. For most of his adult life, people had commented on his way with kids. He loved kids and had looked forward to having his own for a long time.

Although he'd never have told her so, Desmond had also hidden himself from Ashleigh as he cried over the news of her infertility. He had been slowly dealing with that news in his own way, and had maintained the image of strength and security he thought Ashleigh needed as she endured her own struggle.

Ashleigh had composed herself again, and returned her gaze to him, her eyes indicating that she expected a response. "I made vows, Ashleigh. I made a vow to forsake all others, and be faithful only to you."

"You also vowed to obey me," Ashleigh retorted. "If you don't do this for me, you're not forsaking all others, you're forsaking me. You're leaving me unable to have children, yet tied to a man who won't have them for me."

"Ashleigh—"

"That's not all. After we got my diagnosis, you told me that there was nothing you wouldn't do to fix this, but you didn't have any answers. We have an answer now, Desmond. I don't want my husband sleeping with another woman, but that's something I'm willing to deal with because I know there's nothing *I* wouldn't do to 'fix' this. Hannah is on board too. The only question left is whether you meant what you said. Are you willing to do whatever it takes for us to have a baby?"

Ashleigh stared up at Desmond with big, expressive eyes full of hope and expectation. She could sense the warring within him as his moral compass battled with his sense of duty as a husband. Ashleigh already could not believe that Hannah was willing to be her surrogate, and on her specific, intimate terms. She felt the same sense of joy and excitement that she'd felt when she and Desmond first started trying for a baby, and now stood pleading with the only obstacle between her and motherhood. She could not bear to have this sense of hope and joy ripped from her once again, just as the doctor's diagnosis had done a few months ago.

Desmond drew a breath and could feel the weight of his next words as they hung in his chest. However, even sensing that weight could not prepare him for the wailing grief they would visit upon his wife, once spoken.

"Ashleigh, honey, I won't do it."

• • •

Desmond pulled his jacket closer as a cold wind bit at his skin through his shirt. The day had been much warmer, and he was unprepared for the sudden drop in temperature so common during Baltimore's springtime. Through violent sobs, Ashleigh had ordered him to leave the house, and he hadn't had the opportunity to change or grab a jacket. Spots appeared on the footpath as heavy rain started falling around him. He charged through the city on foot in the late evening. As he moved closer to the harbor, he had only one destination in mind.

The rain was scattering tourists, and the increasing winds caused the docked boats to bob up and down in the water. He pushed past two taxi drivers arguing over a fare, and ignored their heckling as he entered a modest hotel by the water. With his fist clenched tightly, he punched the button in the foyer elevator to take him to the fifteenth floor. He watched the numbers illuminate as he passed each floor, and his anger rose with them. He stormed out of the elevator when the doors had barely parted far enough to admit him, and he stepped heavily along the carpeted floor until he stood in front of Hannah's hotel room door. He banged hard on the door three times with his still-clenched fists.

Hannah, barely dressed, eventually answered the door. "Desmond?"

He pushed past her and stormed into the hotel room, illuminated only by the filtered light of a desk lamp, his rain-soaked clothes and dripping-wet hair leaving a trail of wet spots in his wake.

Hannah shut the door behind Desmond and turned to face him. His face wet from the rain, and he raised a pointed finger at her as he yelled in a seething, wide-eyed fury: "What the hell were you thinking?"

"Excuse me?" Hannah asked, annoyed.

"Offering to be Ashleigh's surrogate without discussing it with me beforehand! Do you have any idea what you're doing to my marriage?"

Hannah raised a finger of her own and kept her other arm folded across her chest. "First of all, don't you storm into my space, unannounced and uninvited, and start yelling at me. Second, put your *damned* finger down."

Desmond realized he was still pointing at Hannah and lowered his arm.

She dropped her own pointed finger and crossed her arms again. She maintained her firm tone, "Now, if you want to have a conversation, we can do that. If you're going to be rude and accusatory, however, you can leave." Hannah pointed at the door, unintentionally exposing one of her breasts beneath her sheer robe as her crossed arm slipped lower. Desmond averted his gaze.

"A conversation then," said Hannah, her firm tone now a touch more relaxed. "Excuse me, while I go change."

Hannah exited the room, and Desmond kept his eyes fixed on the floor. He stood in the center of the room and noticed he was shivering. The room was still unnaturally cold, and he was soaked. "Would you happen to have something I can change into?" he called to Hannah in the next room.

Hannah reentered the small hotel living room, wearing more modest clothing, and carrying a men's white business shirt. She handed it to him and turned around to give him some semblance of privacy as he changed. She realized that she could still see him through a mirror on the other side of the room, but Desmond had his shirt off before she could say anything.

She'd never seen him shirtless before, and she quickly found herself examining his reflection in the dim lighting. His broad shoulders sat atop powerful back muscles, which stretched and flexed as he pulled his wet shirt overhead. His arms were muscular, and his biceps bulged as he bowed his arms to button the shirt. His chest and stomach were visibly firm. The moisture on his body from the rain had caused the shirt fabric to stick to him, and become see-through in odd places. Hannah's head tilted to one side in a moment of appreciation, and she found herself briefly reminded of the dream she'd been enjoying only minutes earlier. Her stomach fluttered.

"You always bring men's shirts with you when you travel?' Desmond asked, snapping Hannah out of her steamy recollection.

It took her a moment to respond. "I sleep in them," she answered.

"They belong to an ex?" he asked, as he finished buttoning the shirt.

"No." Hannah saw Desmond had finished dressing, and she turned around to face him. She realized too late that this would indicate that she'd watched him change, but he didn't seem to notice. "I'm a big girl, Des," she smiled wryly. "I can buy my own shirts." There was a small couch in the hotel room. Hannah gestured for Desmond to sit, and she sat beside him. "So, what happened?" Hannah asked. She had already assumed what had happened, but figured that giving Desmond the opportunity to narrate what had transpired after her call would help keep the discussion logical, rather than emotional.

"Well," he started, "Ashleigh asked me to sleep with you, and I said no."

Hannah nodded.

"And I told her that I thought that she hadn't thought this through properly."

"Have you?" Hannah asked.

125

"Of course not! I only found out a few hours ago that you two were contemplating all of this. Even in that time, I've come up with a million questions about how all of this would work, and not an answer for a single one of them. Even if all my questions were answered, I made vows, Hannah. This whole suggestion goes against everything I think it means to be a husband. I promised I'd forsake all others and be faithful only to her. What would it say about me as a husband and as a man if I did this? What does it say about me that I'm even here talking about it with you?" Desmond buried his face in his hands, and Hannah placed a reassuring hand on his shoulder.

His face still hidden, Hannah spoke. "I've never been one for marriage, Des. In truth, even when I was younger, and the other girls were talking about the 'ideal' age and time to get married, I never thought I'd get married. But that doesn't mean I haven't given thought as to what it means to be married, and the promises that are made when a couple exchange vows."

Desmond sat up and listened.

"Did you ever wonder why you say both 'forsaking all others' *and* 'be faithful only to you'? These aren't the same thing, as most people think. Being faithful only to one person means don't cheat on your spouse. But forsaking all others, Des, that means ourselves too. That vow is a promise to renounce ourselves and our interests, our preferences, our everything, in favor of the other. When you made that vow, you didn't just promise not to cheat on Ashleigh, you promised to put yourself aside too."

Desmond threw his hands up in frustration. "Then they're contradictory!"

Hannah smiled slightly. "Are they? Are you being unfaithful to her if she's permitted—no, demanded—that you break that vow? I can't answer that for you. But I think that in refusing her request, you might actually be failing in your promise to obey her *and* to forsake all others."

Desmond shifted uncomfortably in his seat and his face twisted in curiosity. "What do you get out of this, Hannah? Why the push to make this happen? You don't still ... you know... do you?" he asked, hinting at her confession in his office several years earlier.

Hannah let out a single, genuine bark of laughter. "I don't have feelings for you, Desmond," she answered honestly, "and I'm not trying to change your love. Trust me when I tell you that this is not ideal for me either. Before I called your wife, I thought long and hard about her suggestion to sleep with you. Let me be clear: I am not comfortable with the idea. Just like you're sitting here wondering what it says about you as a man, I wonder what this says about me as a woman." Hannah turned introspective. She looked straight ahead, and her gaze drifted into space. "I've never told anyone this," she began, her gaze shifting into the past, "but I once slept with a married man."

Desmond sat in silence, understanding that this confession was difficult for her.

"Mind you, I didn't know he was married at the time. We dated for almost a year before I found out he was married, and I broke things off immediately when I did find out. But I tell you, I was beside myself, not because the relationship was over, but because of how it made me feel to be the other woman. I never want to feel that feeling again, and I'm afraid that this whole ... arrangement ... might do just that."

This time it was Desmond who put the reassuring hand on his friend's shoulder. "Hannah, if you're afraid that this could hurt you, why are you willing to go through with it?"

Hannah smiled, but it was a weak semblance of a smile. "So what if it hurts me, Des? What does it matter if it *breaks* me? If I die right now, if the world swallows me whole, so what? Even if I don't go through with this, there are other things what will hurt me instead. I have spent my life running toward the good things in life, rather than running away from the bad

127

things that inevitably come. I promised myself that I would always run toward, pursue, and experience everything this life has to offer until my feet ran out of ground! But I feel like that's what happened. My feet ran out of ground to run along. Then, out of nowhere, you and Ashleigh showed up and revealed another path —a path that allows me to experience pregnancy, childbirth, and motherhood without the relationship or commitment that follows. A unique opportunity for another adventure! That's why I'm willing to do this, and why I'm not scared off by the thought that I might get hurt along the way."

Desmond thought he understood. "Well, I admire that." He was genuine. "But my vows, you, all of this aside, there's one more thing that holds me back from this."

Hannah turned to face him once more. "What's that?"

Desmond sighed, and he looked down at his feet as he spoke. "Ashleigh is the only woman I've ever been with. I feel her in my bones. I don't want to share that feeling with anyone else. What if by sleeping with someone else, with you, I don't just feel Ashleigh in my bones anymore? What if she has to share that?"

Hannah was startled by the confession, and her eyes widened for a moment. She was glad Desmond wasn't looking and did not notice. Had he waited for her? Had his harbored feelings for her prevented him from being with anyone before Ashleigh? Or was it something else? In college, Desmond was not an unattractive boy. He lacked confidence and was a little dorky, but not unattractive. Adulthood had obviously shaped him into a handsome man, and his legal practice seemed to have given him the confidence he'd lacked in his youth. But knowing that he hadn't met Ashleigh until several years into his practice, Hannah was shocked to discover that Desmond hadn't slept with anyone before his wife. He raised his head and looked to Hannah for an answer.

Hannah sighed. "I can't really empathize there, Des. However, what if … what if by not giving her this, you lose her completely? Not just in your bones, but in your house, and in your life? Or, even if this doesn't defeat you, or her, or your marriage, do you think it'll be the same after this?"

"No," Desmond answered flatly. He knew his wife well enough to know what the future held if he refused her proposal. "She'll resent me for the rest of our lives. She'll think that we had a chance to have a baby and I stood in the way."

"Do you think you are?"

"No! I think she's being ridiculous! If we were going to do this, we could do it manually. There's no rational reason why we have to do this the old-fashioned way."

"So, why would you?"

Desmond sighed and looked up at the ceiling. He knew Hannah was helping him to process and organize his thoughts. "Because it's what she wants," he answered with resignation. He looked back at Hannah, his eyes seeking reassurance. "Would you do it, if you were me?"

Hannah shook her head and laughed. "I'm not answering that!"

"Why not?"

Hannah shifted on the couch, so that she was now sitting on her legs, and began counting on her fingers in front of him. Her small hands were barely visible in the dim light. "First, because I'm not you. Second, I have no idea what it's like to be married. Third, this is a decision you have to live with either way, and it's not appropriate for me to answer that question when I'm … involved."

Hannah and Desmond sat next to each other in the dark. Each could feel the warmth of the other as their bodies defeated the cold around them. They sat in mute silence for a moment, each silently acknowledging the conclusion at which they'd arrived. Through the dark, Hannah could feel Desmond's eyes on her body. At last, they held each other's gaze, and with nothing left to say, Desmond spoke. "I should go."

Standing in the doorway Desmond promised to return the buttoned shirt Hannah had loaned him. She could sense his heavy heart and saw distressed lines under his eyes. She felt an urge to comfort him but didn't, so as not to draw further attention to the physical contact they both knew they'd soon share.

Desmond returned to the foyer of the hotel, and the taxi driver who heckled him upon his entry was now smiling at him and offering his services to drive him home through the rain. Desmond wasn't sure if the driver failed to recognize him, or if he was just eager for the fare. Either way, he caught the cab home.

He stood under the canopy above the front door of his house, insulated from the heavy rain that fell around him. He let out a heavy sigh and entered his home. It was dark, save for a single light which came from the living room. He found Ashleigh asleep on the living room table, tissues scattered everywhere, and photo albums laying open around her. The closest album was open to their wedding photos, a slightly younger Ashleigh and Desmond beamed at him from behind the protective plastic film. He lifted his wife out of her chair and began to walk to their bedroom. She roused as he carried her, and she pulled herself closer to him, not noticing the perfume emanating from the borrowed shirt.

"I'll do it," Desmond said, without looking down. Ashleigh looked up at her husband through sleepy, bloodshot eyes. Desmond looked down at her and repeated, "I'll do it."

• • •

A few miles to the south, Hannah was standing at the window of her hotel room, watching the rain fall and thinking about what was to come. The harbor was dark, and the heavy rain obscured her vision beyond a few feet. She spied the blank page on the desk next to her, and sat down. She picked up her pen and began filling the page, and then another, and another. Perhaps it was her nap earlier that day; maybe it was the sudden burst of inspiration. Whatever it was, the next thing she knew, the morning sun was rising in the distance, visible through clear skies. She'd written all through the night.

CHAPTER 12

THE ARRANGEMENT

A shleigh, Desmond, and Hannah had met in her New York high-rise the following weekend to discuss what they'd all come to refer to as "the arrangement." Desmond had spent the last week working day and night on the Poe case, and the little time he'd spent at home was occupied by Ashleigh's incessant talk about the arrangement.

Although she spoke non-stop about it, Desmond rarely heard her. The notion that Ashleigh might be a mother within only a few months excited her, and that excitement seemed to insulate her from the dark reality of the arrangement. Her spirits were high, and whenever she spoke about the impending relations between her husband and his friend, her voice was peppered with enthusiasm. Was she feigning levity to compensate for her discomfort with the arrangement she'd designed? Did she see through the grimness of it, see it only as a necessary means to a happy end? Or, was she truly just ignorant of the abhorrent reality? Desmond couldn't tell, but he knew for certain that he was not hiding his discomfort, that he could not see this arrangement as a "necessary" means to a happy end. In fact, he thought that it might break him, and he secretly hoped that Ashleigh would come to her senses, change her mind, and permit them all to manage the insemination manually and in private. He was not ignorant to the abhorrent reality of the arrangement, and his lack of sleep each night for the past week was almost exclusively caused by his inability to reconcile what he'd agreed to do with the bearing of his own moral compass.

Desmond sat at the new table in Hannah's living room. After their last visit, she'd replaced the small one-seater table that had failed to accommodate the three of them. He leaned forward with his elbows on the table and a hand on each side of his face. He looked visibly distressed. The lines on his face were deeper and were now joined by dark, sullen bags beneath his eyes.

Ashleigh and Hannah were casually answering some of the many unanswered questions, some of which Desmond had mentioned to Ashleigh when she'd first proposed the arrangement to him. They'd unanimously agreed, without much discussion, that Hannah would be allowed to stay in the child's life, and Hannah had offered to pay for all of the pregnancy and birthing medical expenses: "tax-deductible work expenses," according to her. The attorney in Desmond doubted whether the validity of this, but Hannah seemed sure of herself. Hannah had already started taking prenatal supplements, and Ashleigh had asked Desmond to maintain his workout regimen to keep his sperm in optimal health. Hannah had also agreed to relinquish all parental rights soon after she'd recovered from the birth, and Ashleigh would legally become the adoptive mother. The conversation then turned to the logistics of the conception.

"When you're having sex, I don't want anything involved that doesn't relate to conception," Ashleigh voiced casually.

"So, no oral sex, and no toys, obviously," Hannah responded. "What about kissing?" She had a pen and notepad in hand, but Desmond couldn't tell if she was taking notes or simultaneously working on her next show. She'd been consistently writing and taking oral notes on the voice recorder she kept in her handbag since leaving Baltimore the previous Sunday.

Ashleigh's mouth moved to one side as she contemplated Hannah's clarification. "I suppose it'd be a bit weird if you're having sex and not kissing. I'm okay with kissing."

"No kissing!" Desmond interrupted gruffly. Both women looked at him. He sat up slightly and took his hands from the side of his head. "Ash, I was a virgin when we met. If we're doing this, then at least let me keep kissing just between us."

Hannah looked at Ashleigh and raised her eyebrows once. "No kissing then." Hannah looked back at her notepad and ticked off an item. It seemed her notepad was a list of questions she'd prepared.

Desmond wondered if the making of the list was a measure of her "professional" role in the arrangement, or whether she just wanted to make sure she didn't cross any boundaries. *Any more boundaries*, Desmond corrected himself, returning to his slouched position and leaning on the table.

"Next thing," Hannah continued. "Ashleigh, do you want to be in the bedroom when we're trying?"

Ashleigh looked at her friend thoughtfully. "Do you mean watching, or like a threesome?" Ashleigh replied.

Desmond shook his head slowly to himself, increasingly uncomfortable with the candor in their voices.

"Well, that's up to you," Hannah said. "I've been with women before, but only when I was younger and experimenting a bit. Even then it was always with strangers. If you were there, I wouldn't be … touching you."

"No. I thought about this," Ashleigh said. "I don't want to be there. I want the baby to be born of love—not some sexual tryst. Actually, while it's on my mind, I should mention that I don't want this taking place at our house. I don't want to be able to picture it at all, let alone picturing it happening in our marital home. I thought perhaps Desmond could come up here to you, and I'll stay in Baltimore. He can stay in another hotel and just come over when you send word."

"For goodness sake! Would you listen to yourselves!" Desmond was on his feet, and he kicked his chair out from behind him. "This is wrong, Ashleigh! It's crazy. You're casually sitting around and talking about what sex I can and can't have with my would-be mistress. It's insane!"

Hannah was hurt at being called a mistress, and she wondered if Desmond was making a reference to the confession she'd made to him about having dated a married man. She maintained her composure. She could appreciate Desmond's growing discomfort, but for her, this was strictly a professional venture. The amount of writing she'd produced in the past few days was a personal affirmation that she was on the right track.

Desmond continued. He was tired, and tripping over his words at times. "Ashleigh, you don't want to be able to picture it. I have to *live* it! For me, it's not going to stop after it's done, either. I'll have to carry around this guilt and have these images tear at my soul for God only knows how long!"

Ashleigh leaned back in her chair coolly. "Oh, come on, Desmond. Most husbands would jump at the chance for an 'arrangement.' And any hot-blooded man would be attracted to Hannah. She's beautiful. Don't pretend you don't notice."

This comment made Hannah uncomfortable, though she maintained her professional repose.

"Not me!" Desmond retorted. "I want nothing to do with this arrangement." He was wide-eyed and waved a finger at his wife. "I've resisted your terms for this surrogacy from the start." He pointed the finger at Hannah's notepad. "Here's a question that I can't imagine is in that list: What do you think is going to happen to us if we go through with this? Have you given any real thought to that? I don't even know if I can come back from this—if I'll still be myself after I tear myself away from what I think it means to be a husband and a man—let alone if *we'll* still be the same afterward. What do you think will happen if we do this!?"

"What do you think will happen to us if we *don't* do this!?" Ashleigh was also on her feet now, and she raised her voice. "If I refuse a surgical surrogacy because of my principles, and you refuse a non-surgical one because of yours, where does that leave us!? The only difference between your principles and mine is that mine have concern for the personhood of our *child,* not just who *I* am as a woman and wife. Your principles are about *you,* and everyone else at this table is willing to sacrifice a part of themselves to make this happen except *you!*" Ashleigh and Desmond locked eyes from across the round table.

Hannah broke the tense silence. "Could you both please sit down? It's uncomfortable being the only one seated, and I think if you sit down together, you're more likely to work this through."

Ashleigh began taking her seat, but never broke her husband's gaze. "Desmond, I promise you that if you give me this, I will not see you any differently. This won't make you any less of a man or a husband, or diminish who you are as a person. All it will do is make you a father…something we've both wanted for a long time. But if you deny me this, I don't know that I could ever forgive you."

Desmond stood with his back against the wall adjacent to the table. He breathed in heavily and looked heavenward. That he might lose himself if he went through with the arrangement—this covenant of consensual cheating—was not his greatest concern. He was most concerned about the effects it would have on his marriage, something he was certain his wife was failing to appreciate. He wondered which path offered the greatest risk of losing his marriage—denying Ashleigh her opportunity of motherhood, or giving in to her on terms he thought unspeakable. He shook his head to himself before lowering himself slowly into his seat.

"I hope you're right about that, Ashleigh. I really hope you know what you're doing, for all our sake." He leaned forward, elbows on the table once more, his hands supporting his head. He spent the rest of his time at Hannah's silently enduring the conversation he allowed to pass between Ashleigh and Hannah as they casually made their way down the list of intimate questions.

• • •

A week later, Desmond was standing in Hannah's living room. He turned and watched as the steel elevator doors came together in front of him, closing him in. At their last meeting a few weeks ago, the three of them had "agreed" that Desmond and Hannah would try at least twice a month to conceive, with Desmond making the trip up to New York on the weekends during Hannah's "fertile week." Ashleigh had remained in Baltimore and had arranged to go out with her friends so she wouldn't dwell on what her husband was doing.

Desmond surveyed the room around him. The setting sun was casting vivid hues across the New York skyline, and it caused the white tones of Hannah's open room to reflect an otherworldly orange. He untied his shoelaces slowly and placed his shoes by the closed elevator doors. *This won't be the last piece of clothing I take off tonight,* he thought. His nausea intensified. The room was silent but for the soft howl of a light breeze playing against the living room window.

The knot in his stomach, the soft white carpet beneath his feet, and the setting sun reminded him of Coogee, the beachside town in Australia, where he'd proposed to Ashleigh. Coogee was famous for its beach, and coastal walk along the ocean side cliffs. Ashleigh had spent a summer in Australia a few years before meeting Desmond, and told him about it when they were dating. She'd described it as her "favorite place in the world." He remembered her telling him about how she had climbed over one of the railings on the cliff side walk, and found a secluded outcropping of rock where she'd read, or just be alone with her thoughts above the crashing waves.

Desmond remembered his heart racing in his chest as he and Ashleigh had walked along Coogee beach at sunset, toward the cliffs. He'd used Google Maps to figure out where Ashleigh's favorite outcropping was, and he'd planned to propose to her there. He had walked awkwardly, unsuccessfully trying to hide the bulge in his pocket formed by the small wooden ring box he'd managed to keep concealed from her since they'd left BWI airport in Maryland. An oblivious TSA agent had begun congratulating him when he'd noticed the ring as it passed through the airport X-ray machine and had almost given him away. A drone had passed overhead, and Desmond tried to distract Ashleigh from its whirring. Ashleigh hadn't seemed to notice the drone, for as he climbed over the cliffside railing and helped her to follow him, she'd already begun to cry. She'd figured out that he was about to propose, and was shocked and overwhelmed that he'd remembered her favorite place, and designed to get down on one knee there. The drone that had flown past them was controlled by someone he'd hired to fly it over the water, and capture a photo of him down on one knee.

The picture photo from that moment still hung in their living room back home, and the thought of it pained his heart as he stood watching a similar sunset in the home of another woman. Though identical in all aesthetic qualities, the evening in front of him now felt as far from the one he'd seen in Coogee as Australia was from this New York high-rise. Desmond sighed. Never in a million years would he have expected that a version of himself, the same man who had stood on that cliff, would one day agree to this.

"I'm in here," Hannah called to Desmond from the bed-room. "Don't worry, I have clothes on."

Desmond tore his eyes from the radiant colors the sunset cast across the sky, and walked solemnly toward Hannah's bedroom. His steps were heavy, and he hated himself more and more each time one foot was placed in front of the other. He stood in the doorway of the bedroom, his shoulders sunken and his face weary. It was an extravagantly large room, larger than any bedroom he'd ever seen. He knew Hannah was sitting on the bed, but he couldn't bring himself to look at her.

He glanced around the room as he'd done the first time he'd seen her apartment. The bedroom was dominated by bright tones—whites and creams. The walls were off-white, the lowered blinds were ivory, and the white carpet continued underfoot. The large king-size bed covered in a pure white duvet was cradled by a tall ivory headboard that matched the blinds. The sheer brilliance of the light colors in the room betrayed the dim lighting cast by a glistening chandelier, hanging from the ceiling toward the center of the room. Desmond noticed for the first time just how high the apartment ceilings were.

"Are you okay, Des?" asked Hannah, as she came to her feet. Desmond looked at the ground before bringing his eyes up to meet hers. He looked at her for the first time since their private discussion in her Baltimore hotel room.

Hannah had noticed that he hadn't looked at or spoken directly to her a single time during discussions about the arrangement. As she looked at him, she was shocked by his condition. His normally blue eyes were now more of a dull gray, and the overhead lighting threw shadows across his every harried feature.

Desmond didn't answer. He merely looked away and shook his head. His throat was tight, and he suspected his voice might break if he tried to speak.

Not knowing what to say, Hannah unconsciously played with her hands in front of her. She thought Desmond might need a moment to himself, so she quietly said, "I'm going to freshen up and change into something more … appropriate. I put a bottle of water on the bedside table for you." She stepped softly into the adjacent en suite bathroom, and closed the door. A small *click* followed as she locked it behind her.

Desmond took off his jacket and placed it on a chair in the corner of the bedroom. He walked over to the bedside table where a bottle of water stood waiting. Condensation on the outside of the plastic bottle sparkled as it reflected the chandelier light. He noticed a copy of *What to Expect When You're Expecting* laying on the bed, a bookmark wedged through roughly three-quarters of the pages. Desmond grabbed the bottle of water and gulped down several mouthfuls, his shaking hand causing him to spill a little as he swallowed. The en suite door opened a little as Desmond placed the bottle of water back on the stand.

"Desmond … are you ready?" Hannah called through the small opening.

"No," Desmond replied. "But I don't think it makes a difference. I don't think I'll ever be ready for this."

Hannah stepped out of the darkened bathroom, and into the light wearing a men's white button-up shirt, and champagne colored sockettes. She was never more self-conscious of her mangled, broken-looking feet than when she was intimate with a man. Because of this, she wore something on her feet, even when sharing her bed. All but the top two buttons of her white shirt were buttoned, but it was obvious she wasn't wearing anything underneath. She pulled gently at the front of the shirt to add length and make sure she was covered, but the stretching exposed tanned skin through the opening between the buttons.

She walked over to Desmond until she stood in front of him, and he straightened his posture and looked over her head. Soft, gentle hands rose between them as Hannah reached up to the top button of Desmond's shirt.

He felt the shirt loosen as she flicked it open. She looked up at him as she continued her way down his shirt. His face was hard, and his jaw was clenched. He continued to stare at nothing but the far wall. He remained impassive as she finished unbuttoning his shirt, and removed it over his broad and muscular shoulders.

She noticed for the first time a small, circular scar on his shoulder from an old burn. Hannah looked away to the side as she slowly moved her hands to the top of her own shirt and began unbuttoning. The white shirt inched open, exposing her bosom more with each dispelled button. Her shirt hung loosely upon her shoulders as her hands came halfway through the unbuttoning, her nipples barely covered by the pale cloth.

Desmond could feel his trousers tightening in a purely physiological response to Hannah's partial nudity, and he felt ashamed of himself. Her shy hands finished unbuttoning her shirt, and she pulled it back over her slender shoulders. She let it drop onto the floor beside them, and stood naked in front of him.

Even without looking at her, Desmond could see her body in his peripheral vision. She was tall, and firm. Her figure was complemented by full, round breasts, and a small waist. Her stomach was toned and flat, and her pink nipples were semi-hardened. Strong thigh muscles hugged her legs tightly beneath smooth skin, and her blonde locks glowed beneath the light. She was a gorgeous, radiant woman, and despite this, she stood shyly in front of an old friend with whom she was about to sleep for the first time.

"Stop! Stop!" Desmond cried suddenly. "I can't do this."

Hannah quickly gathered the shirt at her feet and pulled it back on. She pulled the open sides of the shirt together to cover her exposed breasts, and turned quickly to begin buttoning up its front. The quick turn caused the bottom of the shirt to flutter and briefly expose her pert cheeks. Although Hannah understood Desmond's reaction, she was surprisingly hurt by it. Every other man she'd undressed before had hungrily examined her, eagerly consumed her image. Desmond had roundly rejected her without so much as glancing at her, and it hurt her pride. She felt like a self-conscious young woman, naked in front of a man for the first time.

Desmond made for the en suite and closed the door behind him. He leaned over the sink, expecting to vomit. He realized quickly that his nausea was not going to manifest itself outwardly, and reached into his pant pocket to remove his phone. His shaking hands were barely able to unlock the phone, and so he used his auto dial to call Ashleigh.

Ashleigh was in a restaurant in Bethesda when she got the call. She quietly excused herself from her friends, and stepped outside before answering the ringing phone.

"Ash, I can't do it," he sputtered. "I just can't."

Ashleigh sat down on the steps outside the restaurant. She figured that her husband was in Hannah's apartment as they spoke, and it hit her like a blow to the stomach. "Des, we talked about this. I told you I didn't want to know when it's happening."

Desmond sank against the wall so that he sat on the bathroom floor. "Ashleigh, I don't want to do this! If this is what it's going to take to have kids, then I don't want it. I only want you. You're enough for me!"

Husband and wife both blinked back tears.

Through a tight throat, Ashleigh squeaked the words, "It's not enough for me." She screwed up her face. She knew her words would sting her husband. She knew she was guilting him into doing something to which he was fundamentally opposed, but she was desperate for a child of her own.

Silence hung between them for a moment as Ashleigh's words weighed heavily on Desmond's conscience.

She broke the silence, "Des, I know this is hard for you. It's hard for me too—"

Desmond cut her off. "Even though you want me to do this, Ashleigh, I don't think I *can*."

Ashleigh pinched the bridge of her nose and nodded in understanding. "Just … just turn off the lights and pretend it's me. Remember, you're not doing anything wrong."

"But I know that I am, Ash! No amount of pretending is going to change that. It's not like turning off the lights is going to make me forget what I'm doing and with whom."

Ashleigh covered her mouth with her hand as tears began to fall silently down her cheeks. "Desmond, I'm turning off my phone now. I hope…" she paused a moment as she choked on her words. "I hope that when I see you tomorrow, you don't tell me that you couldn't go through with it. I love you." Ashleigh hung up the phone and burst into tears. A couple avoided looking at her as they stepped by her and into the restaurant.

Desmond heard the line cut off.

"I love you too," he whispered into the phone.

"Ashleigh, there you are!" Heather had come outside the restaurant and was standing in the doorway, holding the door open behind her. Ashleigh quickly wiped the tears from her face and turned around.

"Heyyy!" She put on her best fake smile as Heather lead her back to their table where none of her friends suspected she'd been controlling fitful sobs only a moment earlier.

Several minutes later Desmond emerged from the en suite. The chandelier lights had been turned off, and night had fully fallen, delving the room into pitch-black darkness. "I'm sorry, I didn't mean to eavesdrop" came Hannah's voice through the darkness. "The bathroom just tends to echo."

Desmond realized her voice was coming from the near side of the bed. He was startled as he felt her small hand slip into his own.

"I don't mind if you pretend I'm Ashleigh, Des. I know this is hard for you, and I'm sorry it has to be this way." She began leading him toward the bed, and he stumbled over her white bed shirt as they walked. Naked but for her sockettes, she sat on the bed facing Desmond, and began unbuckling his belt.

"I'll do it," Desmond said through the darkness. Hannah released his belt buckle and leaned back upon the bed. She heard the chinking of the belt's metal clasp as Desmond unwound the leather through the loops of his trousers. Next came the low hum of Desmond undoing his zipper.

Hannah climbed under the white bed sheet, invisible in the darkness, and was followed by Desmond a moment later. His bulk tilted the mattress slightly, and she unintentionally rolled toward him. She could feel his naked thigh beneath her own. Any illusion that Desmond was lying beside his wife was broken as Hannah was thrown against him. Her perfume was sweet and intoxicating, and he'd noticed it only now, as the two were pressed together.

This was not his wife's scent.

Hannah gingerly reached into the darkness and grabbed Desmond between his legs. His penis was only slightly hardened—at half-mast, her girlfriends had always called it. Even at half-mast, however, his bulk was impressive. She hadn't given much thought to what Desmond looked like naked, as her premonitions of this moment had always centered on her own insecurities. Her hand stroked his smooth and shaved skin gently and she felt him stiffen both in her hand, and beneath her. She briefly wondered whether she should climb on top of Desmond so that she could control the insertion, but thought that he should be the one to decide when he was ready.

"When you're ready," Hannah said quietly in the darkness. She released him and slowly lowered herself, so she lay on the bed beside him. Her fear of pain redoubled the nervous feelings not felt since she was about to lose her virginity. Her heart raced in her chest, and she tried to slow her breathing as she mentally prepared herself for him.

They lay beside one another for another minute as Desmond warred within himself. He was already so ashamed. No matter how hard he tried to pretend that Hannah was Ashleigh, or that what they were doing was okay, it didn't work. Even as his friend lay naked beside him, he knew he could still get up, leave, try to get Ashleigh to reconsider, and try to forgive himself for what he'd already done. However, he knew that from the point of penetration there could be no turning back. If he was going to turn back, this was his last chance.

Seconds stretched into silent minutes, and Hannah wondered whether she should end this for the sake of Desmond's conscience. She could feel the mattress move beneath her as Desmond's heart pounded with enough force to make it shake. She was about to call out to him in the darkness when she felt him move beside her. For a moment, she thought that he was about to climb out of the bed and abandon the arrangement altogether, but he moved closer and propped himself above her. She realized for the first time just how large a man he really was. His powerful arms straddled her sides, and even through the darkness, she could see that the size of his penis matched the size of the man. He had always been such a gentle person, and so she'd never realized just how large and ruggedly powerful his body was.

"Are you ready," he whispered quietly, only inches from her face. She could feel him twitching at her entrance, and her body reacted to the fluttering coupling of fear and excitement she felt in her stomach. Her heart pounded, and she breathed a quiet, "Yes."

Desmond pressed himself into her, and his full length slid inside of her. Hannah let out a small cry. Even though her body was ready, it tightened beneath him, and she grabbed his forearms instinctively with both hands. Desmond also let out a deep groan as he entered her, and just like Hannah's cry, his groan was one of pain. He felt something inside of himself break, and it took a great deal of his strength not to tear himself away and collapse into despaired tears.

As he slid into Hannah, he felt the dark caress of someone new against his skin. He closed his eyes and fiercely tried to pretend that he was moving inside of Ashleigh, but everything about this was different. He could tell that the sheets beneath his legs were not those on his marital bed. The hands that grabbed his arms were smaller and lighter than Ashleigh's, and through the darkness, he could see golden locks splayed out on the pillow beneath him. He closed his eyes to rid himself of the face that looked up at him with wide, emotional eyes, and his awareness of her perfume intensified. He continued to thrust, and with each slow movement of his body, he hated himself more and more, his soul becoming a black mass as dark as the room in which he'd committed himself to adultery.

Hannah tried to ignore the sharp ache between her legs, and relax her body. Long and uncomfortable minutes passed, and the two bodies failed to fall into a rhythm. She felt Desmond's thick mass of flesh move inside her and press against her every contour. Her soft skin stretched and retracted with each stroke she accommodated, and it truly felt like her first time once more. Her hands moved from his forearms to his toned sides as she tried to brace herself against his continuing movements. She lay in the bed silently, unable to remotely enjoy the act even as the painful thrusts became pleasurable intercourse, as her heart broke for the grief of the man inside of her.

Desmond made no sounds but for his breaths of exertion. His mind flickered over images of Ashleigh as he fought to concentrate on her, and it was at this moment he realized that his wife had been wrong: if Hannah were to conceive tonight, the child would not be borne of love—the only emotions in the room were pity, grief, and hatred. The silent sex in the dark was without passion. It was cold, cerebral, and ironically sterile. As the two bodies crashed together with each fitful movement, Desmond could only think of his wife, and with each thought of his wife, his hatred for himself redoubled.

When Desmond returned home, Ashleigh did not have to ask if he'd gone through with the arrangement. She could see the self-hatred within himself, and sensed in his eyes—when he could finally bring himself to look at her—nothing but resentment.

Even though he'd showered several times in his hotel room after the act, he showered again as soon as he returned home. Desmond and Ashleigh had privately agreed that they would not discuss his meetings with Hannah, and for this he was grateful. As he stood motionless beneath the bullets of water that showered down upon his body, he gratefully realized that he would not have to explain to his wife that he'd been unable to finish. He'd become so overwrought with grief as he'd lain with Hannah that he had lost his erection, and they'd been forced to abort the attempt. He would not be forced to confess that Ashleigh's grief, Hannah's pain, and his own anguish were all for nothing.

CHAPTER 13

OUT

Desmond returned to New York in the weeks that followed as he attempted to conceive with Hannah. His conscience still begged at him with each waking moment, and a sickening feeling stuck to his stomach from the minute he pulled out of the driveway on his way to New York, and remained with him until he was distracted by his work the following Monday. Despite this feeling, he had come to somewhat of an agreement with his conscience: from the second he left his hotel room in New York to visit Hannah until the moment of his return, he would be deadened and dulled to his actions. His face was set in a stone mask of impassiveness, and he would commit all that was required by the sinister arrangement, but not allow himself to feel or experience any dark portion of it until he returned to his hotel room.

Upon his return, the full weight of his suspended emotions— the guilt, the fear, the anger—would all descend upon him at once, and plunge him into a dark pool of despair. He would drown for hours in his grief and sorrow in private, and once finished, he would return home to Baltimore—a hollow shell of himself—but having spared Ashleigh from his inner turmoil.

He had shared Hannah's bed five or six times (by now he'd lost count) and each time, he had been unable to finish. His inability to complete had been, at first, a silver lining. A part of him believed that his failure to complete might perhaps be his subconscious at work, stopping his body from inseminating a woman who was not his wife. However, it was now apparent that without completing, the objective of his sexual encounters with Hannah could never be met, and so their meetings would continue. Upon that realization, any silver lining that may have existed had immediately vanished.

Every time Desmond came to visit, Hannah was shocked by his appearance. Although he always stepped into her apartment well-groomed and freshly showered, there was always something less about him each time he arrived. Each time they had sex, he seemed to lose another part of himself, and for this, her heart broke. Hannah also felt guilty, and had to make a conscious effort to maintain her usual tenor whenever she and Ashleigh spoke on the phone.

However, despite concern for her friends, Hannah was also conscious of her own feelings. Her meetings with Desmond had taken a toll on her as well. The sex she shared with Desmond was regular, but emotionless. There was no levity, no excitement, and no joy in their moments together—no passion or desire. She did not find it surprising that Desmond had been unable to complete during any of their attempts, as the sex was thoroughly *unenjoyable.*

She had not expected the sex to be fun or intimate by any measure, but his cold impassiveness reduced their intercourse to the mere function of two bodies coming together, and this seemed to prevent their bodies from *coming* together. The regular, but unfulfilling sex had also left her feeling frustrated, and unsatisfied. Here she had an attractive and fit man coming to her doorstep as often as twice a week to bed her, and on the few occasions she found herself beginning to enjoy the experience, all pleasure would be removed from the equation as her counterpart would lose his ability to perform.

She was doing her part in the arrangement, so Desmond's inability to do his was frustrating. Frustrating because her body was becoming increasingly restless—eager for an orgasm from sex, almost begging for it. Frustrating also because, aside from her body's cry for satisfaction, she felt used. She had a man in her bed as often as twice a week, and yet he showed no emotion during any of it. He showed no affection, no care; certainly no love. In fact, he showed her barely any recognition at all. He would arrive in her bedroom, strip himself and climb into her bed expectantly. If she wasn't already in the bed waiting for him, she would unclothe herself in front of him and climb into the bed to lie next to him. As she stripped, he would make a point of averting his gaze. As he slid inside of her, he would look away. As he moved inside of her, he would close his eyes. And when he'd finally announce that he could not finish, he would climb out of her and her bed without another word to her. She would be left lying there, sore and ignored, as he got dressed, and left her apartment.

While Hannah did not expect to feel love or intimacy in their encounters, she did expect to be acknowledged: for him to address her, to speak to her, or at the very least, *respect* her. She was not sure whether Desmond was conscious of his treatment of her. Perhaps his feelings rendered him ignorant to hers, but while this might explain his indifference toward her, it did not excuse it.

She had hoped that as she and Desmond continued to sleep together, and the initial shock and cognitive dissonance evaporated, that he might become more comfortable with her, and their sex could become at least a little more personal. However, as time wore on, Desmond seemed as harried, uncomfortable, and detached as ever.

The morning after Desmond's most recent failed attempt, she and Desmond tried again. Desmond had spent longer than usual in the bathroom, and Hannah wondered whether he was warming himself up, or whether he was steeling himself against the moral fallout that came with his every visit. She had left the bed to grab a bottle of water from the fridge and was standing next to the bed as Desmond exited the bathroom. His eyes showed his surprise as he pulled the door open and found Hannah standing naked in front of him. It was the first time he had really looked at her, the first time he had *seen* her and registered her presence since their first night together.

He was naked but for his underwear, and as Hannah climbed into the bed and covered herself with the white bed sheet, she wondered if Desmond had liked what he had seen. She looked at his groin to see whether, if by nothing other than physiological response, by the mere increase of blood flow, he might acknowledge her. He didn't. Desmond climbed into the bed and removed his trunks, reaching out of the sheets to place them by the side of the bed. He propped himself up onto one side as he normally did in preparation for climbing on top of her.

Hannah was angry. She was desperate for *something* from Desmond. *Touch my hand, kiss me on the cheek, say my name, say hello, for goodness sake. Please! Look at me for just a second. Just give me something before you use me*, her voice cried in her head. She was done being used, and abused. For a moment, she hated the man that lay next to her as he prepared to have dispassionate sex with her yet again. She was done being used, finished with being left unsatisfied, and she'd had enough of his refusal to acknowledge her. She didn't want to deny him her body; she just wanted him to *acknowledge* her.

Desmond leaned further over her, and she placed a firm hand on his chest. She pushed his bulk away from her body, and as he leaned back, she pressed him down into the mattress so that he lay on his back. She gathered some of the sheets in her hands to allow her some movement on the bed, and she climbed on top of him. Each of her long legs stretched to his sides so that she straddled him, and the sheets fell from her shoulders. The top half of her body was inescapably in full view in front of Desmond, and her weight on top of him held him in place. He tried in vain to avert his gaze, but his vision could not escape the view of her full bosom in front of him. Her pert and supple breasts rocked with her body as she shifted her weight on his, and her pink round nipples stared him in the eyes.

The muscles beneath her tight stomach twisted and toned as she lifted her weight on top of him. Hannah lifted herself with her legs and reached beneath her to grab at Desmond. She finally received some recognition from Desmond, some vindication that she was, in fact, present, when she found that Desmond was already hard. She held him in place with her legs as she lowered herself onto him. Her legs quivered, and she let out a sigh as she drove him fully inside of her, and as he reached up into her, she began to rock her hips against him.

Desmond would not look at her, but this time Hannah made sure to look at him. He hadn't shaved that morning, and his grizzled jaw was speckled with whiskers. His muscular chest rose with each of his deep breaths, and his powerful hands grabbed the top of her thighs in support as she moved against him. She noticed for the first time that he had a mole just above his belly button, but it was hidden by the slight shadows cast by his abs flexing beneath her.

Unable to escape the image of the woman riding on top of him, Desmond closed his eyes. Tired of his ignorance, Hannah closed her own eyes. She tried to focus on her own feelings and to ignore the space beneath her. That's what he became in these moments, just space. He wasn't truly present, just a kind of man-shaped hole in the world. She continued rocking her hips and gyrating against him. She shook her head as she tried to rid herself of the thoughts and the insecurities that came into her bedroom with him. It didn't work. She tried moving her body faster, but the thoughts kept pace. *What is he thinking about? Why doesn't he look at me? Does he realize how this makes me feel? Why do I care so much?*

Despite taking the dominant role in this tryst, she found herself unable to enjoy it. In fact, she could barely feel that there was anyone in the room at all, let alone inside of her. She shook her head violently once more, and placed both her hands against Desmond's chest, so she could feel him beneath her, some reassurance that he was actually there.

She could feel him penetrating deep inside of her. The feel of his muscular frame beneath her hands, the feel of his hands on her thighs, and the image she imagined they created suddenly gave her butterflies. She increased the pace of her gyrations once more. Her hips moved at a near-furious pace as she dragged herself back and forth against him, her powerful legs pulsing on both sides of him. Her body had stretched and shaped to the contour of his penis, and she could feel him dragging tightly in and out of her. Her breathing became heavier, and though she wasn't aware of it, she'd begun to make noises. She was finally beginning to enjoy herself, beginning to feel Desmond beneath her, inside of her, beginning to feel his presence, and perhaps even beginning to feel his eyes upon her. One of her hands clawed at his chest, and the other clutched unconsciously at her own.

She began to feel weeks of pent-up frustration building between her legs when Desmond made a noise. His grunt interrupted the rhythm and intensifying tingle she felt, and she opened her eyes to find Desmond lying rigidly beneath her. His eyes were open, but his face was still stone-like and impassive. His unfocused eyes stared, looking at nothing, and Hannah suddenly realized that he was coming inside of her. Her eyes widened in surprise, and her stomach fluttered, but the moment was taken from her as she noticed Desmond's reaction. He was ejaculating, but it was without pleasure. In fact, the look on his face, if one was there at all, was one of disgust. The butterflies in her stomach stopped flapping their delicate wings, and she ceased the movement with her hips as she felt his pulsations cease inside of her.

She leaned forward and pressed her body against his. Her head rested at the top of his chest, and she quickly realized that she was craving his closeness. Hannah had never before had a man finish inside of her without him wearing some kind of protection, and she was not sure if it was this, or something else that momentarily bonded her to Desmond. She wanted to be next to him, to touch him, even if it was just for a moment. She could not see it, but Desmond lay on his back and stared blankly at the ceiling, barely conscious of her body against his. Without thinking, Hannah raised her head up and tried to kiss him. He turned his face away from hers, and she was forced to climb off of him quickly as he moved to climb out of the bed.

"No kissing," he reminded her coldly, and without looking at her. He reached to grab his discarded clothes from the floor. His rule on kissing seemed ridiculous to him now.

Hannah covered herself with the white sheet, and her eyes were wide with emotion. "I'm sorry," she said softly, in a voice barely more than a breath, "I wasn't thinking." Desmond said nothing as he continued to dress. She looked away under the pretense of giving him some privacy, but did so to hide her hurt. The lack of intimacy between them—the lack of *any* show of feeling between them—stung, especially in this moment.

Desmond left Hannah's apartment without another word and without noticing, or perhaps without caring, that she was upset. As she heard the steel elevator door close behind him, Hannah laid on her bed, wrapping her arms around herself, once again feeling sore, used, and alone. A single tear bled onto her pillow.

Desmond rushed back to his hotel and watched impatiently as the elevator took him to his floor. The fly of his trousers was still unzipped, and he felt weak and shaky. As he entered his room, he ran to the bathroom. Unable to make it to the sink or toilet in time, he vomited on the bathroom floor. Struck by the weight of his suspended emotions now permitted to descend, he spent the next hour crying to himself as he cleaned his integrity off the cold tile floor.

• • •

A few weeks later, Desmond finished his run through Baltimore, and he collapsed onto a bench at Mount Vernon Place. He'd spent most of his time alone over the past few weeks as he threw himself into his work. The Poe case was progressing steadily, and he worked late into the night, even when he didn't have to. When he wasn't working, he spent much of his time working out, using his anger and aggression to fuel intense and exhausting workouts. The results were immediate. His chest blew out into muscular pectorals, his arms bulged even when resting, and his chiseled abs created a 'v' as they descended deep into his groin.

After Desmond's first night in New York with Hannah, Ashleigh had consistently remained in a state of ignorant euphoria. She talked incessantly about "when" Hannah would get pregnant and had resumed her habit of devouring motherhood literature with an insatiable appetite. Desmond secretly enjoyed the abysmal working hours, and exhausting exercise. Work acted as a distraction from his scarred conscience and Ashleigh's ignorant bliss, and the workouts often left him in an exhausted stupor and too tired to think about how much he hated himself.

On this day, he'd combined the two, having gone for an exhausting run through the city on the lunch break he normally didn't take. He sat on the bench and breathed heavily as the hot sun beat down on him. Thoughts of his nights with Hannah pervaded his mind once again, just as it did every time his hands or mind were unoccupied. While his long hours and frequent exercise were exhausting, nothing seemed to leave him as fatigued as the lack of respite from his guilt-ridden conscience.

He looked around at the gardens next to the Washington Monument—not the one in the District of Columbia, but the original monument in Baltimore. It was late spring, and the well-manicured trees and grass were in full bloom, creating a new contrast of green against the dense stonework common among the heritage-listed city streets and buildings. The scent of freshly watered grass cut against the hot and heavy air that tended to hang in city streets. He normally enjoyed visiting these gardens, but found himself unable to do so on this visit despite the warm weather and the fact that he occupied the bench seat on his own, which was a rare indulgence. He shielded his eyes as he looked up at the figure of George Washington, arm outstretched, pointing into the distance as he watched over Baltimore. In some ways, Desmond could relate to George Washington. Washington had assumed the role of Commander of the Continental Army at the Second Continental Congress at a time when his success with managing large military units was limited. Sure, he'd had the most military experience among the delegates that appointed him Commander-in-Chief, but by European standards, his military expertise was almost non-existent. Desmond felt some affinity to this—the idea of a man who had assumed more responsibility than he was realistically qualified, but whose deft management had proven him capable in the end.

Since the beginning of his legal career, Desmond had always thought of himself as a bit of a fraud. The law seemed to come to him easily, too easily in fact, and he always thought it was only a matter of time before someone realized that he was bluffing his way through his career and was inescapably in over his head. However, exposure never came. He won or settled almost all of his cases, and he was well-regarded in the profession. He now sat on the verge of becoming a partner, and it was only recently that he felt like he was competent at his job. He wondered if Washington had ever had these feelings, and at what point in the Revolutionary War he might have realized that he was a genuinely capable commander.

Desmond thought it strange that men could relate to strangers centuries removed from them. The sun eventually became too bright for his eyes, and he was forced to look away from Washington's statue. He looked to his right, and saw a number of tourists walking backwards, almost onto the road and into the path of moving traffic, to take photos of the bronze-colored statue of Lafayette. Desmond shook his head at their obliviousness before turning his attention to the church standing at the corner of the street, adjacent to the Washington Monument. It was an old, grand sort of church, the kind common to an era when stonemasonry was a well-practiced art. It was well-designed: its colors complemented the surroundings, and its tall, grand spires grew high into the sky, like the branches of an old tree. They gave the impression that the architect had tried to reach the heavens with his spires, having faith that, if tall enough, they'd be able to touch God. Desmond had visited the church several times, but had never been inside of it.

Being a Christian man, he found solace in the idea that the church was able to occupy such a prominent piece of land in one of America's oldest cities without being disturbed. He imagined that in an age where "faith" and "religion" were considered unpleasant or mystical words, petitions probably flew to have the cross removed, or for the building to be torn down to make way for a cafe or business center. That the cross remained atop of the highest spire of a church, which itself stood on top of the hill and overlooked the city, gave him comfort and reminded him of the resiliency of his Maker.

He made a mental note to try and attend church more regularly, and once again, he felt the now-familiar pang of guilt as he was reminded of his nights with Hannah.

Thou shalt not commit adultery, he thought, as he stared at the cross on top of the church building. The idea was important enough that it was recognized in the Ten Commandments, and it was one he'd never thought he'd break. His conscience took note that the commandment did not add, *unless your wife tells you to do it*. There were no exceptions, no caveats, no ifs or buts. The commandment was absolute in its forbidding. He imagined himself trying to explain the arrangement to God on judgment day, and the look on His face as Desmond tried dumbly to justify his actions. Thinking of Adam and Eve, he expected that God would be thoroughly unconvinced by the sort of "but she *told* me to do it" argument he imagined himself making as he pleaded for the sake of his soul. He was forced to look away from the cross as a sick feeling struck him. He was distracted momentarily as the tourists he'd spotted earlier walked in front of him, and he pulled his legs beneath him to clear the path for them.

As the tourists passed him, his focus shifted, and he spotted another bronzed statue directly in front of him. The statue was not well-known outside of Baltimore, but locals knew it well because of the ire it attracted. There were never any tourists taking photos of this statute, and unlike the church, petitions abounded for its removal year after year. The statue depicted Roger Taney, a former chief justice of the United States Supreme Court, sitting in a large chair with his left hand placed on top of a bound copy of the U.S. Constitution. His shoulders were draped in the official robes of his office, and his right hand clutched a tightly wound parchment scroll.

The people of Baltimore hated the statue because they hated the man. Being an attorney, Desmond knew well that Chief Justice Taney had written the decision in the controversial case of *Dred Scott v. Sandford*. Dredd Scott was a man who had sued for freedom from slavery for himself and his family on the basis that he'd lived in a territory where slavery was illegal. Taney, writing for the Supreme Court, determined that African-Americans, having been considered inferior when the Constitution was first drafted, could not be considered citizens of the United States, and therefore could not bring a freedom suit to the U.S. Federal Court. Taney and the majority of the Court had dismissed the case on what many described as a jurisdictional technicality.

The case was widely considered to have set back race equality in the United States by decades—if not a century or more—and for this, Taney and his monument were despised. Desmond looked at the statue of the judge, and noticed for the first time the look of profound sadness on his face. The bronze man seated in front of him seemed to sit sunken in the chair, and his gaze was locked wearily toward the ground. This downcast gaze was distinct from the statues of Washington and Lafayette, whose gazes looked upward and outward, triumphantly looking over the bay as watchful sentinels guarding their citizens. If Washington and the horseback-riding Lafayette were the images of triumph and pride, Taney was the epitome of misery. Desmond wondered if the statue's depiction of Taney reflected his likeness after he had published his decision on the Dred Scott case, and the ire of an entire nation had descended upon him.

Desmond knew that save for the Dred Scott case, a decision which he found abhorrent, Chief Justice Taney had been a wise and capable magistrate. His judicial career was a long and exalted one, and yet his reputation was destroyed by one decision. *One decision destroyed the man*, Desmond thought. *Twenty-eight years on the bench of the Supreme Court, and he's remembered for one decision. His reputation, his memory, and his character, all destroyed by ONE decision.*

He suddenly panicked. Is that how he would be remembered? Would his decision to sleep with Hannah come to define his character and become his dark legacy? Had it done so already? Desmond was on his feet, and he stood with a locked jaw as he looked up at the lifeless and miserable face of Taney in front of him. His heart raced in his chest as he looked at the representation of a man rendered undignified by a single decision made in the folly of man's imperfect nature.

Was Taney's decision wrong? Of course, it was. But should *one* wrong decision destroy the man and his memory? Desmond tore his eyes away from the statue and began to run back to his office at a faster than normal pace. He ignored the heat that pressed against him, he ignored the pain that burned in his tired legs and lungs, and at times he even ignored the streetlights as he sprinted across the road and around traffic. What he couldn't ignore, however, was the realization that he no longer identified with the pure white statue of George Washington that stood proudly on top of the world, but with the dark, defeated, and sulking figure of Chief Justice Taney, collapsed in his chair. Desmond ran harder than he could remember ever having run. He wasn't running for exercise anymore—he was running away from his imagined future.

• • •

Late one afternoon, Ashleigh stood in the kitchen of her home on the phone with Hannah. She heard the front door open, and stepped out to see Desmond coming into the house as he returned home from work. She mouthed the word "Hannah" to him, and pointed at the phone with her free hand. His face didn't seem to give any indication that he understood, his features remaining placidly unmoved. He didn't nod or smile. He didn't even say hello. She watched as he headed for the

A Part of You

stairs, and she returned to the kitchen to resume making their evening meal.

She heard the sound of running water as Desmond stepped into the shower, and she turned her attention back to the phone. "He hasn't been the same," she said softly. "Ever since this started, he just hasn't been himself. I've tried keeping high spirits, trying to appear happy about all of this in the hope that it can help him focus on the positives, but it's not working. He doesn't talk. He barely eats. He just works and exercises, and he showers *all* the time." Ashleigh's voice began to catch in her throat. "He won't even look at me, Hannah. We've barely spoken in weeks." Her voice went low. "He hasn't touched me since this started. I've even tried initiating things, but he won't have any of it. It hurts to be ignored so intently, and it's exhausting trying to act happy all the time while it's happening."

Hannah didn't know what to say, and so she remained silent on the other end of the line. She had felt uncomfortable around Ashleigh ever since their conversation in the sauna, and she found it strange that the young woman was confiding in her at all about such intimate matters. It felt especially uncomfortable to be having this conversation now that she was playing an integral part in Desmond's and Ashleigh's difficulties. The long pause between them indicated that Ashleigh expected some response from her. Hannah suppressed an irritated sigh. It wasn't her responsibility to resolve Ashleigh's issues, and she hated that her call had interrupted her fervent writing. She didn't have any answers, so she answered with a question. "Are you okay, Ash?" Hannah's voice convincingly concealed her irritation.

Ashleigh gave an involuntary sigh, and she held back unbidden tears. "No, I'm not." She grabbed the nearby onions she needed for their meal and began cutting them. If Desmond unexpectedly came downstairs, she could blame any tears on

161

them. "I'm having a hard time. I struggle every time I think of where Desmond is going on the weekend and what he's doing. I question my insistence that the surrogacy be non-surgical. I'm frustrated every time we find out there's been no conception and that this has to continue. I'm exhausted at trying to appear positive and keep it together all the time. And I hate that the only person I can talk to about this is the woman sleeping with my husband!"

More silence.

Ashleigh continued venting. "Desmond is just ... absent, even when he's here. He seems incapable of talking to me about these things; none of my friends would understand, or be able to listen without judging. I just need *someone* to talk to, and quite honestly, I hate that it's you!" Ashleigh bit her lip hard, wishing that she could stuff the words back into her mouth. She was afraid that if she pressed Hannah too hard, then she might pull away from these conversations, or worse, that she'd pull out of the arrangement entirely. "I just really need a friend right now," she said softly to Hannah.

Hannah suppressed another sigh. She was having a difficult time trying to deal with her own hurt feelings, and the idea that she might have to help manage Ashleigh's mixed feelings as well had her teetering on the edge of an emotional breaking point. She tried to reconcile that Ashleigh was having as hard a time in the arrangement as she was. It was clear that each of the women participated in the phone conversations as eagerly as they participated in the arrangement, each begrudgingly accepting that neither of them could have a connection to what they loved without the other.

Hannah took a deep breath and reminded herself that all of this was a part of her professional pursuit for inspiration. "I know what you mean," she said. "I know it's not easy for you to talk to me about these things with me being involved and all. It's not easy for me either."

Ashleigh smiled with watery tears in her eyes. She might be speaking to the woman with whom her husband was sleeping, but at least Hannah understood. She wiped at the tears with her sleeve to clear her vision. There was another long silence between them, and it seemed suddenly strange that two women who could share a man could have nothing to say to each other.

"Hannah, are you okay?" Ashleigh asked cautiously, afraid that her outburst was making Hannah reconsider her role in the arrangement.

Hannah was caught a little off guard. She had spent so much of her time alone and was used to dealing with her own emotions and insecurities within the silent confines of her apartment. It was strange to have someone, especially Desmond's wife, ask her how *she* was doing, but she welcomed it despite the pit that dropped in her stomach at the question. "I'm okay," she managed to say.

Ashleigh could tell by Hannah's voice that this was a half-truth, at best. She remained quiet in the hope that Hannah might fill the silence between them. The voice that came back to Ashleigh sounded strained, as though Hannah was trying to force her spoken words to be delivered evenly.

"I'm just lonely." Hannah felt uncomfortably vulnerable at the confession.

Ashleigh heard something in Hannah's voice that made her sound distant and sad, the kind of distant sadness attached to a woman who'd spent too long in an unloving relationship, but who couldn't bring herself to end it. "Hannah, would you like to come down to Baltimore for the weekend?" Ashleigh asked, starting to feel sorry for Hannah. She heard the water shut off upstairs, followed by footsteps as Desmond got out of the shower. She moved the onions to one side. "My class breaks for the summer on Thursday. If you come down on Friday, we can spend the day together and have a girls' day. We can go for a boozy brunch with mimosas, have fun, and if you feel like it, we can talk about things. But only if you feel like it."

Hannah looked down at the writing pad in front of her. She had been writing notes about the male lead in her next show. She had little interest in having a girls' day with the wife of the man with whom she was having regular sex, and had absolutely no interest in talking to her about it. "I don't know," she answered a little reluctantly. "I'm a little busy working on my next show right now."

"Oh, that's completely understandable." Ashleigh answered quickly, a little embarrassed. "How is it coming along?"

"It's going really well," Hannah answered with an unbidden smile, her tone immediately becoming brighter. "I always do my best writing at times when I'm down or emotional, and I've written *volumes* of work for a new show in the past few weeks." There was another awkward pause between the women, and Hannah felt guilty that Ashleigh had inquired about her work immediately after she'd declined her invitation.

"You know what?" Hannah began, breaking the silence, "I think I will come and join you on Friday. It's been a while since I had someone to talk to."

Ashleigh turned as Desmond entered the kitchen behind her. He was wearing headphones, and his eyes avoided hers. "Me too, Hannah. Me too."

• • •

Desmond stood outside of Hannah's Baltimore hotel room and hung his head. She and Ashleigh had spent the previous day together in the city while he worked. He didn't understand how they still managed to maintain any kind of relationship given their circumstances, let alone a functional one. Ashleigh had come home from her day with Hannah with a renewed sense of happiness. He wasn't sure if she was genuinely happy or putting on a facade, but either way, it was annoying him to have her acting so chipper while he wallowed.

She returned from her date with Hannah and told him that they had agreed that he should visit her and try to conceive while she was conveniently in the city. He had told her that he didn't want to, the thought of Chief Justice Taney's statue still haunting him. However, she'd insisted that he attend Hannah this evening, telling him that, unlike his nights in New York, he could come straight home to her afterward, and that she missed waking up next to him in the morning without either of them having to rush off to work.

"And then," she'd told him, "maybe tonight or in the morning you and I could ... you know." She had smiled at him suggestively.

Desmond had let out a half-hearted chuckle. At his age, he doubted he had the stamina for repeat performances, and even if he did, he didn't think he'd have the heart to sleep with his wife on the same night he bedded another woman. "Maybe in the morning," he'd told her. "I'm looking forward to waking up next to you too." He meant this. He genuinely missed the connection he used to share with Ashleigh, and perhaps sleeping next to her and having a lazy Saturday morning with her was just what they needed. He'd kissed her on the forehead before leaving their house and tried to give her a reassuring smile as he left.

After he'd left, Ashleigh immediately began preparing for his return. She cleaned the house, prepared a bottle of wine and a quick meal, exercised, showered, shaved her legs, put on a tight dress, and placed a sexy outfit in their bathroom ready to change into when he came home. She went to great lengths to get everything ready for his return. Partly because she was excited at the prospect of sharing some intimacy with Desmond for the first time in several weeks, and partly as a means of distracting herself from what he was doing. She hadn't confessed it to anyone, but a part of her wondered if Desmond's distance was because he was no longer attracted to her. She reassured herself that the arrangement was just difficult for a good man like her husband, but Hannah was a beautiful woman, and Desmond, while a good man, was still a man.

Desmond raised a reluctant hand and knocked on Hannah's hotel door. It was the same door he'd angrily banged on several weeks earlier on the night Hannah had offered to be their surrogate.

"It's open," came Hannah's voice from beyond the door. Desmond opened the door and stepped into her hotel room. He noticed features of the room he hadn't noticed on his first dimly lit visit. The carpet had a strange brown and red pattern across it, the ugly type of pattern only ever found in hotels, and the walls were an uneven burgundy color. He wondered why a woman of Hannah's means would choose to stay in such accommodations when he knew she could easily afford to stay at one of the nicer waterfront hotels just a few hundred feet away. The writing desk in the corner of the room, the same one that possessed a single, blank sheet of paper on his last visit, now had tens of papers scattered across it, with several more strewn across the floor around it, some of them crumpled into paper balls. "You've been busy," he said flatly.

Hannah came into view from the bathroom. Her blonde hair was made dark by its dampness, and she wore a white bathrobe tied tightly around the waist. Despite appearing to be fresh out of the shower, Hannah nonetheless wore her trademark sockettes to hide her disfigured feet. She gave a half smile, surprised that he'd noticed her work on the writing desk, and more surprised at the fact that he'd spoken to her. She squinted at him appraisingly. Had he finally realized that his behavior was making her feel used?

Desmond stripped next to the unmade bed and climbed under the sheets. "Ready when you are," he said coldly.

I guess not, she thought, answering her question. She untied the damp bathrobe and threw it back over her shoulders and onto the floor on the spot. She stood proudly in the center of the room. She had nothing to be ashamed of. She was a beautiful, successful woman, dedicated to her work, and helping an old friend and his wife have the baby that circumstances and a defective reproductive system had denied them.

She strode over to the bed and climbed under the sheets to join Desmond. He lay there, looking up at the ceiling as usual, and didn't move. She rolled her eyes. Did he expect her to take charge and climb on top of him every time now just because it worked last time? She lay next to him, waiting. After a long minute of silence and stillness, she realized that something was off. Desmond's eyes, locked on the ceiling, no longer showed quiet deadness, and his breathing was shaky and heavy. This version of Desmond was different, even off-putting. He didn't seem distant or cold. He seemed almost scared. She thought that he might once again need her to take charge, and she rolled over toward him and prepared to throw one leg over his side.

"Wait." His voice was commanding.

She retreated from him and resumed her place lying next to him. To Hannah, his eyes appeared to be staring at the ceiling, but Desmond was looking past the ceiling, across the city, and into the bronze eyes of the sad and defeated figure of Chief Justice Taney. *I don't want this. I don't want to lose Ashleigh. I don't want to lose myself. I don't want to do this at all*, he thought. "I can't do this," he said aloud in the same commanding tone.

"I know Desmond, but—"

Desmond cut her off. "No, Hannah," he turned his head to look at her. "I *can't* do this."

Hannah looked down at the sheet resting over Desmond's groin, and saw he was completely flaccid. "Oh!" she said as she understood. "I see."

Desmond breathed in heavily. "I'm sorry. There's just too much going on right now... Ashleigh, you, me, work." *Justice Taney.*

Hannah smiled back at him, a genuine, sweet smile. The fabric of the pillow showed a spreading patch of wetness as her still-damp hair rested against it. "I have an idea," she said excitedly as she threw off the covers and got out of the bed. She looked back at him, ignoring both of their exposed nudity. "Get dressed."

• • •

Hannah took Desmond a few hundred feet down the boardwalk beside Baltimore Harbor to the bar on the ground floor of one of the nicer hotels. She'd discovered this bar on her previous visit and found that she felt comfortable here. It was expensive enough that the younger crowd, college kids and the like, avoided it in favor of the cheaper pubs and bars downtown, and it wasn't as crowded as some of the harbor side restaurants and dedicated bars tended to be. The bar was dim, but not dark. Ravens-purple and Orioles-orange lights lit the walls and glowed fluorescently against the night outside. A pleasant, cool breeze blew in from the harbor, and a soft tattoo of music echoed throughout the bar. The music was another reason Hannah liked this hotel bar. Not only was the selection good—the artists played real musical instruments unlike the beatbox and mechanical noise common to contemporary music—but it was also soft enough that she could have a conversation without needing to yell over unnecessarily loud and invasive music so common to weekend nights at other venues.

She sat on a stool at the bar and Desmond took the stool beside her. Despite being out on the town with another woman, it didn't feel like a date. He wore a plain gray T-shirt and casual pants, and Hannah was wearing an old T-shirt, blue denim jeans, and very little makeup. She'd thrown some on very quickly, and tied her hair into a simple ponytail just before she and Desmond left the hotel room. To the casual observer, this was simply two friends hanging out, not a date. The bartender was busy with another customer at the other end of the bar.

"I'm sorry," Desmond said to Hannah. He leaned closer to her, so she could hear him more clearly. "I'm sorry I've been treating you poorly throughout this whole thing."

She turned her head over her right shoulder to look at him, the first time they'd made eye contact in a long time. "I didn't think you'd noticed," she answered pointedly. Her diamond eyes were emotionless.

Desmond furrowed his lips; her answer showed she'd noticed his poor treatment of her since their first night together. "I'm sorry," he repeated. "I don't know how to be a guy that's capable of doing this while also being a nice guy. I don't know how to be myself in all of this."

"You could try just not being an ass, Des. Say hi when you come over, ask me how I'm doing beforehand, and ask me if I'm okay afterward. Just … be sweet about it. I'm not expecting you to romanticize this because there's nothing romantic about it, but don't make me feel so … used. I'm a person, Des. I have feelings. Just respect that."

Desmond began speaking, but Hannah held a finger in front of his lips. He stopped trying to talk. "You don't need to say anything else Des," she said. "You've said you're sorry, and I've told you how it could be different. And so, it's done. It's fine. I'm fine. We're fine." She smiled at him and placed her hand on top of his for a moment before releasing it to flag down the now-free bartender.

Desmond was a little flustered, but otherwise relieved. She had called out his poor behavior and dealt with it calmly and swiftly. Her straightforwardness and casual candor dismissed the tension between them, and with just a few words, his guilt and discomfort around her vanished. He was smiling to himself when she looked back at him.

"I figured we could use a night out," she began. "We've been doing this incredibly intimate thing together and we haven't really talked in weeks. We're making this a lot harder than it needs to be. So, let's have tonight off, have a few drinks, forget about the arrangement, and just be two friends catching up." She looked genuinely excited by the idea.

Desmond saw the bartender approaching and leaned toward Hannah. "I'm not supposed to drink," he reminded her. "Ashleigh doesn't want alcohol to affect my boys, remember?" He leaned back and found Hannah looking at him with a humored *are you serious?* face.

She let out a single, delighted laugh. "Des, we don't need to worry about that. At least not tonight."

"Orders?" asked the bartender without taking his eyes off of Hannah. She looked at Desmond with a smile and waited expectantly for him to order first.

Desmond looked at the bartender. "Do you know how to make a Vesper martini?"

Hannah let out a hilarious giggle. "Still! You still order Vespers? Because of the Bond thing?" Desmond had started ordering Vespers at bars during his final year of college when *Casino Royale* was released. Back then, he thought that the strong cocktail was sophisticated and manly. Hannah was still laughing. "You couldn't even drink them before. You'd take a few sips and have to leave the rest because it was too strong!"

Desmond smiled and laughed back with her. "Well, I like them now." The bartender took the order without joining in their frivolity.

"And you?" he asked curtly to Hannah, his interest in her dissipating now that he assumed she was spoken for and on a date. Hannah looked wryly into Desmond's eyes—a challenge. "I'll have the same."

Desmond put up a hand to the bartender, gesturing for him to wait before taking the order. "Hannah, it's not exactly a light drink! It's harsh and very strong."

"So?" she asked.

"It's really strong, Hannah, and you must weigh one hundred and twenty pounds soaking wet. You'll get drunk just from the fumes."

Hannah threw her shoulders back in an exaggerated movement, and waved her finger in front of him in mock indignation. "And how, exactly, would you know how much I weigh!?"

Desmond raised an eyebrow at her knowingly and turned back to the bartender, "Two Vesper martinis please!" Ordering the drinks changed the subject: he had laid on top of her and her on top of him more than once, and neither of them needed reminding of that right now.

The night wore on, and patrons came and went while Hannah and Desmond sat at the bar swapping old stories and drinking. The bartender placed another Vesper in front of each of them.

Hannah twirled the glass on its bottom rim, and its contents began to swirl. "There's something I always wanted to ask you," she said, without looking up from the glass. "Why didn't you ever ask me to stay whenever I came to visit you? I left on another adventure after every time I came to you, and I'm sure you knew it." Desmond nodded, looking into his own swirling drink. "So, why didn't you ever ask me to stay?

Desmond took a deep breath and sipped his fresh drink. He felt the cool liquor burn its way down his throat, and he winced. "Did you want me to?"

Hannah, knowing that he'd answered her question with another question to buy himself some time, turned and smiled. "I wouldn't say that I *wanted* you to ask me to stay...Well, maybe on that last occasion." She paused to see if he remembered what she was talking about—if he remembered the time she'd arrived in his office just a few short miles away from where they sat now, and told him that she was ready to be his. If he remembered, he gave no indication.

"I guess a part of me always hoped you'd ask me to stay. What woman doesn't want a man to tell her, 'Don't go. Stay with me.' That his feelings for her are so strong that he can't stand the thought of being without her? I never needed you to tell me to stay, but considering you had all those feelings for me at the time, I always wondered why you didn't."

Again, Desmond breathed in and followed with a large gulp from his quickly disappearing drink. He opened his mouth to speak, closed it again, and turned his head with a smile as he searched for the right words. "Hannah, you were always 'hold,' but never 'have.' And I was always 'had' but never 'held'."

Hannah burst out laughing mid-sip, and sprayed a mouthful of her drink into the air. Wiping the remnants of liquid from her smiling lips, she turned to him and tried to speak through her laughter. "What does that even mean?"

Desmond laughed with her and sighed wearily, "I guess it means that my feelings just weren't strong enough to ask you to stay. I just wasn't that guy."

After a few hours and several more martinis, they were tipsy and laughing hysterically together. Desmond suddenly turned to Hannah and spoke in as serious a tone as his slight slur would permit. "Han, why're you doin' this for us? Why put yourself through all this?"

Hannah took a deep breath as she tried to think clearly. "Why not? I get to help you and Ashleigh, I get some help with my work, and everyone wins. Plus, I'm getting to that age where having a baby carries greater risk. It's like I told you before." She took another sip of her martini.

"I get that," said Desmond, "or at least I get that you'd agree to this if you were a *normal* surrogate, but why agree to it with the sex involved?"

Hannah shrugged. "Still, why not? All those other reasons are the same. So what if we have a bit of sex to get the whole thing started?" She smiled at him cheekily. "At least that's what I thought before I realized the sex would be so bad!" Her smile widened as she teased him.

Desmond leaned back, feigning shock and hurt, and her cheeky smile broadened to flash brilliant white teeth. She gave him a cute look through blonde strands that had fallen to cover half her face. "Y'know, Hannah," he slurred. "I'm not normally like that. It's just the circumstances. I'm normally much better in bed. Normally very good. The best, in fact."

Hannah looked at him suggestively. "Everybody thinks they're good in bed, Des."

He matched her increasingly intense gaze. "I don't think I'm good," he offered playfully. "I said I'm the best. And I have references!"

Hannah threw her head back as she downed the rest of her martini. She slammed it down on the bar with a bang and looked Desmond in the eyes with a hungry, fiery gaze. "Oh yeah?" She smiled. "Prove it."

• • •

Desmond burst into Hannah's hotel room carrying her in his arms, her legs wrapped tightly around his waist. Her thighs, made powerful from years of dance, tensed and flexed as she pressed herself into him. She squealed as she raked fingers down his large, powerful arms swollen larger by carrying her. Her nails left red marks on his skin from under his short sleeves and down his forearms, and he let out a deep growl as the stinging red lines gripped his arms tightly.

Hannah breathed heavily, and the scent of liquor mixed with her sweet breath enveloped his mind in an intoxicating, lustful cloud. With Hannah's weight supported by her legs, Desmond freed his hands from beneath her and reached behind her back. He tore her shirt in two in a single, fluid motion and threw the ripped remnants into some distant, non-existent corner of the room. He felt her black bra press into his chest as she reached behind him with fumbling hands. He had thought she was reaching for the base of his shirt, but her hands ventured lower and grabbed his buttocks through his jeans. She let out a delighted, near-maniacal laugh as she squeezed.

He carried her further into the dark hotel room, and into her bedroom, turning on the lights with one blind hand as they entered. Despite the powerful grip her legs had around his waist, he lifted her easily and flung her onto the bed. She giggled as she bounced once upon the white duvet. Desmond stood at the base of the bed. The marks she'd clawed into his arms only moments earlier were an angry, fiery red.

Her eyes darted up and down his body as she took in his powerful figure, and she could see the difference that his furious workouts had made on his body. She remembered watching him change through the reflection of the mirror in the next room. He was toned then, but now his muscles were firm, bulging, and it gave him a primal, manly, and violent appearance. As she appreciated the way his T-shirt hung from broad shoulders and clung closely to his sculpted torso, she found it hard to imagine that this was the same Desmond she had known in college. She flicked the button of her jeans open and locked her eyes with his hungry gaze as she grabbed the waistband with two hands. She let the fly open by itself as she slid the jeans down her long, smooth legs.

Desmond grabbed the blue fabric as it reached her ankles. As he pulled them over her feet, the denim collected around her socks, and they came sliding off with the jeans, exposing her mangled feet. Her eyes went wide in a moment of instantly sobering alarm. "Lights!" she yelled in near panic. "Turn them off!"

Desmond allowed her jeans to drop to the floor at the base of the bed. He followed her terrified eyes with his own and saw her feet. "Lights?" he asked softly. "What for?" He grabbed one of her delicate, broken feet, held it softly in his rough hands, and began to knead the sole gently with his knuckles and thumbs. "You have nothing to be embarrassed about," he assured her. "You're beautiful."

Hannah slowly pulled her foot free of his gentle grip without taking her eyes off of his face. She tucked her feet gently beneath herself as she rose up on her knees and held herself in front of him. She reached down and grabbed the base of his T-shirt with both hands. Desmond raised his arms in the air as she slowly raised the shirt along his abdomen, over his chest, and he disappeared from her as the fabric hid his face. The shirt caught itself as she attempted to lift it above his head so that only his chin and mouth were exposed.

He laughed at himself, but hidden from his view, Hannah stared intently at his lips. She drew herself closer to him, closing the gap between their bodies. The heat coming from his body was intense, and she felt sweat forming on her skin. Desmond's laughter subsided, and for a brief, hidden moment, he thought he could feel her warm breath lightly dance on the exposed portion of his face. Time paused for Hannah as her lips hovered barely apart from his. She wanted to kiss him. Deeply, passionately. But she remembered his rule and the embarrassment that had followed the last time she had unconsciously tried to break it. She breathed him in a little as she leaned in to place her wet lips against his, but she fought against the urge at the last second and pulled herself away as time unfroze.

Desmond reached higher to lift the shirt fully over his head, and she came into his view as the shirt disappeared. Still standing beside the bed, he looked down at her beautiful face and their eyes locked.

For the first time in months, Desmond's eyes were his own once more—that deep, ocean blue. Still partially clothed, Hannah felt more vulnerable under his present, piercing gaze than she had felt any other time she'd been with him.

His large hand moved the lone strand of hair that covered her face behind her ear so that he could see her fully, so that he could count the lines upon her face, so that he could drink in the image of the woman before him without the slightest obstruction. His hand lingered by her ear as the rogue strand fell into place. His hand began to fall, to trace its way down her delicate neck, and found its home behind the nape of her neck. Their bodies leaned slowly toward the one another, like magnets held barely within range, until yearning lips hovered barely apart. The inch between them was electric, charged with everything that had accumulated between them over the past few months, over the years of absence, and over the decades of friendship and unrequited feelings.

She raised one of her hands into that electric space and placed it lightly on his chest. She had expected to feel his heart pounding inside of his chest, to feel it racing, like hers. Instead, she could feel it beating a calm, steady tattoo beneath the skin, as though his heart thought nothing of the encounter, of the electricity building within and between their bodies, as if it thought that everything was right with the world. "Desmond?" Hannah whispered.

Desmond's other hand found her exposed waist, and he pulled her effortlessly toward him, and wet lips found their counterpoint. His mind recoiled reflexively as if it had just brushed against a livewire, and yet his lips remained fully grasped to it, allowing the electricity to pass through his entire body. His kisses were slow and intentional.

She pressed harder into his rough lips and felt his arms wrap around her, making her feel small and safe. There was something incredibly arousing and simultaneously comforting in the way his strong hands treated her so delicately and sweetly. She leaned back, breaking away from his passionate kisses so that she could look at him. He had a slight stubble growing through, and it caused the blue of his eyes to burst in contrast. She watched as those eyes examined her. Watched as they pierced through her physical beauty and drank in her every nuanced detail. She placed her hands on both sides of his face and invited his eyes to meet hers, afraid that after breaking his rule his eyes would no longer belong to him. She had learned over the preceding weeks that he was losing himself a little more each time they touched, and she was afraid that his kiss might have him feeling as though he had lost himself completely. She poured herself into his eyes, and watched as they curved into the half-crescents of an adoring smile. She returned the smile with a truly nervous, vulnerable one.

She released his face, and he leaned in to continue kissing her. His kisses traced the edges of her lips, along her cheeks, and down her neck. She pulled the elastic from her hair, and undisciplined blonde locks fell behind her and over his face. She felt his hand on the small of her back. It stroked its way slowly along the dimples of her spine until it found the clasp of her bra. The clasp came undone with a flick of his fingers, and the straps went limp on her shoulders. His hand traced its way back down her bare back, navigating its way along the smooth skin to the small of her back.

His gentle palm supported her as she leaned back onto the bed. His lips followed hers, and his body followed his lips as he joined her on the bed. Moments later, Hannah lay on the bed with Desmond, feeling more naked than she had ever felt before. The remainder of their clothes had joined the other discarded items, lost in the oblivion that existed beyond the edge of their mattress. Her breath was shaky as Desmond hovered above her. Excitement and nerves stirred together like the familiar and unfamiliar mixing in each of them. She had known Desmond, the boy.

Desmond, the friend.

Desmond, the man.

Desmond, the reluctant participant of their obscene "arrangement."

But never Desmond, the lover. And from the way he looked at her as he entered her, she wondered whether she had ever really known any lover. Her shaking breaths turned into a startled cry as she felt him move within her, and his groan matched her cry. This time, there was no pain. There was no shame, no guilt, no guile. They discovered the island within one another and found an easy rhythm as their souls collided. She held onto him tightly as he moved above her, about her, and within her.

She loved him with her body in the same way that he, at some time, she thought, had loved her. He had given to her his years, his prayers of affection, his thoughts, his energy, and his silent devotion, and she repaid him with her smile, the arch of her back, the curling of her toes, the dimples above her hips, and the crescendo of her womanly body. She lost track of how long they spent together in blissful unity, and of how many times her body had tightened and released against his. As her body was automatically capable of singing along to the music their bodies made together, she instead tried to focus on the song itself, trying to make sure that she would not forget how it sounded when it was over. Desmond's muscles tightened all over as his primal body did what it had learned to do without being taught. His powerful arms—those powerful arms that could move her any way he wished as easily as tear her apart—straddled her protectively as his body breathed its life into hers.

And when it was over, when their bodies continued to quiver against the other, they held each other in their arms and the embrace of their eyes. His arms continued to protect her from the bulk of his weight as he laid suspended above her. As he hung motionless above her and the lines between their bodies unblurred, her hands materialized once more, and she reached up and caressed his rough cheek. With her other hand placed lightly against his chest, she leaned up, closed the few inches between their faces, and kissed him once more on the lips. The kiss lacked the frenzy or passion of those that had preceded it when their bodies were one. It was tender, soft, and alone. He lowered himself so that he lay beside her, and she coiled into him, grabbing his arm and placing it around her. Twenty minutes later, once the room had stopped spinning, Hannah and Desmond were asleep, his arm remaining around her through the night.

• • •

Desmond woke the next morning with a start. His head pounded with a dull ache, and the light coming through the bedroom window hurt his eyes. Hannah remained asleep, still cuddled into him under his arm. He glanced around the room, desperately looking for a clock or timepiece. It was daylight. He knew that much. His stomach sank as he remembered what Ashleigh had said to him about wanting to wake up next to him.

He gently removed his arm from around Hannah, and peeled himself out of the bed so that he did not disturb her. He quickly dressed, rushed to the bathroom to smooth his appearance, and made ready to leave Hannah's hotel room. He caught a glimpse of Hannah's face as she dreamed wearily on the bed in front of him, her still features caught somewhere between a placid smile and peaceful serenity.

He felt guilt toward both women, he realized. He didn't want to be the jerk both he and Hannah knew he had been on their previous times together, and have her wake up to an unexpectedly empty hotel room, once again feeling used. He ran over the writing desk in the corner of the next room and went to scrawl a quick note, but what should he say? He knew last night was a mistake, that it was different from their other nights together. If he wrote *Thank you for last night*, would she take that as an affirmation of what transpired? If he just wrote *Sorry*, would that make her feel used once again? What if she didn't think that last night was a mistake, or any different to their other nights together? He found himself familiarly conflicted, trying to reconcile the jerk with the nice guy.

Whatever he wrote, he had to get back to Ashleigh. Her opinion of him was the only one that mattered. He scribbled the only thing he could think of, tore the sheet of paper from its ledger and placed it gently on the pillow beside Hannah before leaving the hotel room.

A few minutes later, Hannah stretched and reached out for Desmond. Her outstretched hand fell into the warm indentation he'd left in her bed, and found the note. The smile she woke with vanished as she read Desmond's handwritten message: *Thank you. I'm sorry.*

• • •

Desmond rushed back home. His heart was racing, and he felt nauseated. He knew that last night was different from the others, that much was obvious. Last night lacked the regret and deadened dispassion that he'd brought to Hannah's bed on other nights. This time was different.

This time, he'd cheated.

On the short drive home, he decided he was going to confess everything to Ashleigh. He'd tell her everything that had happened between him and Hannah, and beg for her forgiveness. He'd tell her that he's done with the arrangement. Tell her that he wants nothing more to do with it, that his soul and conscience—and their marriage—can't bear this any longer.

He pulled up in his driveway and felt the sting of Hannah's claw marks on his arms and shoulders as his shirt and the seatbelt bristled against them. He ran into the house, panting and in a cold sweat. He came to a stop in the doorway as Ashleigh stood waiting for him. She still wore the tight dress she'd put on the night before, and dinner was set in the fine dining area behind her.

Mascara-streaked tears cast black lines down her face, and she pointed at Desmond with her cell phone in her hand. "You!" she screamed, as fresh tears scrolled unrelentingly down her face.

His pulse quickened, and he braced himself against her next words.

"What did you do!?" She screamed again, her voice tense, loud, full of anguish. He opened his mouth to speak, but Ashleigh cut him off. "Hannah just called me. What did you *do*?" She let out a low moan as she stood and continued to cry.

Desmond put his palms out in front of him in an attempt to usher in calm. "I'll tell you everything. I was going to tell you everything" he began.

Ashleigh threw the phone onto the ground angrily, and its broken pieces bounced in different directions on the floor. "What's there to explain? It's done! Our family, it's over!"

Desmond's tight features broke as Ashleigh turned away from him and collapsed in a chair at the dining table. She pushed the cold food out of the way and cried into the arms she placed in front of her. "It's over," she cried loudly into her arms.

"No," Desmond said softly as tears came to his own eyes. "Don't say that." He moved to crouch beside her and placed a hand on her leg. Ashleigh lifted her head to face him, and her face showed the grief he'd only seen once before—the day they'd received her infertility diagnosis.

"She called," Ashleigh blubbered, referring to Hannah. "She told me..." She choked on her words and she wailed harder. She grabbed Desmond's hand from her leg and threw it back at him. "She told me she's out!"

Desmond stood and took a step back. "What?" he asked, looking down at Ashleigh.

Her smeared face looked up at him, and she repeated, "Hannah, she says she's out. She won't sleep with you anymore. *What did you do?*"

Desmond stumbled backward, and his back hit a wall. He slid down it and collapsed into a numb pile on the floor. Hannah knew what he knew.

They didn't just have sex last night. They'd made love.

CHAPTER 14

POE

Six weeks later, Ashleigh left the house to grab a coffee and have some alone time. She'd ignored the breakfast Desmond had made, and left out for her. He wasn't home, but even if he had been, she wouldn't have spoken to him or told him where she was going. They had barely spoken since his last night with Hannah in Baltimore.

It was the middle of the week, and as school was on summer break, Ashleigh had most of the days to herself. She parked her car and strolled to a cafe near Desmond's building. She didn't want to travel so close to Desmond's office, but the best coffee in Maryland happened to be served by The Legal Grind, a cafe set up close to the Federal Court building. She took her time as she walked through the city toward the cafe, even stopping by many of the boutique stores on the side of the roads.

When she did reach the cafe, she took a seat at one of the outdoor tables and ordered a latte. The hot sun shone overhead, and it caused her tanned skin to sweat on contact. Her large-rimmed sunglasses covered at least half of her face, and her bright yellow dress contrasted against the dull black and gray suits worn by so many of the other patrons.

Probably lawyers, she thought. Her phone rang again. She took the phone out of her handbag, which hung from the side of her chair and saw the caller ID indicate that it was Hannah trying to call her—again. She ignored the call, silencing the ringtone and placing the vibrating phone back into her bag. It was the fourth time Hannah had tried to call that morning, and she'd lost count of how many of her calls she'd ignored in the past few weeks.

They hadn't spoken since Hannah called her after spending the night with Desmond. Ashleigh was mad at her. Hannah had allowed her to build up her hopes of mothering a naturally birthed baby, only to shatter those same hopes, but not before sleeping with her husband several times.

She shook the thoughts from her head and took the latte delivered to her table. It was a beautiful day, she was on summer break, and she didn't want the thought of Hannah, her husband, or Hannah *and* her husband, to rob her of her ability to enjoy yet another summer day. She grabbed one of the nearby magazines and began flipping through the pages, reading the odd article as she sipped at her coffee. She turned the page of the magazine and a gasp of breath escaped quickly from her lungs. The pages showed a series of pictures of Hannah and Desmond in a hotel bar, and on the street just a few short miles away from where Ashleigh now sat.

The photos showed the two of them in various states: one of them sitting at a purple-and orange-lit bar and laughing as they shared a drink, and another showed Hannah's hand on Desmond's leg as she gave him a lustful look; yet another showed her leading him by the hand down the street. They both looked drunk. Her eyes pored over the pages, and unimaginable anger squeezed her chest. She found breathing painful, and she was short of breath. Her lip curled, and she briefly looked around to see if anyone had noticed her. She was thankful for the wide-rimmed sunglasses she wore.

Here was her husband and his mistress, their exploits from *that* night on full display for the world to see. The images burned in her eyes, and the photos began to move in her mind as she imagined where these images must have lead next. She tore her eyes away from Hannah's lusty stare and began to read the accompanying article.

How to Enjoy Retirement
By Jack Katan

Most spend their retirement playing golf, going on cruises, and ticking items off a bucket list long neglected during their professional years. Then again, most people don't retire in their thirties like Hannah Lenore, the successful but recently retired choreographer and playwright known for her unique fusion of classical ballet and musical theater. The writer of hit ballets such as Free *and* Don't Go *appears to be enjoying her retirement by traveling around the country and making up for lost time.*

Though not seen since her unexplained disappearance from her final show in New York City months ago, the infamously reclusive playwright was spotted meeting this mystery man at the Marriott Hotel bar on Baltimore Harbor before leading him off to her hotel at the other end of the boardwalk. The writer showed these pictures [inset] to the door staff of Ms. Lenore's expensive park-side estate in NYC, who confirmed that this mystery man had been making nearly weekly trips to Ms. Lenore's penthouse suite on weekends, only to leave an hour or less later.

The author is not one to speculate on what occurs in the private confines of any person's living quarters. However, the reported weekly meetings, along with the suggestive body language seen here, leave little to the imagination as to what is transpiring between these two. This writer certainly does not judge or condemn the exploration of a single woman's sexuality, and this story in itself would be rather innocuous were it not for the fact that this mystery man is married.

Desmond Mathews [pictured] is an attorney for the prom- inent Baltimore law firm Rennick, Spectre & Co., the very same law firm newly representing the infamous Kristen Poe in the controversial IVF case. Perhaps Ms. Lenore is seeking to fill the void left by her recently concluded career with the cheap

thrill of sneaking around with a married man? Perhaps Mr.
Mathews is seeking to make a name for himself both inside the
courtroom, and out? Perhaps an adaptation of Poe v. Maryland
IVF Clinics is coming soon to a theater or stage near you?

Whatever is happening in these photos (however clear that
may be), the traditionally reclusive Hannah Lenore sure knows
how to enjoy retirement, and she's generous enough to make
sure that we can all enjoy it too!

Ashleigh was breathing heavily, almost hyperventilating.
The cafe swirled around her as she felt dizzy and lightheaded.
The surrounding noises left her feeling confounded and dazed.
Her mind whirled with questions: Was *this* the reason Hannah
had been trying to call her? Had her friends or family seen this?
What would they say when they found out? Had Desmond
been enjoying his rendezvous with Hannah this whole time as
these photos suggested? Had he just been pretending to
struggle? What was this about his firm representing the woman
in the IVF case? Is he working on the case? Why hadn't he told
her about this? For how long had he known? Ashleigh was
embarrassed; publicly humiliated. She wanted answers to these
questions, and she wanted them now.

Rolling the magazine and clutching it in one hand, Ashleigh
grabbed some money from her purse with her free hand and
threw it down onto the table; enough for the coffee plus a little
extra for the magazine. She grabbed her bag and poured her
unfinished coffee into a takeaway cup as she left the restaurant,
and began to make her way toward Desmond's office building.
She wanted answers, and he was going to give them to her.

• • •

"I hate lawyers," Kristen Poe snapped to Desmond as they sat
down at a restaurant cafe outside of his office building. They
had been meeting in his office with her quadruplets when one

of the children began crying. The shrill screams of the infant had awoken his brothers and sister, and soon the entire floor was deafened by the cacophony of bedlam. She tried to soothe them for fifteen minutes without success—Desmond stopped his billing clock during this time—and Rennick had appeared at Desmond's glass office door. He entered and asked Desmond to resume the meeting elsewhere, as several other clients were complaining about the noise.

She had let fly a barrage of profanities at Rennick before Desmond managed to calm her enough to get her moving toward the office elevator. He'd picked up the lone girl among the quadruplets and rested her against his chest as he carried the case briefs in his other arm. Poe had pushed the other three infants in her four-seater stroller. By the time they reached the elevator, the baby girl in Desmond's arm had stopped crying and was nuzzling against his chest as she drifted back to sleep.

"I'm sorry, Ms. Poe. I booked the soundproof deposition room for our meeting, but another attorney's deposition was moved up by a court order, and so we lost our booking," Desmond had said as he returned the sleeping girl to the stroller. He'd then picked up two of the crying boys from the stroller before taking a seat in the cafe, sitting opposite his client. His case briefs laid upon the table between them. Poe sat at the cafe table and was breastfeeding the child who had awakened his siblings. A single breast hung out of her shirt in full view, and the child quieted as he drank hungrily from her nipple. The two boys in Desmond's arms soon settled. One of them fell asleep in Desmond's rocking arm, and the other looked lackadaisically at his surroundings with wide, blank eyes.

Poe looked at Desmond as he sat with the two calmed babies in his arms. "You have kids?" she asked pointedly. Desmond opened his mouth to answer, but Poe continued talking. "I know we're not supposed to ask that in today's age of 'political correctness'." She made air quotes with her free hand.

"But who gives a damn. If something I say offends you, well that's your problem so far as I see it. If you don't like it, don't listen. Or, listen and disagree. People seem to have forgotten that it's perfectly fine to disagree about things. These days, if you disagree with something as innocuous as the spelling of your own name then you're branded racist, sexist, homophobic, transphobic, ignorant, a bigot, or one of the many other -ists or -phobics they have these days." She looked down at the feeding baby.

"I don't have kids," said Desmond flatly, answering her previous question. Poe looked up at him and rolled her shoulders in a half-shrug, "What do I care?"

Desmond gently laid each of the now settled boys in the stroller and grabbed the case brief as he resumed his seat. He looked at the pages he'd clipped to the front of the file, a list of questions from the other side. "Ms. Poe," he began.

"Call me Kristen," she interrupted, without looking up from the baby.

"Kristen," he continued, "you understand that the other side served you with interrogatories—"

"What are those?" she asked abruptly.

"They're a list of questions they want us to answer," Desmond clarified. "But neither you, nor your former attorney, answered them."

"I remember. I told my old attorneys not to answer them."

Desmond face showed confusion, if not quiet irritation. "Why?"

"Have you read those questions? Some of the things they're asking about is none of their business!"

Desmond had read the questions and thought most of them were rather benign. He held the piece of paper in front of him and read the first interrogatory aloud, "What are the identifying particulars of the father of the children forming the subject matter of these proceedings, including but not limited to name, address, telephone number, fax number, cell, and social security number."

Poe laughed. "That one doesn't even make sense!"

Ignoring her comment, Desmond placed the pages back on top of the case brief. "I appreciate that these may be intimate questions, but they're relevant to the proceedings which *you* have initiated."

"You want to know who the father is?" Poe looked furtively askance. "There is no father!" Her eyes returned to meet Desmond's. "It's the twenty-first century Mr. Mathews; women don't need a man to have children. I was turning thirty, I wanted kids, and so I had them, you sexist pig."

Desmond blinked away the irony as he recalled Poe's comments only a moment earlier about people being branded sexist so easily, and often. The tension between them broke as a waiter approached to take their orders. As he wrote down their choices from the menu, his eyes continued to dart to her exposed breast.

He folded his black leather-bound order booklet and spoke to Poe. "Madam, is there something I can get for you to preserve your modesty?"

Poe stared at him blankly as though not hearing him. "My what?"

The waiter leaned in closer. "Is there something I can get you to cover yourself with?" He gestured to her breast with a nod of his head.

Poe let out a loud and haughty laugh which startled the waiter upright. "Kid, I abandoned all modesty when I became a mother. These tits don't even belong to me anymore. No, thank you." The moment of joviality seemed to calm her.

She sighed and returned her attention to Desmond. "What happens if we don't answer those 'interro-gorror-oraties' … or whatever those questions are called?"

Desmond answered. "Well, they've already filed a Motion for Immediate Sanction. It means they've notified the court that you haven't answered their questions within the time limit, and that they want some form of punishment."

"What kind of punishment?"

"It depends," Desmond answered. "The court has wide discretion here. It could hold you in contempt, it could order that you pay the costs of the other side's wasted time, or it could dismiss your whole claim." She seemed uncomfortable with this news and shifted her weight in her seat. Desmond continued. "However, we're in the Circuit Court, and they tend to be a little more lenient. If we give your answers to the other side before I have to go to court to respond to their motion, then the court will be a lot happier with us."

"And what if I don't care about making the court happy?" She was quickly slipping back into her abrasive character, and Desmond was growing impatient with her.

"Ms. Poe. Kristen. If you don't care about making the court happy, then you're wasting my time and yours. Let me remind you that *you* initiated these proceedings and brought all the parties together. If you're going to use the court as the forum to resolve your dispute and try to get some compensation, then whether you like it or not, you're going to have to play by the court's rules."

Poe sighed. "I hate lawyers." She locked eyes with Desmond to let him know that she included him in her ire.

Desmond pinched the bridge of his nose and sighed. "Why?" he enquired against his better judgment.

"Why what?" Poe replied with disdain.

"Why do you hate lawyers?" Desmond had to stop himself from snapping his words at his client, his patience worn thin by her blasé attitude.

She concealed her breast and placed her son over her shoulder to begin burping him, taking her time with each movement to make Desmond wait on her. "It's because you profit off other people's misery!"

Desmond leaned back and rolled his eyes as Poe continued. "Someone's dead or dying? You need an estate lawyer. Marriage failed? You need a divorce lawyer. Gravely injured? You need a compensation lawyer. Parasites, every one of you! Just parasites, attaching yourselves to, and feeding on the tit of misery." She did nothing to hide the disdain burning within her eyes as she glared across the table at Desmond.

"Oh, I see," Desmond began sarcastically, leaning over his case briefs to bridge the gap between them. He'd encountered enough people who'd had bad experiences with lawyers and had endured his fair share of lawyer jokes from friends-of-friends to know how to deal with people like Poe. "I guess you only go to see a doctor when you're feeling healthy then? Perhaps you take your car to the mechanic when it's working perfectly fine? You call the police when you're completely safe, do you?" He leaned back to resume his normal posture, and a satisfied smile began to creep across his face in a half-smirk as he watched his words register across his client's face.

"I'm no parasite, Ms. Poe. It's just the way the world is. Circumstances create a need for a service, and someone steps in to fill the need. Lawyers are no different from any other service provider."

The pair heard a hiccough come from the baby slung over Poe's shoulder as he spit-up on the cloth draped beneath him. Poe reached into the stroller for a wet wipe without breaking Desmond's gaze.

"Yeah, well lawyers are the only ones who seem to enjoy the misery which causes the unfortunate to call upon them."

Desmond, by this stage extremely irritated with her repeated challenges, was on the verge of informing her of the misery her lawsuit had visited upon his own life—that his wife was no longer speaking with him or his friend because of the arrangement they'd had to make because of *her* lawsuit. He knew he ought to refrain, lest Poe see the matter as a conflict of interest, so he swallowed his pride and decided not to pursue the matter further. His introspection was interrupted as the waiter returned with their lunch orders.

He turned back to Poe as the waiter left. "Now, if we're done challenging each other, let's get to work."

• • •

Ashleigh's fingers clutched the curled magazine and still-hot coffee in each of her hands. She held the magazine so tightly that her knuckles were white, and she tried to remember every one of the questions that circled through her mind, so she could demand answers to them in a few moments. As she crossed the street just outside Desmond's office building, her attention was grabbed by the loud, echoing cries of four babies in the outdoor seating area in front of a nearby restaurant cafe.

She looked over at a frazzled red-haired woman trying frantically to soothe the crying children as other patrons looked on and complained loudly about the noise. She noticed Desmond was with the woman as the red-head pushed him away from the stroller. Ashleigh approached her husband and the stranger at the front of the cafe and removed her sunglasses.

Desmond's face turned a ghostly white at his wife's approach, but no one noticed amid the infantile furor.

"Would you like a hand?" Ashleigh asked the frantic mother. Poe looked up at Ashleigh. Her overwhelmed face showing disbelief.

"Please!" she responded urgently, the complaints and passive aggressive comments from other patrons in the restaurant after hours of answering interrogatories with Desmond were wearing her thin.

Ashleigh placed her coffee and magazine on the table beside her and moved to stand on the other side of the stroller. She knelt down so that her face was level with the baby in the front seat. Its little face was red and scrunched into an angry ball of lines. It's small, open, and gummy mouth showed that the baby was teething. Ashleigh brushed the baby's cheek gently with the back of some of her fingers. She applied a little pressure against the cheek and softly massaged the gums through the chubby cheeks and small lips. The baby began to settle. Its lips straightened, and the teary eyes opened. She cooed and smiled at the infant and moved slightly to one side, so she could repeat the technique with the sibling in the next seat.

As the four children began to settle, Ashleigh stood up and spoke to Poe. "*Quadruplets*! I don't know how you manage. You must be a supermom!"

Poe smiled and shook her head. "Do you have kids?" she asked Ashleigh, as she brushed frizzy strands of hair from her face that had fallen out of her loosely tied bun. Ashleigh looked coldly in Desmond's direction.

"No. No, we don't. Do we Desmond?" she said sardonically as she grabbed her magazine and coffee from the adjacent table.

Poe looked at Desmond and then back to Ashleigh. "You know each other?"

Ashleigh smiled a mirthless smile. "I'm his wife."

Poe looked at Desmond and laughed before looking back at Ashleigh. "Lemme give you some advice. Don't have kids!"

Ashleigh's humorless smile vanished, and all sarcasm left Poe's manner, replaced by a deadly seriousness as she spoke. "No, really. I wanted kids for the longest time. Before my IVF procedure, there was *nothing* I wouldn't have done or sacrificed to be a mother. But now ..." She paused as she looked at her quadruplets in the four-seater stroller and a nostalgic sadness crossed her tired, overworked face. "Now there's nothing I wouldn't give to go back. You know how people tell you that everything changes after you have kids? They tell you not to have them and that you can't give them back. No matter how much people warn us about how different things will be, how tough, time-consuming, and exhausting it is, we never listen! I'm telling you, having these kids was the biggest mistake of my life. I lost everything, and gained nothing."

An awkward silence settled in, and one of the patrons of the nearby tables yelled, "Some quiet! About damned time."

Poe shot an angry look at the nearby tables, unable to see where the voice had called from before she continued, "I wanted kids, but I didn't want … *them*." She gestured toward her children and seemed to shrink within herself. A crestfallen, dejected aura enveloped her entire person. She shied away from Ashleigh's piteous gaze. Ashleigh looked down at one of the infant faces looking up at her. She couldn't imagine ever feeling that way about any child, let alone her own. The baby looked up at her with wonder in its eyes, and Ashleigh's anger momentarily broke as she smiled down adoringly.

Without raising her spirits, Poe turned her attention back to Ashleigh. "I'm sorry if I'm talking a lot. I don't get many chances to speak with adults these days, and just having an adult conversation is the highlight of my day."

She extended her hand to Ashleigh. Desmond's heart stopped.

"Kristen Poe. Nice to meet you," she said as she introduced herself to Ashleigh.

Ashleigh looked up at Poe, still wearing the adoring smile she shared with the baby. She glanced at Poe, then back to the four children in the stroller, and then to Desmond. Her smile vanished, and a venomous scowl took its place. Her grip around the magazine tightened as Desmond's second betrayal registered in her mind.

She realized that she was speaking with Poe. *The* Kristen Poe. The monster from the IVF lawsuit which had barred her access from every IVF clinic and treatment in the country. The same Poe whose selfish, desperate, and shameless money-grabbing lawsuit all but forced her to concede the awful arrangement between her husband and Hannah.

Her eyes turned to daggers, and she shot them at Desmond, whose hardened face stood ready to accept a torrent of abuse. Ashleigh looked down at Poe's extended hand and smacked it away with the rolled-up magazine. She raised the magazine and pointed it at Poe, dangling the rolled-up pages mere inches from her startled face, and breathed in a seething, menacing tone, "You cretin. Do you know what your selfishness has visited upon the lives of countless women in this country? You don't deserve these children, you don't deserve a damned penny from the IVF clinic, and you sure as hell won't get me to shake your hand, you miserable bitch!"

Poe pulled her hand away from Ashleigh, and her face showed shock as she started to speak, "What are you—"

Her voice was cut off as Ashleigh unleashed a furious slap across her face with the magazine, the sound of the paper cracking against her resounded through the restaurant and startled the children in the stroller. Poe's eyes watered. Her cheek stung and was quickly turning a deep crimson where the makeshift weapon had struck.

Ashleigh turned to Desmond and threw the coffee at him with her other hand. Her throw missed, and a waiter behind Desmond was forced to dodge the spilling projectile. Ashleigh stepped in front of Desmond, as shocked and silent patrons watched the confrontation.

"And you..." she seethed, her face knotted in disgust. Desmond looked down at his wife's glaring eyes and said nothing. She leaned back slightly and spat in his face. He barely flinched. He didn't even wipe away the saliva that splattered and dripped down his face. Ashleigh turned on the spot and stormed out of the restaurant.

One of Poe's babies gave a muffled whimper as though it was about to start crying again, and the noise broke the surreal silence that enveloped them after Ashleigh's departure. Poe bent over to pick up the child, and as she straightened up with the baby in her arms, Desmond saw she was crying. Poe turned to him and patted the baby on the back soothingly as tears rolled down her face, and onto her shirt. "I wasn't always a monster," she blubbered to Desmond, her crying now edging towards piteous sobs. "I was a nice person. I was kind to people."

Desmond closed the gap between them, and placed a reassuring hand on her shoulder as he tried to apologize for Ashleigh. He tried to comfort her, but his attention was locked on the image of his wife storming up the street.

Poe shook her head. "I don't blame her. I'd have done the same thing before all of this. I'm sorry I was so mean to you, and I'm sorry I upset your wife. I just wanted children. I just wanted to be a good *wife*! I didn't think he'd leave me like this!"

Her crying had turned to hysterical sobs, and someone at a nearby table groaned. Desmond barely registered her reference to a husband. "I lied before," Poe confessed. "There is a father. Of *course*, there's a father! He left a month before *they* were born, saying he 'couldn't cope' with four kids. *He* couldn't cope! He just left me, eight months pregnant and no means to support myself."

As Ashleigh moved out of view, Desmond returned his gaze to Poe, looking down at her as she cradled her baby. Her reddened and bloodshot eyes darted around frantically; she looked like a lost child. Her red hair was tied up in a lazy bun, and split ends abounded—a thousand thin strands shot off in as many directions. She was very pale, and her skin gave off a sluggish, gray color beneath freckles that sat atop her pockmarked face. Her clothes were old and dirty—dried spit up marks rested on her shoulders, and what looked like food stains were visible all over her pants.

"I was a good person," she consoled herself through a shaky voice. "I was a nurse, for goodness sake!" She looked at Desmond. "Tell your wife I know it's wrong to sue the IVF clinic, but I don't have a choice. I have four babies to look after, and no lawyer husband ready to look after us like she does. I don't want to do this, but I have no choice. Tell her!" Poe grabbed the stroller handle with one hand and began to walk out of the restaurant with one child still over her shoulder. Still crying, she walked down the street in the opposite direction from which Ashleigh had left. A middle-aged man looked over at Desmond and raised his arms in triumph as he watched Poe depart the restaurant with the stroller.

Ignoring the rude, overweight man, Desmond quickly threw some cash down on the restaurant table and gathered his case briefs. He hurried out on the sidewalk to the restaurant's entrance, and looked both ways. On his left, he could see Ashleigh walking in the distance toward the harbor. Her arms were bundled around herself, and she walked with haste. On his right, Poe was struggling down the street with her baby in one arm and a bulky stroller loaded with three children and a nursing bag in the other. He wanted desperately to pursue his wife and try to fix things between them. To speak to his wife—while she still was his wife—and try and save their marriage. However, he'd made an oath to serve his client's interests above his own and walking in the opposite direction of Ashleigh was a sad, scared, and overwhelmed mother looking for a solution to the terrifying reality in which she had unexpectedly found herself. Desmond looked back at his wife one more time, and winced as he took off at a light jog down the street after Poe. He helped her with the child, and she let him take the stroller from her hands. She barely managed to sob the words, "Thank you" as he helped her. She covered her mouth with one hand

and continued to stifle shaking cries as she walked back to Desmond's office.

A hundred feet away, Ashleigh stopped in the street and looked behind her. Tears streaked her cheeks beneath the sunglasses she'd put back on in a vain effort to hide her heartbreak. She could see her husband helping Poe with her stroller in the distance, and watched as he gave her a reassuring hug. Ashleigh turned back toward the harbor and continued toward her parked car at a quickened pace, accelerated by her anger and frustration. Once again, her husband was leaving her behind to chase after another woman.

• • •

Ashleigh climbed into the driver side of her car and removed her sunglasses. She leaned forward and sobbed piteously against the leather steering wheel. *How did it come to this?* she screamed the words in her mind as her painful groans echoed outside of the vehicle. Her mind replayed the series of events over the preceding few months over and over until they felt like hallucinations.

She watched herself tell Hannah that any surrogate would have to be willing to have sex with Desmond. She looked on as another version of herself from just a few months back asked Desmond—begged him—to sleep with Hannah. She watched as he informed her that he would hypothetically represent Poe in her IVF case. She let the pictures in the magazine come to life in her mind, and she watched Hannah lead her husband up to her hotel room and watched as the two had intimate, loving sex, laughing maniacally at her ignorance to the romance she'd orchestrated. And finally, she heard Hannah's voice echo across time through the speaker of her cell phone. "It's Hannah. I can't do this anymore. I don't want to sleep with Desmond again. I'm out. I'm so sorry, Ashleigh."

Ashleigh's hallucinations materialized as she heard her phone ring once more from her handbag. She pulled the phone

A PART OF YOU

out and saw that Hannah was calling again. She answered the phone angrily. "What?" she barked, overwhelmed by emotion. "What is it? What do you want?"

Hannah's meager voice came back to her. "Ashleigh, I'm sorry. I've been trying to call you for weeks—"

Ashleigh cut her off in a distressed, impatient tone. "To tell me about the article and the photos? Yeah, I've seen them. What a fool I've been, right?"

Hannah's voice came back through Ashleigh's phone in a forced but even tone. "There was that. I'm sorry, Ash. Katan is an ass and a sensationalist. I'm somewhat of a gossip favorite of his. You can't trust everything he says."

"And the photos?" Ashleigh said. "What about the photos?"

Hannah sighed. "Ash, everyone nowadays has a camera on their phone. Everyone's a paparazzo now. People snap photos and sell them to the tabloids. The tabloids just make up whatever story they think will sell and use the photos as supposed proof."

Ashleigh cried hard into her phone. She didn't know what to believe. The article had been right about a number of things. How would she know that the photos weren't exactly what they looked like? How would she know if Desmond and Hannah had only been trying to conceive, and not carrying out some illicit affair? Hannah's voice broke Ashleigh's brief reverie.

"I wasn't calling about the article though, Ash. There's something else I have to tell you. I would have preferred to tell you in person, but you won't take my calls."

"Oh gosh," Ashleigh cried, "What else is there?"

There was a long pause between them. Ashleigh quieted briefly and heard anxious breathing on the other end of the phone. "It happened, Ash," Hannah answered. "You're going to be a mother. I'm pregnant."

Ashleigh ended the call without another word. She leaned forward, finally releasing her tight grip on her steering wheel, and she cried softly and alone into her hands.

PART THREE

CHAPTER 15

WORDS OF WARNING

A shleigh sat uncomfortably in the foyer of the marriage counselor's office. The room was small and cramped, and the leaves in the potted plants placed around the room wilted and hung lazily as they succumbed to the oppressive heat of the room. The ceiling fans rattling overhead did little to combat the heat wave that the dying days of summer had unleashed on the east coast, and she could feel her sweaty skin sticking to the leather of the couch seat. She fanned herself with the clipboard the receptionist had given her to fill out. She had left one question unanswered— Family Structure: Unmarried, Traditional Marriage, Nuclear Family, Alternative.

She looked at the question with no small measure of contempt. She had always thought of herself as traditional, and the idea that she might fit under the vague description of "alternative" made her uncomfortable. She glanced sideways at Hannah seated next to her. Hannah rubbed her slightly distended belly lazily as she fanned herself with a magazine she'd grabbed from the adjacent end table. A little more than a month had passed since Hannah had called Ashleigh with the news of her pregnancy, but no one looking at her would guess she was pregnant. Her skin continued to glow with its natural radiance, and but for a belly that looked like she'd simply had a large lunch, her body remained unchanged. Desmond sat on the other side of Ashleigh with one of his hands placed on her leg. She pushed the hand off so that it flopped heavily toward the floor. He gave her a look: part confusion, part hurt.

"It's too hot," she lied, as a quick excuse. Since the day Hannah had told her she was pregnant and she'd discovered Desmond was working on the Poe case, Ashleigh and Desmond had struggled to connect, and had steadily drifted apart. Desmond had focused his attention heavily on Ashleigh in a vain attempt to rekindle the joy of being together, but she always felt his gestures were too laden with apologetic overtones. She missed her husband. She remembered what it felt like to get caught up in the excitement and joy of their happy marriage, and the absence of that feeling now left her feeling empty.

As more time passed, however, that emptiness was filled with the joy and excitement of Hannah's pregnancy, and she found herself caring less and less about Desmond's seemingly insincere presence. She tapped the pen impatiently on the clipboard she held in front of her. She realized that she was angry—or, if not angry, she was annoyed. The heat of the room annoyed her; the overly watchful gaze of the receptionist annoyed her; even the stupid way in which her stupid husband sat beside her annoyed her, and she felt a sudden urge to break the clipboard over his head and tell him to stop breathing so loudly. She didn't though. She knew herself well enough to know that she was simply still angry at Desmond for hiding his involvement in the Poe case from her, and for doing whatever he had done to Hannah to make her pull out of the arrangement after their last night together. She was annoyed that Desmond never came home that night. She was annoyed that even now, more than two months afterwards, the memory of these events still felt like a knife to the heart. She hadn't forgiven him for these things. She had tried a little, but she didn't know what exactly she'd be forgiving him for when it came to his night with Hannah. What's more, Desmond didn't seem sorry enough for hiding his work on the Poe case to warrant her forgiveness.

She glanced at Hannah and Desmond on either side of her, and sighed angrily. *There is nothing "traditional" about this arrangement,* she thought. She placed a cross in the box next to "alternative" on the form, and rose quickly to give the clipboard back to the receptionist.

"Thank you," said the young receptionist with a wry grin. "The doctor will see you now."

Ashleigh looked at the closed door that led to the counselor's office and then back to the young receptionist. "He was just waiting for me to fill out the form?"

The girl nodded.

Ashleigh shook clenched fists in front of her. "If I had known that, I wouldn't have spent twenty minutes deciding on the answer!" She tried her best to show that her frustration was not aimed at the girl.

The receptionist shrugged her shoulders. "It's part of the process, Miss."

Ashleigh took a long, deep breath and thanked the girl as she turned to join a now standing Hannah and Desmond. She had arranged the visit to this counselor. Touted as the best marriage counselor on the east coast, he had many quirks and rules, one of them being that he refused to see any couple more than once. Despite this, his consults were notoriously successful. Ashleigh avoided Desmond's hand as it reached for hers, but she played it off as though she simply hadn't noticed.

As they stepped into the counselor's office, she was disappointed to discover that it was no cooler inside the office than it was in the scorching foyer. A lone figure to the side of the room sat with his back to the trio, and he pointed silently to the leather couch and unmatched chair across from him. Ashleigh and Desmond sat on the two-seater couch, and Hannah sat gently on the adjacent seat. Ashleigh felt the leather stick once again to her exposed skin, and she wondered how Hannah managed to look so immaculate and serenely comfortable as she sat pregnant, in an oversized chair, in a hot room.

She was surprised as she realized for the first time how spacious the counselor's office was. Their chairs and the adjacent end tables sat in the middle of the office, and an expanse of space enveloped them on all sides until it was interrupted by the walls of the room. Against the faraway walls sat shelves filled with a library of books, and a small, lone wooden chair sat in front of a closed window looking outside at the scorching sun. There was a Willy-Wonka-esque feel to the office, though the focus seemed to be more on utility than quirkiness. There was nothing in the office that didn't serve some distinct, functional purpose. Nonetheless, Ashleigh gave a quick second look around the room to make sure there wasn't a hat rack or picture frame cut in half.

The counselor remained silent in front of his computer with his face buried in the book in his lap. The emptiness that surrounded them gave Ashleigh the impression that they sat silently on a small island of their own, and as her feet dangled over the floor beneath them, she felt exposed and vulnerable, almost childlike.

The counselor closed the book in his lap, and it gave a sharp clap as the pages quickly came together. "Apologies," he said, clearing his throat and returning the book to its spot in the bookshelf. "I hate finishing in the middle of a chapter. It took you longer than I expected to answer that family question on the form, and so I'd started to read another chapter."

Ashleigh's ears perked up. "You knew we'd struggle with *that* question?"

The counselor chuckled. It was an ugly, hollow laugh that sounded like he had learned to laugh from a description of one in a book. "Of course," he answered. "I read the file notes from your call to book the appointment with me. I customize every questionnaire form for every visitor. Judging by your response, I assume you selected 'alternative'?"

Ashleigh nodded slightly, with her mouth hanging slightly agape.

The counselor smiled to himself as he moved his chair closer to the threesome. To Ashleigh, the room suddenly became much smaller. The counselor sat opposite her and Desmond, his face half-hidden behind hands pressed together, forming a pyramid with his fingertips. He squinted at them through thick, clear glasses. His narrow gaze gave an appraising, if not displeased, look. His features were wizened with age, but his skin was still taught, deftly holding onto the responsibility of keeping shape and form where others' skin might have started to sag or become loose. The top of his head was bald, and this might have given his already high forehead an almost comical height if not for the wrinkles which parsed the two hemispheres of his skull. The hair on each side of his scalp was dyed the same color as his black beard, and the two joined at the high point of his jaw. His silver eyebrows showed his hair's true color, and magnified the intensity of his gray, appraising eyes, which darted back and forth.

Ashleigh shifted in her seat uncomfortably. The counselor sat perfectly still but for the steady movement of his calm and even breathing, and the quick darting movements of those pressing eyes. He noted that Ashleigh and Desmond sat with more than a foot between them, despite the small size of the couch.

She's displeased with him, he thought. He noticed Ashleigh was leaning ever so slightly away from Desmond. His half-hidden eyes moved to the hand Desmond had placed on the couch in the space between them.

Guilt, he thought. *He is unconsciously trying to bridge the gap between them.* Desmond was leaning forward on the couch and looking intently at Ashleigh. *He wants to fix this. Very badly, it would seem.* The counselor's eyes flicked over to Ashleigh. *Not sure about her though, leaning away from him, avoiding his gaze, her legs crossed away from him.*

He paused as he examined her further, her eyes avoiding his. *Presentably dressed, jewelry, wedding band is still on her finger.* His eyes narrowed further so that they looked barely more than slits on his pale face. *But she's not dressing up for him.* His eyes drifted quickly to Hannah, who sat smiling at the quirky old man. *She's dressing up for her, like a competition."*

His eyes glanced upward at the overhead ceiling fan and then over to the window which nearly vibrated in the baking heat of the afternoon sun. *It's too damned hot.* The counselor removed his hands from in front of his face and sat up stiffly. "I have questions," he said to the couple and the woman seated in front of him, sharing his gaze between them. "These questions assume certain matters. I would appreciate it if you could please try and answer my questions, even if you think that the assumptions upon which they are based are incorrect. Answer them honestly. The quicker, the better. I want your honest, gut-reaction responses. Understood?"

Everyone nodded.

"Desmond, what did you do that has you feeling guilty?"

"Wait," said Ashleigh, shaking her head in disbelief. "You don't want to hear about why we're here? About what's happened?"

The counselor gave a knowing half-smile, and looked at Ashleigh. "Ms. Mathews, why you think you're here is far less important than you think it is. I do not ask my visitors why they think they come to me, because they so often do not know. The reason they *think* they have come to me is usually wrong, or at least irrelevant."

Ashleigh leaned back into the chair feeling embarrassed, and the counselor turned his head to face Desmond.

Desmond met the counselor's gaze and did not look away as he answered, "I slept with another woman."

The counselor did not react. It was not an uncommon confession in his office.

"That's not all—" began Ashleigh until hushed by the counselor's hand, raised once more to quiet her.

"In time," he answered. He lowered his hand and kept his attention directed toward Ashleigh. "Ms. Mathews, why do you feel like Desmond's infidelity is your fault?"

Ashleigh stared at the counselor in mute shock.

The counselor put his hands out in front of him with his palms facing upward in empathetic gesture. "It's not uncommon, Ashleigh," he said, switching to her first name to appear more personable. "It's not unusual for wives to blame themselves for this kind of behavior, at least in part. Sometimes they think they haven't given their husband's enough attention, haven't stayed in shape, haven't noticed the signs..."

"I told him to do it," she answered flatly and without embarrassment, also without breaking the counselor's gaze.

Interesting development, he thought without showing his surprise at Ashleigh's answer. He continued his questioning. "Desmond, do you intend to have sexual relations with this woman again?"

"No."

"Do you want to?"

"No."

The counselor paused. He leaned forward in his seat and stared intensely into Desmond's eyes. *He's telling the truth. Curious.* "Do you intend to see this woman again, Desmond?"

"I suppose I'll have to."

"Why?"

Desmond gestured toward Hannah. "Because she's our surrogate, and she's pregnant."

The counselor turned his head in Ashleigh's direction and briefly looked at her abdomen before looking at her face. "You're infertile?"

Ashleigh nodded, perplexed at how the counselor had managed to glean so much information about them after so little inquiry. The counselor leaned back in his chair and grabbed a black, leather-bound notepad from his side table. He remembered the notes taken from when Ashleigh had called to book the appointment with him. He'd been informed that a surrogate was involved, but not a non-surgical one.

"Non-surgical surrogates," he said aloud to no one in particular. He began writing in his pad. "You're not my first, though I pray you'll be my last."

Ashleigh looked at Desmond and then back to the counselor. "How did you—"

The counselor cut Ashleigh off, fixing her with a knowing look over the rim of his glasses. The counselor looked back at his notepad, and spoke as he continued to write. "Standard surgical surrogacy—artificial insemination—can be a messy affair. Non-surgical surrogacy is … more volatile. I wish you'd come to see me before embarking on this. We could have mitigated the negative emotions that can arise, but nothing can be done about that now."

He took off his glasses and looked at the couple on the chair before him. "Your marriage is in dangerous waters. You are both about to experience a wave of new and conflicting emotions over a prolonged period. Desmond, as the father of this child your paternal instincts are going to kick in, and you will naturally care for the welfare of the child in order to ensure that your offspring remains healthy. This will instinctively mean care and concern for its vessel, the surrogate." He nodded at Hannah.

"At the same time, you will have responsibilities to Ashleigh. She is no longer just your wife, but the intended mother of your child. She is owed your care and affection, but because she is an adult and can fend for herself and your child cannot, you will likely diminish in your mind the emotional reliance that she has in you. Additionally, Desmond, now that the surrogate is pregnant, and you have accomplished the objective of your sexual encounters, all involved would expect that Ashleigh is once more owed your fidelity."

Desmond nodded. "That's not going to be a problem," he said firmly.

The counselor leaned forward toward Desmond. "I believe that you believe that, Desmond. I really do. That you love your wife is obvious, and it was one of the first observations I made after you stepped into my office. However, your emotions are about to become unbalanced—redistributed, if you will—as you begin to experience a new kind of love. A paternal love. There is a risk that you may confuse these new feelings for your child with feelings for the surrogate."

The counselor held his hand up firmly against Desmond's protest, incredulity and indignation painting his voice and stare.

Ashleigh looked at Desmond and then to the counselor. "You think he's going to develop feelings for Hannah?" she said softly through the lump that had formed in her throat.

The counselor lowered his hand. "No. Not quite. The heart does not have room for more than one. We are capable of loving our spouse and having a love for all of our children and our friends, and we can love these people at one time. There are many different kinds of love."

Ashleigh winced, as Hannah's similar words from her interview echoed in her mind. If the counselor noticed Ashleigh's reaction, he did not show it. He continued. "However, the *romantic* heart has room enough only for one love, Ashleigh, and the heart can change."

Ashleigh lowered her face and held Desmond's hand as he placed it on her lap and reached for hers.

"Ashleigh, I tell you these things not to dishearten you, but to ensure that you can arm yourself against them. It is only by knowing the risks that we may prepare against them. Desmond's are not the only feelings that will be tested. Just as he must be careful not to confuse his feelings for the child as feelings for the surrogate, you will need to be conscious of your own emotions. As Desmond spends time with this woman and your unborn child, you will naturally have feelings of jealousy. However, you must be careful not to confuse these with feelings of abandonment."

"How?" she whispered. The marriage counselor touted as the best on the east coast had all but informed her that the next seven months would be hell, that her husband might develop feelings for Hannah, and that *she* would be the one that needed to keep her emotions in check. They had waited weeks to see this marriage counselor, and during that time their marriage had deteriorated despite their efforts to reconnect. Ashleigh had come to this office hoping that she and Desmond would leave as happy as they had been before receiving her infertility diagnosis. Now she felt disillusioned. The counselor's words had not been of hope and encouragement but of warning. She felt more hopeless than before, defeated before the battle had even started. "How are we supposed to get through this?" she said imploringly.

The counselor smiled sympathetically and placed his hands together once more in the shape of a pyramid. It was an ugly smile that stretched across his lips like a scar rather than a measure of reassurance, but it was sincere. "Take heart, Ashleigh. The way to assuage the feelings I have warned against, and the way to reconnect throughout this process is fairly simple: remember that this is *your* baby. Ashleigh, if you remain cognizant that this baby is yours, then it will be easier

212

for you to tolerate the time and attention that Desmond must now naturally give to the surrogate. Desmond, if you remain cognizant that this baby is Ashleigh's, then you are less likely to confuse your newfound feelings for the child.

"To answer your question, Ashleigh, the way we manage this is for you both to be *involved* in the pregnancy. I suggest that both of you, and the surrogate, join the surrogacy support group at the Ellicott City Community Center, just outside of Baltimore. This should allow Desmond the opportunity to develop his paternal feelings for the baby in your presence, and help associate those feelings with you, rather than the surrogate. Being so intimately involved with the pregnancy should also foster increased maternal bonding between you and the baby. Finally, it should provide a safe space for you all to discuss and manage the surrogacy and to tackle the obstacles that will invariably arise throughout the pregnancy."

"What about me?" Hannah chimed in. Everyone's face turned to see her sweet smile shining at the counselor. "I assume there is a reason you insisted I attend this marriage counseling session? You've told Ashleigh and Desmond what to look out for and what to guard against, but what about me?" Even when demanding answers, she sounded sweet and delicate.

The counselor's scar-like smile pursed, and his eyes showed a deep sympathy. "You seem like a lovely woman, Ms. Lenore. That is why it pains me to tell you that your role in all of this will be the most difficult."

Hannah maintained her smile, but her large, expressive eyes reflected something resembling concern.

"*Powerful* maternal instincts will kick in, if they haven't already, and will only continue to intensify as *Ashleigh's* pregnancy progresses. And it will be at the precise moment that these instincts peak—the childbirth—that you'll be required to hand the child to Desmond and Ashleigh. You really cannot imagine how horrible this will be."

Hannah looked down at her small baby bump and realized too late that she was instinctively rubbing her stomach as the counselor spoke.

"This is not all, Ms. Lenore," the counselor continued.

Hannah ceased the caressing of her abdomen and gave her attention once more to the counselor.

"As the pregnancy progresses, your hormones will be in a great state of flux. You should not be surprised if you find yourself having feelings for the child's father throughout the pregnancy."

Ashleigh tried not to shoot Hannah a distrustful look and failed.

The counselor made a mental note of the already blossoming jealousy and continued, "However, Ms. Lenore, like Desmond and Ashleigh, you must be ever-conscious of your feelings so that you do not confuse them. The feelings that will develop for the child are for the *child*, not for Desmond."

Hannah looked at Ashleigh and gave a sweet, reassuring smile before looking back to the counselor.

"Thank you, Doctor," Hannah began stoically. "I've known Desmond for many years, and he's not the kind of man who ever brought romance to mind, even throughout all of this."

Desmond's brow furrowed slightly, and his eyes flicked briefly to Hannah. She continued to look directly at the counselor.

The counselor's scar-like smile returned. "If all three of you are prepared to attend the surrogacy support group, then I am finished speaking with you as a group. Ashleigh, Hannah, if you could please wait outside—I need to speak with Desmond alone."

The two women rose together and made for the door to the waiting room. Desmond watched the women as they walked together in awkward silence and left the room. As the door closed behind them, he turned his attention to find the counselor now sitting closer to him and staring at him intently.

"I asked you why you feel so guilty, Mr. Mathews."

Desmond looked confused and affronted, "And I told y—"

"No." The counselor cut him off. "You told me a half-truth. What's the other half?"

"I told you," Desmond came back firmly.

"Don't waste our time, Desmond. I can't help your marriage if you're not going to be honest."

Desmond finally broke the counselor's gaze in shame. His answer was slow as he struggled to give life to his confession with words. "I resisted this…arrangement, as we have come to call it. I hated it. I really did. I hated it so much that there were times where I was completely unable to perform. I was hurting my wife, I was mistreating Hannah, and this whole dark arrangement was breaking me."

The counselor continued to stare at him unwaveringly.

"However, on the last night I shared with Hannah, it wasn't just different. It was intimate. I slept with Hannah not because Ashleigh told me to, but because I wanted to. On that last night, I cheated on my wife." All expression left Desmond's face. It was the first time he'd confessed this aloud, and the reality struck and gutted him. He abhorred cheating, and never in a million years would he have expected these words to leave his mouth. He raised a hand to touch his lips as he remembered breaking the rule on kissing, and for a moment he could feel Hannah's soft lips against his own. He removed his hand and wanted to spit the bad taste the memory left in his mouth.

The counselor nodded impassively. "But you haven't told your wife about this."

Even though this was not a question, Desmond shook his head solemnly. "I couldn't. I was going to. I was going to tell her everything. But by the time I got home, Hannah had already called her to say that she was out as the surrogate, though we didn't know she was already pregnant by that time."

"Have you spoken to Hannah since?"

"Hardly."

"You haven't discussed that night or talked about it?"

"No."

"Good. Don't. I think it's in the best interest of your marriage not to talk with Hannah about that night. The deed is done, she's pregnant, and there is no longer any need for the two of you to talk about the nights you shared. As for your wife, Desmond, you *must* tell Ashleigh about that night. You cannot rebuild your marriage on roots tended with deception."

"And if she leaves me because of it?" Desmond asked, almost frightened.

"Then that would be her right." The counselor's tone could easily have been mistaken as cold or uncaring, but it was simply factual. "If a man could share with another woman something as reserved for his wife as intimacy, then he no longer has any claim on her forgiveness. Tell her, Desmond, and bear the consequences. I do not think she will leave you, but even if she does, she deserves to know."

Desmond began to argue. "I think—"

The counselor became instantly irritated, and he raised his voice. "Mr. Mathews, what you think is far less important than you think it is. That woman out there," he pointed to the office door through which Ashleigh had left, "do you know what she wants? All she wants is for your relationship to be what it used to be. For you to be the man you were before all of this. Do you realize what a big deal that is? Ashleigh is a woman who was so desperate to be a mother that she had her husband sleep with another woman, and now even with a baby of her own on the way, all she wants is you. And here you sit trying to rationalize why you shouldn't be honest with her, even though it's the guilt you feel that is coming between you and your wife. Tell her, Desmond. If not for the sake of your marriage or conscience, then simply out of respect for your wife."

Desmond sat up and met the counselor's eyes once more, "I think—" He caught himself as his words brought a reproachful look from the man in front of him. "I think you're right."

The counselor wheeled his chair away from Desmond and crossed one leg across his lap. He settled back into what Desmond realized must be his usual pose, with his fingers making a triangle in front of his face. "We're done, Mr. Mathews. Please send in your wife."

Desmond made to leave the office and paused as his hand held the doorknob of the door leading to the foyer. He could hear Ashleigh and Hannah conversing through the wooden panels of the door. He turned just enough to catch the counselor's eyes watching him, and he gave a single nod as he turned the handle.

Ashleigh entered the counselor's office wearing a forced, but hopeful smile. She resumed her seat in the middle of the lounge, and the counselor remained comfortably seated away from her. "Ashleigh," he began, "earlier you said, 'That's not all' when we were talking about why Desmond might be feeling guilty. It was important for me to know what Desmond felt guilty about, but now I am curious about the other reason or reasons *you* think he *ought* to feel guilty. What did you mean when you said, 'That's not all'?"

Ashleigh proceeded to tell the counselor about the IVF case. About her discovery that Desmond was representing Poe, and her feeling of being betrayed by Desmond for concealing his involvement in the case. The counselor nodded and patiently listened as she told him through a rising voice and broken tears about her surprise and hurt. About how she felt guilty for striking and insulting Poe, and then felt angry at herself for feeling guilty.

He waited and listened in mute silence as she bore detail to her shame and vulnerability after her infertility diagnosis, and exhausted his supply of tissues as she expressed her loneliness and helplessness each time Desmond left her to visit Hannah. She sobbed as she recalled her shame for begging Desmond to sleep with Hannah, and her dismay that Desmond could betray her feelings by helping Poe, the woman who had caused her so much grief.

As Ashleigh reached into the now empty tissue box, the counselor reached into his jacket and removed a handkerchief. He handed the cloth to Ashleigh and spoke, "Ashleigh, part of the reason I asked to see all of you privately is because what I have to tell you will be difficult to hear, and I expect you will hear it better without the distracting noise of embarrassment or worry about what others think of it."

Ashleigh blew her nose into the handkerchief and looked warily at the counselor. He sighed. "Ashleigh, you're not upset about Desmond's involvement in the Poe case, or about him concealing his involvement. That is to say, you're not as upset as you think you are."

Ashleigh's head recoiled slightly, and her face looked as though an odor had wafted in from the window.

"Ashleigh, what you have done is transferred your hurt and frustration. You are upset and frustrated at Desmond having sex with the surrogate, and probably frustrated that he hasn't had sex with you since, but you feel as though you cannot rightly feel or express this because you demanded it from him. So, you transfer this hurt to something which you feel vindicated in feeling angry and hurt about—his involvement in this lawsuit. I'm not excusing his concealment or suggesting that you're not vindicated in being hurt by that. What I am saying is that you're not going to move past this if you're focusing on the wrong cause. Search your feelings, and you will likely find that now that the Hannah is pregnant, and you will soon have your baby, that you care less about this Poe woman and her lawsuit than you think you do."

Ashleigh closed her eyes briefly and saw Poe's frayed red hair. She could still imagine the force that vibrated through her arm as she slapped her with the magazine. And suddenly her heart was crushed as she remembered the face of Poe's sweet baby looking up at her and the thousands of women across the country who, because of the lawsuit, couldn't have children like those Poe regretted conceiving. Her eyes snapped open. "I don't just worry about Desmond's involvement in this case. I worry that he'll win."

"So what if he does?" The counselor shrugged. "If he wins, the clinics will have clearer and standardized instructions regarding insemination procedures. If he loses, the clinics will reopen their doors and continue their procedures as normal. Do not confuse yourself as one of these mothers-in-waiting unable to have children. Now that Hannah is pregnant with your child, the Poe case is far removed from you. If you feel for the other would-be mothers who cannot have children for the time being, then realize that it is a problem for those women, and not for your marriage.

Ashleigh wrung the handkerchief in her hand. "I hate her," she said coldly as she thought of Poe.

"Then hate her, but do not transfer that hate to Desmond. Hatred has no place in a marriage, and your marriage has enough to worry about with your child growing inside of another woman. You and Desmond will need to work together to manage this surrogacy and all that is to follow, and you cannot hope to make it through this surrogacy with hate in your marriage.

Ashleigh sighed. She knew the counselor was right. "I'm not ready for this," she admitted softly as she stared out the nearby window.

The counselor smiled warmly, the ugly quality of his smile now all but vanished, "No one is ever ready for parenthood, Ashleigh, even those who think they are."

Silence hung delicately in the office for a few moments before the counselor spoke. "I have one more question for you, Ashleigh." She turned away from the window. The counselor continued. "If you could, would you go back and stop yourself from asking Desmond to sleep with Hannah?"

Ashleigh smiled. She knew the answer immediately. "There are a lot of things I would give up if it meant that Desmond would look at me with those eyes once more: like I was the only thing that mattered and the only thing he could see…like I could disappear, and it would make his world crumble. But would I give up the baby—*my* baby?" she corrected, "the one growing in Hannah's womb? No. Not for a second. Because whenever I think about that baby, it's all that matters to me. Having that baby means I have it all."

The counselor nodded slowly, and although his lips remained impassive, his eyes were smiling. "Remember that," he said softly. "That is all for us, Ashleigh. I wish you every happiness. Please send in Ms. Lenore as you exit."

Ashleigh let out a deep sigh, suddenly feeling like a weight had lifted from her shoulders. As she stood, she reached out and offered the folded handkerchief, into which she had blown her nose, back to the counselor.

The counselor chuckled and politely raised his hand in objection. "Please, keep it." Ashleigh laughed back. She thanked the counselor as she wiped the mascara stains from her cheeks and exited the office.

As she pulled the door open, she could see Desmond sitting next to Hannah with his hand placed on her stomach, as though trying to feel for the child's kicking. Her lungs quickly filled with air as the pang of jealousy rattled her heart, and she forced a smile as the two looked up at her. "It's too early for that, Des. Hannah, he wants to see you." Desmond stood quickly and helped Hannah to her feet. Ashleigh tried to keep her immediate emotions in check as Hannah stepped into the counselor's office and the door closed behind her. *He's just taking care of the baby*, Ashleigh reminded herself as she took the seat left empty by Hannah.

"It's very hot in your office," Hannah informed the counselor as she lowered herself into the familiar leather couch. "Did you know that?"

The counselor smiled. "People tend to be more honest when they're uncomfortable, Ms. Lenore. You get used to it with time." He stood and moved over to the nearby window and opened it. A cool breeze began to filter the heat from the room. Hannah smiled in appreciation at the counselor's cleverness.

"What can I help you with?" she asked sweetly.

The counselor sighed as he looked out the window at the fading daylight. The sigh was one of fatigue rather than one of irritation or impatience, though to Hannah it sounded like it could have been either. "Have you ever been pregnant before?" the counselor asked stoically as he returned to his seat.

Hannah's face creased in confusion, "What do you mean?"

"I mean have you ever had an abortion or miscarriage?"

Hannah hesitated. She looked over her shoulder to make sure that the door to the lobby was closed and turned back to the counselor to find him watching her with his piercing gray eyes. "What I'm about to tell you," she began cautiously, "you have to realize that I've never spoken to anyone about it."

The counselor nodded slowly, somehow silently communicating that he would hold whatever she had to say in the strictest confidence.

Hannah continued. "There was a time when I was dating a man. A married man. I didn't know that he was married, and I broke it off as soon as I discovered the fact. But before I broke it off, I was late. I was really late. I thought I might be pregnant. I found out after the breakup that I wasn't. But for that time where I wasn't certain, I was hoping ... even praying that I wasn't pregnant. I was relieved when I knew I wasn't. At the time, I didn't know whether I was relieved because I didn't want *his* baby—the baby of a married man—or because I didn't want kids at all. All I knew was that I was relieved. That relief quickly turned into guilt. A part of me felt like I had willed my body into not being pregnant—like I had been, but that I had forced my body to reconsider. I know that doesn't make any sense, but that knowledge never made it any easier. So, to answer your question, no. I have never had an abortion or miscarriage, but I'd be lying if I told you I hadn't felt like I had."

A quiet pause hung in the air between them when Hannah finished speaking. She looked imperceptibly out the open window and into the warm distance beyond. "Why did you ask?" she said as she came out of the past, and returned her attention to the counselor.

The old man squinted once more as he looked at her. "I'm trying to understand why you would agree to participate in a non-surgical surrogacy. I thought that if you had lost a child in the past, that the desire to 'replace' the child you lost might motivate you to help a couple to avoid the kind of emptiness you may have experienced as a result. I don't understand your motivation."

Hannah smiled in response, and the sunlight coming from the window lit her face and gave her pregnant glow an even warmer appearance. "My work is very important to me," she began. "I had run out of ideas to write about. I had no inspiration for my next piece of work. So, I hoped that I could find inspiration in being a surrogate. Surrogacy would allow me to experience pregnancy, motherhood, even love, and I had hoped those experiences would give me the inspiration I needed for a new show."

"And did it?" asked the counselor.

Hannah nodded slowly to herself, but her head rocked to one side as she did. "I think so. It's hard to tell. I've certainly written and composed more than I could have hoped for since we started the arrangement, but in truth, most of my writing began before I even fell pregnant. Since I discovered we'd conceived, I haven't written as much as I had thought I would. Sometimes I think it's because I never had what Ashleigh has—"

"Desmond?" the counselor cut in.

"No," Hannah answered curtly. "That organic desire to be a mother." She continued to finish her interrupted thought. "And because I never had that desire, being pregnant doesn't move me like I think it would move her."

"Then what desires do you have?" the counselor prompted.

Hannah's dangling feet danced above the ground, another smile crossing her lips as she spoke. "I wanted to dance. I wanted to explore the world and reduce what I had seen to music. I wanted to live and be free to do whatever I wanted. And I wanted my work to give those feelings I experienced to other people, to allow them to live. My initial motivation for participating in the arrangement was to continue these things."

The counselor's squinting gaze softened as Hannah spoke. He'd learned something from her answer. "Ms. Lenore, I asked you what desires you *have*, and yet you talk about your desires in the past tense. You told me about the things you 'wanted.' You also described your work as being the 'initial' motivation for your participating in the surrogacy. Was there another motivation? Or, did your motivation changed along the way?"

Hannah's placid expression showed signs of discomfort around the edges. She didn't realize that she had spoken in the past tense. She had also never considered the possibility that she might have unconsciously had another motivation for her participation in the arrangement, or that motivation might have changed during it.

Sensing her discomfort, the counselor asked a less rhetorical question. "Hannah, if the desires you talked about were past desires, then what do you desire now? You mentioned that you had hoped that experiencing pregnancy, motherhood, and love would give you the inspiration you sought for your work. Are these things you simply want, irrespective of your work?"

Hannah's mind rewound time. Her lip twisted as she remembered her interview with Katan outside of her most recent show in New York. Remembered the way he had seen right through her and given life to her fear of never finding love. "I want …" she began hesitantly. "I want what I've never been able to find, or perhaps what never found me. I want love. I want what Ashleigh has when she talks about having a baby. I want to feel what I see when Desmond looks at Ashleigh. And if I'm really honest, I want to feel that for myself, not for my work. I didn't realize it until now, but I guess part of my motivation was the hope that this baby would give me the love I want to feel."

The counselor watched as Hannah discovered and examined these feelings for the first time. "Have you ever felt that before?" he asked. "Have you ever loved, or felt the kind of love you desire?"

Hannah's eyes drifted and hovered absently over the seat vacated by Desmond. "Perhaps," she whispered shyly. "I don't know."

The counselor shifted in his seat, and for the first time, he showed some body language that wasn't carefully controlled. He looked almost uncomfortable. "Ms. Lenore, what I have to tell you is not easy for me to say, but it is my duty to say it nonetheless. I believe that everyone deserves to love in this life, to know what it is to give it and receive it. True love is never unrequited. However, as a surrogate, you must understand that you have committed the child in your womb to Ashleigh, and you must respect that Desmond is her husband. It is my sincere hope that you find the kind of love your heart desires. It is also my hope that you do not try to find it with either Desmond or the baby, for neither belong to you."

Hannah nodded unconsciously, not really hearing the counselor's words. She was still processing the revelation their conversation had brought to her consciousness. The counselor hid his face once more behind his pyramid fingers. "That is all I have for you," he said heavily. "I wish you every happiness, Ms. Lenore. You may leave when you are ready."

Hannah looked behind her at the door to the lobby before turning back to the counselor. "Am I allowed to ask questions?" she asked cautiously.

The counselor smiled his scar-like smile once more. It was rare that his clients felt comfortable or bold enough to ask their own questions of him. "Of course," he said cheerfully. "I will answer as best I can."

Hannah paused as she organized her thoughts enough to form a question. "Are you married?" The counselor nodded, and his smile broadened wide enough to show yellowing teeth for the first time. "Fifty-two years," he said with pride. "I have the best marriage in the world. Married over fifty years. I have loved my wife with all my heart every single day and remained utmost faithfully hers. Like I said Ms. Lenore, the heart only has room for one, and she was my one. She's actually quite a big fan of your work."

Hannah smiled, flattered. Her smile faded as she bit her lip nervously and prepared her second question. "I have one more question," she began. Something the counselor had said earlier had bothered her when she was waiting outside in the lobby. She leaned forward in her seat, conscious of the life inside of her.

"You said that we were not the first non-surgical surrogates to come and see you. What happened to the ones before us?"

The counselor's controlled expression failed him as his eyebrows pinched slightly into a small frown. He waited a moment, carefully considering his response. "I can't discuss my other clients, Ms. Lenore. Doctor-patient privilege," he said mechanically.

"Oh," said Hannah, visibly deflated. "I had hoped that if they were okay at the end of it, then it might mean that we will be too. Things have got pretty messy, and if what you've said is true, then this is only the beginning." She pushed herself up from the chair as she made her way to leave. The sunlight passed over her face, and its absence darkened her already crestfallen eyes.

The counselor looked up at her as she rose, and he sighed, deciding to give her some final measure of reassurance before her departure. "I can tell you that they're all living happily in Massachusetts—husband, wife, mother, and son—all of them. All of them just fine."

The corners of Hannah's lips rose slightly in a small smile, but the shadows in her eyes persisted. "That's wonderful," she offered, trying to sound hopeful. "Thank you for sharing that." With the small amount of hope restored to her, she rose fully from her seat and placed a hand on her stomach. "Please give my best regards to your wife."

The counselor watched as Hannah walked on soft steps out of his office, and he buried his face in his hands when the door closed fully behind her. He thought of his previous non-surgical surrogate clients, and when he remembered what became of them, he wondered whether he did the right thing in lying to Hannah. He always hated lying.

As dusk fell a few hours later, the counselor walked the familiar route through the cemetery next to a church he no longer visited. When he reached his wife's grave, he knelt down painfully on knees that ached under his own weight and lovingly stroked his wife's headstone. He pulled up the chair he left against the tree by her grave and sat down wearily.

"You'll never guess who I met today, sweetheart," he said sweetly. As the sun faded behind him in the distance, he began to tell his wife about his day, just as he had done every day for almost fifty years.

CHAPTER 16

SEX WITH STRANGERS

Desmond paced back and forth rigidly in his living room. He checked the clock for the third time in as many minutes. *She should be home soon.* He watched the minute hand tick one stroke deeper into the evening. Ashleigh had gone out alone after the session with the marriage counselor. She had said she wanted to be alone to process everything the counselor had told her.

Desmond looked at the small suitcase he had packed, and fought the urge to pack some more things. He had packed a few clothes and essentials into a suitcase, just in case Ashleigh ordered him out of their house. He glanced at the clock once more and swore at himself. He was waiting for his wife to come home so that he could tell her about what had happened on his final night with Hannah—about what he did, and what he had felt. His heart renewed its racing as he heard the front door unlock. He had spent hours trying to think of what to say, and he still hadn't managed to find the words. His mind began to race as he heard the sound of Ashleigh's footsteps inside the house. *Oh God, what am I going to say? What is she going to say? Is she going to leave me? Where would I go? What's going to happen to the baby? Oh God, here she comes.* His final racing thought became a prayer, *God, help me!*

Ashleigh came into view as she turned the corner and entered their living room. Her soft smile vanished when she saw

Desmond standing in the middle of the room. She looked him up and down, immediately sensing that something was off. His blue eyes seemed locked on her face, yet unable to meet her eyes, and his body was awkwardly rigid, locked in a furtive stance.

Something in the corner of her eye caught her attention, and she turned briefly to see a small, but bulky suitcase set on the floor to the side of the room. She drew a deep breath. "Hi, honey," she said with skeptical gaiety. "What's the suitcase for?" She had entered their home in a good mood, maybe even a hopeful mood—a mood that was rare enough these days that she wasn't prepared to have it taken from her so easily.

Desmond closed his eyes, tilted his head to one side and rubbed his forehead with one of his hands. An awkward silence hung between them as he searched painstakingly for the right words. When the right words didn't come to him, he spoke with the first words that came to his head. "Can we sit?"

Unsure of whether she wanted to be seated so close to him, Ashleigh obliged her husband and sidled silently into a chair at their dining table.

Desmond sat on another side of the table so that he sat diagonally from her. After a moment of looking down at the tabletop, he finally brought his gaze to meet hers. His eyes seemed more focused as he examined her face, and as she sat patiently, waiting for Desmond to collect himself, she could tell that he was slowly becoming more present.

During the time that she had all but forced him to sleep with Hannah, Ashleigh had watched as Desmond warred within himself, and deteriorated as his conscience was constantly racked and battered with guilt. The guilt-ridden and hollow version of her husband had slowly disappeared after Hannah announced her pregnancy, though it had suddenly returned and found a seat across from her. She forced a weak smile and extended her hand on the table. Her hand reached for Desmond's.

Her forehead creased slightly at the effort of maintaining her calm expression. "Des, it's okay."

Desmond seemed to awaken at the gesture, and his eyes showed a mixture of surprise and hurt. He grabbed his wife's hand. He squeezed it hard as he tried to wring out what might be the last measure of warmth he'd ever feel from his wife. His first words choked him as he tried to speak through the knot in his throat. The reassurance of his wife's hand in his gave him strength, and his voice broke free. "Ashleigh," he said, seemingly short of breath, "there was a time when I believed that I was incapable of cheating on you. Completely incapable, because I loved you with every piece of me, and the idea of sharing any piece of me with another person horrified me. That was, in part, why the arrangement with Hannah was so difficult for me."

Ashleigh's mind briefly flicked over the memory of her own feelings throughout the arrangement, and she consciously buried them, so that she could focus on her husband's.

Desmond sighed deeply, and it came out in shaking breaths. His heart broke as Ashleigh gave his hand a reassuring squeeze, and he looked deeply into her brown eyes on last time, hoping that his mind would remember what it looked and felt like to have her love reflected in them. He felt tears brimming in his own eyes, and he fought to get his confession out before he found himself completely overwhelmed.

"I cheated on you, Ashleigh." His words fell despondently into the empty room surrounding them.

Ashleigh reflexively yanked her hand away from his grasp, and her face showed the pain of betrayal. Desmond continued, his discarded hand still laid between them. "The last night I spent with Hannah was different than the others. I slept with her because I wanted to, not because I had to."

Ashleigh's eyes were wide, and she looked heavenward as she tried to fight back the tears brimming in her eyes.

"I can't honestly say that it was only because of the alcohol. The part of me that should have known that I was doing something wrong didn't stop me, and I can only assume that it was because that part wasn't there that night. I'm so s—"

Ashleigh held up a hand and gestured for Desmond to stop speaking. She held her other beneath her nose as she tried to stifle the crying. "Stop," she managed to get out. She turned her body away from him and leaned forward as though kicked in the stomach. Taking a deep breath, she turned, and returned her gaze to Desmond without wiping the tears from her face. "I know," she confessed softly.

Desmond wiped at the tears that had fallen down his cheeks. "What?" he asked with confusion. "How?"

"There were photos in a magazine, Des. I know that look on your face and everything it means. I know what happened because I know you, because I know my husband."

"But you didn't say anything?" said Desmond, the inflection in his voice suggesting that his words were a question, though more a question to himself than to her.

Ashleigh sighed wearily. "I wanted you to tell me. I needed to hear it from you," she confessed softly. The silence in the room was thick as husband and wife stared at the empty table space between them. Ages passed around them in silence as they wondered how they had come so far from the couple they used to be.

When Desmond spoke, his voice was low and husky. "I'm sorry, Ashleigh. I'm so sorry."

He looked up to see her staring blankly at the table and shaking her head slowly. "No," she said without looking up. "I don't want your apology." Desmond feared what this would mean before his wife continued, "I have felt ... betrayed ... sickened ... and hurt by the fallout of all the things that have passed between us since my infertility diagnosis. And yet as much as I have tried, I haven't really allowed myself to feel these things as though you caused them, because you didn't. I did. It wasn't enough for me that Hannah should be our surrogate. I had to have you sleep with her too. It didn't matter, or it didn't matter *enough*, that forcing you to sleep with her was tearing you apart. Tearing *us* apart. I feel these things because of me, and even now as you tell me that you cheated, I blame myself. I blame myself because I forced you into her bed, and I can't really be so angry with you if somewhere along the way you went there willingly."

"Yes, you can!" interrupted Desmond. "This was *my* fault, Ashleigh. All mine."

Ashleigh sighed and shook her head absentmindedly once more. "I suppose it doesn't matter whose fault it is, Des. It's done." She paused and looked at him pointedly, staring into his eyes with a fierce, piercing gaze. "It *is* done, isn't it?"

"Yes," Desmond replied firmly. "Never again."

"Do you still want her?"

"No."

"Do you have feelings for her?"

"No."

Ashleigh continued to stare into her husband's eyes, searching hard to see if a different truth was hidden within. She leaned back and shook her head once more. "I don't want your apology for this Desmond, but I do want something."

"I'll do anything," Desmond replied sincerely. "Just say the word."

Ashleigh pushed herself back from the table and came to a stand. She took a step toward her husband, grabbed his T-shirt by the collar with both hands, and lifted him out of his chair. "Make love to me, Desmond. I want to *feel* you. Make love to me. Not like your wife, but like a woman you have to have.

Make me feel wanted. Do you understand? Make love to me, and let's put all of this behind us."

Desmond nodded with tears in his eyes. He kissed her deeply, lifted her easily off her feet, and began to carry her to their bedroom. She couldn't help but start crying again as she felt Desmond's lips search hers with loving kisses. *He's here!* she thought to herself with relief as the bedroom door closed behind them.

Ashleigh reluctantly let her hands unclasp behind Desmond's neck as he lowered her onto their bed. He rose again in front of her and pulled his shirt over his head. The dim light in the room cast dark shadows across the fiber of his every muscle, though Ashleigh barely even registered his shirtlessness. She breathed in slowly to compose herself as her aching heart raced painfully in her chest. Her breaths came out shakily. She reached out to her husband and gestured for him to join her on the bed.

As soon as he was within her reach, Ashleigh pulled him tightly toward her, and she pressed all of his weight onto her as she hugged him tightly. His arms wrapped around her so that they hid the space between her body and the mattress, and he hugged her back. The tears that she had tried to control a moment earlier, the same tears that had started on the stairs only moments ago, came flooding out once again. Ashleigh sobbed against her husband's exposed shoulder. Partly in grief, mourning the love lost between them in recent months. Partly in fear, scared of the hope he brought to her with his embrace. But mostly, inexplicably, from the realization that the words that echoed in her mind were true: *He's here, and he's all mine!*

She continued to sob into her husband's shoulder, and the harder she cried, the tighter he pulled her toward him. In this moment, Ashleigh lost her guard. As her walls came crashing down, she exposed to him the measure of grief, pain, and loss that she had walled within herself and hidden from him.

She had let him see snippets of this pain in the moments that she'd lost control of the anger that lived within it, as it broke through small cracks and lashed out at him, only to be brought back under her control and forced to languish within the confines of her body. But now, cradled in the safety of her husband's embrace, the need for those walls disappeared, and they disappeared with it.

Ashleigh eventually peeled her face away from Desmond's shoulder and looked up at him with puffy, bloodshot eyes. He didn't say anything. She didn't want him to. What words could describe what she'd endured in his absence? What words could fix it? His warm lips touched her face as he kissed the lines that her tears had drawn down her cheeks. He traced those lines as if each streak were an open wound, as if his lips held the power, if not to heal them, then at least to close them and stop the bleeding. Ashleigh grabbed the side of her husband's face to bring it in front of hers. The rough stubble of his cheeks rubbed against her soft hands as he looked down at her with attentive blue eyes. She whispered softly as she returned his gaze, "I've missed you."

Ashleigh raised her leg to change position just as Desmond was climbing onto the bed again after removing his trousers. The knee of her lifted leg connected with his temple. The jarring strike, the stunned look on his face, and the unfamiliarity of the clumsiness between them combined to make her laugh. She giggled and pulled her laughing husband closer toward her. It was the first time in many months that laughter had visited their bedroom.

The laughter continued as they struggled to find a rhythm with each other. Desmond had lost his balance and fell into her awkwardly at the moment of penetration. At another point, their heads collided with an audible *clunk* as they motioned into one another. She had finally burst into hysterics when Desmond mistook her saying, "You're on my hair," as "Oh yeah, right there." None of this was what she had had in mind when she told him to make her feel wanted, but it did better than that. It made her feel at home and in love. The space around them quieted in the darkness.

As their laughter subsided, their bodies rediscovered their rhythm. Their souls resumed the connection recently broken, and they moved together as the rest of the world floated away in the darkness. The reconnection shocked her consciousness. She found herself barely breathing, afraid that even the faintest noise might unthread the fragile fabric that had entwined them. To Ashleigh, even the mattress beneath her had floated away with the rest of the world, and she hung suspended in space with her husband, all at once hopeful, devoted, and caught up in the moment. Her chest felt fit to burst, and breathless, she refused to adjust her breathing. Their matching, racing heartbeats were the only sounds in their floating darkness. With every movement inside of her, she felt Desmond pick up another scattered piece of their broken marriage.

And yet, despite Ashleigh's best efforts, the floating, rapturous, and suffocating illusion was shattered with a single thought that flooded her mind when finally forced to breathe: *I wonder if he's thinking about her.* The thought pulled her consciousness like gravity and threw her back into their bedroom, back into the light. The thread that had reconnected them was unraveling. *Even though he's picking up the pieces, will the picture still look the same? Will pieces be missing?*

Her body fell out of rhythm with his. He didn't notice. *He must be thinking about her. Stop it! Just stop it, Ashleigh. Stop ruining this moment!* She fought hard against her consciousness and closed her eyes, trying once more to get back to that floating paradise. She could feel his eyes on her body and suddenly found herself wishing he'd closed his eyes too. *She has a better body than me. How could he not notice? Is he even attracted to me anymore? God, why can't I stop thinking about her?* Only moments earlier she had been enjoying the laughter, enjoying her husband's presence, and enjoying the feelings that came with their attempts to find their way back to intimacy. But now, the harder she fought to get back to that feeling, the faster she was fading out of their connection. *Is this how it's going to be from now on? Will we ever get back to how we were, or do we take what's left and try to move on?* Ashleigh gave up on trying to get back to the connection she'd held onto breathlessly, and when Desmond finally stiffened and groaned in completion, she was just glad it was over.

In the early light of the next morning, Ashleigh looked up at her husband as he lay naked and sleeping beside her. She had slept in his arms as they cuddled together throughout the night, and she had awoken before him. Ashleigh peered through the morning light as she tried to get a better sense of his features in the gloom. She quickly realized that what she felt as she looked upon him was no longer hatred or something akin to hatred, which is what she had felt each time she looked at him over the past few months.

She lay in silence, continuing to look at him as she tried to put a name to what she was feeling. She lay staring at eyelids that hid blue eyes that used to make her go weak in the knees. His scent permeated the air around her, and his familiar warmth radiated into the sheets she lay upon. She had expected that their lovemaking the night before would make her feel closer to him, would perhaps allow her to look upon him and see her incorruptible and good-natured husband, unspoiled by the events of recent months. It hadn't.

Even though the Desmond lying next to her was the same in all aesthetic qualities, even though everything about being cuddled against him in the morning had a familiar feeling to it, she couldn't help but feel that the man lying next to her failed to fill the hole her husband left in her bed just a few short months ago. She realized that whatever she was feeling was not hatred. *After all*, she thought to herself as Desmond stirred beside her, *it's very hard to hate a stranger.*

CHAPTER 17

TODD & KATELYNN

Dusk had fallen in Ellicott City, but a warm summer breeze still survived the darkness. The breeze caressed Desmond, Ashleigh, and Hannah as they stood outside of the community center. Desmond squinted in appraisal as he looked up at the brown blocky building. "Looks like a dump" he said flatly.

Ashleigh drew a deep breath and let out a sigh as she tried to remain optimistic about the counselor's recommendation. The three of them stepped inside the building and were forced to shield their eyes as they adjusted to the harsh fluorescent overhead lights that lit a hallway. The dull green laminate flooring lead to various rooms that branched off from both sides of the hallway, each room hosting a different kind of support group according to the directory on the wall.

"Third on the left," Hannah advised as she read the directory. "Is anyone else excited about this?"

Ashleigh allowed Desmond to take her hand in his own and the three walked down the hall to their room.

As they stepped into the room, the first thing Hannah noticed was that they were the oldest by several years. They would come to learn that with all IVF activity suspended across the country due to the Poe case, couples desperate for children were willing to pay quite a lot of money for healthy surrogates, and many young women with limited options were ready and willing to give up nine months, and the freedom of their bodies to cash in on the seemingly limited opportunity. Upholstered chairs were arranged into a crude circle in the large room. Hannah, Desmond, and Ashleigh took a seat, Desmond sitting between his wife and friend, and the meeting began. A middle-aged man leaned forward on the edge of his chair and identified himself as the meeting administrator.

"Good evening, everyone. Thanks for coming. My name is Shaun. As you're aware, this is a support group for surrogate mothers. If you are not a surrogate and you're looking for the support group for your own pregnancy, please move to the room down the hall and two doors on the right."

When no one in the room moved, he continued in a rehearsed, disinterested drawl. "All right then, welcome. Let me start by saying that the purpose of this group is to assist surrogates throughout their pregnancy. We do this by supporting each other, and by supporting each other, we also find support ourselves. I want everyone to take turns introducing themselves, and then share something that you're currently struggling with, or concerned about. This helps to foster vulnerability and trust within the group and allows these bi-weekly sessions to be more productive. We'll do this at least once each trimester. You, in the pink dress," he pointed at a young girl seated next to Ashleigh. "Please go first. Tell us who you are and share something you're struggling with." The girl was young, in her early twenties at best. The pink dress she wore was rather faded, and it seemed the young girl had tried to dress up for this first meeting. She wore a *Hello, My Name Is* Jen sticker on the bust of her dress. She shook her head shyly and muttered, "Please, not first."

Hannah raised her hand eagerly. "I'll go first."

The shy girl across from her mouthed the words 'thank you,' and Hannah winked at her in return as she lowered her hand. "My name is Hannah. I'm the surrogate for my friends

Ashleigh and Desmond here. I'm about twelve weeks along and, though I haven't shared this with anyone yet, I am *struggling*. So far, I've been pretty wary about expressing how shitty I feel now that I'm pregnant. You know, there are people out there who are struggling to conceive or can't have children, and I don't want to offend anyone, but if there's an appropriate place to talk about these things, then this is it."

Hannah glanced briefly at the faces watching her as she spoke to make sure she hadn't offended anyone. Seeing no one's expression change, she continued. "It's hard! I'm a bawling mess one minute and crying for no reason, then I'm a psycho to the people trying to help me or cheer me up, and then I'm back to crying again, usually because I've been mean. And then there are the hormones! Damned hormones! I am craving random things all the time—things I don't even like! Sometimes I crave them so badly I can almost smell them, and then the smell makes me feel sick. I feel like I need a nap *all the time*, and that's somewhat inconvenient because of the morning sickness, so I'm desperately in need of a snooze when I'm in the middle of vomiting. Sometimes I try to rest my head on the toilet bowl and sleep, hoping that if I vomit in my sleep, it will just go into the toilet. And my boobs hurt." Hannah briefly paused as she pressed a hand into one of her breasts. "My boobs hurt a lot. Sometimes they hurt in a nice way. Not now though. Now they just hurt like a bitch." Hannah sighed. "That felt good ... and now I want asparagus!" Hannah threw her arms up in the air in exasperation before putting a hand beneath her nose to stifle the imagined smell.

The other women seated in the circle began to laugh, clap, and cheer. When the low cheers and applause had ceased, the administrator spoke up and addressed the group, "Thank you for your candor, Hannah, but that's not quite what I had in mind when I asked everyone to share."

Another girl in the circle cleared her throat pointedly and grabbed the group's attention, "Shaun, unless you're pregnant too, shut up. You don't understand."

Shaun leaned back in his chair with a sardonic smile across his face. "All right Nicole, why don't you share, then?"

Nicole shook her head and returned the smile, "No need. I think Goldilocks here just about said it all."

Shaun made his way around the circle once more until he came back to the girl in the pink dress. "Are you ready?" Shaun asked the girl.

She nodded shyly. She sat upright, but continued to look down as she spoke. "My name is Jen. I'm nineteen, and I'm about nineteen weeks along. I was … um … I was dating a not-so-nice guy. He wasn't good to me, or even nice to me really, but I loved him, or I thought I loved him. I don't know. But when I found out I was pregnant, I knew my baby wouldn't be safe if I stayed with him, so I left. He didn't seem to care, even when I told him about the baby. I can't look after a baby on my own; I know that. So, when I have the baby I'm giving it to my older sister and her husband. She can't have kids." She looked up when she finished speaking, and her eyes scanned those looking at her for judgment.

"And…" Shaun broke in and made a prompting gesture with his hands.

"And what?"

"What's something you're struggling with?" Shaun intoned.

Jen looked confused. "Everything. I'm struggling with everything. I'm nineteen and pregnant to a man who used to beat me. Everything is a struggle. Everything's always been a struggle."

Shaun furrowed his lips and forced himself to look away. He recognized that Jen's circumstances didn't quite meet the definition of surrogacy. However, even though the rules dictated that he remove her from the group, he didn't have the heart to eject the poor girl. Jen looked visibly relieved when he mumbled his thanks to her, and moved to the next girl in the circle—Ashleigh.

"Hi everyone, my name is Ashleigh, and Hannah is my surrogate. We found out a few months ago that I can't have kids. After I recovered from that news, Hannah generously offered to carry our baby. There are a lot of things that I've struggled with in this pregnancy." She glanced briefly at Desmond. "However, if I'm honest with myself, the thing I struggle with the most is the thought that maybe I'll want another baby after this one. We've gone through hell just to be pregnant with this first child, and I'm afraid that once it's here, I'll want another. Maybe it's selfish, but I'm afraid that I'll be willing to go through everything all over again to have another baby, but that I'll be alone in that desire."

Hannah could feel Ashleigh looking over at her as she finished speaking. Ashleigh's confession had surprised her, and she couldn't bring herself to meet the imploring gaze she expected to find if she looked up and faced her. She was thankful when one of the girls at the other end of the circle spoke up, breaking the flow of the attendees speaking in turn.

"Excuse me," a girl with tattoos over her arms and pink-dyed hair addressed Ashleigh in a thick Baltimorean accent. "I'm sorry, I must'a misunderstood. Are you saying that you're the receiver of that chick's baby?" She gestured at Hannah with a nod of her head.

Ashleigh tore her eyes away from Hannah's averted face and turned to the girl addressing her. "I'm sorry, what do you mean by 'receiver'?"

The girl seemed slightly irritated, "I mean are you gonna be the mom for the baby she's gonna have? Will you *receive* it when it's born?"

Ashleigh turned back to Hannah briefly, who nodded in affirmation. She turned back to the irritated girl. "Yes, that's the plan."

The girl threw her hands up in the air in annoyance. "What the hell, Shaun? What's she doin' 'ere?"

Ashleigh turned to Shaun. "I'm sorry, is there a problem?"

Shaun groaned and turned to Ashleigh. "Here's the thing, Ashleigh…Normally we don't allow what the group calls 'receivers'—the women expected to *receive* the baby when it's born—to be part of this group. The group is supposed to be a safe space for the surrogates to share their feelings, and this can often involve the expression of resentment or jealousy for the woman who is going to … take their baby away."

Ashleigh was confused. "But the doctor told us to come here! It was his suggestion. I just figured—"

Shaun had his hands out and was ushering Ashleigh to stop speaking as he interrupted her. "Yes, yes, yes, Ashleigh, I'm well aware of your referral. It's just that some of the other women might not feel comfortable—"

"He's right," Jen accidentally muttered under her breath. She quickly clasped both hands over her mouth as all faces in the room turned to her. Unclasping her hands, she continued, "I'm so sorry. You seem like a real nice lady, and I'm real sorry you can't have kids. It's just that I don't know that I'd feel comfortable talking about my receiver, even though she's my sister, knowing that there is a receiver sitting right here with us. Do you understand?" A murmur of concurrence filtered through the room.

Ashleigh's eyes turned wide in confused panic, and she looked to Desmond.

Desmond, next in turn to speak in the circle, took to his feet and cleared his throat. "Hi, my name is Desmond," he began firmly. A polite hush quieted the murmuring room as each attendee was distracted by the quick resumption of the introduction protocol. "Ashleigh is my wife, and Hannah is my surrogate. I understand that some of you might take umbrage with the fact that Ashleigh is going to receive the child when he or she is born. I can appreciate that. I can also appreciate that you might feel uncomfortable talking about your receivers with one sitting close by. However, what I will ask all of you to appreciate is that it took a great deal from the three of us just to be here tonight. My wife can't have children. In our desperation for a child, we sought out a surrogate, and Hannah very generously stepped in as our non-surgical surrogate."

Desmond looked firmly into eyes that judged him as he continued to speak. "I'm sure that many of you can imagine what this arrangement has done to Ashleigh, to myself, to our marriage, and to Hannah. It hasn't been easy, and by all reports, it is only going to get harder. We have come to this group to seek the support we need through this process. So, what am I struggling with? I am struggling with the idea that if you don't accept my wife into this group simply because she's a receiver, then it may spell the end of my marriage, and destroy the future home for my child."

Desmond looked down at Ashleigh as he concluded. "My wife is a strong woman—she'd have to be to endure everything it has taken just for us to be here tonight. I am confident that she can endure what you have to say about your receivers without taking it personally. Her presence here—*our* presence—should not detract from your own need for support, and I trust that we can all manage just fine if we remember the purpose of this group." Desmond sat down and held Ashleigh's hand.

It was the girl with tattoos who spoke first. "I know who you are, Mr. Mathews. Big, fancy attorney helping that Poe chick, right?"

Desmond nodded, and the girl threw her head back, laughing in disbelief before she continued in a mocking tone.

"You're such a hypocritical piece of shit! Have you noticed how you and your wife are the only ones here wearing wedding rings? That me and the other girls don't have no one here to support us like your surrogate does? It's because, 'cept for Jenny 'ere," she said pointing at Jen with her thumb, "rest of us are paid surrogates. Pay jobs. Rich, fancy people like yourselves want a kid and will pay real handsome-like for it while the clinics are shut. We need this group 'cause we don't get no support elsewhere. But hey, me and other girls wouldn't be knocked up and making so much bank if not for your girl Poe, so I guess we owe you that. S'long as you three don't get in the way of the support we actually need, y'all can stay."

The tattooed young woman looked around the circle of surrogates. If she was searching for resistance from anyone else, she didn't find it. She looked back at Desmond and challenged his casual, steely gaze. "Make no mistake though, big shot, I don't like you, and as much as I have you to thank for the opportunity to lease out my womb to the highest bidder, I don't owe you shit. Understand?"

Desmond nodded sternly once more, and her grimace softened to a smile that would have been convincingly sweet if not for the words that followed it. "Good. Now get lost, old boy."

She gestured at the door with a nod of her head. "Your face is annoying me, and I wanna talk to your girls without you."

Shaun interceded angrily. "Eileen! You're not in charge here. I am! You don't get to choose who stays and goes. I do! I won't let you boss everyone around, the way you did during your last pregnancy!"

Eileen leaned back in her chair and shrugged her tattooed shoulders. "Settle down, Shaun. I just don't want to look at him right now is all. I'm all hormonal and pissy, and his stupid face is distracting. I've said my piece, and I'm fine for them to stay. We'll be all fine next session. Best of friends, scouts honor."

Eileen held three fingers up in a mocking gesture of the scout's credo.

Shaun was about to speak, but Desmond cut in first. "It's fine. I don't want our presence to upset the group. I'll wait outside for tonight's session." He looked back at Eileen, "Then we're good?"

Eileen nodded once in resignation.

"Good." Desmond rose and proceeded out the door as the group began a muttered murmur behind him in the background. He stepped out into the fluorescent hallway once more and leaned against the wall next to the open doorway he'd just walked through. He closed his eyes and pinched the bridge of his nose. "Why is everything so damned difficult?" he groaned to himself.

"I wouldn't take it personally," a voice sounded to his left. "There's a lot of fresh faces in there, but she's gone through this before. I think she's just being protective."

Desmond opened his eyes and was startled to see a man leaning against the opposite side of the door frame just a few feet away from him. He hadn't noticed him when he'd stepped outside. The man was pale and lanky. His eyes were sunken and carried deep, dark bags beneath them. He was completely bald but for a few wispy patches of dark hair, and he looked deathly skinny. His pale, lanky, and skinny features combined to give him a sickly appearance.

Despite his somewhat creepy appearance, his gray eyes were friendly, and his broad smile gave life to his hollow cheeks. Desmond couldn't help but return the smile. "You were listening?"

The lanky man nodded his head, and it seemed to move his entire body. "Name's Todd," said the man as he extended a skeletal hand. The skin over the hand was pale to the point of translucence, making his blue veins visible.

"Desmond," he replied as he took Todd's hand and noted the weakness in his grip. Desmond leaned off the wall and peered into the room full of surrogates. "Which one is yours?" he asked.

Todd smiled again. "None of them." Anticipating Desmond's confusion, he elaborated. "I'm supposed to be in the cancer support group down the hall, but it's too damned depressing, and it gets me down. Take a walk with three depressed people, and I guarantee you'll become the fourth! In there, it's all death and fear, so I find it nice every so often to come and stand by the surrogacy support group. Here it's all hope and life. You didn't think I was naturally this handsome, did you?" The joke seemed to break the momentary awkwardness Todd had sensed from Desmond. "How does a non-surgical surrogacy work, anyway?" Todd asked.

"I had sex with the surrogate," Desmond answered flatly.

"Really? That sucks," Todd replied equally as flatly.

Desmond raised an eyebrow in surprise. "You're the first one who's said so. No one else I've told understood. They either think it's awesome, telling me I should try and 'make the most of it,' or 'stretch it out,' or 'have a threesome.' Or, they think it's disgusting and label me a cheater."

"Sheesh," Todd said as he looked upward, the fluorescent lights casting ghostly shadows across his sunken features. "There's nothing I wouldn't do or give for my wife, so I can understand why you did it. I wouldn't have enjoyed it either."

Desmond was dumbstruck. He recalled in vivid detail how co-workers and friends he'd told about the arrangement had reacted to him. Some had lauded him, others derided, but no one had ever really understood. He looked across at Todd. *Finally, someone who understands!* He found himself smiling. The two men listened in silence as the women inside the room continued the support session. Hannah was back to the subject of cravings once more, and told the other girls about her newfound love for Ledo pizza.

"Hey, Todd," Desmond began.

Todd turned his attention to Desmond. "Yup?"

"Do you like Ledo pizza?"

"Never tried it."

"Are you kidding me? Ledo Pizza, the pillar of Maryland pizza? The epitome of the perfect slice? 'Never cuts corners'?"

"'Fraid not."

Desmond shook his head. "Unbelievable." The men continued to talk as the conversation inside the support room rattled on behind them.

Fifteen minutes later, the two men heard the surrogacy support session wrapping up as the women repeated a support mantra dictated by Shaun.

"I'd best get back to my room before Katelynn catches me out here again. She thinks it's creepy," Todd said as he pushed himself off the wall.

"Was good talking to you," Desmond said as Todd began a slow walk down the green-tiled hallway.

Todd called back over his shoulder, "You too, bud."

The hallway soon filled with people pouring out of their classes. Eileen exited first, spotted Desmond, and called out to him, "Hey you!"

Desmond turned around and prepared for a fresh barrage of taunts or insults. Eileen came and stood before him. Standing up, she was noticeably very short and small. People exiting their classes and sessions filtered through the hallway around them. "I'm sorry I was a bitch in there. Hannah was telling the truth: hormones do throw you all over the place and can make you crazy. I spoke with your girls. They say you just came into all of this Poe nonsense in the middle of the shit storm."

"It's fine. We're good."

"Sweet. All us girls are going out soon. So, you'd better be good to Ashleigh and Hannah, else I'll hear all about it." Eileen winked at Desmond and faded into the crowd bustling around them.

He spotted Ashleigh and Hannah waiting for him near the exit, and they left the building as he joined them.

"Everything okay?" Hannah asked, as they stepped into the warm night. "We spoke to Eileen inside. Her sister can't have kids because of the Poe case, and it caused a bit of a falling out between them because she wouldn't act as her sister's surrogate unless she got paid. Said she didn't want to miss out on the money she could make being someone else's surrogate, so the case is a touchy subject for her."

"What'd I miss?" Desmond asked, trying to change the subject. "What'd you all talk about while I was gone?"

"Most of it was about your case, to be honest," Ashleigh replied. She bit her lip nervously. "It got a bit heated in there at times." She stopped walking and grabbed Desmond's arm to make him stop beside her. "Des, there's a lot of people out there really upset about your case. Eileen recognized you immediately, and so I have to imagine that other people know who you are now." She looked around nervously. "Is being involved in this case putting you in any sort of danger?"

Hannah's eyes reflected the same concern, and she caressed her belly with one hand.

CHAPTER 18

INSPIRATION

Two more months passed, and the hot summer days had given way to lofty breezes that carried fallen leaves through chilled air. Hannah, now twenty weeks pregnant, had rented a hotel room in Baltimore on a long-term basis to stay close to Ashleigh and Desmond throughout the pregnancy.

She had also found an old warehouse in the industrial district around Baltimore Harbor to begin preparing her next show. Developing the show away from New York allowed her to prepare in private, and she delighted at the thought that when she finally announced the premiere, it would come as a shock to the entire industry. Of all of Hannah's remaining dancers, only Jacqui was willing to follow her to Baltimore. While Jacqui was busy recruiting local dancers and setting up the warehouse studio with the appropriate outfit, Hannah was hard at work trying to write the rest of her show. However, but for a few scenes, she had once again hit the wall with a lack of inspiration.

Todd and Desmond had continued to catch up during each of the surrogacy sessions and had quickly formed a friendship. At their last meeting, and after Desmond's incessant nagging, Todd had agreed to come out with him to try Ledo Pizza on the condition that Desmond shut up about it.

They entered the pizzeria through a curtain of air chilled by the overworked air conditioning unit blowing hard overhead.

The air conditioning was unnecessary, as the days had already begun to turn cold, and it chilled Todd to his increasingly exposed bones. His chemotherapy had caused the last tufts of his hair to fall out, and his eyes sported permanent black rings beneath them, giving him an Uncle Fester-esque look.

"I'm confused," Desmond said as he and Todd sat down at a table.

"It's not that confusing."

"You're telling me that you've lived in Maryland your whole life, and you've *never* tried Ledo pizza?"

"I don't see why that's so confusing. Besides, you promised you'd stop talking about it if I came here."

Desmond called a waiter and placed an order for a large cheese pizza with jalapeños.

"How come I've never met your wife?" asked Desmond. "Seems a little weird after all this time that we've never met."

Todd shrugged. "It's hard to find the time, I guess. When she's not working, she's often busy with doctor's appointments and checkups with the pregnancy." Todd noticed Desmond's shocked expression and continued, "Yeah, she's pregnant. I didn't mention that? Oh yeah, she's in the pregnancy support and preparation group at the community center."

"Why don't you attend the classes with her?"

Todd paused. "It's a support group for single mothers. We're preparing for Katelynn to raise the baby on her own."

"I'm sorry."

Todd waved him off. "Don't be. How could you know?" Todd sensed the unasked question and answered flatly, "I have stage three leukemia."

"Shit," said Desmond. "I'm a medical negligence attorney, so I … well, I don't *understand*, but—"

"I know what you mean." Todd cut him off. "I was a veterinarian before I had to stop working. I've seen every kind of cancer in every kind of animal. I know what this is, and that's why we're preparing for Katelynn to … you know. I appreciate it too, by the way, what you were going to say. But you don't have to say anything. In fact, I'd prefer that you didn't. That's actually one of the reasons I like talking to you. Looking the way I do now, it's hard to speak to people. Even talking to people that I know is awful because all they want to talk about is how terrible I look, or how sorry they feel for me. Why the hell would I want to talk about how bald and creepy I look?" Todd laughed and continued, "But you don't. You speak to me like a regular guy, and I appreciate that. In fact, I kind of need it. Even Katelynn has been a bit doom and gloom lately."

"How so? If you don't mind my asking," asked Desmond.

"She keeps bugging me about making these videos for the baby. Kind of like recorded messages in case I die before the birth date. Something like, 'Hello, I'm your dad. I died. Blah, blah, blah.'"

"So why don't you make them?"

Todd smiled, enjoying Desmond's inquisitiveness. "I have reasons. I'm not ready to talk about that stuff just yet."

Desmond nodded in understanding.

"What about you. How's your case going?"

Desmond sat back, a little annoyed. "How do you know about that? How does everyone know?"

Todd smiled. "You're the talk of the community center. Not just because of the case—also for using a non-surgical surrogate, which is just interesting—but mostly because of the case. Still, I recognized you as soon as I saw you in the hallway. Everyone does." Todd nodded toward a couple sitting at another table, and Desmond turned to briefly catch them staring at him and muttering to each other before they looked away.

Todd leaned over the table and spoke a little more softly. "Desmond, you remember OJ's trial, right? OJ is remembered far more for his court case these days than anything he ever did in football. His case got so big that it didn't just make his lawyer famous, it made his lawyer's *kids* famous. I'm not saying that this Poe case is the same, but this is the biggest case in America since the abortion case in the seventies, although Roe had the good sense to use a pseudonym. You shouldn't be surprised if the whole country learns your name or knows what you look like."

Their pizza arrived amid a cloud of steaming melted cheese, but not even Desmond's favorite pizza could dispel the uneasy feeling that Todd's words had brought him.

• • •

A few miles across the city, Hannah was meeting with the other women from the surrogacy support group for a girls' luncheon. Ashleigh wasn't invited. Most of them had swapped stories of the strange and awkward requests they had received from the benefactors of their surrogacies, including Eileen, who shared that her receiver's husband had insisted on administering his sperm sample himself.

They had laughed in hysterical horror as she reenacted the moment, playing both roles. Jen was next, and everyone turned quiet as they expected her to retell the somber tale of how she had got pregnant by her ex forcibly raping her during one of his drunken beatings.

However, Jen was smiling broadly, and her cheeks were flushed pink. "I met someone!" she squealed excitedly. The other women looked at one another and let out a collective, "Woo!" Jen laughed, and continued. "His name is Jason. He's in the army, and he's just got back from a tour overseas. He's ... whoo," Jen fanned herself with her hand, and her cheeks flushed a deeper crimson. "He's a real man. He's big and strong, but so sweet and sincere."

"What does he think about your pregnancy?" Nicole asked excitedly.

Jen's smile fell from her face, and she twisted her hands together. "I haven't told him yet."

"What?" yelled Eileen. "How has he not figured it out yet? You're huge!"

"I am not!" Jen retorted with indignation.

"Fine, well you're not huge, but you're clearly showing. Has he been away on tour so long that he forgot what a woman's body s'posed to look like?" The group gave a shocked giggle.

Jen, visibly uncomfortable, whispered back, "We haven't been physical yet."

"How long have you been seeing him?"

"Almost two months."

"TWO MONTHS?" Eileen sputtered. "By God, woman. If I had a man like the one you described for two months, I'd already be pregnant with the next baby!" The group laughed once more.

"I'm afraid," Jen said, and the laughter stopped. Tears started to appear in her eyes, "Sex doesn't mean to me what it means to all of you. To me, it means being choked to the point of unconsciousness with my last thought being whether he'll let go once I pass out. It's learning how to contour my makeup to cover up the swelling and bruises I'd get for resisting. And it means pain—and not just physical pain." Jen looked down and rubbed her belly. A tear fell onto her slightly bulged stomach and made a tiny wet spot on her loose-fitting dress.

Hannah's voice broke through the silence that followed. "Tell us more about Jason, hon."

Jen looked up and smiled at Hannah, breaking another tear in the process. "He's just so sweet. He asks me how my day was, and surprises me at work with little gifts and notes." She sighed. "That's why I'm so afraid to tell him about the baby."

"Y'know he's gonna find out eventually, right?" Eileen intoned.

"But what if he leaves me?" Jen asked, throwing her hands out.

Eileen shrugged. "What if he wants you to keep it?"

Jen went quiet, suddenly struck by a notion she hadn't previously considered. Eileen noticed Jen's sudden reverie and so turned to Hannah to keep the conversation going, "What 'bout chu, ballerina? How was it for you getting pregnant?"

Hannah laughed and shook her head, sending blonde curls in all directions as she did, "Oh no. We're not going there!"

"Oh, come *on!*" Nicole begged. "That's the whole reason we didn't invite Ashleigh. We're all dying to know what it was like being a non-surgical surrogate. All of our surrogacies came from having sex with an improvised turkey baster. It's hardly interesting stuff, except in Eileen's case with her weirdo." Eileen shot Nicole a dirty look. "Ashleigh's not here. Tell us!"

Hannah looked around nervously. All eyes were on her expectantly, eagerly awaiting more details about a relationship about which they had learned little. "Okay," she said reluctantly. She told the group about how she had known Desmond in college. How she would come to visit him before leaving on her adventures. About how he had rejected her on her final visit, how they had only reconnected after Ashleigh found out about her infertility, and about how Desmond's devotion to Ashleigh had made the sex so horrible in the beginning.

"You mean it got better?" Nicole asked with a wry grin.

Hannah returned an embarrassed smile, and her face flushed at the unwitting confession.

Eileen, now intrigued, beckoned Hannah for more details after their friends had calmed down from all of the laughter that followed.

"It was ... gosh. How do I describe it?" Hannah asked rhetorically as she looked up at the ceiling searching for the words, her fingers unconsciously moving their way to her exposed neck. "It was incredible." She let out a sigh as she let her mind return to that night for the first time. "It was everything you expect sex could be when you first discover sexuality. It was sensual and intimate, scary and exciting, and totally consuming all at once." Her heart started to race in her chest. "There was just something so primal and manly about him that night! You wouldn't know it by looking at him, but he's a hulk of a man under his clothes! I was all over him, and he was ... ugh ... really just about to *take* me, you know what I mean? And then, all of a sudden, it became really sweet. It was adoring, like he lov—" Hannah stopped herself and came back to the present to find all eyes transfixed on her, her friends staring enviously, almost longingly at her. "But," she continued as her memory ticked over from that night to the next morning, "that night should never have happened. At least not like that. When we first started having sex and trying to get pregnant, it was terrible. He loved Ashleigh so much that it ruined him to sleep with another woman. That last night was different though. It was like there was no Ashleigh. Like he was giving his love for her to me. That wasn't something that I was ever meant to see. That belongs to Ashleigh. So, after that night, I told Ashleigh that I was pulling out of the arrangement and wouldn't have sex with Desmond anymore."

"Wait, *what*!?" Nicole exclaimed as she broke free from her lusty stupor. "You mean you wanted out *before* you found out you were pregnant!?"

Hannah bit her lip and nodded, and her friends looked at one another in disbelief.

Jen, breaking out of her own reverie and rejoining the conversation broke in, "Do you ever think about maybe keeping the baby, and running away with him?"

Hannah didn't get to answer as the group erupted in a collective furor, all memory of Hannah's story forgotten. Eileen's steely voice broke through the yells of their other companions, and she raised a pointed finger at Jen. "Now listen here, Jenny. We get that's your baby in your belly, but any talk about keeping the baby is taboo for surrogates. Do you get me? It's hurtful, and we don't wanna think about it. Never again!" She lowered her hand, but maintained eye contact with Jen, who was now shaking slightly with fear.

"I'm sorry" she whimpered as the crowd quieted. "I'm sorry."

Hannah barely registered the voices clamoring around her or Jen's apologetic expression. Her eyes darted among the faces of the other surrogates and her mind ticked over their stories, their reasons for becoming surrogates, and the circumstances that had brought these very different women together. As the other surrogates frowned, yelled, and muttered to one another, Hannah's lips broke into a smile. She had found another piece of inspiration she needed for her show.

• • •

Ashleigh angrily pressed the red button on her phone to cancel her call to Hannah, which had once again gone to voicemail. She had tried to call Hannah three times that afternoon, and all of her calls had been forwarded to voicemail. She made this fourth attempt during her drive home at night. It was unlike Hannah to leave her calls unanswered without at least texting her to say that she couldn't answer.

She grabbed her purse from the passenger seat after parking her car in her driveway and headed inside. As she opened the door to her home, the house was lit with fairy lights and candles. She placed her purse on the bench by the door and found a small card with the words, *Come to the loft.*

All thought of Hannah forgotten, Ashleigh followed the lights upstairs through the otherwise dark house. As she climbed the stairs, she could hear soft music coming from the roof. She took the stairs from the second floor to the loft two at a time, and as the loft came into view, she found Desmond waiting for her, standing with a bottle of champagne in his hands and surrounding by twinkling lights. The soft flickering lights of nearby candles shimmered across his face and masked his age.

"We never celebrated the pregnancy," he said quietly to her in answer to her questioning expression. "You waited for this for a long time, and I think it's something we ought to celebrate." The cork blew off the bottle with a loud *pop*, and Desmond poured the bubbling liquid into a flute glass with a strawberry in the bottom. He continued, "Except this way, you still get to drink!" Ashleigh smiled at her husband as she took the glass from his hand.

An hour later, the bottle was empty, and Ashleigh and Desmond sat on the couch among the lights, sipping the last remnants of the champagne still in their glasses. Their conversations had been light and happy and reminded Ashleigh of their life before her infertility diagnosis.

Suddenly, Ashleigh sensed a change in Desmond as he went quiet. "What is it?" she asked as she watched him place his glass on the table in front of them. He turned to her, giving her his undivided attention, and took her free hand into his. "You know Ash, I prayed for you. I prayed for you and us, long before we even met. I prayed that you were safe, that you were happy, and that if you were with someone else, that you'd quickly figure out that they couldn't love you like I do. Most of all, I prayed that when we finally met, that I wouldn't disappoint you. I still pray that last part, and I'm sorry that I did."

Ashleigh placed her glass on the table and repositioned herself on the couch so that she leaned against her husband. He wrapped her in his arms, and she was comforted by his familiar warmth. "Des, things aren't the same between us, and I'm beginning to think that maybe they never will be. You're not the same man anymore. In fact, I don't think either of us is the same person we were when we got married. But that's okay. Now it's even exciting sometimes. It's like I'm getting to know this alternative version of you, and I get a chance to fall in love with you all over again. You did disappoint me, but the way I see it now, it was the former version of you that disappointed me. We're starting fresh. We're not just Desmond and Ashleigh anymore; we're mom and dad. I want us to focus on who we're about to become, and not who we were." She twisted herself so that her lips could find his, and soon the night consumed them.

CHAPTER 19

HEARTBEATS

H annah shivered as the obstetrician squeezed cold blue gel onto her bare, pregnant belly. Now twenty-two weeks along, her bump had grown to the size where she was noticeably pregnant, despite maintaining her frequent exercise regime. She smiled at the doctor, and silently reminded herself to take mental stock of the emotions that ran through her throughout this experience. She had found inspiration for her new show as each stage of the pregnancy progressed, and those parts of her show that she'd already written were being put into the early stages of production.

The doctor moved the transducer around Hannah's stomach, painting her skin with a thin translucent veil of gel. The doctor's face furrowed, and she let out a "Hmm" as she restarted her search for a heartbeat. Hannah's heart began to race. She forgot about her show, and the presence of Desmond and Ashleigh beside her. Her baby's health now her only concern. Her thoughts turned to the time she accidentally bumped her belly into the corner of a high table, the nights early into her pregnancy where she'd slept on her stomach, and to the impossible ways she'd twisted and thrown her body as she demonstrated basic form to her new dancers in preparation for her show. A thousand fears swept through her in an instant as the doctor navigated the transducer over her skin.

Many more minutes passed, and the doctor tried to keep her concern in check, making every effort to hide her worry behind the focused creases she forced across her features. Tears welled in Hannah's eyes as her fear intensified. She turned to Desmond. "I'm scared," she confessed in a shaking voice. She had intended to say more but found herself muted by an internal preparation for the news she expected the doctor to deliver after just a few more moments of torturous silence from the transducer.

Desmond took his eyes off of the ultrasound screen and looked into Hannah's. He took one of her hands into his own and gave her a reassuring smile. She gripped his hand tighter, intertwining their fingers as she returned her focus to the ultrasound screen. She poured her energy into that screen, hoping that by sheer force of will she could make the ultrasound screen find her baby and speak the heartbeat of her unborn child. She was so focused on the screen that she didn't notice the doctor's hand had stopped moving the transducer on her skin, or that Ashleigh had begrudgingly moved to her other side to place a hand on her shoulder. The room fell silent.

Hannah held her breath, and Desmond kept his reassuring gaze on her as the black-and-white kaleidoscopic image on the screen became static. The long silence broke as the doctor adjusted the transducer held just below Hannah's belly button, and a warbling sound echoed from the screen's speakers. All eyes turned to look at the doctor as she offered a relieved smile, "That right there, Ms. Lenore, that's your baby's heartbeat. A perfectly healthy baby."

Hannah released Desmond's hands as she covered her face and began crying heavily. Ashleigh, also crying softly, removed her hand from Hannah's shoulder and placed it over her mouth as the sound of the baby's heart beat around them. To Hannah, months of secret fears and latent maternal instincts made their presence known in an instant. Since the beginning of the arrangement, she had detached herself from the pregnancy, willing herself to believe that she was merely a vessel carrying her friend's baby.

But now, in one striking instant, her fear for the well-being of the child made her feel it. This was *her* baby, not only a part of her body, but a part of who she was. The face, the hands, and the little feet forming inside of her womb were a small part of herself, with parts of her old friend thrown in. Although the little life had grown inside of her for months, she had not realized how much the child had meant to her until she heard its little heartbeat beneath the cadence of her own.

Her concealed tears continued as she confronted questions she'd unconsciously pushed aside in self-preservation. *What will he or she look like? What kind of person will this child become? Will it love music and dancing like me? Will I get to hold him or her? Will I be able to let go?*

The doctor smiled sweetly at the two crying women before turning to Desmond. "Would you like to know the baby's sex?" she asked him, with a full grin.

Desmond looked back at both women and shrugged, words struggling to escape his lips, "I—I don't know! We never discussed it!" His focus darted between Ashleigh and Hannah.

"What do you think?" he asked looking between them.

Hannah uncovered her face. It was puffy and red from the furious tears that still beat their way down her cheeks. Hannah looked up at Ashleigh and opened her mouth as a measure of automatism took control. She had intended to tell Ashleigh that she should decide whether or not to know the baby's sex, as it was her baby. However, her focus shifted slightly, and she once again noticed the image frozen on the ultrasound screen behind Ashleigh's shoulder, the words refused to leave her lips.

As she looked upon the little life growing inside of her, she forgot all about Ashleigh and the sex of the baby. "Oh," she sighed involuntarily, once again feeling the intense pull of emotion for the little life. "I can't." Tears overwhelmed her once more, and she covered her face again to hide the image of the baby that she wasn't prepared to see.

Ashleigh mistook Hannah's reaction as relief for the baby's health, and she turned to Desmond with a smile, forgetting her surrogate. She found him also staring at the screen. "What do you think?" she asked him. "Do you want to know the sex?"

Desmond, never taking his eyes off the screen shook his slowly in answer. Ashleigh smiled and shook her head. "I don't want to know either!" she said gaily as she moved over to her husband's side, and hugged him.

As Desmond and Ashleigh stared lovingly at the image of their baby on the screen, the doctor pressed a button on the ultrasound machine so that it froze the image, and she removed the transducer from Hannah. Despite the euphoria emanating from Desmond and Ashleigh, the doctor sensed a confused mixture of love and pain from Hannah, and rose in sympathetic understanding. "Mr. and Mrs. Mathews, I think Ms. Lenore would appreciate a moment alone."

A muffled sob from beneath Hannah's hands was the only convincing they required. The couple allowed the doctor to usher them quietly from the room. As she heard the door click behind the doctor, Hannah rolled onto her side, pulled the screen to face her, and cried alone in the room as she looked upon the baby she'd never raise.

• • •

The next day, Desmond stood by his office window and watched the city streets move below him. He smiled to himself and sighed heavily. The medical clinic had put forth a motion to have Poe's case dismissed. Desmond had defeated this final challenge, and a trial date was set for early December. He relished the moment as, after months of hardship, everything seemed to be going his way. His relationship with his wife was the best it had been since her infertility diagnosis, and she was the happiest he had seen her in a long time. The ultrasound showed a healthy baby, and Hannah had been working feverishly at her new warehouse studio to prepare her show, which was now in full development.

Desmond breathed a sigh of relief, as, for the first time in a long while life was good, even easy. His reverie was interrupted by the ringing of his office phone and its red blinking light. He picked up the receiver and heard the firm's receptionist. "Ms. Lenore on line one." Her tone was filled with the same contemptuous reproach that textured his interactions with many of his colleagues after they'd learned of his arrangement with Ashleigh and Hannah. The receptionist transferred the call without waiting for his approval.

"Hannah, is everything okay? Why are you calling my work line?" His tone echoed his concern.

"Des, it's about your work. My publicist just received a tip that Jack Katan is going to call Poe and ask her to do an on-air interview. Des, you can't let her do it. You don't know Katan like I do. He'll destroy her."

"I just got back from court. Poe is on her way to my office now. She should be here any minute. Hannah…"

"Yes."

"Thanks for the heads-up."

Poe's face appeared on the other side of the glass wall to Desmond's office as he hung up the phone. She was wearing an old, moth-eaten coat, and her familiar wiry red hair frizzed in all directions above her fatigued face. Even without the quadruplets with her, she looked like a woman on the verge of breaking. He beckoned her quickly inside.

Poe smiled as she sat in the chair in front of Desmond's desk, and she jerked a thumb over her shoulder. Her smiled exacerbated the deep wrinkles that marked her tired face.

"Your receptionist doesn't like you, does she? I asked her to let you know I was here, and she told me to let myself in and 'just follow the stench.'" Poe gave a little laugh and Desmond could only smile.

"I have something for you," Desmond said gaily as he reached beneath his desk. He lifted a large box onto his desk in front of Poe. The bright colors of the gift wrapping and adorning bow glowed against the dull monochromatic colors of the office. Desmond answered Poe's confused expression. "Your babies. It's their first birthday today."

"You remembered?" Poe asked, obviously touched by the gesture.

"Of course," Desmond replied, still smiling. "I mean, it's written all throughout the briefs, but yes, I remembered."

Poe's voice broke as she spoke. "I couldn't afford any gifts for them. Thank you, Desmond."

The moment between Poe and Desmond was interrupted as her phone rang in her handbag. Desmond's eyes went wide as Poe reached curiously into her bag. "Don't answer that!" Desmond yelled, freezing Poe in her tracks. Poe's ringtone, the tune to the song "Keep Holding On," continued to play out as she looked at Desmond waiting for an explanation. The ringtone eventually died, leaving them in silence.

The silence was brief, as no sooner than the ringing of Poe's phone died, Desmond's office phone rang once more. He pushed the speaker button so that Poe could hear the exchange. "Mr. Jack Katan on one." The firm's receptionist put the call through once again without waiting on Desmond's consent, and Katan's voice filled the office. "Mr. Mathews. I had a feeling you'd get to Poe before I could. Kudos to you."

"What do you want, Katan?"

"Thought you'd never ask. Now I know that you're obliged to communicate all matters concerning the case to your client, so listen closely as I don't like to repeat myself. I want to do an on-air, live interview with Poe. The offer is one hundred thousand dollars for a one-hour interview. She has one hour to accept."

Desmond laughed. "Bullshit, Katan. You and I both know that your offer doesn't expire in an hour. I know you want this interview, so cut the crap."

Katan laughed back. "What can I say? You've got me there. I do want this interview. But figure this: if Poe doesn't call me to accept my *generous* offer within the next fifty-nine minutes, then I won't pay as much. In fact, now the offer is ninety-five thousand dollars. Congratulations, you just cost your client five grand. Talk to your client quickly Desmond. I'm an impatient man, and the clock is ticking. Oh, and Desmond, one more thing. Say hi to Hannah for me, will you?" Desmond and Poe heard the phone click as Katan hung up the phone.

Desmond clenched his jaw in irritation. *Does Hannah have history with Katan?* he thought. *Is that why he's obsessed with her?*

"I accept!" Poe's words brought Desmond's attention back to his client. "Desmond, I *need* that money."

"Kristen, Katan doesn't care about you. He's trying to take advantage of your desperation."

"I don't care! I *need* that money! You have no idea what it's been like! Do you have any idea what diapers cost for four infants? I'm so broke I had a cab drop me off two blocks away and then ran here because I couldn't afford the fare." Her face showed her disappointment in herself, but no sign of shame or embarrassment. She bore the look of a woman capable of standing firm in the face of judgment as she was grounded in the knowledge that she did these things only out of necessity, and not by any defect of her character.

Desmond carefully examined her face as she leveled his gaze. He noticed that the smile lines at the corner of her eyes were becoming less conspicuous and that the lines of bitterness at the edges of her mouth were darker and more profound than their last meeting.

He tried to imagine what she looked like before her insemination procedure. He pictured a young, happy woman, lost in the idea of having a child with the man she loved. His imagination erased the lines beside her mouth, gave color back to her skin, and silkened her hair to remove its frizz and fray. The contrast between the Poe that sat before him and the one he imagined from little more than a year ago was upsetting. He knew that Poe was only twenty-nine—the same age as Ashleigh—and yet she looked older than him.

"Kristen," Desmond began, trying hard not to let the sympathy he felt for the woman infect his tone, "I know you need the money, but this isn't the solution. This interview will give you a temporary solution to your money troubles, but it will adversely impact your chances of winning the case, and winning the case is the long-term solution."

Poe looked at her watch and began to protest, but Desmond held up both of his hands to invite her to let him finish. "This interview with Katan, it's not a puff piece. It's an exposé." He sighed as he fought for a different way to phrase his next sentences. He found none. "America hates you, Kristen. There are tens of thousands of young women, maybe hundreds of thousands, who right now can't have their dream babies because of your lawsuit. Now, I understand that you didn't ask or expect for the clinics to close their doors to insemination procedures, but the public sees it as your fault. In their eyes, you're the woman with buyer's remorse for her babies. The woman who wants the world's latest abortion. Katan doesn't want to share your story or level the playing field by humanizing you. He wants to cash in on America's hatred for you for himself. I've seen him do this before. He will twist your words and make you trip over yourself. He is an expert at misrepresenting people, and if he has the chance to do this to you, he's going to give the parties on the other side of your lawsuit ample ammunition to use against us in court. More than that, if his interview gets enough traction, he will poison the minds of every potential juror out there. Remember, the jury is there to protect you from the wrong judgment, but they won't protect you if they don't like you."

Poe looked at her watch again. Another fifteen minutes had passed. "I'll be careful!" she barked back in a panicked voice.

"It's not that simple," Desmond retorted in an equally panicked voice. He was afraid he was losing Poe to the luster of the money promised to her. "Kristen, when we go to court we can't just win on the law. Even if we're right on the law, a jury that doesn't *like* you won't decide *for* you. Do you understand? If Katan gets his interview, our chances of winning your case plummet."

Poe was resolute. She looked firmly at Desmond and shook her head. "I need that money."

Desmond shook his head slowly back at Poe. "No, what you need to do is think about your kids, forget this interview, and focus on winning your case. I need you to trust me on this. We can win, but you need to trust me."

Poe looked at her watch once more before looking back at Desmond. Something about her bearing changed, and her eyes shot daggers into Desmond's. "You don't get to tell me what I need, Mr. Mathews, and you sure as hell don't get to tell me what *my kids* need! I'm thinking that maybe this interview is less about my case than you're saying. Maybe you're just upset that all this money from the interview will go to me, unlike if we win my case where you and your firm take a big, fat chunk of *my* winnings!"

"No, Kristen, I care about you and those kids! Not just because of my professional obligations, but because I care about what happens to all of you!"

"Your obligations," Poe began stoically. "You have to do what I tell you, right? As my attorney, you have to follow my instructions?"

Desmond looked painfully at Poe. He knew he'd lost her. "Yes," he answered in a low voice.

Poe drew a deep, shaking break as she tried to calm herself. "Mr. Mathews, as my attorney, I instruct you to call Mr. Katan and accept his offer. After that, tell him to call me directly and that you are prohibited from discussing the interview further with him. I will take care of it on my own."

"Kristen—"

"*AND*, you will call me Ms. Poe. Understood?"

"Ms. Poe," Desmond said imploringly, "at least let me negotiate the terms of the interview and write a contract for you. Let me protect you!"

Poe stood as she made her way to leave Desmond's office. He remained seated and looked up at her as she spoke. "No, Mr. Mathews." Poe looked at the wrapped gift still sitting on his desk. "You've done right by me compared to my other lawyers. You're nice to me, and while I trust you with my case, I don't trust you with my money. Thank you for the gift, but I can't accept it. Make sure you call Katan within the next ten minutes." Poe turned on the spot and walked out of Desmond's office without looking back at him.

Desmond reached past the rejected gift sitting on his desk and pressed a button on his phone system to dial the receptionist. "What do you want?" her voice barked through the speakers.

Desmond picked up the phone receiver and answered her angrily, "Get me Jack Katan. After that, you can either lose the attitude, or your job. Your choice." He slammed the receiver hard into the phone console before sitting back in his chair, and preparing himself to deal with Katan.

CHAPTER 20

CHOICES

D esmond pulled on a fresh pair of trousers as he changed out of his business suit and into more comfortable clothing. It was late in the fall, and despite the relatively early hour, the sun had already set, plunging them into early nightfall.

Ashleigh sat on the bed next to Desmond with her back against the headboard. The blue blouse she had worn to work that day was half-unbuttoned, exposing the bare cleft of her breast, her bra having been removed the second she got home from work. The white duvet concealed the fact that she wore only panties underneath. She set her book down on the bedside table next to her glass of red wine, and turned to Desmond as he continued to change his clothes. "Do you have to go?" she pined. "I haven't been to that support group for weeks, and no one seems to have noticed. Surely you can miss this one meeting, and stay in with me?"

Desmond sighed. He was within just a few weeks of the final hearing in Poe's case, and the preparation workload was taking a toll. He was tired. "I want to," he replied casually, "but you know I have to go."

Ashleigh swung her legs out from under the blanket so that they hung over the edge of the bed. Her long, smooth legs dangled daintily in the lamplight as her feet lightly danced upon the soft carpet of their bedroom. "Desmond ..." she teased to get his attention.

He looked up at her as he began buttoning up a fresh shirt. Ashleigh caressed her exposed neck with one hand and allowed it to trace its way down to the still connected buttons of her blouse. She flicked a button open so that it exposed more flesh between the fabric of the slowly opening blouse. As the final button came undone and the blouse skirted open, she hopped off the bed and made her way over to him. She planted a kiss hard on his lips and fondled his crotch through his trousers.

"Stay with me," she whispered, as she led her kisses to his neck. "I need someone to stay with me and keep me warm on this cold night, and all of my best parts are so cold," she teased as she bit him lightly on the earlobe. She felt his hands reach under her blouse and plant themselves around her waist, but her coy smile was short-lived as Desmond used his grip to push her gently away from him.

"I have to finish getting ready," he said regretfully in answer to her dismayed expression. "Believe me, Ash, I want to stay in, but I can't. Hannah has been having a hard time since the ultrasound, and I need to be there for her."

Ashleigh grabbed the parsed ends of her blouse and pulled them closed in front of her. "And you think I'm not having a hard time too? It's not easy you know, always watching your husband leave you alone at night to go and look after another woman!"

Desmond paused and shook his head, his mouth slightly twisted. "That's not fair, Ash. I'm leaving to support Hannah because the counselor *told* us that's what we should do. We went to the counselor because the pregnancy made things weird between us, and Hannah is pregnant because you insisted on how you wanted us to get pregnant. All of this has happened because you were so particular about how you wanted a baby, not because I have any desire to leave you and run around with another woman."

"Oh!" Ashleigh cried, "So this is all *my* fault? You always do this! You always turn the tables around so it's my fault so that I can never be mad at you! Because you're the innocent one in all of this. *You're* just a victim in this whole scheme, and I'm just your baby-crazy wife! Right? Well, I'm not the only one who wanted the baby Desmond. You did too! So, stop pinning all of this on me."

Desmond raised his hands up in a placating gesture and spoke in a calm tone. "I'm not saying this is your fault, Ash. You just accused me of wanting to run off and be with Hannah tonight, and I'm just saying that it's not what I *want* to do, it's what I *have* to do."

"What you also *have* to do is take care of your wife, Desmond," Ashleigh said coldly. "And this isn't all my fault either. I'm not the one leaving tonight, and I'm not the one who got Hannah pregnant."

Desmond shook his head. "I thought we were past this. I never wanted it to be like this. I wanted a normal surrogacy, but you forced my hand!"

"I didn't force it inside of her though! You went there all too willingly on your own." Ashleigh's voice was cold. Normally when she got this angry, she couldn't help but yell and scream. This time her voice was deathly even, and her eyes stared into his with an icy menace. "Tell me I'm wrong, Des. Tell me you didn't put your hand inside of her. Didn't kiss her. Didn't pull her head back by the strands of her blonde hair while you *fucked* her that night. Tell me you didn't enjoy it."

She stood her ground, staring Desmond down as he glared back at her furiously. After failing to respond, Ashleigh answered for him, "And if you can't tell me I'm wrong about those things, dear husband, then don't you dare try and tell me that all of this is my fault!"

Desmond reached out one of his hands to touch Ashleigh, but she shied away from him to avoid his touch.

"No," she answered, "I know where they've been." Desmond dropped his arm heavily. Ashleigh turned from him, climbed back under the covers of their bed, and grabbed her book from the bedside table. She gave the pretense that she resumed her reading, but she was too hurt and angry for the words to mean anything to her as her eyes glazed over them. Desmond stood motionless next to the bed, just watching her as he tried to find the right words. "Just go," she said softly without looking up. Her anger was quickly subsiding, and she wanted him gone before it was replaced with heartache.

Desmond finished getting dressed and made for their bedroom door. As he stood in front of the open doorway leading to the black darkness of the hallway, he turned and said, "I don't just have obligations to care for you, Ashleigh. I also have to take care of our baby, and that's where I'm going tonight." He turned again, left the room, and disappeared into the darkness.

As Ashleigh stared at the seemingly blank pages of her book, she wondered if by "our baby" Desmond had meant his and hers, or his and Hannah's.

• • •

Desmond arrived late to the surrogacy support meeting, and he took his seat next to Hannah as he quietly slipped into the room. There was an odd, quiet tension in the room the likes of which he'd never before noticed in the group. He looked at Hannah and saw that her blue eyes were wide, and fixed on Jen. He glanced around the room and found everyone else similarly transfixed on the young woman, except for Shaun. Shaun had his head buried in his hands as he rubbed his face slowly, as if severely fatigued. Desmond sat back in his chair and turned his attention to Jen as she continued speaking to the group.

"I know you all told me I'm not supposed to bring it up, but this group is supposed to be for my support too, and I need to talk about this." Her voice had a firmer quality to it than her usually timid and soft voice, but it still shook as though she was not sure of herself. "I told Jason about the baby, and he didn't flinch. He thought I was going to keep the baby, and he still stuck around. That's a big deal for me. I'm not used to people sticking by me. Even when I told him I was planning to give the baby to my sister and her husband, he supported me. He's going to respect and support me in whatever choice I make with the baby. This whole thing got me thinking though that ... well, maybe I want to keep the baby and raise it with him. It's my baby, and even though I told my sister that she could have it, I only told her that because I didn't think I could raise the baby on my own. Maybe now, I don't have to. Maybe with Jason, I can give the baby a good life and I don't have to give him up?"

"Jenny," came Eileen's voice.

"I know, Eileen! I know I'm not supposed to talk about this, but I need to, okay? I need to talk this out, and just because you had a fallout with your sister about surrogacy doesn't mean I shouldn't be able to talk about things with my sister."

Eileen shook her head. "Nah, Jenny. That's not what I was gonna say." To everyone's surprise, Eileen spoke in an even, almost sympathetic, tone. They had expected she would get upset, just as she had at the bar during their luncheon. "Jen, how long have you known Jason? Three, maybe four months? You're talking about a decision that will affect you, your baby, your sister, and her husband, for the rest of your lives. You're gonna make this decision for someone who's been in your life for a few months? Not only that, but you hardly know the guy. What do you know about him? Sure, you know he was in the army, and he's a nice guy when he's with you, but what about when he's not? When you're not around, is he still nice-guy army-man Jason? Is he the kind of man he was when he got sent away to the army? Or someone completely different? You're young, Jenny, and you don't have a lot of experience with men. In the first few months, sometimes years even, they can put on an act and make you think that everything about them is wonderful. It's after you've fallen for them that they flip the switch, and you see the real version of them. If you think I've just had bad experiences, ask the women in this room. Ask your friends here."

The eyes of every woman in the room glazed over as they reflected on the men in their own pasts.

Jen was getting more upset as Eileen went on. "Don't you tell me that," she said softly to Eileen. "Don't tell me I don't have experience with men when you know what my ex did to me!" A few tears broke away, and traveled down her pale cheeks.

"Jen, sweetie," Nicole broke in next to her. "That's what she means. How long was it before your ex hit you? How long did he seem like the perfect guy before he got drunk or lost his temper?"

Jen sniffled and wiped away another tear as she remembered the first time her ex's fist crashed against her cheek. It had fractured her cheekbone and left her with a bruised eye for two weeks. He had apologized and given her flowers, even promised her it was an accident and wouldn't happen again. He kept his word the next time, sort of. The next time he took to her, he punched and kicked her in the stomach, not the face.

"More than a year," Jen whispered somberly, as a tear rolled over the spot where the fracture had healed. "We'd been together over a year the first time I saw him like that, and it was almost two years before he hit me. After that, it was like it never stopped."

Eileen got up from her chair and crouched awkwardly in front of Jen, her own growing baby bump making the position a challenge. "Jenny, sweetheart, I'm not saying that Jason is a bad guy. Everyone here hopes he really is the perfect guy for you. I'm just saying that a decision to keep the baby isn't one to make lightly, especially when you're still in the honeymoon period with a new guy. As for keeping the baby for yourself, sweetie, there's not one of us that don't think about keeping the babies we have inside of us. That's why it's so upsetting when you talk about it. They're a part of who we are, and we get nine months to prepare to rip that part out of our hearts and hand it to someone else. It's not easy, but it's the right thing to do most of the time. Maybe next time you think about keeping the baby, or telling your sister your decision, ask yourself whether it's the right decision for the baby, not just for you."

Jen nodded slowly, but didn't look up at Eileen. Her face still hung low so that her chin rested on her chest.

Desmond's attention was averted as he heard Todd's voice just outside the door to the corridor. As he had done at most of the meetings, Desmond quietly excused himself from the group as he stepped outside to see Todd, who would come to visit him outside the room during nearly every session. Desmond expected that the surrogates would be more comfortable continuing their conversation without him there, anyway.

As he stepped through the doorway, he saw Todd speaking with a punchy, short blonde woman with a round pregnant belly. "Katelynn, you can't slap a pregnant woman!" Todd said, referring to one of the surrogates who had left the group before Desmond to step outside and smoke.

"Why not?" Katelynn retorted. "I'm pregnant too. It's an even playing field. Besides, that cigarette she's smoking is doing a lot more damage to her baby than my hand will!"

The exchange ended as Desmond stepped into the dimly lit green corridor. Katelynn turned to him and smiled. "Aha!"

she yelled triumphantly, pointing at Todd with a sardonic smile. "I knew it! I knew you were skipping out on your group to talk to him!" She turned to Desmond. "Desmond, I presume?"

"Yes?" Desmond responded furtively, looking at Todd.

Todd smiled. "This is my wife, Katelynn."

Katelynn extended her hand toward Desmond. Her extended arm was slightly elevated away from her, as she was so much shorter than Desmond. "Good to finally meet you, Desmond. Todd talks about you a lot."

She had wide, light-blue eyes beneath long blonde hair pulled back into a ponytail. Freckles dotted her nose and spread onto one of her cheeks, the asymmetry giving her a unique and flattering appearance. She shook Desmond's hand and stepped back toward Todd's side. He put his arm around her and pulled her toward him. It would have been a sweet image, Todd hugging his heavily pregnant wife toward him, if the image didn't create such a heavy contrast between the two of them, and highlight Todd's sickness.

Katelynn was visibly energetic, her movements were animated, and her grin radiated her affection for her husband. Next to Todd, however, her vitality gave him the look of a dead man brought to life. His clothes hung off of him, and the weight of the fabrics seemed ready to overcome him. His skin was gray and colorless, and the dark rings around his eyes made it look like he sported twin black eyes. As much as Katelynn's appearance expressed the radiance of the life growing inside of her, Todd's expressed the slow expiration of his own.

"As you know," Katelynn continued excitedly, "I'm not fat. Just pregnant. Okay, maybe I'm a little fat too. The baby likes Twinkies."

"And buffalo chicken dip," Todd added, looking down at her lovingly.

"Oooo, and that!" she said looking back up at him, her appetite reflected in her blue eyes. "Actually babe, do you think we can grab some on the way home?"

Todd laughed. "I think we have the time."

The reference robbed Katelynn of the genuineness of her smile. She forced some curvature to her thin pink lips, through the awkward silence that followed. She shook her head slightly to rid herself of her thoughts and turned back to Desmond. "So, Desmond, what is so important between the two of you that Toddy continues to ignore my request for him to make videos for the baby?"

"Sorry?" Desmond asked, unsure of how to answer.

"Well he skips his classes to see you, and he's out to lunch with you all the time. I have to assume something is going on that's important enough for him to risk my continued nagging for the videos."

"Not now, Katelynn," Todd begged.

"Yes now," Katelynn insisted. "Now and always. I don't think you realize how important this is to me. We don't have much time left, and your child needs to know who you are! Look at me!" she said, reaching up high above her head to reach his chin. "Todd, I need this. We don't know when it will happen."

Todd looked down at his wife's pleading expression and turned back to Desmond. "Des, we need a moment. I'll see you next week."

"Not if I don't have my videos by then, you won't!" Katelynn half-teased as she looked back at Desmond.

There was something in the way she looked at him that suggested she was asking something of him. Her round eyes begged at his consciousness to intercede...to perhaps cancel his meetings with Todd so that he could focus on the video, or to use them to encourage him to get them done—he couldn't be sure which. "It was nice to finally meet you, Katelynn," was all he could muster before turning and rejoining his surrogacy meeting. As he closed the door behind him, he could hear Katelynn talking to Todd as they walked off, hand in hand, down the green corridor.

When the support group session ended, Desmond escorted Hannah out of the building and toward his car. She had remained silent throughout the entire session, and during their walk out into the parking lot. The session had centered around the surrogates' respective temptations to keep their babies, and how they had handled those moments. Eileen and Hannah were the only ones who had declined to share.

Desmond started the car and began the drive back to Hannah's place in Baltimore. They traveled each mile in uncomfortable silence, which continued long after he had parked in the garage beneath Hannah's hotel, and walked her to her door. He stood awkwardly as she searched for her keys; the only sound coming from her hand rummaging through her handbag.

Desmond recalled the first time he had stood outside of Hannah's hotel room door, drenched in rainwater and pounding impatiently against its panels. He looked at her, starting from her pregnant stomach and allowing his eyes to continue up her body until he saw her face. "Hannah, is everything okay?"

"I'm fine," she answered flatly as she lifted her handbag higher to let in the light. She found her key and pressed it against the electronic panel to unlock the door. Suddenly, Desmond's hand reached forward and grabbed hers. She looked over her shoulder at him, unsure of his meaning. His face showed a grave concern, and at once she could see every line that pressed itself along his features.

"Hannah," he began softly. "The ultrasound ... and tonight. Are you—" He caught himself, unsure whether he wanted to finish his sentence. "Have you ever thought about keeping the baby for yourself?"

Hannah jerked her hand free of his, and he stepped away from her reflexively. Her pink lips pressed together, and she fought to keep her eyes from welling up with tears.

"You're so stupid, Desmond," she said softly. She pushed on the unlocked door, entered the room, turned, and slammed the door in his face.

• • •

The next day, Hannah headed to her warehouse studio in Baltimore, still hot-headed and offended by Desmond's question the night before. She spent much of the night penning a new scene for the show. She always wrote best when she was upset. The show was now all but finished, or at least written down.

She had almost composed the entire show, but the two halves had seemed unconnected, as though they marked the beginning and end to two different stories. However, the new scene, written just the night before, was exactly what she needed to connect them, and now she could focus on perfecting the choreography her dancers had been rehearsing for weeks.

She stood on a parapet that acted as a makeshift observation deck and screamed down to her dancers who had again attempted their routines, and failed to meet her standards. "No! No, no, no, no, no! Jacqui, where did you find these girls!? Run it again!"

A stagehand reset the music, and the dancers returned to their starting positions and began again. Only a moment into this attempt, Hannah made a 'cut' motion with her hand over her neck to the stagehand. The music shut off abruptly, and the dancers stood exhausted in the middle of the floor as Hannah descended the parapet to join them.

"Girls, what is going on? Jacqui, you're my lead. I expect more power when you make that jump. Ghada, learn the difference between a pirouette and a fouette. You keep your foot in, pointed against the side of your knee in a pirouette. You keep your leg out to the front, open it to the side, and then in like a pirouette for a fouette. Randa, your routine is step, pause, pivot, step, step, turn, pause, pivot, step, pause, and brace. Not step, pause, pivot, step, turn, pause, pivot, step, turn, and pause. It's not hard! My shows are successful because I demand perfection. Unless you can all deliver me perfection, GET OUT! UNDERSTAND?"

While most of the dancers were new, and didn't know that Hannah wasn't herself right now, Jacqui had never seen Hannah with anything less than perfect composure. When the dancers again tried and failed to demonstrate the routine to her satisfaction, Hannah ordered them to step down from the stage, and stand on a line demarcating where the front row would sit. She made them wait as she shuffled slowly offstage behind a curtain and sat heavily on a bench. Alone behind the curtain, she brought her feet up to her lap as best she could and removed her shoes. She peered around her cautiously to make sure that no one could see her before removing her socks and stretching her mangled toes. Her feet, deformed and ruined by a lifetime of rigorous dancing, were made worse by the pain and swelling from carrying around the added weight from the pregnancy. Still, she crammed her feet into an old pair of pointe shoes and shuffled her way back onto center stage in front of the crowd of dancers.

Jacqui saw the pointe shoes on Hannah's feet beneath her rounded stomach and began to weep. "Madame Hannah, no!" She knew all too well the pain that came from feet like Hannah's, and unlike most, she had counted herself lucky to have never seen Hannah dance herself. To try and dance at the beginning of the third trimester would be nothing short of excruciating.

"It's okay, Jacqui," came Hannah's voice as she gestured for the stagehand to reset the music. "I want this to be perfect. This number means too much to me." As the other assembled dancers realized what was about to happen, they began to protest. A cacophony of cries broke out as others in the warehouse studio came to the stage to investigate the source of the commotion, and soon their cries joined those of the protesting dancers.

Hannah heard none of them. She was lost in her silent world as the ultrasound images flashed in front of her eyes, as she felt Desmond's lips on hers, and as she heard his voice echo in her mind as he asked her if she'd thought about keeping the baby for herself. The cries of protest drowned as the crash of music washed over the stage. Hannah's form sprang into life in answer. Even with the sizable belly, she was balanced and graceful, swimming through the air like she was made of music.

Hannah ignored the pain screaming from her feet and ankles as her emotions, now set free on the tide of the music, took control and racked her body around the stage in a manner that was simultaneously furious and delicate. *This* was Hannah Lenore. More than the sum of the smutty articles published by Katan, more than an aged-out has-been, more than just a dancer, and more than just a surrogate. She was the agent that married the human spirit with music, and gave it fresh form. She was beauty and grace, whose movements set to score told a tragic story of pain and loss the likes of which was unimaginably, brutally cruel.

The music faded and brought an end to the rehearsed number, and almost every face in the studio was matted with fresh tears. Jacqui rushed up the stage and helped to support Hannah as she came off pointe with shaking legs. "That," she said proudly looking out at the tear-splattered rapture on the faces looking up as she leaned on Jacqui for support, "is how I want your dancing to make the audience feel. This scene is about heartbreak. I need you to show in your dancing that it isn't easy. That the way out isn't clear. Show me that you were just fine this time yesterday, and how it's impossible that you could feel so overwhelmed and confused now; that you would give anything to have that person stay with you while you fall asleep, just to give you peace. Show me that you know the pain of a heart breaking, and that you never fully healed. If you can't dance for me like that, then you've never really had your heart broken."

Hannah leaned heavily against Jacqui as she was helped over to the bench behind the curtain. After slowly and painfully changing her shoes, Hannah eventually swapped places with her dancers. She sat on a chair placed on the front-row line as her dancers took their places on the stage. They attempted the routine once more, this time allowing their own experiences to wash through them and guide their bodies through the choreography. Hannah looked at the pain reflected on the faces of each of the dancers. She watched her choreography performed as intended, and her heart began to race.

For the first time, she felt her baby move inside of her. The movement startled her at first, and when a second kick came, the stage and the dancers in front of her dissolved. She was alone with her baby amid the music. "Oh," she whispered to herself as she felt life move inside of her. *So, this is what it feels like.* She sat, sharing the music with her unborn baby until the music and the movement ended together.

She came back to the present as her dancers stood on the stage, awaiting her feedback on their performance. Hannah smiled and blinked back tears in her eyes, "My goodness, girls, that was wonderful. I um—" she cleared her throat, "it seems I've upset myself. I'm just so proud of you all, and so excited to see you pull that off so well. If you'll excuse me ..." Hannah stood and made ready to move to her private office at the other end of the makeshift studio when one of the newer dancers on the stage called out to her.

"Ms. Lenore?" Hannah turned to face the young girl. "Ms. Lenore the way you dance … the way you teach … Well, you're going to make a wonderful, beautiful mother is all."

Hannah fought harder to keep her tears back. She smiled up at the girl and managed a meek, "Thank you Rita," before turning and hobbling toward her private quarters. As she closed the door to her office behind her, she leaned her back against the cold door, overcome with heartache. She kept one hand on her inflated belly and used her other hand to cover her mouth to muffle her violent, shaking sobs.

CHAPTER 21

THE INTERVIEW

P oe stood nervously at the side of the set where she would sit for her interview with Katan. Worried that Katan's dressing team would work against her, she opted to dress and groom herself. Not having had the time or luxury to put on makeup for more than a year, her makeup was thick and uneven, and her dress was old, out of fashion, and clung too tightly against her body in odd places. She had bought the dress long before becoming pregnant, and had not accounted for the physical changes that came with being a mother.

Poe unconsciously bit at her nails as she watched faceless people scurry about the set, adjusting lighting, placing potted plants and other props in the backdrop, and fluffing the cushions on the two seats in the center of the room. Poe felt out of place. She watched the set get put together in a matter of minutes, and the sleek style and sharp lines drew a sharp contrast to the mess of an apartment she was never able to keep clean or tidy.

Katan stepped out of a door at the other end of the set, with an entourage of makeup and hair artists in tow. One of his assistants was still pressing a lint roller along the sleeve of his jacket as he walked. He kept his eyes leveled on hers as he made his way toward her, and his stare made her feel smaller and smaller with each step he took. He shooed away his entourage with a wave of his hand, and they vanished into the darkness behind the many spotlights suddenly set upon her. "Ms. Poe!" he began gaily. "I'm so glad you accepted my offer. Mr. Mathews wasn't too pleased with me when last we spoke. It hurt my feelings." Katan exaggerated the offense by placing a hand over his heart. He was a tall man, and he looked down upon the nearly cowering woman in front of him.

Poe was forced to drop her gaze, partly because looking up at Katan strained her neck, but mostly because she was intimidated by his presence. "Where is it?" she demanded, trying to sound strong.

Katan stooped down and tried to place his face in front of hers as he attempted to resume eye contact. "Where is what?" he asked firmly, but quietly enough so that only she could hear him. Poe looked up quickly, and it forced Katan to step back quickly to avoid being head butted.

"Don't!" she commanded him. "Don't play with me! You know what I'm here for, so don't play dumb. Where's the check? I told you, no interview unless you pay me up front. I don't want to play any games."

Katan gave a smile that was more threatening than sweet. "Now, now, Ms. Poe. We're here for the *children,* remember?" he chided her with thinly veiled condescension. He pulled an envelope from his jacket pocket with a flourish, and leaned in as he handed it to her, speaking louder than was necessary. "I'm hoping that this small gift will help to support your little miracles."

Poe snatched the envelope from Katan with shaking hands and shoved it into her handbag. She looked around nervously as though she were doing something wrong, and checked her bag twice more to make sure the envelope was still safely secured in her possession.

"Okay," she said to Katan as she tried to match his gaze. "Let's get this over with. You have your hour."

Poe sat opposite Katan on a seat that was too large for her. Katan sat on a bright red and stylish chair that was too gaudy for her liking, but which contrasted flatteringly with his dark suit. A stagehand had come close to her to try and remove her handbag, which lay on the ground by the side of the chair, but she refused to let it, or the check, out of her sight. It would remain on the ground by her side whether it was in the frame or not. She recalled that the interview was being streamed live over the television and the internet, and tried to remain calm as Katan made some long-winded, unnecessary introduction.

The interview had been extensively advertised around the country on all mediums from the moment she had agreed to participate. Radio shows talked about it incessantly, fielding calls from outraged strangers, and television and internet commercials promoted the interview at every opportunity. Although advertised for only a brief period, the level of attention it had garnered was astonishing.

Poe hadn't spoken to Desmond since the last time she'd left his office, and just as Katan was wrapping up his introduction, she found herself wishing that he was beside her, or at least that she'd visited him to prepare her for Katan. Desmond had always been so calm and reassuring, and she needed both of those qualities now more than ever. Katan's perfectly manicured features glistened in the spotlight as he finished his introduction, and turned his attention to Poe.

"And so, to hear from the infamous woman herself, here is Kristen Poe." He briefly paused to subtly emphasize the conspicuous absence of applause. "Kristen, you began your lawsuit against the insemination clinic more than a year ago, and since then, every single clinic in the country has shut its doors to the hundreds of thousands of American women who use their services every year. In fact, in the year before you filed your lawsuit, over one hundred thousand American babies were born through the use of in vitro fertilization. Over one hundred thousand babies were not born because of you, and over half a million women have been denied the chance to try for one. Please tell us, how did we get here?"

Poe wondered if Katan would begin all of his questions with damning exposition. She tried to clear her throat before speaking, and in doing so, she accidentally coughed up some phlegm which caught itself on her chin. She quickly wiped it away with her sleeve, and even Katan's lifetime of rehearsed composure couldn't hide his disgust. Poe stammered as she tried to recover. "I, um ... my ... my husband and I tried for years to have a baby, and it just wouldn't take. It just never happened for us. So, we saved for a long time—a real long time—to try and afford a professional insemination procedure. We scrounged all the savings we had, and then some. When we were at the clinic, they told us that the best chance at conception would be the insemination of multiple fertilized eggs—the embryos. My husband and I knew we could only afford one shot at it, and so we agreed. They never told us how many they were going to implant. They just kept saying the word 'multiple.' We found out later that they implanted four, and all four took." Poe let the sentence trail off as she remembered when the clinicians first told her that all four embryos had attached.

A model of empathy, Katan nodded. "Kristen, thank you for sharing. I wonder though if that answers my question...How did you get from the insemination to the lawsuit? Please help me to understand. And ... and, let me finish. Where is your husband?"

Poe looked at Katan, a little confused. She hadn't tried to interrupt him as he asked his question. "He left," she answered flatly. "I was about a month from the due date when he told me he couldn't cope anymore, that he never expected he'd have to support so many mouths. I came home from a checkup with the obstetrician—he was supposed to be there too, but he just wasn't—and when I got home, he had some bags packed, and he left. I haven't heard from him since, and I don't know where he went."

Katan gave an overly forlorn look and touched her knee sympathetically. His reaction was so painfully forced that Poe wondered if his viewers couldn't see right through his act. "Now, I don't want to make light of your tragedy, Kristen, but a lot of women experience this. You're not the first woman to have the father of their children walk out, or refuse to pay child support. In fact, some might suggest that you had it better than others: that at least your husband gave you the courtesy of telling you he was leaving, instead of just going out for some milk and never coming home."

Poe looked around uncomfortably. She wasn't sure if that was a question, or if she was supposed to answer, but Katan stared at her expectantly. She answered as best she could. "Well, I was pregnant with quadruplets. I don't think that experience is easy for any woman or mother, but I was pregnant with quadruplets. *Quadruplets*, Jack. Everyone talks about how hard it is to have one baby. I had four at once, on my own, and with no money. So, no; I don't think I had it any easier."

Katan tried to hide a smile of self-satisfaction. "Kristen, you brought up the matter of money. There are a great many people who think that this lawsuit is all just about money for you. You know, you're not the first woman to have quadruplets or have the father walk out, so what makes you so special that the insemination clinic—a state-sponsored organization— should pay for the costs of raising your children?"

Poe pushed herself back further in her chair, feeling increasingly uncomfortable. "I don't … I don't think I'm special. Do I look special to you?" Poe answered, with a low-sweeping gesture to herself.

Katan nodded once more. "I don't think you're special. Let me be clear, Kristen. I don't think you deserve any special treatment, but it's not for me to decide. That's what juries are for. Now though, when I said that people think that your lawsuit is all about money, you didn't deny it. So, it is all about the money…Correct?"

Poe shook her head in shock. "No," she half-pleaded, looking about her for someone who understood the words coming out of her mouth. "This isn't about money. The clinic made a mistake!"

Katan tilted his head mockingly and looked directly at the camera that came zooming closer toward them from an overhead arch boom. "That's a little disingenuous now, isn't it? Just denying it after-the-fact because you admitted it here?"

"I didn't admit anything!" Poe cried, the little color in her face quickly draining.

Katan leaned forward on the edge of his seat, bridging the gap between them. "But Kristen, didn't you demand payment for this interview? Didn't you say that payment of a substantial gift was a precondition of us speaking together?"

Poe was flustered and began to panic. Sweat patches began to noticeably seep through the fabric of her dress under her arms, giving her an overheated, sickly appearance to the viewers. "Yes, but … oh God. That's not what this is! The children have expenses that I can't meet on my own!" she cried, her voice nearing hysteria.

Katan continued, "In fact, I did a little research myself and found that you filed your lawsuit three months before the babies were born. And yet, you just told us that your husband left you less than a month before your children were born. How could any of this have been about expenses and making up for your husband's deficits when he hadn't even left yet, and the children weren't even here?" Katan's voice was rising, his tone accusatory.

"These aren't the same thing!" Poe cried. "I never said this was about the clinic making up for what my husband left me with!

The lawsuit is about their mistake, and the payment for this interview was for the costs! They aren't the same thing!"

Katan leaned back in his chair and shrugged. "How can anyone know, Kristen? You've spun so many lies that it seems that even you can't keep track of them all. But I want to move away from money. I know that's difficult for you, but please, let's move on."

Poe clenched tightly at the fabric of her dress that draped over her knees. She fought hard to keep back the tears of exasperation forming in eyes bloodshot from too little sleep. *Just do it for them*, she told herself. *Just thirty minutes more and this is over. You'll have enough money to keep the kids going for several months. Thirty minutes more and it will all be easier.* Poe made a slight whimpering noise as she tried to control her breathing.

Katan softened his tone and approach so as not to appear opportunistic or cruel to his viewers. "Kristen," he continued, "I want to talk to you about the children. What are their names?"

Poe breathed out heavily once more to calm herself. She looked up at Katan's mockingly expectant gaze. *Don't let him beat you*, she reminded herself. *You let everyone beat you. Don't let him.* "The boys are Logan, Andre, and Kevin. My daughter's name is Olivia."

"That's sweet," Katan said almost convincingly as he gave her a pleasant smile. "And in your lawsuit, it's your position that the clinic simply implanted too many eggs, correct? That they made you have too many babies?"

Poe nodded cautiously, and Katan continued, "I have to ask: how many children would you have been happy with?"

Poe looked back at Katan reproachfully, trying to examine what his angle might be. "I did my research," she started, starting to find her composure once more. "I did my research. It's only in those cases where there's a bad prognosis of conception that they're supposed to use four or five embryos. I wasn't a bad case. Most clinics would have inserted one or two embryos. I think we would have been okay with twins. My husband and I had always talked about maybe having two kids."

Katan cut in, "Mmhmm, mmhmm. So, two children?" he confirmed with another slow, cautious nod from Poe.

"So, out of Andre, Olivia, Logan, and Kevin, which two would you choose to get rid of?"

Poe sat quickly upright in her chair, shocked by the question. "What!?" she barked.

Katan maintained a placid, expressionless face. "You just said that you would have welcomed two babies—that the clinic made a mistake in giving you four. So, if you had it your way, which two would you sacrifice?"

"That's disgusting," Poe spat indignantly. "I wouldn't harm any of my children."

Katan put his hands up defensively. "Whoa, Kristen. I never said anything about harming or killing your children, and I'd appreciate if you didn't speak like that. You're upsetting a lot of viewers with that kind of talk."

"Stop twist—" Poe began to yell in frustration but was cut off by Katan.

"All I'm saying is that if four children are too much to support, and two would be comfortable for you, why not adopt them out? Through your lawsuit, you've denied thousands of couples across America the ability to have their own children. Any one of them would jump at the chance to adopt your unwanted babies."

"I didn't say I didn't want my children!" Poe cried, once more overwhelmed.

"Yes, you did!" Katan corrected her. "And all of America heard it! Now, answer my question! Why didn't you adopt out any of your children?"

Poe finally lost control of the emotions she'd kept in check for forty-five frustrating minutes of Katan's misrepresentations, and a defeated tear rolled its way down her cheek as she recalled the one time she had thought about adoption when the children were first born, the one moment she considered giving up any of the children she'd learned to love. "I didn't want to put any of them up for adoption because I couldn't stand the thought of them being raised by a stranger."

Katan shook his head slowly in exaggerated disbelief. "One minute you want your children, and the next you don't," he said almost pitifully. "Which is it? The decision to have the children was yours. The decision to keep them was yours. And yet, you want the someone else to pay for them. Other couples have twins, triplets, even quads, all the time. They don't sue anyone." Katan's tone and pause showed he expected an answer.

Poe sighed. The interview was draining her. "I didn't choose to have four," was the best answer she could give, and Katan took hold.

"Well, neither did they! That's just the hand that nature deals sometimes. At least you got a warning! You knew the risks with IVF, and yet you pressed on. You even knew you were pregnant *weeks* before most women make the discovery. You had other options Poe, and yet you want the clinic to compensate you because you're not happy with the outcome of the option you chose."

"Termination," Poe said sternly, glaring at Katan, "wasn't an option!"

Katan matched Poe's glare, staring her down. "I don't like to discuss abortion publicly, Ms. Poe. It upsets too many people. But seeing as *you* brought it up, why wasn't it an option?"

Poe receded in her chair and dropped her face into her chest, succumbing to Katan's overpowering stare. She weighed her words carefully, trying to make sure that she could not be misunderstood or misrepresented. "Because life is too precious," she answered softly, sadly, and without looking up.

Katan leaned back in his chair, knowing that he had her beat. "Even yours?" he said coldly. His straight face didn't move, even as Poe looked up at him with something more than offense painted across her face. She looked back at him with something more severe, more personal. Something closer to anguish. Her eyes were wide and filled with pain, and though the rest of her face was a stone mask, her eyes welled fully, and tears began to roll freely down her face.

"You're a monster," she whispered. Her arms shook as she pushed herself up from the chair and she ripped the microphone away from the top of her dress. She threw it to the ground and stormed off and away from the set. She didn't hear the smug mockery that Katan delivered as he wrapped up the interview with a self-congratulatory closing monologue to his audience.

Poe wept freely and let her tears roll off her cheeks to splatter on the floor as she stood in what she hoped would be a private nook near one of the stage room exits. She stifled whimpers and wiped her runny nose on her sleeve. Wanting to see with her own eyes the check that would make enduring the traumatic interview worthwhile, Poe reached into her handbag and removed the envelope Katan had given her. She ripped it open and removed the check. As she looked at the numbers on the check, she blinked back the fresh tears still forming in her eyes to make sure she was seeing them clearly—the check was for only one thousand dollars. Her breathing reached a hyperventilated pace, and her heart raced in her chest. She held the envelope to her face to see if there were more checks stuck inside. Seeing none, she gritted her teeth and clenched her fists, crumpling one of the corners of the check still held in her hand, and yelled quietly in frustration.

Dazed, she looked around the studio and saw stagehands already scurrying around, dismantling the set. The spotlights were turned off, the chairs had been removed, and men were at work taking props away from the backdrop. Katan was nowhere in sight. Avoiding the set and the stage room exit closest to her, she walked quickly through a corridor and found Katan's dressing room. There was nothing on the closed door to suggest that it belonged to Katan, but she could hear his mocking laugh through the door.

She turned the unlocked doorknob and pushed the door open. Katan sat in a large cushioned chair in front of a lighted mirror and was surrounded by a small entourage of admirers. The group turned and saw a ragged, tear-streaked Poe standing in the doorway with the check clenched in her hand.

"Get security," Katan said calmly to his entourage, "and get the door."

The group quickly stepped into the corridor from which Poe had arrived, each giving her pitiful and disdained looks as they passed. The last of them shut the door behind him. Poe was alone with Katan in the room.

"What is this?" Poe screamed hysterically shaking the crumpled check high above her head. "This only says one thousand! What happened to the fifty you promised me!?"

Katan opened his hands in front of him as he continued to sit casually in his seat. "Fifty?" he asked. "I never said anything about fifty! And you have nothing to prove otherwise. We have no contract. No witnesses. Nothing. As far as anyone knows, that one thousand dollars was a gift paid to you for the interview in the interest of helping your children. And anyone who watches the interview or reads the payee on the check will see just that."

Poe pulled the check in front of her eyes and saw that it was issued in the names of her children. "You bastard," she cried softly. "The only ones who suffer for this are my children.

Do you understand that? I let you use and humiliate me for an hour out there for the sake of providing for my children, and this is what to you? Just some trick? Some publicity stunt? My children are *starving* because of you!"

"No!" Katan yelled getting to his feet. "Your children suffer because of *you*! Because *you're* selfish. Because *you* can't put them first. Because *you* smell money and you come running like a bitch in heat! Everything that comes to your children comes to them because it's what *you* deserve! Consider yourself lucky I agreed to pay you anything up front. You don't even deserve the thousand you've got. You promised me sixty minutes, *and then walked off in fifty-two!*" Katan was screaming at full volume and shaking furiously. His face was red, and the pictures adorning the walls shook as his voice boomed around the room. He glared at the scared image of Poe as she became smaller to him.

Two security guards burst through the door to the room and seized Poe roughly by her arms. Katan swept his hair back into place and flung his arm in the general direction of the exit. "Get her out of here!" he ordered. "Make sure she doesn't steal anything on her way out."

The security guards lead Poe down to the foyer of the building. Panic struck through her emotional numbness as she looked through the glass panes of the building's facade. Several crowds had braved the cold rain that poured outside to gather at the building's entrance and form one giant mass of bodies, all fighting for space. She could hear some of them cry a muffled chant and saw the bleeding ink of messages scrawled on colored cardboard signs held over their heads and collapsing from the wetness.

Those fighting for space at the front of the crowd were press, clearly annoyed at having been relegated from their carefully picked spaces at the entrance of the building to standing with protesters. They stood with cameras pointed toward the front of the building, waiting for Poe to exit after her humiliating interview. Those in the front of the crowd saw her through the glass, and their cries agitated the balance of the crowd. They began to push against the barricades that had been set up between the crowd and the building, and police and building security worked together as they tried to control the press of soaking bodies attempting to make their way through them.

"We'd better get her out of here," one of Poe's guard escorts said to the other. "Management wasn't expecting so many protesters. Call Ethan and tell him to get more police here...Now!" The other guard nodded and ran off in another direction.

"I don't know that you're worth all this trouble, lady," the remaining guard said to her as he looked out at the police clashing with the crowd.

A voice sounded to their right, "Of course she is!"

Poe and the guard turned on the spot, the guard reaching for a baton hanging on his belt. The voice was Desmond's. He approached the pair quickly, his umbrella leaving drops of water on the tiled floor in his wake. "Let me take her," he ordered the guard firmly.

"And who the hell are you?" the guard barked back indignantly, his hand still reaching behind him.

"I'm her friend!" Desmond barked back. "Your job is only to get her out of the building. Let me do it for you." Desmond turned his back to the guard and leaned forward so that he was eye level with Poe. "Are you okay?"

Poe shook her head and looked out at the crowd. The team of guards and police were quickly losing control. The barricade was quickly deteriorating. "There's no way out," Poe said with her eyes glazing over. "There's no way out."

Desmond turned to the guard. "I have a car parked next to the building. North Charles Street. Is there an exit that opens onto that street?" The guard nodded and led them quickly into a fire exit to the side of the building. They opened the door slightly and peered outside to see if anyone might be waiting for them at the more discreet exit.

The coast was clear.

Poe was dazed, not fully registering everything going on around her. Desmond turned to her, threw his jacket around her shoulders, and shoved the umbrella into her hand. "Put this on. Everyone knows what you're wearing."

Poe didn't move.

"Kristen!" he shouted, jolting her attention back to him. "My car is only a hundred feet up the street. You're going to walk ahead of me. I'll be right behind you, and I'll unlock my car right as you get to it so that you know which one to get in. I want you to keep the umbrella held low, so it covers your face. Walk like you're just walking down the street, not like you're in a rush. Don't look around, okay?"

Poe nodded, but Desmond wasn't sure if she had truly heard him. He pushed the door fully open. Rain pelted down from the black clouds overhead, and he could hear the muffled yells and screams from the front of the building. Poe stepped out onto the street with the umbrella held low and walked slowly up the sidewalk. Desmond walked a few steps behind her, his hands in his pocket. His shirt was quickly soaked through without his jacket, and he had to fight the urge to look behind him. He unlocked his car as Poe walked near to it, and she looked back at him to make sure it was his.

Just as she turned around, a loud crashing noise echoed from the front of the building, and screams broke through the torrent of rain. Desmond whirled around and saw people running away from the front of the building and down the street toward them. "Get in the car!" he yelled to Poe, and she climbed into the back seat with the umbrella still open.

Desmond threw himself into the front seat and quickly maneuvered away from the curb and sped off down the street.

A few thuds echoed behind Poe as projectiles hit the retreating vehicle, and Poe turned to see a few people giving chase on foot. After turning down several streets and getting safely onto the highway, Desmond looked into the rearview mirror at Poe. She sat with her head against the window pane and stared blankly outside, not seeing anything. Her makeup was streaked down her face, even though no rain had touched it. She was the image of a woman absolutely defeated, too numb and weak at this point to cry anymore.

"I'm sorry I didn't listen to you," she said softly as they drove along in silence.

Desmond took his eyes off her and focused on the road in front of him - too ashamed to look upon her in such a crushed state. "Me too," he said softly in answer, though not for the same reason.

• • •

Desmond stood wearily in the elevator on the ground floor of his office building, and pressed the button to take him to his office. The purple bags under his eyes from his late night, coupled with a poor night's sleep gave him a disheveled appearance, and as he caught his reflection in the clean steel of the closing elevator doors, he realized too late that he'd forgotten to shave. He gripped the leather handle of his briefcase and pinched the bridge of his nose as he tightly closed tired eyes, and fought the vertigo caused by the quickly rising elevator.

The partners had sent him an email immediately after Poe's interview had finished. *Meet with us tomorrow. Large conference room. 8:00 a.m.* The elevator doors opened, and the busy office foyer stood still as all eyes fell on him. He ignored the loud echo his footsteps made on the tile floor and the muttering he heard behind him as he made his way toward the large conference room. He saw through the glass walls of the conference room that every one of the partners had gathered to address him, a rare and foreboding sight.

The door made a sucking sound as he opened it, the soundproof lining along the frame breaking temporarily. It made a whooshing sound as he let it close behind him. The receptionist had called ahead to the conference room to alert the partners of Desmond's arrival, and it was as silent as the rest of the office floor. Desmond let the partners' eyes follow him as he moved at his own pace to the only vacant seat at the end of the table closest to the door. Rennick sat at the other end of the table, and as Desmond briefly caught his gaze, he knew what his eyes were saying. *I can't help you.*

Desmond placed his briefcase on the empty seat and turned to face the men and women waiting for him. "I'll stand," he said flatly. Some of the partners visibly bristled and shifted in their chairs at his defiant attitude.

Rennick remained fixed to his seat at the head of the table, seemingly motionless but for the movement of his passive features as he spoke, "Desmond, a great many of the partners have come to me and expressed concern for your management of the Poe case."

"The interview?" Desmond asked.

Rennick nodded slowly. "Some of your colleagues had come to me to discuss your case management before last night's interview, but yes. After last night, the echo of complaints and concerns reached a pitch that I could not ignore. Thus, I called this meeting." *But I didn't want to…*Rennick's eyes spoke the last words of the sentence. "We are surprised that you allowed your client to participate in that interview."

"The *client*, as you put it, was adamant about her participation. She was very firm in her instructions on this point," Desmond shot back defensively.

Rennick's eyes narrowed, perturbed by Desmond's interruption. "Part of what we expect from partners is the ability to effectively counsel a client, and steer them away from making unwise decisions. Your client was adamant in her instructions because you let her hear what Katan said about his offer. You put him on speaker, and let her hear your conversation with him. I read your case notes, Desmond. You failed to control the delivery of his offer, and *that* is why your colleagues are concerned about your handle on this case."

"That's not all," cut in another partner seated next to Desmond. "I am getting complaints about your appearance," she inclined her head toward Desmond, "your attitude, even the way you spoke to the receptionist last week! None of this is becoming of a senior associate vying for partnership. All of us are worried that you're losing this case before the jury is even empaneled!"

She looked around the room at the other partners and met nodding heads and a general murmur of concurrence. "This case is huge Desmond, and I have to wonder if—"

"Silence!" Rennick shot to his feet, his booming voice making the glass walls shake. He was staring down at the female partner with wide eyes, cutting her off immediately. She sat back in her chair, staring back at Desmond reproachfully. Rennick raised a finger as he continued to address the partner. "How *dare* you! I told all of you that you were not to go there before Desmond arrived, and in this office, my word is *law*! Is that clear?"

The female partner looked back at the angry old man at the end of the table and nodded solemnly. The room was silent, but for Rennick's heavy, near panting breaths.

"What is it?" Desmond asked as he and Rennick stood at opposite ends of the table.

Rennick shook his head. "It's irrelevant," said Rennick as he began to calm down.

"I want to know," Desmond answered, his tone making it clear he was not asking.

"I said it's irrelevant!" Rennick answered with a firm and irritated tone. His eyes elaborated, *I don't want to answer.* The two men leveled each other's stare from across opposite ends of the table.

"I want to know," Desmond repeated. He began to look at each of the faces in the room. "If this meeting is to address my performance and handling of the case, then I want all the cards on the table. I can't defend myself or my conduct against allegations if they're hidden from me." He returned his level attention to Rennick, "I want to know."

Rennick looked to the ground and sighed. His anger seemed to leave on his breath, deflating his frame. When he looked up at Desmond, he looked pained by the words about to leave his lips. "Desmond, a number of the partners are concerned that your circumstances are clouding your judgment on this case. That you're too involved."

"My ... circumstances?" Desmond asked, as he felt anger rise within. He felt the muscles of his jaw tighten as he clenched his teeth. "What circumstances would those be?"

Rennick had to look away from Desmond in shame. "Your wife's infertility and everything that has gone along with it."

The partners in the room had stopped looking at Desmond, each staring at the ground, the table, or into middle space. Rennick's confession had made public their complaints and concerns previously exchanged only in secret emails and hushed conversations. Desmond looked around the room, and didn't meet a single set of eyes. He looked back to Rennick. "What about you? Do you share this concern?"

Rennick sighed. "Desmond, I'd be lying to you if I told you it hadn't crossed my mind."

Desmond's knuckles turned white as he gripped the back of the seat in front of him. The air in his chest roared as his breaths came on beleaguered heaves. "I want to make something abundantly clear to everyone in this room," he snarled. "My personal life is none of your *damned* business! I don't bring my personal life into this office, and that right sure as hell doesn't fall to any of you. A year from now, long after I have won this case and I am sitting among you as a partner, you will all do well to remember that." Desmond grabbed his briefcase and left the conference room without waiting for their leave.

As the door whooshed shut once again behind Desmond, Rennick took his seat and addressed the remaining partners. "If any of you had meetings planned in the next hour, cancel them now. If you think that was difficult to endure, well then, brace yourselves. You all just pissed me off."

• • •

Hannah thanked her driver as he parked outside the front of Desmond's office building. She still felt bad about the way she'd left things between them outside of her hotel room, and wanted to explain how she'd been feeling since the ultrasound. She stepped out of the vehicle and was greeted by the scents of cinnamon and pumpkin spice carried on the cold fall breeze from the nearby cafes and restaurants. She pulled her jacket closed around her and hurried into the building foyer to escape the cold.

Although Thanksgiving was a couple of weeks away, winter seemed to have started early. Not even the bright rays of sun shining down and kissing her face were able to warm the air after the downpour the night before. She had come straight from the studio where'd she'd hosted a discreet teleconference with the owners of one of the theaters just off Broadway in New York.

Another production company had suddenly declared bankruptcy, and as a result, had vacated its reserved use of the theater. With her show almost finished, and knowing that the theater would not remain available for long, she had instructed her agent to organize a teleconference with the owners as soon as possible. She'd quickly struck a deal with the theater owners, as they knew as well as she did that any available theater would jump at the opportunity to host her "coming out of retirement" show, as they had put it. The only condition was that she'd have to be prepared to premiere her new show by the end of December, a little over six weeks away. This wouldn't be an easy endeavor, but she knew that even with her reputation, anything close to Broadway wouldn't become available for some time. After striking a deal with the owners of the theater, the cat was out of the bag.

Almost immediately after ending their teleconference, Hannah's phone began to ring endlessly; her "secret" production was obviously no longer a secret. Hannah's phone buzzed in her hand as she received a text message from her publicist: *Katan and his people keep calling. Not happy he missed the scoop on your show. He's still in Baltimore following a recent interview.* Hannah smiled to herself as she read the message. It wasn't often she got one over on Katan, and she delighted in this occasion.

Hannah still wore the brilliant smile as she entered Desmond's building, and heads turned as she strode confidently through the foyer in her gray business jacket, matching pencil skirt, and heels, which clicked with each step of her long legs. Her smile vanished, however, and she stopped dead in her tracks as she saw a man leaning against the wall in the space between the two elevator doors.

It was Jack Katan.

"Why hello, Hannah," he said with a smile as he pushed himself off the wall, and walked toward her.

Hannah sighed impatiently. "Seriously, Katan? What are you doing here?"

"It's insulting to ignore my calls," he began. "One might begin to think you're avoiding me."

Hannah laughed, "I'm not avoiding you, Jack. That would require me to be thinking about you in the first place, and as you've heard, I have better things to think about."

Katan looked over his shoulder at the closed elevator doors and then up through the ceiling to where he imagined Desmond would be sitting. "Clearly," he mocked.

"What do you want?" Hannah asked, impatience once again returning to her tone. "Have you seriously just been standing by the elevator, waiting for me?"

Katan looked back at her and shrugged. "You or him. One or the other. It didn't matter which. I knew I'd run into one of you here before I flew back to New York."

Hannah shook her head, unsure of whether she should humor him with her question. "To what end?"

Katan shook a finger at Hannah and made a chastising sound. "Tsk, tsk, Hannah. You know I don't like secrets. Secrets are horrible things. Everything's better when it's out in the open. I've built my whole career on helping to get things out in the open! Things like ... I don't know. The sex of your baby?" Katan's eyes dropped so that he stared at her bump.

He was briefly stunned as Hannah's hand crashed against his face in a quick and furious slap. "Don't you *dare* talk about my baby!" she said, seething. "Not to me, not in your bullshit articles, not to *anyone*. Understand?"

The doors to one of the elevators opened in front of Desmond just as Hannah slapped Katan. Still fuming from his meeting with the partners, Desmond rushed over to her, dropped his briefcase, and grabbed Katan by his collar in two bundled fists. "What the hell are you doing here?" he hissed through clenched teeth. "It's not enough that you humiliate a poor defenseless woman on TV, now you have to harass a pregnant woman too?"

Katan smiled and spoke calmly even though Desmond held him off balance. "What's the problem, Desmond? You can hang around my office foyer, but I can't hang around yours?"

Hannah's small hands reached up on top of Desmond's, and she softly gestured for him to lower Katan. "Desmond, don't. He knows the sex of the baby. Don't give him an excuse to tell you."

Desmond released Katan's collar and shoved him backward. "How could you know that?" Katan smiled, and stretched his arms out in front of him. "I have connections everywhere. How do you think I stay so well informed?"

"What do you want?" Desmond demanded. "What are you even doing here?"

Katan's smile broadened. "Why, I was explaining that very thing to Hannah before you interrupted us!" he said brightly, seemingly unperturbed by being roughed up by Desmond. "I was just telling her that I hate secrets. Secrets hurt people! Just like Hannah hurt me by keeping her show a secret. It was very embarrassing to be one of the last to know about this show, and she could have avoided that by just picking up the phone and letting me know ahead of time. A bit of professional courtesy, you know? And after all the history we have! Why, when I discovered the sex of your baby, I figured I'd lead by example and tell at least one of you ahead of time what my next story will be. It's going to be about your little arrangement—your sordid affair with Hannah to have a baby, and get past the clinic doors your client closed with her lawsuit. Oh, the irony! It really makes for fantastic reading!"

"That's what phones are for," Desmond barked, his anger mounting. "Why are you *here*?"

Katan's face relaxed, and he leaned in toward Desmond, speaking just loudly enough for Desmond and Hannah to hear his voice. "Why, simply to see the look on your faces when I tell you it's a girl!"

It took a moment for Desmond to register Katan's words. A wave of shock ran through him as his anger was briefly displaced. He looked over at Hannah. Her face showed a mixture of shock at the news, and anger that it should be delivered against her wishes, and by Katan of all people.

The culmination of the blows delivered by Katan—the articles, the interview with Poe, and now this—rose up quickly inside of Desmond, and he lashed out in uncontrolled fury. His face twisted into a mask of pure hatred. "You bastard!" he yelled, and he leaped forward with his arm raised to take a swing at Katan's smug face.

Hannah quickly grabbed his arm as it reached behind him, and she swung herself in front of him. She held her face close in front of his and placed her hands on its sides so that she filled his field of vision. She felt Desmond drop his arm behind him and she looked deeply into eyes. His deep, blue eyes, marred with anger and hurt, trying to look through her at his target.

"Look at me," she whispered to him, her face barely an inch from his. "Just look at me. Stay with me. Stay here with me." She watched his eyes focus on hers, and the anger left them, leaving them filled only with pain. "Don't let him take this moment from us," she whispered. "We're having a girl, Desmond. A beautiful baby girl. Don't let him take this from us."

Tears began to scroll silently down her cheeks as Desmond's face filled her own field of her vision, and his gaze spoke to her the measure of pain and heartache hidden inside of him. "This wasn't meant for him!" Desmond whispered to her, his voice hoarse and deep. "This moment, it was supposed to be private, happy...only between us when she was born." His voice quivered as he spoke the word "she" for the first time in reference to his daughter. "He's *robbed* us of that moment, Hannah. He took that from us."

Hannah stroked his grizzled cheek affectionately with the thumb of one the hands that held his face in front of hers. "Has he?" she asked, a sad smile breaking across her pink lips. "It's just us here. He hasn't taken anything. He lost." She leaned forward slowly and kissed the part of his cheek left uncovered by her hand before releasing him. "Let's go," she said, taking his hand in hers and leading him away from Katan.

Katan called out after the retreating pair. "You know, the only unfortunate thing in all of this is that I wasn't the one to get her pregnant," he scoffed. "She might seem all prim and proper, but boy, is she an animal in bed!"

Hannah's arm fell as Desmond released her hand, and she turned to see him land a punch squarely on the side of Katan's face. The powerful blow rocked Katan backwards, and he fell onto the ground, holding his jaw. A trickle of thick, red blood began to ooze slowly out of one of his nostrils, and his split lip poured out with more of the same onto his shirt. "That's assault!" Katan yelled, as Desmond stood over him. "That's assault! You're done. Finished! I'm going to sue you to oblivion!"

Desmond smiled as he looked down at the cowering man, suddenly made small on the cold ground. "I'm a lawyer. Give it your best shot. I just gave you mine." Desmond grabbed his briefcase as he turned to rejoin Hannah. Katan could only watch as they left the building side by side.

CHAPTER 22

THE RIGHT WORDS

Todd sat at his kitchen table with his arms propped on the glass in front of him, and his heavy face held in his tired hands. He'd collapsed into the seat over an hour ago, and was still trying to summon the strength to get up and get ready for his meeting with Desmond later that day. "I told you," he said quietly to Katelynn as she sat opposite him with a look of frantic frustration. "I don't have the right words."

She had once again brought up the matter of the video recording she wanted him to make for their baby. This was a conversation they had argued about several times over the preceding months, and it was clear that Katelynn was becoming impatient, if not desperate, for those recordings. "You keep saying that" she responded with angry irritation rising in her voice, "You keep saying that you don't have the right words. But it's getting to a point where it doesn't matter, Todd. Look at you!" She examined her husband, and the tormented sadness she hid every day from him revealed itself once more, "You're wasting away."

Todd's body had become so weak from his sickness that his hands and arms shook under their own weight. The friendly eyes that normally shone brightly in the black hollows of his skull-like face had dulled and grayed, and his breathing was labored and desperate — a trait he tried vigilantly to hide from Katelynn. She stood up from her seat and moved to hug him from behind, his pale skin cold against the warmth of hers. "And I don't just mean physically. You're wasting away. Your you-ness is leaving you day by day. You don't smile or joke as much these days. You don't flirt or touch me playfully when we're in the same room, and I know that has a lot to do with you feeling weak, but still. You're becoming a ghost of yourself. An echo. And I have to wonder, what happens if too much of you has left by the time you make the recording? Will our daughter know the real you? The one I fell in love with? And what happens if you wait too long and there's no recording at all? Our girl needs her father, Todd, even if it's only just to say good-bye."

Todd raised his face from his hands and touched the arms wrapped around him. His voice shook as he spoke, but more from the emotion he felt from his wife's words than the effort it took from him. "I should go. Desmond is probably waiting for me."

"*Desmond?*" Katelynn cried out angrily as she released him, and stood indignantly erect behind him. "Desmond? I'm here begging you for recordings, and you're going to waste more time with him? I want my recorded video, Todd. To hell with Desmond!"

"Katelynn, I can't," Todd answered softly, still seated with his back to her.

"Why?" she begged painfully.

"You know why. Because—"

Katelynn cut him off angrily. "Because you don't have your right words? Damn it, Todd. It doesn't matter anymore! Don't you see that? I want any words. Any! Just get the damned camera, push the red button, and say *something*! Say anything! Read her a story. Tell her what you're thinking. What you're feeling. Tell her what you had for lunch. I don't care! I just want her to know your voice!" She was shouting now. "Give me anything! To hell with your right words!"

Todd rose slowly from his seat and turned to face Katelynn. His face showed he was trying to hide his pain, both physical and emotional. "You don't get it!" he yelled back in a tone matching his wife's, and the force of his raised voice racked his body. "You want me to tell her what I'm thinking? What I'm feeling? The only thing I'm thinking and feeling is that cancer sucks! That life is just one big and unfair experience. That we spend our entire lives enduring these horrible realities just so that we can feel the fleeting good moments that are few and far between. I want to give our daughter *something*. Something real she can hold on to. But right now, whenever I think about recording a message, all I can think about is how *angry* I am, and how unfair life is, and *that* is something our daughter doesn't need to hear from me. The world will teach her this all on its own, and I won't be here to protect her from any of it! To hell with my right words? Do you realize how many moments there's going to be in her life where even the *right* words won't be enough? How many moments there'll be where words don't reach? How many moments where I can't reduce my presence to words for her? Where there's simply no substitute for just *being* there?"

Todd brought a hand in front of his body and began counting on his fingers. "Her first day of school. When a boy breaks her heart. The day she comes home wondering if she's pretty. Her college graduation. Her wedding day."

Katelynn held her eyes closed tightly and shook her head violently as tears escaped. Todd resumed. "Those are just a handful of big moments. What about the difficult conversations she'll need to have? How do I tell her, when I don't even *know* her yet, that she shouldn't give up when her faith in life is beneath her knees? That it gets better. It gets easier. Even if she can believe a complete stranger, because that's all I'll be to her. How can she trust what I'm saying when it didn't get easier for me? When the 'better' I worked and waited for my whole life was just cancer? If she does give up, how do I tell her that she was created for something great? How do I tell her that I wanted something more for her than just a nine-to-five while she tries to find a man in her spare time? How do I look her in the eye across time, through the lens of a camera, and answer her when she asks me if God is real?

"I mean, for goodness sake, Katelynn, I'm only thirty-three! I thought I'd have more time! I haven't even had enough time to answer these questions for myself, let alone my daughter. I can't record a video yet because I don't have the answers to the questions she's supposed to ask her dad! I was supposed to have an entire lifetime to be ready for these questions. To be ready to be her dad, and keep her safe from the world. But I don't! I get a couple of months to condense as much fatherhood as I can into a single video that lasts a couple of minutes. I haven't made the video yet because I don't have the right words. The *perfect* words. Because if she's not going to have me around, then she at least deserves that." Todd was panting when he finished speaking, and it muffled the sound of Katelynn's quiet sobs.

She threw herself into his arms and buried her face into his thin chest, and the force almost knocked him over the table behind him. He stroked her blonde hair slowly with his skeletal fingers as she tried to memorize what it felt like to be held in her husband's arms. When at last she leaned back from him, she looked up at him with strands of blonde hair stuck to her cheeks from the dampness of her tear-streaks and said, "Say hi to Desmond for me."

Todd kissed her softly on the forehead before bending low on shaking legs and kissing the tip of her pregnant belly. "Daddy's waiting for you, sweetheart. Don't be late," he whispered softly into her stomach, and the message caused Katelynn to break into a smile and fresh tears. Todd kissed

Katelynn once more, and a minute later he'd grabbed a hat to cover his bald scalp, and walked out the front door.

As Katelynn watched him leave, she couldn't help but feel that he'd somehow left another part of himself behind at the kitchen table. The version of her husband that walked away from her was ghostlier than the man she'd just held in her arms.

• • •

"I'm fine!" Todd shooed Desmond away from him after he'd risen quickly from his seat, and tried to help him walk the last ten feet to their table at the cafe.

Desmond went back to his seat and watched furtively as Todd carefully navigated his way around his chair before collapsing heavily into it.

"Should have gone to Ledo's again..." Todd said with a sarcastic smile. "It's closer to my place."

Desmond gave Todd a wry grin and had to stop himself from mentioning the pizzeria in observance of the promise he'd made earlier. "You look rough," said Desmond. "Not rough in terms of appearance—just rough like you're having a hard day."

Todd nodded with wide eyes. "You're not wrong! Katelynn brought up the recording again." A waiter approached them and took their orders. Desmond ordered his usual coffee, and Todd requested a pot of decaffeinated green tea.

"Tea?" Desmond asked as the waiter left with their order. "Never known you to order tea."

Todd nodded. "Coffee exacerbates my shakes these days. The slightest bit of caffeine and I'm shaking harder than a widow's vibrator." Todd chuckled at his own joke. "Besides, the doctor has been trying to get me on green tea since he first diagnosed me."

The waiter came back with their order, and each took the first sip of their beverages. "So," Desmond began, "the recording. How's it going?"

Todd squinted at Desmond appraisingly. "I thought lawyers were supposed to be subtle when prying out information."

Desmond shook his head. "Nah, you're thinking of psychiatrists. Normally when we want information, the other person is under oath and obliged to answer, so there's no need for subtlety. Last time I tried talking to you about the recording, you said you weren't ready to talk about it. Given how you look after your conversation with Katelynn, I figure you might like to talk it out; so, I hope you're comfortable talking about it now."

Todd smiled back at Desmond and nodded. "You're a negotiator Des, so let's negotiate. I'll talk to you about my recording if you talk to me about a topic of my choice."

Desmond grinned as he wiped some coffee foam from his lips with the back of his hand. "Do I at least get to know what the topic is beforehand?"

"Nope, there's no fun in that."

Desmond scratched the back of his head as he weighed his options. "Hell Todd, I guess I'd talk to you about anything anyway. Might as well get a story out of you in exchange. Deal. So, what's happening with the recording?"

Todd removed his hat and rubbed the side of his bald head. "It's hard. Katelynn wants a recording. She keeps reminding me that I'm going to die soon, and I ought to hurry up. It's not that easy though. I don't have the right words yet."

"Right words? I'd have thought that in these circumstances any words would be right, or at least that none could be wrong," interjected Desmond.

Todd reflected on the conversation he'd just had with his wife. "Consider this, Desmond, if I didn't have cancer, I'd have at least one year to think about what to say on her first birthday, eighteen years to think about what to say to her on her prom night, twenty or thirty years to think about what to say to her on her wedding day. And none of what I'd have to say would have anything to do with death, cancer, or anything sad. Those moments would get to be completely happy. Yet now in one video, I'm supposed to deliver some emotional wisdom that is not only relevant to all of these moments, but which makes up for my absence and erases all the times she'll think to herself, 'I wish Dad were here.'"

Desmond nodded. "So," he began, unsure of what to say, "You're having a daughter too?"

Todd slumped back in his seat smiling. "Yeah, I am."

Desmond shook his head. "Goodness, help us both, then!" The two men laughed together until the effort turned Todd's laugh into a gasping wheeze.

When Todd regained control of his breathing, he slammed an angry fist into onto the table. "Y'know Desmond," Todd began stoically as he wiped away the spit that had accumulated at the side of his mouth, "When I was a kid, I had a dream. When all the other kids talked about what they wanted to be when they grew up—an astronaut, a firefighter, a pilot—I just dreamed about being a good man. My dad was an alcoholic. A gambler. A bitter and sad man who blamed his son for his wife leaving him instead of his habits. So, I just wanted to be better than him. I wanted to be a provider for my family, put a roof over our heads, and not have my kids worry whether the money would come out or not every time we'd go to the ATM. And I did it. I'm a good man, I think. I became a vet not because I wanted to, but because I was told it paid well, and now Katelynn and I don't have to worry about money.

"But this wasn't supposed to be the end of my story. My end goal was never to just be comfortable. I was supposed to be somebody! Building a comfortable life as a good man was just act one. It was supposed to give me the freedom to have that internal discussion that everyone else got to have as a kid. It was supposed to be *my* turn to decide *what* I wanted to be, not just *who*. But now ... now I don't get to. And I've accepted that, for the most part. If what I expected to be act one is my whole story, then my daughter will be the sequel. *She* is going to be somebody.

"But returning to the recording again, here's the thing: if I never got the chance to figure out how to be more than ordinary, how can I teach my daughter how to do it? I keep thinking that as I get closer to my death, that I'll receive some divine clarity, some perfect wisdom that I'll be able to leave her. But nothing's coming, and it has me thinking that perhaps I lived my entire life without learning anything worth teaching to my daughter. I'm starting to think that maybe she'd be better off not hearing from me at all."

Desmond broke in. "Come on now, Todd. Let's say your little girl had you around her whole life. She wouldn't just be coming to you for you to impart some 'divine wisdom,' as you put it. She'd come to you just because you're her dad. She'd come to you to hear all those life stories that you're saying were all a waste. And she wouldn't ask to hear them because there's a hidden lesson to be learned. She'd want to hear them just because they're about you. If you don't let her know you and your stories, where else is she going to go to get that?"

Desmond stopped abruptly as Todd held an outstretched finger in front of him. His lip quivered, and his face twitched as he tried to control the muscles in his face and hold back the tears welling in his eyes.

"Don't!" Todd begged, "Don't go there, please."

"I'm ... I'm sorry," Desmond sputtered. "I didn't ... I don't know what you mean."

Todd caught the droplets on his face just as they broke free and wiped them away impatiently with his hand. He looked around at the cafe guests to see if anyone noticed him.

"You have to understand, Desmond. I haven't told anyone about this." Todd half-hid his face in the hand he propped on the table as he spoke, his voice shaking with emotion. "I'm not just struggling with the fact that I won't be around for all these moments with my daughter."

Desmond heard Todd's breathing turn heavy as he cried, hidden beneath his hand.

"Desmond, who's going to walk my daughter down the aisle? Who's she going to call 'Dad'? Who's my wife going to wake up next to years from now? Katelynn's young and beautiful, inside and out. I can't expect that she won't find love again. You see, it's not just that I won't have these moments, it's that someone else will have them in my place!"

Desmond looked away, trying to give his friend a measure of privacy as he recomposed himself. He tried to speak evenly, carefully trying to sound understanding without being overly sympathetic. "Todd, I don't pretend to know what it's like to be confronted with these things. That said, I find it very hard to imagine that your family would so readily forget or replace you. You think it won't be your photo on the mantle in your home? That it won't be you that your daughter thinks of on Father's Day? You're wrong. Now, you know Katelynn better than me, but I've seen the way she looks at you. If … *if* she ever decided to be with someone again, don't dare think for a second that she wouldn't trade that for just a few more minutes with you. You are and always will be, your wife's husband and your daughter's father."

Todd sat upright and wiped the napkin across his blood-shot eyes one last time. "I don't want to talk about this anymore." Desmond nodded and tried to quickly change the topic and tone of their conversation. "Well then," he began, "we made a deal. You can ask me about whatever it is you wanted to talk about."

Todd smiled in appreciation at the quick change in topic, and at the fact that Desmond didn't seem to care that he'd been bawling just moments earlier. It was one of the reasons why he continued to spend so much time with his friend. Desmond stood alone as the only person who didn't treat him like a dead man walking—who didn't tiptoe around his sickness like some taboo reality that could be erased if everyone just ignored it for long enough. Sometimes he needed to talk about it, but even Katelynn would avoid the topic as though such avoidance would make Todd forget all about his sickness and his inevitable, impending death. No one else understood why he had spent so much time with Desmond in recent months, but the simple truth was that Desmond was a person to whom he could talk about anything, without judgment or coddling.

Todd made a gesture with his hands to ask for Desmond's help in pouring more tea into his cup, as he couldn't lift the pot. Desmond quickly poured more of the liquid into his friend's cup as Todd looked on helplessly. Todd picked up his teacup once more and leaned back in his chair comfortably. "I want to know what's going on between you and Hannah."

Desmond raised an eyebrow, "Me and Hannah? I don't know what you mean."

"That's fair," Todd responded with a grin. "I guess maybe you haven't seen it. Y'know, Ashleigh hasn't been to the surrogacy support sessions for weeks, and I don't know if you know it, but I'm often by the door of that room watching long before you notice and come out to talk to me. You're different with Hannah lately. I don't really know how to explain it, but you're more…protective. Almost affectionate, without actually being affectionate."

"That's not much of an explanation at all!" Desmond retorted, still confused.

"Well, that's why I wanted to talk about it. I was hoping you could help me understand what I'm seeing. Maybe I'm going about this the wrong way ... being too direct?" Todd continued. "Let's look at it from another angle. How're things between you and Ashleigh?"

Desmond sighed. "Now that's even more complicated."

"Then simplify it. Try and tell me in a sentence or two. You'd be surprised at how that can uncomplicate matters."

Desmond looked heavenward as he tried to answer, "More and more it feels like we like each other, but don't love each other. Or, maybe it's the other way around. Whatever it is, it doesn't feel right. It doesn't feel like it used to, or like it should."

"And why's that?" Todd continued.

"Well, Ashleigh keeps telling me that I'm not the same man anymore. That I'm a different man ever since Hannah got pregnant," answered Desmond.

"And what do you think?"

"I think Ashleigh doesn't know what she wants. She wants a child at all costs, and that meant she wanted a child using a non-surgical surrogate. But then, she still wants me. Not just me though—she wants the version of me that would never do something like that. But she still wants me to do it. So, she wants a version of me who'd refuse to sleep with another woman, but who'd still do it, so she could have her baby. She wanted this. She just didn't want it to change me!"

"And do you think it has changed you?" Todd intoned, keeping the train of thought in development.

"I don't know," Desmond answered earnestly. "It's hard to tell. I don't feel any different. But if I have changed, I wouldn't even know if having sex with Hannah is what did it. The whole arrangement changed things between Ashleigh and me. I wonder if I changed, whether that's what changed me."

"And do you still love Ashleigh?" asked Todd as he stared straight at Desmond from behind his cup.

"What? Are you serious?" Desmond asked, shocked.

Todd nodded empathetically and put a hand up defensively. "Well, hold on a second. I'm not implying anything. I just wonder if you've asked yourself this question. You just said you're not sure if you like or love Ashleigh, or whatever. So, do you still love her, or are you just afraid of letting her go?"

Desmond made a noise like he was about to answer, but then paused. Todd made a gesture with his hands as if to say, *see, there's something to this.*

Desmond continued, "It's not that ... you don't understand!"

Todd cut in. "No, you don't understand. I'm not judging you, Desmond. There was a time where I'd have rebuked you for feeling this way, whether that's feeling something less for Ashleigh or something more for Hannah, but not so much now. Now my clock is winding down and my time is running out. Perhaps my attitude has changed. Perhaps it hasn't. It doesn't matter. All I'm saying is that life is too short to be spent the wrong way. Or with the wrong person—"

Desmond spoke indignantly over Todd. "Now hang on, Todd! I'm not at all suggesting that I'm unhappy, or with the wrong person! I'm still in love with Ashleigh, and I want to be with her!"

"Do you also want to be with Hannah? Do you love her too?" Todd asked seriously.

Desmond let out an irritated sigh. "Why does this keep coming up!?"

"That doesn't answer my question," Todd observed. "Do you love her too?"

Desmond sat silently for a moment, staring at Todd's face. "No," he answered flatly. "Not like that."

"Not like that?" Todd repeated. "So, you do love her, just not in the same way you love Ashleigh?"

"Why are you so interested in all of this?" Desmond asked. "What do you care?"

"Why are you so afraid to say how you feel about Hannah? Look, you could say that you love Hannah as a friend. You could say that you love the baby growing inside of her. There are many different kinds of love, and a million legitimate ways to say that you love Hannah, none of which would be considered inappropriate, or as though you're cheating on Ashleigh. So why are you so afraid to say how you feel about her? Can't you see that your reluctance to admit *any* kind of feelings for her is the *exact* thing that makes all of this just a little suspicious?"

"What do you want me to say?" Desmond barked.

Todd shrugged, a little exasperated. "I just want you to be honest with yourself. Life's too short, and I just wanted to make sure that you're taking the time to consider these things. So that you don't spend your whole life in a routine and miss out on discovering and pursuing what it is you really want."

"And you think that what I really want is Hannah?" Desmond asked.

"I don't know what you want, Desmond," answered Todd. "How could I? How could anyone? I just think that maybe you don't either. I just want you to be honest with yourself and ask yourself these difficult questions, so perhaps you can figure it out."

"You want me to be honest?" Desmond answered defensively, his annoyance clear in his tone. "I don't want to talk about this anymore. How's that for honesty?"

Todd shrugged once more. "Fine by me, Des. You helped me in our conversation about my video recording, and I just wanted to try and return the favor in something I thought I saw in you."

Desmond bristled in his seat. He was still trying to calm himself, and it took a moment for Todd's words to sink in. "What do you mean? How did I help you with your recording?"

Todd gave a broad, genuine smile as he lowered his cup from his lips and placed it back on the table with two shaking hands. "You gave me an idea, one I think I can pull off with your help, but only if you know how to keep a secret."

• • •

Desmond returned home from his meeting with Todd late in the evening. Ashleigh sat reading in their bed with the covers draped over her legs, and a nightgown over her shoulders. Although she sat comfortably in a warm bed and propped up against the cushioned headboard, there was something stiff in her posture suggesting that she was anything but comfortable.

"Where were you?" she asked Desmond without looking up from her book. Her tone was more curious than accusatory. She didn't understand how he could have spent so much of the day and evening with Todd.

"I was with Todd," Desmond answered with a yawn as he removed his shirt. He shivered in the cold room when he finished undressing and adjusted the thermostat before climbing into the bed to join his wife.

Ashleigh put her book down on her bedside table and rolled onto her side so that she faced Desmond. He lay on his back staring up at the ceiling with his arms folded behind his head.

"I miss you, Des."

He rolled onto his side so that the two faced each other. "Miss me? I'm right here, Ash. I always am."

Ashleigh shook her head slowly. "No, you're not. Between work, the surrogacy support group, and your time with Todd, it feels like I never get to see you anymore. Almost like you have time for everyone but me, and everything but us."

Desmond reached up and stroked his wife's cheek with his hand. "There's just a lot going on right now, Ash. All of those things are temporary though—the case, the pregnancy…" He paused as he looked away. "… even Todd," he finished sadly. He looked back into her eyes, "But us, we're forever," he said smiling.

Their quiet moment in bed was interrupted as Desmond's cell phone vibrated with an incoming call on his bedside table. He grabbed the phone and sat up, concerned. "It's Hannah," he said aloud before he answered the call.

Ashleigh rolled her eyes as she moved onto her side and listened to Desmond's half of the conversation. She shook her head in irritation as her husband interrupted even more of their little time together for the sake of someone else. "Tell her to call back at a decent hour!" she said loudly enough for Hannah to hear on her side of the call.

Desmond covered his free ear to hear Hannah's voice better, "I'm on my way" he said before ending the call.

"Are you kidding me!?" Ashleigh cried as she propped herself up in the bed. "You *just* got home! Look at the time! What's so damned important that you have to go over there right away?" Desmond climbed out of bed and grabbed the shirt he'd taken off only minutes earlier.

"She said she's having cramps—"

"So, tell her to call a doctor! An ambulance! Have her driver take her to the hospital!" Ashleigh yelled.

Desmond turned so that he was facing Ashleigh. His shirt was only half-buttoned, and the bottom of it flapped around his abdomen as he moved to find his pants, "Ashleigh, when the woman *we* got pregnant calls and asks for my help, I'm not going to say no, or play twenty-questions. She's worried that something is wrong. Frankly, I'm surprised that you're not worried too. This is *our* baby." Desmond made sure to use a gender-neutral term to describe their child. He hadn't told Ashleigh about his encounter with Katan, or that he and Hannah knew they were having a girl.

"What you don't understand is that these days I'm *always* worried," Ashleigh retorted.

Desmond came around to her side of the bed and leaned down to kiss her quickly on the forehead. He was so rushed that he didn't even realize that his kiss missed, and that he'd pecked thin air. "I won't be long," said Desmond as he made his way to the door. "Don't wait up."

Desmond disappeared in the darkness beyond their bedroom door, leaving Ashleigh alone in their bedroom. *Don't worry,* she thought to herself as she stared into the blank space where Desmond had left. *I'm done waiting for you.*

Early the next morning, Ashleigh stood alone outside Hannah's Baltimore hotel suite. She had gone there unannounced, and after knocking, could hear someone moving inside the hotel room. Hannah peered through the peephole before opening the door with a broad smile. "Ashleigh!" she exclaimed as she opened the door fully. "It feels like it's been ages! Come in! Come in!" Ashleigh gave a weak smile as she stepped across the threshold of the suite and entered the room.

Hannah closed the door behind her and pulled her robe closer about her front. Placing her handbag on a nearby table, Ashleigh turned to face Hannah. She was wearing a lilac robe that was obviously expensive. It hugged her arms and waist tightly, and her belly protruded from the opening at the front. However, besides an exposed baby bump and slightly larger breasts, there hadn't been a single observable change to the siren-like finesse of her surrogate's appearance, and she somehow managed to look attractive even in her morning mess. *Gosh,* Ashleigh thought to herself, *that's not even fair!*

Hannah made her way back to her kitchenette and called back to Ashleigh, "I was making some herbal tea. Would you like some?"

"No, thanks," Ashleigh called back to her. "I won't be here that long."

Hannah emerged from the kitchenette with a mug in hand and a slightly confused and disappointed expression on her face. "Oh, I thought perhaps you wanted to come to the warehouse and see what I've got coming along. Everything's in full swing now. It's done! It's all come together so quickly, but now we're just perfecting routines and designing set pieces and costumes before the premiere!" Hannah regaled excitedly.

"No," Ashleigh answered flatly. The change in Hannah's expression made her elaborate, "I mean, I'm very happy for you. That's all exciting. But that's not why I came here."

"Oh?" came Hannah's response. She gestured to a table which she'd repurposed on one side with a couch instead of legged chairs, and she and Ashleigh took a seat opposite one another. Hannah sat comfortably on the couch seat, and Ashleigh sat stiffly on a harder, higher chair. Although the moments that passed between them immediately after taking their seats were brief, they were awkward in their silence, and the air between them was pregnant with the expectation of confrontation.

Ashleigh cleared her throat. Now that she was here, sitting in her pregnant surrogate's abode in the early hours of the morning and without invitation, she felt stupid and wondered if she wasn't overreacting. "I wanted to talk to you about last night ... with Desmond."

Hannah cupped her hands around the warm mug standing on the table in front of her and winced as she nodded slowly. "I know. And I'm really sorry. By the time Desmond got here, the cramping had pretty much stopped, and I felt like such a pain in the ass."

"Do you have to call on him like that though?" Ashleigh asked, trying her hardest not to sound petty. "I mean, I get it. You're pregnant. It's just that I get so little time with him as it is, and as soon as I get him, he's off to be with you again. I need him too, Hannah. You're his friend, but I'm his wife. I feel like

I'm the only one not calling out to him for help, but in doing so, I'm the only one not getting any."

Hannah moved one of her hands from her mug and placed it on Ashleigh's. The heat from the mug had warmed her hand, and it radiated into Ashleigh's. "I'm sorry Ashleigh. Last night was the first time I've called on him like that, but it wasn't the first time I've wanted to. I've tried my best to deal with this pregnancy on my own as much as possible. You know, most women have someone to support them throughout this whole process. Someone to hold their hair back when they're having morning sickness. Someone to massage their feet from carrying around the extra weight all the time. Someone to run to the grocery store to grab something to satisfy a craving or comfort them when their hormones are going crazy. I don't. Last night I called and asked for Desmond's help, but by and large, I am on my own."

"That's not entirely true," Ashleigh answered pointedly. Hannah removed her hand from Ashleigh's, and Ashleigh continued. "You're not alone in this. If anything, *I'm* the one who's alone! Everyone seems to have someone to support them, except me. Poe has Desmond to support her; Desmond has Todd and me to support him; Todd has Desmond and Katelynn; and you have Desmond, me, *and* the support group. But for me? Who's there for me? Desmond is off running around supporting everyone else, you're busy with your show, and I'm left to fend for myself for all the things I'm dealing with."

Hannah nodded slowly, and her features hovered somewhere between skepticism and sympathy. "Ashleigh, the surrogacy group was there for you as well, but you stopped coming."

Ashleigh snorted. "They were not there for me! They made that clear on the first night. I stopped attending because no one wanted me there. No one wanted to hear what a *receiver* had to say or what I was struggling with. That group is there for you and Desmond, not for me. I have no one!"

"You have me, Ash!" Hannah offered sincerely. "I could be there for you. Just call me."

Ashleigh tried to force a smile. "That's sweet of you to say, but that's not true. You're so busy with your show these days that I hardly hear from you unless Desmond's somehow involved. Don't get me wrong, I don't blame you or anything. I know you've needed to move things along with your show to have it ready by next month. And I know that this show of yours is one of the reasons you agreed to be involved in this pregnancy in the first place. Still, I can't help but feel so *alone*."

Hannah frowned. "You're right. I'm sorry. I'll try not to call on Desmond again."

Ashleigh looked down at Hannah's exposed bump and felt a hot flush of guilt. "No," she answered reluctantly. "You're pregnant. You need help too. It's just…" she paused. "It's just, why do you only call on Desmond? Why don't you call me to help you? I'm supposed to be getting involved so that this pregnancy feels like it's my own, but more and more it feels like it's just something between you and Desmond."

Hannah smiled at Ashleigh. "Ashleigh, there isn't something between me and Desmond."

Ashleigh recoiled slowly, and slightly away from the woman seated across from her. "What? That's not what I said," she said skeptically, her eyes narrowing slightly. "I said that this pregnancy is starting to feel like something just between you and Desmond, not that there *was* something between you and Desmond."

Hannah smiled again, this time awkwardly. "Sorry," she began. "I must have misheard you."

Ashleigh leaned forward in her chair to better appraise Hannah's response. "Hannah, tell me the truth. Do you have feelings for Desmond?" Ashleigh watched as Hannah broke eye contact and noticed her cheeks flush. Hannah overcompensated as she tried to keep her body appearing relaxed, and it gave an awkward rigidity to her posture on the couch seat.

Hannah didn't want to lie, but she was afraid that she didn't know the answer to the question. "Ashleigh," she began, her voice a little higher pitched than normal, "my hormones are all out of whack. Ninety-nine percent of the time I don't know what I'm feeling, or why."

"That doesn't answer my question," Ashleigh said sternly, without breaking her appraising gaze.

Hannah met and leveled Ashleigh's gaze, and for the first time, the difference in their age was apparent. Hannah looked into the eyes of her younger counterpart and answered evenly. "You wanted the truth, Ashleigh. That's the only answer I've got."

Ashleigh's eyes narrowed, and she reached for her handbag on the table as she rose from her seat to leave. "I don't think I'm comfortable supporting you anymore, Hannah. And given your answer, I don't think it's appropriate that you call on Desmond for his help either. I don't want you to spend any more time alone with my husband. Is that clear?"

Ashleigh's words cut through Hannah deeper than she'd have expected, and the baby kicked hard inside of her in response to her racing heartbeat. She bent over in pain, uttering a small groan, and placed one hand around her stomach. She rubbed the spot where the baby's foot was pressing, and looked up at Ashleigh as she spoke between pained, panting breaths. "I understand ... I won't call on Desmond. I'll deal with this on my own."

CHAPTER 23

INNOCENT MISTAKE

D esmond stepped outside of his home and pulled his coat tighter around him. A cold December chill swept around the street on the wind. The clear night sky was reflected in the thin layer of ice on the footpath in front of his doorstep as the day's rain froze in the evening chill. When he saw that his windshield was covered with an opaque sheet of ice, Desmond mentally kicked himself for parking his car on the street instead of in his garage.

He felt his phone vibrate in the breast pocket of his coat, and he pulled one of his gloves off with his teeth before reaching inside with quickly numbing fingers and pulling it free. He read the new text message from Hannah and his face furrowed in confusion.

I'm having my driver take me to the surrogacy support session. I'll meet you there. Don't pick me up.

He stuffed the phone back into his pocket and climbed into his frozen car. *What brought this on?* he thought, as he turned the car's heater on full blast. *I've always driven her to the sessions and back. Why the sudden change?* He continued to ponder Hannah's text message as he waited impatiently for the car's heater to melt the ice off of his windshield.

• • •

Hannah was lying on her bed in her hotel room. She glanced at the bedside clock and let out an audible groan. She was already late for the support session and still hadn't started getting ready. The baby had been stretching its legs inside of her and was making a habit of pressing painfully hard against the inside of her abdomen. She continued to massage the spot where she could feel what she thought was her baby's foot to encourage her to retract it. *I wonder if the baby keeps pressing because it likes the massage?* she thought absently to herself.

She grabbed her cell phone lying on the bed next to her and called her driver. She listened as the phone rang several times before clicking over to his voicemail. She waited patiently for the recorded message to finish before leaving her own message after the beep. "Kaled, I'm not feeling well. I won't need your services tonight. Nothing serious, just a bit of pain. Say hello to Merna for me, won't you? Goodnight." She ended the call with a shudder. She had always hated leaving voicemail messages. She'd always felt an unnatural need to sound overly jovial in her messages, and she was sure that the forced enthusiasm made her messages sound disingenuous.

She tossed the phone lazily onto the bed and began to lie back down on the soft mattress once more. Not a moment after her face touched the pillow, a gentle rapping came from the front door to the hotel room. Hannah wearily lifted her head from the pillow. "Is that you, Kaled?" she called, thinking he may have been on his way to help her downstairs before she'd made the call.

She heard no response, and another set of knocks rapped against the wooden door.

Hannah sat up uncomfortably in the bed before making her way to the door and peering through the peephole. She opened the door impatiently and placed a hand on her hip. "I told you not to come!" she said with annoyance to Desmond.

He stood alone in the hallway with his coat draped over one arm.

"I know, but have you seen how icy it is outside? I didn't want you to slip while you made your way to or from your car."

Hannah turned on the spot and walked back into her room, leaving the door open behind her. "I'm not even going tonight, Desmond. The session already started anyway. How did you know I'd still be here?"

"You were always late when you traveled on your own," Desmond answered as he entered behind Hannah and closed the door. She turned to face him. "Well, just let yourself in," she said sarcastically as she threw her arms out in front of her.

Desmond squinted slightly as he looked at her, "What's going on?"

Hannah sighed. "Nothing. I'm just ... annoyed." She looked down at her bump and placed frustrated hands on its sides. "She keeps *kicking* me! Like, all the time. Not even kicking really, it's like she sticks her leg out and keeps it there. It's painful." She sighed again.

Desmond threw his coat onto the back of the dining chair next to the nearby table. "That's why you're not going tonight?"

Hannah had her hands back on her hips again and rocked them to one side as she stood in indignant displeasure. "I don't need a reason, Desmond. If I don't want to go, I don't have to. Your wife didn't seem to need a reason when she stopped coming." She breathed heavily out of her nose. She was irritated at her attitude and felt cruel for referring to Ashleigh as "your wife," instead of by her name. "It's painful," she said flatly. "I hurt all over. She keeps poking my insides, my feet are *killing* me—and you know that it must be excruciating for *me* to complain about sore feet—my back hurts from carrying around the extra weight, and something is up with my neck." Hannah moved her neck around as if trying to get it to crack. "I'm having trouble sleeping. It's so bad."

Desmond pursed his lips on one side. "Are you ever giving yourself a break?" he asked.

Hannah shook her head slowly and looked off to her side. "You know I'm not. I'm supposed to open the new show in New York in a few weeks, and between keeping up with work, the pregnancy ..." *and Ashleigh!* she thought. She sighed. "Even you, Desmond—I'm overwhelmed, and I really do need a break tonight. Okay?"

"Okay," Desmond answered openly without any trace of offense. He unbuttoned the cuffs on his business shirt and began rolling up his sleeves.

"What are you doing?" asked Hannah with tired exaspera- tion. Desmond continued rolling up his sleeves without answering. "Desmond!" Hannah began again, her exasperation quickly turning into annoyance. "I just told you I need a break tonight. Even from you."

Desmond finished rolling up his sleeves. "I know," he answered. "But here's the thing. I know you well enough to know that if I leave here now, you won't spend any time relaxing. You'll throw yourself into your work late into the night again. If you need a break, I'm here to help. I won't even be "here." We can get your favorite ice cream out of the freezer, set your tablet up with your favorite trashy shows, and I'll massage your feet and neck in silence. It'll be like I'm not even here."

Hannah thought about her conversation with Ashleigh— about how she'd said she didn't want her calling on Desmond for help anymore. It didn't matter to her that she hadn't called on him this time, or that she'd told him to leave. She wasn't going to split hairs. The point was that Ashleigh was uncomfortable with them spending time together alone, and that's exactly what was happening now. Hannah returned her gaze to Desmond, and she shook her head. She opened her mouth to ask him again to leave, but had the wind knocked out of her by another powerful kick from the baby. She let out a deep groan as the baby's leg stayed in place and pressed heavily against her insides. Still in a crouched position, she placed her hands on her sides and tried to think past the pain. She focused on taking deep breaths.

Unsure of what was going on, Desmond rushed to her side and stared helplessly at her with his hands held in front of him. "What's wrong?" he begged, "What do I do?"

Hannah leaned back and twisted to try and get the baby to retract its outstretched foot. "Owwwwww!" she moaned.

She suddenly recalled all of the times she'd complained about period cramps only to be told, "It's better than the alternative." She shook her head to rid herself of the useless memories. "It's like she *wants* to hurt me! This is so much worse than period cramps!" Hannah moaned.

Desmond crouched low too so that he could swing one of his large arms behind Hannah's legs, and he easily lifted her off her feet. With all thought of Ashleigh banished by the pain in her abdomen, Hannah allowed herself to be carried back into her bedroom. Desmond laid her gently onto the bed, and she rolled onto her side, assuming the only position that seemed to give her the slightest relief from the pain when the baby decided it was a good time to stretch out its growing limbs.

Desmond watched as Hannah massaged the sore spot through shallow and painful breaths. He seated himself on the edge of the bed behind her, cracked one of his knuckles, and began to massage her lower back. An hour later, Desmond was still working on the knots and strains he could feel beneath Hannah's skin. He had massaged her back, her neck, and her shoulders. She had refused to let him remove her socks or massage her feet despite him having seen them during their final night together. The baby retracted its leg after about half an hour of torture, but the two had fallen into a conversation, and Hannah was content to let Desmond continue relieving her sore muscles while they spoke.

"I'm telling you," Desmond began, "every single nursery rhyme and children's story is morally corrupt. Jack and the Beanstalk? Jack breaks into the giant's house three times, commits three counts of burglary, and when finally pursued after stealing the giant's means of making a living, Jack's solution is to murder the man. Meanwhile, we all scream: 'Yay, Jack!' as the giant begins to rot at the base of the beanstalk."

Hannah let out a hearty laugh. "What else?" she asked.

Desmond smiled. "How about the tale of the three blind mice? We have three blind creatures running around a farm—not that they'd know that given they're blind—and the farmer's wife decides to chop off their tails. It doesn't even sound like she was trying to kill them! She's just torturing these small, blinds animals."

Hannah laughed again, this time snorting. "All right, what about Snow White?" Hannah asked, trying to find a hole in Desmond's theory.

Desmond laughed. "That's the easiest of all! Snow White is only thirteen years old in the story, but that doesn't stop her living with seven men! That's not even the worst of it! After the apple puts her to sleep, along comes 'Prince Charming' who sees a sleeping thirteen-year-old and thinks it's appropriate to make out with her!"

Hannah laughed again, but this time, less heartily. Between the massage, the comfort of her own bed, and the recollection of all of the children's stories, she was quickly fading to sleep. She smiled to herself absently as she felt the baby inside of her changing position, presumably also trying to find a comfortable position in which to rest.

"The baby is moving," she cooed without opening her eyes. "Not in a bad way," she clarified. "Just moving."

Desmond's hands froze on the small of her back where he'd been massaging once more. "Can I feel it?" he asked softly.

Hannah nodded on her pillow, and she reached behind her to grab his hand and guide it onto her belly. Desmond was forced to climb fully onto the bed behind her to reach her stomach, and the mattress dipped deep where his knees rested.

"Just lay down," Hannah intoned sleepily.

Desmond laid himself on the mattress so that he lay straddled behind Hannah. She let out a contented sigh as she felt his comforting warmth behind her, and she guided his hand once more around her to where the baby was still rustling within. Desmond allowed Hannah to guide his hand beneath the front of her shirt and place it against the warm skin of her rounded belly. Hannah released his hand and placed her own on top of his so that only the fabric of her shirt lay between them. Flanked by her baby and its father, she sighed lazily, and her breathing quickly became steady as she lulled into sleep.

Desmond could feel Hannah rise and deflate with each calm breath, and he froze at once when he felt her stomach quiver from his daughter's movement. The little life stirred mere inches beneath his hand, and a paternal, protective rush ran through him instantaneously. Now and again he felt a slight jolt of movement, and with each micro-interaction with his daughter, he became patiently excited for the next. He kept his hand still and allowed his breathing to match Hannah's as he focused on his hand, eager to feel the movement of his child once more.

However, with his head on the pillow and his breathing matched to Hannah's, he too quickly fell asleep with his arm still wrapped around her and his face buried into her blonde locks.

• • •

Hannah stirred restlessly as a buzzing sound roused her awake. She sat up, and Desmond's hand slipped out from beneath her shirtfront, stirring him awake also. She glanced around in a daze as the buzzing continued intermittently. The buzzing was coming from her cell phone lying on the bed beside her. Ashleigh was calling. "Hello?" she said wearily with a yawn as she answered the call.

"Hannah!" Ashleigh's panicked voice came through from the other end of the call, "I can't get a hold of Desmond. I'm worried his car slipped in all this ice that's on the roads. Do you know where he is? Did he make it to the support session?"

Hannah was slowly coming awake, and the night came back to her as she looked around the room and saw Desmond rubbing his eyes next to her. The clock behind him told her it was almost midnight. Desmond followed Hannah's gaze to the clock behind him, and he jumped out of bed with a start. He patted himself down looking for his phone before running into the next room.

Hannah rubbed the bridge of her nose between her tired eyes. "Ash, everything's fine. He's with me. We lost track of time." There was an awkward pause between them; Ashleigh's panicked breathing became deathly still.

When she did speak, her voice changed from panic to stern irritation. "What do you mean he's with you?" she asked. Even over the phone, it was clear she spoke through gritted teeth.

Desmond came rushing back into the bedroom with his cell phone in hand. "It was in my coat on the chair!" he said derisively. "I've got seventeen missed calls!"

Hannah turned away from him as she continued the call with Ashleigh, "We never made it to the support session. I wasn't feeling well, and Desmond took care of me."

Ashleigh held the phone in front of her face as she screamed into the other end. "You miserable bitch! Did you give *any* consideration to what I told you about calling on him?" She was screaming so loudly and frantically that Desmond could hear her voice through the receiver from across the room. An eyebrow raised on his reddened face as he wondered what Ashleigh had told Hannah.

"You're right Ashleigh; I'm sorry," Hannah replied meekly, not letting on that Desmond had arrived on his own and remained with her at his insistence.

"I've spent the night waiting at home, worrying that my husband is lying dead somewhere in some car crash, and all the while he's safe *in your hotel room*?" Ashleigh spat down the phone.

Desmond stepped quickly across the room and took the phone from Hannah's trembling hand. "Ashleigh, I came here on my own. Hannah didn't call me. And we just—"

Ashleigh cut him off. "You're an asshole." She clicked the line dead without giving him a chance to explain, leaving Desmond and Hannah looking at each other, speechless.

Desmond sped home and found Ashleigh waiting for him at the table in their living room. It was close to 1:00 a.m. Fatigue clearly plagued her, but there was something about her that suggested that it had little to do with the late hour.

"You know," she began stoically as he stepped cautiously into the room, "when you're gone, I sit and I cry with a broken heart, imagining you with her. I sit *here*, and I tell myself that everything is fine, that you're not screwing her behind my back, or worse, that you're in love with her. And when I can't believe my own lies anymore, I tell myself that I'm going to confront you when you get home—like this—and I'm going to tell you that I've had enough of your violent heart. That I want you to leave and take this ghost of a life with you."

Desmond took a step toward her and took a breath to begin speaking, but Ashleigh cut him off by holding up her hand. "But then you get home," her voice started shaking as she looked down to avoid his gaze, "and I see you smile, and I go weak again. I see the way you look at me, and then you start to talk about *our* baby, and I fall to pieces again." Her face broke into a painful sort of half smile as she brought her hands up to her chest and cupped them over her heart. "All you have to do is say hello, and my heart doesn't stand a chance. You make me feel like the girl I was when you got down on one knee and asked me to be yours, and my heart believes my lies again." She reflexively wiped at tears that weren't there. Her mood visibly darkened, and the room seemed to darken with her. "But as soon as I start to feel safe, you're off to go and see her again. I ask you not to go, but your feet are already halfway out the door, and I think to myself, 'Oh gosh, what have I done?' I should have known that this would change us." She looked up at him with angry, grief-stricken eyes. "...That it would change *you!*" She shook her head slowly. "When the baby gets here, I hope it won't be like this."

Allowed to speak, Desmond tried to remind Ashleigh that he had responsibilities to the baby, and an obligation to look after the friend that is helping them have the baby, but she couldn't hear him. She had heard his words before: his explanations; his placations. It all just fell on without meaning on her ears now—she was deaf to his lies. Her consciousness barely registered him as he ended with a promise that he was "still her husband" and "still the same man she married."

She looked up at him absently and simply replied, "No, you're not."

Perhaps it was her impassiveness. Perhaps it was the way her words hit him like an allegation. Perhaps it was the fear that he was becoming everything she had accused him of being throughout the arrangement, but something in his face twisted, and his voice became something akin to a low growl. "Few things in life can destroy a man, and what you asked me to do was one of them! I told you that at the time. Hell, I *begged* you not to make me do this, and yet you *watched* as I killed myself going to her night after night. Now when I still have to go to her, you complain that I'm not the man I used to be, not the man you married. Well if you're right, then it's because *you* killed him. Remember that *you* wanted this, Ashleigh. I was against it from the start."

"I didn't want *this!*" Ashleigh barked back at him, his words finally reaching her. "Not knowing where you are, what you're doing, or who you're doing it with! The man I married would *never* have left me waiting up to worry like you did tonight, and that has *nothing* to do with what I asked you to do with Hannah! Stop blaming me for all the things that you're becoming!"

"And what exactly am I becoming?" Desmond asked, as he stared angrily down at his wife.

But Desmond's anger faltered when it found nothing to strike against. Ashleigh's anger and defiance had dissipated instantly at his last question; in its place was passive apathy. "What have you become?" she repeated stoically. "A man that I can't even hate because he's not here."

Breaking Desmond's gaze, she turned on the spot and began to make her way up the stairs to their bedroom. She paused after taking the first few steps and looked over her shoulder to address him further. "I realized tonight that I would give anything to change your fickle-minded heart back to the one I once owned. I would give anything to go back to the way things were, even the pregnancy. I never thought I'd say that."

Desmond watched as she turned away from him and continued silently up the stairs, closing the bedroom door behind her.

CHAPTER 24

POE V. MARYLAND HEALTH CLINIC

The trial had been grueling. It had taken several days to impanel a jury. Almost everyone had some opinion of the issues at hand. Some had some friends or relatives who'd had their conception efforts frustrated by Poe's case. Others were happy clients of an IVF clinic in the past. Most, however, had already watched Poe's interview with Katan, and formed their opinion of the woman.

After two days of voir dire, only three jurors had been empaneled. In fact, the jury selection process had proved so grueling, and the likelihood of finding twelve impartial jurors and a few alternates had grown so unlikely, that Desmond had started to worry whether the case would be able to proceed in this jurisdiction at all. Fortunately, on the third day of voir dire, there had been a fortuitous run of potential jurors who, by some miracle, had never heard of the case or formed an opinion on the matter of IVF procedures.

The judge, unwilling to endure the drawn-out process a second time in the event of a hung jury, immediately sequestered the jurors. Without sequestration, any number of the jurors might be corrupted or persuaded by the interfering public or heavy media attention the case had garnered now that it was finally before the court.

Not since the Baltimore riots had the city been the central focus of the nation. Once the jury was empaneled, Desmond had spent a little over a week presenting Poe's case. He had called expert witnesses to give evidence about Poe's pre-IVF fertility issues. He'd called countless doctors to give evidence about the medically-accepted insemination protocol, called other doctors to speak about the necessary warnings and disclosures that must be given before fertilized eggs are implanted, and spoken to a statistician about the number of IVF patients who had been forced to raise more children than they'd planned due to multiple eggs taking. Finally, he'd called the doctor from the clinic who had performed the insemination procedure, and through tense questioning, forced him to admit that he never told Poe how many fertilized eggs they were implanting, only that they had told her that "multiple" eggs would be used. To the shock of the court, the jury, and everyone lucky enough to have secured a seat in the public gallery, Desmond closed his case without ever having called Poe to give evidence herself.

A murmur of shock had echoed through the rear of the courtroom as the move stunned all in attendance, and the judge was forced to call order due to the noise made by journalists running out of the room to report the unexpected development of the case.

Desmond had thought long and hard about whether or not to call Poe as a witness. Had she not participated in the interview with Katan, he might have allowed her to take the stand. Perhaps in those circumstances, she might have garnered helpful sympathy from the jury. However, after seeing what Katan was able to do to her during the interview—how easily he had made her trip over her words, misrepresent herself, and destroy her character—there was no way he was going to permit the clinic's attorney to enjoy a similar opportunity.

After a week of presenting their evidence, Desmond and Poe were forced to endure a days-long assault from the clinic's attorney. Armed with the deep pockets of the clinic, medical insurers, and donations from individuals around the country who saw Poe's case as an abomination, there wasn't an expert they couldn't afford. The clinic's attorney brought forward their own top-of-their-field expert witnesses—doctors, fertility specialists, and medical law scholars. They hammered them for days with expert testimony, buried them in legal disclaimers and other paperwork, all signed by Poe and her husband. Finally, to close the case for the defense, they produced Poe's interview with Katan.

Desmond had prepared for this. He objected to the evidence immediately, and after exchanging thinly veiled formalities with the clinic's attorney, the judge ordered the jury and public gallery to leave the courtroom so that a mini-hearing on the admissibility of the interview could be conducted without swaying the jury. The admissibility hearing lasted the better part of a day, and the judge had reserved her judgment on the matter until the next morning.

Despite Desmond's well-prepared objections and legal authority, however, his effort came off as second-best when the judge sided with the defense the next morning. When Desmond asked that only certain portions of the interview be shown to the jury, the judge denied his request, ruling that the entire interview was admissible as a "statement against interest." The interview would be played in full, in front of the jury. As the clinic's attorney gleefully prepared the video footage on the screens around the courtroom, Poe apologized profusely under her breath to Desmond. He ignored her prostration as his mind flipped through how best to respond to this blow to their case.

Quickly making up his mind, he turned to Poe. "Listen to me," he'd said in a hushed but authoritative whisper, "no matter what, do *not* look at the jury while the video plays. Understood?"

Poe only nodded. Desmond carefully observed the juror's faces as the interview played out in front of them. He watched them recoil, their mouths twist in disgust, and at times glare at Poe with wide-eyed disbelief as she shrank in her seat next to him.

Look at me. Look at me, Desmond willed to himself, silently hoping that Poe would follow his advice and avoid accidental eye contact with the jurors while they judged the interview. The brutal defensive onslaught ended with Poe storming off of the stage and a damning closing monologue from Jack Katan. The defense finally rested, pausing the video so that Katan's smug and taunting smile remained frozen on the screens surrounding them.

The judge cleared her throat. "We'll now proceed to closing remarks. Mr. Mathews, would you like to make a closing statement?"

Desmond looked down at the carefully curated closing statement he had prepared weeks earlier. His closing statement had been written, amended, reviewed by Rennick, thrown out, rewritten, reviewed by Rennick once again, carefully manicured by the partners of the firm, and then thrust back into Desmond's hands days earlier. He had memorized its every word and rehearsed its delivery. He knew when to pause for emphasis and which jurors to look at and when. But something about it didn't feel right.

"Mr. Mathews, any closing statements?"

Everyone was watching him: the judge, the attorneys for the clinic, the people in the gallery behind him, and Poe. Desmond scratched a non-existent itch behind his left ear, forcing him to turn and see Poe in his periphery. She was looking up at him, but she seemed to be looking through him. The hope her eyes had worn throughout the trial had left, and she squinted through a dull and vacant stare. As he turned to face her fully, she looked away from him and turned her face to the floor. Her face hung so low that her chin rested on the moth-eaten "suit" she had worn every day of the trial. He'd learned to ignore its smell after the first week of trial. After watching the interview play out in front of the jury, it seemed that the last thing she had left—her hope—had gone.

"Mr. Mathews, I won't ask again." The judge's voice broke the tense silence of the courtroom. Desmond let out a shaking sigh. As he stood and re-buttoned his suit jacket, he turned over his closing statement so that only a blank page stared up at him. He rejected the carefully prepared words, knowing full well that in doing so, he was likely rejecting any chance of becoming a partner of his firm. He cleared his throat.

"I apologize, Your Honor. Mr. Katan always had a knack for putting me to sleep."

The judge tried to suppress a smile at the remark, and a quiet giggle filtered through the gallery behind him.

Desmond took one last look at Poe before turning to face the jurors. "Ladies and gentlemen of the jury, thank you for your patience. This has been a long trial, and I know you are all probably eager to get home to your own families. I know I am. The defense produced a lot of evidence to show that Kristen Poe was made well aware that the clinic was going to implant multiple eggs. The doctor told her that he was going to implant multiple eggs. The disclosure and waiver forms she and her husband signed informed her that the clinic was going to implant multiple eggs. Even in the video you just watched, my client admitted that she knew the clinic was going to implant multiple eggs.

"But you see, that's the problem. Everyone told Kristen that there would be 'multiple' eggs, but not how many. So, how many is multiple? Two is multiple. Four is multiple. Hell, even ten is multiple. The clinic had a duty to obtain *informed* consent from Kristen before implanting those eggs. They would have you believe that they discharged that duty through their warnings and forms. However, what if they'd implanted six eggs? What if they'd implanted eight? Does it seem like Kristen was consenting for the clinic to implant as many multiples of eggs as they saw fit? Of course not! The duty of informed consent required the clinic to inform Kristen of the exact number of eggs they were going to implant, and then let her and her husband decide how many eggs they thought they could handle, assuming they were all successful, and resulted in beautiful little children. But they didn't. The clinic did the same thing to Ms. Poe as everyone else: they took advantage of her. They took advantage of the use of the word 'multiple' in their warnings and notices, and they used it to mean whatever *they* interpreted it to mean.

"I know you're angry about this case and what it's done to would-be mothers across the country. I know you're angry because *I'm* angry too. My wife and I were unable to have children of our own because of this case, and it's tearing my marriage apart. But that doesn't mean that Ms. Poe and her four babies aren't entitled to the relief they're seeking. It doesn't mean that the clinic didn't make a mistake. And it doesn't mean that you should let your personal feelings stop you from making it so that other mothers aren't similarly taken advantage of in the future.

Kristen Poe is here today as a woman who has been taken advantage of by everyone in her life—by her husband, by the clinic, and by Jack Katan. Don't you do it too." Desmond returned to his seat on shaking legs. Kristen was crying quietly in her seat next to him, her face still buried in her chest. Desmond's focus moved from Poe to the jury. None of them appeared moved.

Their stony faces looked upon the crying figure seated beside him with passive apathy. Desmond shook his head slowly in disbelief and placed a reassuring hand on Poe's shuddering shoulder as the clinic's attorney stood to commence his own closing statements. Desmond listened intently as the clinic's attorney battered his case. He felt what could have been the final nail hammered into the coffin of their case as his counterpart closed his case. "No matter how high—or in this case, low—a patient's intelligence might be, anyone with a brain knows that 'multiple' means two *or more*. If Ms. Poe was so stupid or irresponsible so as not to realize that *multiple* eggs might lead to *multiple* babies, then she was never fit to have attempted motherhood in the first place."

Desmond's heart sank as he watched several jurors nod to themselves in agreement.

• • •

The next day, Desmond pressed the End Call button on his phone after leaving another exasperated voicemail message for Poe. He bristled uncomfortably in the rear seat of the law firm's escort vehicle on the way back to court.

"Where is she?" Rennick asked from the seat next to him. "Did you tell her to remain on standby, ready to rush back to court when you called?"

"Of course I did!" Desmond answered without looking up from his cell phone, wishing it would ring.

Rennick grunted disapprovingly from the back of his throat. "I don't know what the hell you were thinking going off-script like that. That was a damned foolish move, boy."

Desmond didn't answer. Rennick and the other partners had been giving him hell since the judge excused the parties while the jury deliberated.

"And where the *hell* is your client, Desmond? I thought you had a real relationship with this woman. Everyone else gave me the impression that you were the only friend she has. You'd better hope she's waiting for us at the courthouse."

Desmond ignored the comment and tried to call Poe once more. He tried to reassure himself as he listened to the sound of the dialed call. With so much evidence produced over the course of the trial, the two sides had left the courtroom with the expectation that it would take the jury a week, maybe two, to deliberate their verdict. However, Desmond had received a call from the court informing him that the jury had returned with a verdict after less than one day's deliberation. This did not bode well for Poe.

Their black escort vehicle rounded a corner, and the Circuit Court came into view. A heavy crowd was gathered at the front of the courthouse, just as there had been every day during the trial. Scores of bodies pressed together in an angry and violent display of protest. Advocates of a dozen organizations had taken the Poe case as an example of the righteousness of their cause. Pro-life advocates touted messages that every woman capable of childrearing should be permitted to have children no matter their circumstances. They repeated chants suggesting that the clinics closing their doors around the country was an unconstitutional barrier against women's freedom to have children.

Pro-abortion activists arrived in scores to protest against the pro-life attendees. Others still brought cardboard signs touting Poe's unfitness to be a mother and suggesting that child services step in to take the babies away. Independent protesters were also present, simply there to express their hatred for Poe. It was these protesters that beat and spat on their car as Desmond's escort vehicle made its way to the curb at the front of the courthouse. Police quickly stepped in to remove the assailants, and their faces next to the car were replaced with camera lenses as journalists quickly stepped in to take their places.

Rennick leaned back in his seat. "Desmond, keep your head low as you make your way up the steps, but make sure you don't cover your face. I don't want you to give any of them the impression that we're afraid of them or what they might throw at you ... literally."

Desmond looked beyond the camera pointed in his face through the glass pane of the window and out to the crowd. "I'm not afraid of them," he answered softly. He looked down at his phone once more. "I'm afraid for Poe."

Rennick nodded absently next to Desmond. "I'll call you when it's over."

Rennick remained in the car as Desmond stepped out of the escort vehicle with his briefcase in hand. The press flooded to him, and the faces beyond them disappeared behind the glass and metal of the cameras and microphones surrounding him. He could barely hear the journalist's questions beneath the cacophony of the shouts, screams, and chants of the crowd. He ignored it all and kept his eyes fixed on the courthouse steps in front of him. A camera to his left was taken out as a brick, hurled from somewhere beyond his field of vision, slammed against it. The cameraman swore loudly and, left impotent without a functioning camera, fell behind as another cameraman took his place.

The shouts and screams intensified as protesters from both sides of the courthouse steps began to fling all manner of projectiles toward him, and the police fought to keep control of the crowds. Desmond fought the urge to hold his briefcase up protectively as water balloons filled with paint began to fly overhead to strike against those surrounding him. An egg cracked on his neck and oozed its yolk down the collar of his shirt. He kept his eyes forward, ignoring the sticky liquid as he made his way steadfastly up the steps.

He felt what he thought was spit strike just below his right eye, and he heard the closest cameraman mutter, "Filthy bastards," under his breath. He wasn't sure if the cameraman was talking about the protesters, or lawyers.

As he reached the top of the steps, Desmond crossed a line of police with riot shields. The crowd fell behind him as the police permitted only him to pass through. As he took a few steps beyond the protective barrier, he stood alone at the top of the steps and turned to look at the crowd that had built and fallen behind him. Camera bulbs flashed in his eyes, men and women stood screaming at him from a cautious few inches away from the riot police, and he could see news choppers hovering overhead just a short distance away. He turned again and made his way into the courthouse, knowing full well that Poe would not be waiting for him inside. There was no way she'd have made it through that crowd alive.

The courtroom was barely less crowded than the courthouse steps. Lawyers shuffled around in blue, gray, and black suits, and the people in the packed gallery bristled. The jurors appeared visibly nervous as they waited for the judge to come out and permit them to end the scrutiny of a thousand eyes by delivering their long-awaited verdict. A loud knock came from the chamber's door to indicate the judge's entry, and the room fell instantly silent as everyone stood.

The judge sat at the head of the court, and all present took their seat. The judge's eyes glanced around the room, and she made an irritated kind of sniff to indicate her displeasure at seeing her courtroom packed with quiet anarchy. "We're here to resume the matter of Kristen Poe against Maryland IVF Clinics Incorporated. Are all parties present?"

Desmond watched as the judge's eyes fell on the empty seat next to him, and then on to him.

"Mr. Mathews, is your client present?"

Desmond stood awkwardly to address the court properly and looked nervously behind him at the closed entrance to the courtroom, "No, Your Honor. She is not."

The judge made another irritated sniffing noise. "Mr. Mathews, where is your client? I would imagine that her presence in my courtroom would be of particular importance to her today."

Desmond stood once more. "Of course, Your Honor. I have been unable to contact her this morning. However, Ms. Poe has four infant children. There are any number of reasons why she might not be here this morning. I offer my sincere apologies on her behalf and ask for the court's indulgence in excusing her absence." He resumed his seat.

Another sniff came from the judge. "Mr. Mathews ... stand when I address you directly Mr. Mathews. Thank you. Mr. Mathews, what would you say if I said I was of a mind to adjourn the delivery of the verdict until your client is present?"

Desmond inhaled deeply, unsure of how to answer. "This is your courtroom, Your Honor," he offered meekly. "I am at your mercy and am a servant for whatever pleases the court." He gestured gingerly toward the full gallery. "I would say, however, that given the gathering both inside and outside of your courtroom, it would appear that everyone's best interests are served by announcing the resolution to this matter as soon as possible."

The judge's expression softened, and she nodded to herself in agreement. "Thank you, Mr. Mathews. You may sit. Counsel for the defendant, I am inclined to agree with Mr. Mathews' suggestion. Do you have any objection to us proceeding in the absence of the plaintiff, Ms. Poe?"

The clinic's attorney leaned barely off of his chair and called, "No, Your Honor."

"Very well." The judge turned to face the jury. "Mr. Foreman, has the jury reached a verdict?"

"Yes, Your Honor."

"And what say you?" the judge called back.

Desmond looked back once more at the courtroom door hoping to see Poe rushing to take her seat beside him, but the door remained steadfastly closed. He returned his attention to the jury. He noticed his heart was racing, and the tension in his chest reminded him of his need to breathe.

The foreman looked over the other eleven jurors before looking with terrified eyes at the crowd packed into the gallery at the rear of the room. Quickly returning his attention to the judge, he sputtered his answer. "In the matter of Kristen Poe versus Maryland IVF Clinics Incorporated, we the jury find in favor of the plaintiff."

The courtroom instantly erupted in a clamor of quiet exclamation, the murmurings of all present compounding together to form a low noise. Desmond, struck frozen in disbelief, stood alone as the only unanimated figure in the courtroom.

The judge called the room to order before stoically turning to the lawyers for the clinic. "Counsel for the defendant, do you wish to poll the jury?"

The now deflated attorney came slowly to a fully standing position and straightened his jacket before answering. "No. I don't think that will be necessary, Your Honor."

"Very well. On to the matter of damages then. Mr. Mathews, your initial complaint was for the sum of one hundred and seventeen million dollars, representing a combination of claims including, but not limited to wrongful life, negligence, and intentional infliction of emotional distress. I understand well your arguments about the need for your client to provide for the children for the rest of their lives. I also understand that your client has had to endure the physical pain of birthing additional children and the emotional distress that comes from them simultaneously. However, I also note your client's previously self-confessed intention to provide for perhaps two of the four children. Accordingly, I am going to exercise my discretion under the doctrine of remittitur and reduce the amount claimed. I, therefore, enter judgment in favor of the plaintiff in the sum of forty million, two hundred and one thousand, nine hundred and eighty-nine dollars. I will reserve my written judgment with reasons for a later date. This court is adjourned. Thank you."

"All rise!" the bailiff called as the judge took to depart from the room. Desmond rose to stand on shaking legs. The judge disappeared beyond the door to her chambers, and Desmond felt all eyes fall on him. The judgment had barely registered in his mind as Poe's absence still nagged at him. He quickly gathered up his briefcase, shook hands with opposing counsel, and rushed outside to the courthouse steps. News of the verdict and judgment had already made its way outside, and the press was permitted to advance beyond the riot police to wait for Desmond as they attempted to quell the riotous crowd.

Desmond was stopped in his tracks by journalists pressing their way toward him as soon as he appeared at the top of the courthouse steps. He tried to move beyond them to proceed immediately to find Poe, but the journalists moved with him. He pushed forward and was forced back as cameras and microphones again pressed toward his face. "Three questions!" he cried out angrily. "I'll answer three questions, and then you'll let me pass!"

His tone made it clear that he was not asking. An older woman with a sharp, beak-like face pressed forward and called to him, "How do you feel about the judge's reduction of the award?"

Desmond answered quickly, "I think we're still to be very happy with the judgment. This money should not only compensate Ms. Poe for the physical, emotional, and psychological hardships she has been forced to face, but will also give her the means to acquire as much help as she needs to adequately support her children."

Another reporter stepped forward to ask their question, "Mr. Mathews! Do you think more IVF users will now come forward to sue the clinics for multiple unwanted births?"

Desmond answered cautiously. "I can't speak to that. When Rennick, Spectre & Co. first took carriage of this case, we invited victims of similar circumstances to come forward and make this a class action suit. No one came forward. I suspect that their willingness to prosecute their cases will largely depend on the judge's written judgment, which is yet to be released. Final question, please."

The mass of press in front of Desmond seemed to part as Katan stepped into the fray, accompanied by his cameraman behind him. "Mr. Mathews," Katan began over the now hushed press, "how do you feel knowing that you are responsible for giving your client—a woman clearly not fit for motherhood—tens of millions of dollars?" Katan's signature sardonic smile followed.

Desmond leveled his own eyes against Katan before looking over the crowds in front of him and beyond. "That's what none of you understand," he began. "None of you! This was never a cash grab. It wasn't 'buyer's remorse' or 'the latest abortion in history.' It wasn't a statement for *them!*" he pointed out to the protesters, "for any of their causes. This was never about being pro-life or pro-abortion, and we never wanted the clinics to close their doors. This was about a woman who was left unable to provide for her newborn children because of the actions of the IVF clinic, and who was so desperate to give them the life that she thought they deserved that she sought legal help. That's it."

He looked back at Katan. "And in your haste to destroy this woman, you all seem to have forgotten that she's not 'my client' or '*that* monster' as you've called her. Her name is Kristen Poe, and she's a human being. No more questions." Desmond pushed through the mass of bodies and broke free at the top of the stairs. He spied the firm's black escort car waiting for him at the curb, and he rushed down the stairs toward it. He climbed inside to find himself alone in the back seat.

"Back to the office, Mr. Mathews?" the driver asked gleefully. "The firm is already celebrating!"

Desmond fumbled in his briefcase for the manila folder Rennick had given him when he'd first taken the case. He pulled it in front of his eyes and answered, reading the details from the cover. "No. Take me to 1101 Russell Street. Take me to Poe's house."

Desmond had spent the entire car ride rejecting incoming calls and trying to reach Poe on the phone without success. He tapped his foot on the floor of the car impatiently as they made their way through the streets of Baltimore, steadily descending into neighborhoods of declining character. They reached an area where every odd house had either collapsed or was propped up by crude timber stilts.

"Mr. Mathews," the driver called from the front seat once more, "I'm not permitted to leave the car idling in these areas."

"That's fine, Andrew," Desmond answered. "I don't need you to wait for me after I get out." The car came to a stop outside of an apartment complex with black, scorch mark stains across the facade. The tanning above the entrance suggested that there used to be a sign, but it had fallen or been ripped free some time ago.

Desmond stepped out of the car, and the thick, acrid smell of marijuana greeted him before his foot fell to the cracked footpath. He quickly discovered the source of the smell. A group of men sat smoking on the small staircase in front of the building entrance. They all eyed him with a mixture of curiosity and disdain, his finely pressed and tailored suit making it clear he didn't belong there. One of the men spat on the ground as Desmond approached. The thick and yellow mucus spattered on the cold ground a few inches away from Desmond's shoe and began its slow freeze on the pavement. Desmond sidled his way between the unmoving residents of the front steps as he heard Andrew drive quickly away down the street, the sounds of the engine doing little to muffle the insults that the men on the steps muttered under their breaths at him.

He pushed past a security door whose lock was smashed to pieces, and the smell of marijuana was quickly replaced with the wretched stench of the garbage bags leaking only what God knew onto the carpet. The bags were piled into the corner inside the security door, and the garbage juice was leaking a thick, dark-brown trail into the now soaking carpet. Its owner had left a crudely scribbled note on one of the bags reading, "Too cold outside." Desmond's shoes stuck to the floor with each squelching step, and he was forced to give his foot a little tug to free it from the grip of the sticky carpet.

Not trusting that the elevator would still be in operation, he stepped hurriedly to the stairs and took them two at a time to the fifth floor. He came to stand in front of Poe's closed front door. He banged heavily on the thin wooden door with his fist, it's thin panels shaking loudly against the force. He looked down both sides of the empty corridor to see if anyone would be disturbed by the noise he was making, but quickly decided that any noise was being drowned out by the blaring music coming from one of Poe's neighbors.

He banged loudly on the wooden door once more and called Poe's name. "Kristen! Kristen! It's Desmond. Are you in there?" He waited long seconds to see if she would answer, and the music coming from the neighbor intensified, it's bass booming enough to make the air vibrate. He banged on the door again, "Kristen! It's Desmond. We won!" he added hopefully.

He stopped pounding with his fists for a moment as he thought he heard something through the door. He pressed his ear to the panel and tried to ignore the interference caused by the neighbor's noisy music. On the other side of the door were the audible cries of Poe's babies. He strained his hearing to see if he could detect the sounds of movement from within the apartment and became increasingly concerned when he heard none. He tried banging on the doors once more and, now deaf to the crashing music surrounding him, he heard the cries intensify from within.

"Kristen. Kristen!" He could feel that something was wrong, and after looking down both sides of the corridor once more, he stepped back and kicked his foot into the door. Its thin panels gave way instantly, and his foot broke clean through to the other side. He hopped awkwardly on the spot before pulling his foot back to himself and kicking again, this time kicking closer to the doorknob. His foot broke through again. He drew back a final time, and with another kick, he broke the door free of the lock on the other side. Splintered pieces of wood littered the floor as the door swung open.

What Desmond found inside Poe's abode broke his heart. The carpet was stained a green-brown color from years old-spillages, the drywall sported old, fist-sized holes in almost every wall, and despite a wintry chill flowing freely through the room, it did nothing to mask the thick and musty metallic smell throughout. The ominous feeling within Desmond intensified as he stepped further into the apartment and found furniture overturned and broken glass on the floor. The cries of the children reverberated against the broken walls and deafened him to all else. He quickened his steps and called out to Kristen several times as he followed the sound of the crying children.

His voice railed against the music fading behind him. "Kat—" his call stopped short as he came to the kitchen and found Poe lying limply on the floor in a pool of her own blood. Her eyes stared blankly at the ceiling, her hands were covered in blood-streaked cuts, and a large knife protruded from her abdomen. The front of Poe's shirt was matted in blood and shone darkest over the stab wound in her stomach. Desmond quickly knelt beside her and, wetting the knees of his suit trousers with her blood, checked her pulse. He felt nothing, and it confirmed what was already clear.

Kristen Poe was dead.

Time slowed for Desmond, and he was struck by a sudden dizziness that left him feeling woozy. Kristen was dead, but why? How? He breathed heavily to stop his nausea escaping from his mouth, and he pressed a hand to the cabinet beneath the sink to steady himself. Coming to stand, he looked down at Poe's vacant, staring eyes. He had seen photographs of dead bodies before for his work. However, in every one of the photos he had seen, death had seemed to bring a sense of peace. The faces of the deceased were always relaxed, the lines in their faces smoothing after finally letting go of their worldly troubles. Not hers though. Although Poe's eyes lacked focus as their stared blankly into space, her face kept that same harried, sad, and tortured look. Even in death, it seemed she'd been unable to escape her misery. Taking one more moment to look upon her, Desmond noticed for the first time that the side of her face was tainted with a faint silver trail. She'd been crying as she slipped away into the darkness.

Unable to bear the sadness reflected back at him, Desmond looked away from Poe. The cries of the children reached his ears through the white noise that had briefly deafened him, and he scrambled through the decrepit apartment to check on each of the children. He found all four of them together in a single crib. The baby girl stood with her small fists clutching the rails while the boys sat in one of the corners holding one another. All four of them were red in the face from hours of screaming, and their little mouths were curled to release the crackling volume of their pitiful wails.

Desmond approached the crib, and two of the babies reached up to him with their tiny arms for comfort. He reached inside the crib and lifted the girl to him, and she buried her face into his chest, and she hugged her arms around his neck. As he bent down to pick up one of the other children, he spotted a small envelope taped to the front of the crib. *Mr. Mathews* was scrawled on its front in Poe's handwriting. Desmond grabbed the envelope with a shaking hand. Still juggling the little girl crying in his ear, he awkwardly opened the envelope, and his heart sank as he read to himself:

Desmond,

I knew you'd come here right after court and find the children. That's just the kind of man I counted on you to be.

When you called me this morning, I knew it was time for the court to make its decision. I couldn't bear to find out if we'd lost. I suppose it doesn't matter one way or the other now. Either way, it seems my children are better off without me. I birthed these children with a husband that couldn't be counted on and without a means to support them. I brought a lawsuit premised on the fact that they were unwanted. And finally, I took that interview with Katan against your advice, and in doing so, I put my children in jeopardy. It seems that's all I've ever been able to do for them. I won't do that again. I used the money from the interview to take out a life insurance policy just in case we didn't win, and for the first time, I feel like I'm finally putting my children first.

I spread all the hate mail and threats I've received over the past year throughout the apartment, broken glass here and there, and tossed my furniture around. Thanks to you breaking down the door, my death will look like a homicide, and the life insurance policy will be paid out. At least this way, win or lose with the lawsuit, my children have a future.

I remember you told me that, as my attorney, you need to follow my instructions. My last instructions to you are to destroy this letter and never tell anyone the truth about my death. Make sure that the life insurance policy gets paid, and in the unlikely chance that we won the case, please make sure that my kids end up with a family that wants children as much as your wife does. You asked me to trust you with this case. I'm sorry I didn't have the strength or hope to hold on just a little longer, but I'm trusting you with this. Thank you for being the only one who treated me like a person, who saw through my poor decisions and still thought that I was worth something. That was worth something to me.

Kristen

Desmond lowered the letter and stood looking at Poe's children, her final tear reflected in their fresh ones. As he stood near Poe's lifeless body, surrounded by the wails of her four infant children, he couldn't help but feel that her victory felt very much like a loss.

CHAPTER 25

I LOVE YOU TWO

"You don't have to do this, really," Todd said in a low voice as Katelynn ran a washcloth along his arm.

"I should be doing this for you. You're the one carrying a baby!" Todd finished.

Katelynn smiled from her seat on the cold tile floor beside the bathtub. "You need help, Todd. There's no shame in that. Besides, your pride and stubbornness still has you walking everywhere unassisted, long after the doctor said you should be in a wheel—"

"No wheelchairs," Todd said softly, looking away from his wife. "I'm a man, Katie. I'll walk on my own two feet for as long as my body will let me, even if I am a little slower these days."

Katelynn giggled at him as she continued to bathe him. "Just a little?" she teased. Todd smiled again and looked back at his wife. Katelynn tried to keep her smile in place as she looked at her husband's face and her heart broke. Although his familiar eyes still glittered at her in adoration, everything else was different—diminished somehow.

His smile cracked the sides of his eyes with deeply recessed wrinkles, and his eyes sat in dark, hollow, and sunken sockets pocked by heavy bags. His pale skin clung to a skeletal frame. Katelyn forced herself to look away as she blinked back tears. The man she had fallen madly in love with years ago was wasting away in front of her, and there was nothing she could do to stop it. All she could do was sit back, watch, and try to etch every moment with him into the deepest parts of her memory.

"What's it like?" Todd asked, looking down at her heavily pregnant belly. Although she wasn't due until the first week of February, her belly had inflated quickly in the past few weeks, and she looked to be near full term. "Being pregnant, I mean," he clarified.

Katelynn lifted Todd's thin arm, so she could wash his armpit, and she smiled as she answered. "It's hard to describe really. It's kind of unique. I can't really describe it because there's nothing else like it. You have to experience it to know what it is, you know? And there are different parts to it. Everyone always kind of talks about the physical aspects— feeling large, not liking the changes to their bodies, the cravings, the weight, and the pain in the back—but there are other parts too."

"Like what?" Todd asked with genuine interest.

Katelynn screwed up her face in deep thought as she tried to think of a way to articulate what she'd meant. "Well, for one, it's pretty amazing having this little life growing inside of you. I really can't describe the feeling that comes from that any better than to say … it's like magic. Honest to God magic. There's a life inside of my womb right now, and it's part you, part me. A life that's made from us, and it's *growing* inside of me."

Todd smiled. "What else?"

Katelynn sighed. "Well, being pregnant with *your* baby makes me love you so much. It's on a whole other level from anything I have ever felt. I think it's because there's a piece of you inside of me, and it's like my soul just knows that it's yours. It just makes me feel so connected to you, and I love it! There's definitely a lot of things about being pregnant that are just plain inconvenient, but these other things—the important things—well, I wouldn't trade them for anything."

Todd smiled with his eyes closed as he listened to his wife's explanation.

"What made you ask?" she asked as she began to run the warm washcloth down his skeletal back.

"I was just thinking about when we first started dating and how we'd spend hours just swapping questions because we wanted to know more about each other," he answered. "I realized that I hadn't asked you what it was like, and I wanted to know."

Katelynn laughed at her husband's curiosity, and from the memories of the two of them lying in each other's arms late into the night trading questions.

"Is there anything you haven't asked me?" Todd asked. "We both know we soon won't have the opportunity, so you might as well ask everything now." Although he spoke about his impending death, Todd's tone wasn't dark or ominous. His words carried the warmth and joy of a man who knew his fate, had accepted it, and simply appreciated the time he had until he met it.

Katelynn had let the washcloth drop into the warm water behind Todd's back and used her washing hand to knead the muscles along his exposed spine. She rubbed her belly with her free hand and paused cautiously with her eyes fixed on his naked body sitting weakly in the bath water. "What is it like for you?" she asked with a low voice. "Knowing that it's coming soon?"

Todd let out a single laugh. "You mean knowing that I'm going to die? We can call it what it is Katie. Not calling it 'death' isn't going to stop it from happening."

"Maybe," she answered. "But calling it that makes it hurt more," she said somberly.

Todd cleared his throat in embarrassment. "Well," he began "that's also hard to explain." He looked heavenward as he sought a way to describe his feelings. "When I was nineteen, I met a woman who had been blinded by disease in her early twenties. Because she wasn't born blind, she knew what it was like to be able to see, unlike someone who was born blind, you see. When I asked her what it was like to be blind, she told me to close my eyes. When I did, she asked me what I saw. I said 'nothing'. Then, she told me that I was wrong. 'No,' she'd said. 'What you *see* is the back of your eyelids; what you *see* is black. I, on the other hand, see *nothing*.' She told me that I couldn't understand what it means to be blind because I can't imagine what 'nothing' looks like. The point of this is to say that I can't explain to you what it's like to slowly die, because you don't know what dying feels like. So, I guess it's much like how you described being pregnant, in that you can't imagine what it's like because there's no object of comparison. Although we're all dying slowly, it's something entirely different to know that it could come at any minute."

Any minute. The words echoed silently in Katelynn's mind. Silent tears slipped down her cheeks, and she started breathing heavily as she imagined what her life would soon look like without her husband. Fully clothed, she stood and climbed into the bath to sit behind Todd, his slight frame making it easy for the bath to accommodate her pregnant bulk. Todd looked behind himself in confusion until he felt his wife's arms wrap around him, and her cheek press into his back.

"You know," Katelynn began softly. "I have loved our time together. Every moment of it. Even these ones. I don't want to get too emotional, but I hope you know how much I—"

"I know Katie," Todd answered with tears in his own eyes. "I love you too."

• • •

"Can you please do me up?" Ashleigh called out to Desmond as she sat in front of the vanity mirror of their New York hotel room. Both she and Desmond had received VIP invitations to Hannah's showcase that night and had been getting ready in their separate bedrooms until she called out to ask for his help with her dress. He came up behind her in a black tuxedo with the bow tie untied around his neck. He silently placed a hand at the base of her back and used his other hand to slowly run the zipper along the teeth up the length of her back. She watched his stoic face through the reflection of the vanity mirror. He hadn't been the same in the weeks since Poe's grizzly death. Something about him had just seemed burdened or damaged, and he had refused to talk about it. Still, as the zipper of her tight black dress reached the top of her back, he placed his hands on both of her shoulders and whispered, "You look beautiful" in a low and husky voice before turning on the spot and making his way to the bedroom door.

"Wait," said Ashleigh. She turned in her seat and walked barefoot over to Desmond as he stood looking at her from the doorway. "Let me do your bow tie," she said as she reached up to grab its loose ends from around his neck. "You've always struggled with bow ties." They stood in silence. Her nimble fingers tied the black fabric into a perfect bow, and he looked over her head into the empty bedroom behind her. She pulled the bow tight, and their eyes locked as he looked down at her. "Des—" she began.

"Thank you," he muttered curtly. He turned on the spot, breaking their gaze, and left her bedroom. Ashleigh watched as his hulking figure made its way into the darkness of the area connecting their bedrooms. *He's hurting*, she thought to herself. She stepped one foot out of her bedroom and into the darkness, about to go after her husband, and then paused. *But so am I*, she thought to herself, and she pulled her foot back into the light of the bedroom, and returned to her vanity to finish getting ready.

• • •

Christmas time on Broadway in New York was always a brightly lit affair, accompanied by merriment and fanfare. Festive lights adorned the already-staged lights of advertisements and gallery boards, expertly decorated Christmas trees appeared on almost every corner, and music caroled overhead to cajole the masses of people scrambling to complete last minute gift shopping. However, the festivities of the season paled in comparison to the fanfare pulled together for the premiere of Hannah's show, *I Love You Two*. Crowds pressed against the barriers that had been set up alongside the red carpet leading into the theater's entrance as Hannah stepped out of a limousine. Her blonde curls bobbed around her exposed shoulders, and her strapless red sweetheart dress hugged her body until it flared with asymmetrical length into a beautiful, rose-like bloom just above her waist. The effect exposed her calves, ankles, and matching red heels from the front, and left everyone behind her truly wondering whether she was in fact pregnant. Her red lips parted to expose a wide and youthful smile, and her blue eyes glimmered in the reflected light of the flashing bulbs in front of her.

Tonight, she didn't care that the hairspray made her hair feel heavy and rigid. She didn't care that Katan would be lingering somewhere among the media reps looking for another interview, and she didn't care that everyone who didn't know better thought of her show as a "coming out of retirement" celebration. Tonight, Hannah Lenore was once again the woman in red, and she reveled in the actualization of the moment she had spent months fearing she would never again experience. She made her way slowly down the red carpet. Fans and journalists alike called her name, and reached out to her with hands and microphones on both sides of the barricades. She waved and giggled excitedly, as though experiencing the fervor and fanfare for the first time. Two-thirds down the length of the red carpet, Hannah looked up at the overhead marquee and the cache of glittering bulbs flashing around the announcement of her show— *PREMIER: I Love You Two - A Hannah Lenore Production.* Her eyes remained transfixed on the marquee sign, and the chasing lights twinkled in her smiling blue eyes as her heart raced, and pride swelled within.

Desmond and Ashleigh had arrived at the theater before Hannah, and had gathered in the vestibule with members from the surrogacy support group, whom Hannah also had gifted VIP tickets. Ashleigh had greeted all of the women by name, and was listening to each of them with genuine interest as they regaled what had happened in the months since Ashleigh had seen them. Eileen had surprised Ashleigh by squeezing her in a big hug and exclaiming, "I'm so glad you're not being a bitch about our pregnancies!"

Laughter followed, and Ashleigh tittered about how much the women's bellies had grown since she had seen them. Noise filled the vestibule, and a cold draft swept through the room as the door leading back to the red carpet outside swung open. Hannah stood beaming in the doorway with bulbs still flashing behind her. Each of the surrogates scoffed and whistled at the woman in red standing in front of them before she made her way over, and greeted each of them with a hug. She moved to embrace Ashleigh last, and the hug was awkwardly accepted.

Releasing Ashleigh from her embrace, Hannah looked to Desmond and Ashleigh and asked, "Can I borrow the two of you? They want to do an interview outside and meet the inspiration behind the show. Ashleigh shuffled on the spot uncomfortably, and looked anxiously at Desmond. "Oh," she said, looking back at Hannah. "No, I ... I don't want to be a part of the limelight." She looked again at Desmond. "You should go though, Des. You're used to the cameras and speaking in public." She looked back at a visibly disappointed Hannah. "It's just not my thing."

"Okay," Hannah said perkily, trying not to let her disappointment take away from the experience. "Looks like it's just you and me, Des." Hannah grabbed Desmond by the hand and led him back outside through the vestibule doors pulled open for her.

Ashleigh watched with irritation as Hannah led her husband away from her, and she squinted as she tried to discern whether the annoyance came more from the handholding, or because Hannah had called him 'Des.'

Desmond looked at his surroundings as Hannah continued to lead him over to a group of cameras and microphones waiting beside a spotlight. He craned his neck over his shoulder as he took stock of the lights, the sounds, the signs, the colors, the screams and cries, the cameras ... and Hannah. In as much as the hollow hallways, the acoustically prepared courtrooms, the briefcases, and the legal controversies were his world, this was Hannah's.

He quickly realized why Hannah had been willing to go to such lengths to find inspiration for this show. They were both performers, albeit on separate stages. Performing in the courtroom gave him the same feeling that performing on the theater stage gave her. There was simply nothing else like it, and he could only imagine the lengths he would go to get it back, were it ever taken from him. Finally, he understood Hannah's part in the arrangement, and her willingness to participate.

Hannah pulled Desmond under the glare of the spotlight and waited as her agent selected which reps could come forward to ask their questions. The space in front of Hannah and Desmond quickly filled with cameras and microphones reaching out to them, and the barrage soon began. "Ms. Lenore! Ms. Lenore! Is it a boy or a girl?"

"That's still a secret known to a select few," Hannah answered, remembering with a broad grin that Katan never broke the story.

"And when's the due date?"

Hannah's grin broadened further. "I'm due in March."

"Mr. Mathews! Over here, Mr. Mathews. What does your ex-wife think about the pregnancy?"

Desmond screwed up his face in a mixture of annoyance and confusion. "I'm not divorced," he said simply. He looked over at Hannah, and she nodded back at him. Desmond turned back to face the journalist and spoke clearly. "My wife and I wanted a baby, but as you all know, until recently, the IVF clinics were closed. Hannah is an old friend of mine, and when she heard about our predicament, she very graciously agreed to be our surrogate."

The comment sent a wave of tittering throughout those within earshot. The crowd erupted into more frenzied questions, which continued to fire until the overhead lights dimmed twice to indicate that the show was about to start. Hannah looked at Desmond and signaled that it was time to head inside for the show, but a familiar voice called to them and caught their attention.

"Hannah! Hannah, please!" Both Hannah and Desmond turned and saw Jack Katan struggling with Hannah's publicist and members of the security detail. Poe's death still fresh in his mind, Desmond saw red, and stepped angrily in Katan's direction. Hannah placed a hand on Desmond's stomach and urged him to stay in place. "Hannah!" Katan called again. "Hannah, I'm running a story on your show, and that's all. I don't need to speak with either of you. I'd just like my camera detail to get a photo for the article. Please."

Hannah looked up at Desmond, and he simply nodded once without taking his eyes off of Katan. Hannah's publicist released Katan with a bit of a shove, and his cameraman lined up with the other gathered journalists to get a photo of the pair. As camera holders planted themselves in place and began to aim their cameras at the pair, Hannah wrapped an arm around Desmond's waist and looked up at him. "I never thanked you," she said to him as the camera flashes began.

"Thank me for what?"

"You didn't have to agree to the arrangement. You didn't have to have a part in any of this. You didn't have to give me this." Hannah gestured with her head to their surroundings. "You always acted as though it was just me giving something to you and Ashleigh. But I got something out of this arrangement too, and I didn't have to lose myself in the process. So, thank you Desmond, for giving me tonight."

Desmond's arm found its way to Hannah's waist, and the pair stood side by side smiling at the cameras and at each other, as the flashes continued to bathe them in intermittent light.

Desmond left Hannah's side, and found his seat in the front row next to Ashleigh. "How did it go?" she asked. "What took so long?"

"They had a lot of questions," Desmond answered. "They didn't seem to know about you, and when I clarified that Hannah is our surrogate, it set off a whole lot of questions. I guess people are just interested in Hannah and her life."

The lights dimmed, and the sound of the opening musical number rose around them, ending their brief conversation. Hannah quickly scuttled into her seat next to Desmond after giving a quick talk to the team backstage, and the stage curtain rose in front of them. Hannah's frenzied applause greeted her dancers over the rising tide of the music, and the show was quickly underway.

• • •

Ninety minutes into the production, Hannah excused herself and ducked low as she made her way to the aisle and retreated somewhere into the darkness of the theater. Ashleigh, seated on the far side of Desmond, was so fixated on the show that she failed to notice Hannah's departure.

Although Ashleigh was still upset with Hannah, and hurt by Desmond, she still found herself more than able to enjoy Hannah's work. On more than one occasion she found herself moved to silent tears by the choreographed numbers produced only a few feet from her front-row seat, and her heart raced in time with the excitement of the music and the movement of the dancers. The stage dimmed to pitch-black once more, and the music softened to a symphonic breeze as the final number began.

A muted light illuminated a bed on the left-hand side of the stage, and a slow, somber tune began. A man in a business suit emerged from the shadows of center stage. Clutching the handle of his briefcase, he made his way over to the bed. He placed his briefcase at its foot, and lifted a brown-haired woman out of the bed. He carried her gently to center stage and lowered her against his body so that they stood facing one another with their bodies touching. They began dancing together in a sort of slow, intimate waltz with the two held tightly together, each looking deeply into the other's eyes.

As the tempo of the music accelerated, their dancing became faster and more violent. The man in the suit ran his hands down the front of her nightgown, and she threw her body into his, leaping into his arms. The man carried the brunette woman back over to her bed and lowered her gently onto its covers. She held her arms around his neck tightly even as he lowered her, and he was forced to pull himself free of her arms as he stood.

The man collected his briefcase once more and began striding to the right side of the stage, his face a frozen mask of steeled resolution. With each stride, the light over the bed dimmed, shrouding the brown-haired woman, and her bed, in total darkness once more. At the same time, another bed was appearing on the right-hand side of the stage. Just as before, the man placed his briefcase at the foot of the bed, though this time he threw his suit jacket onto the bed and lifted a blonde woman from the covers, once again carrying her to the center of the stage. They became embroiled in a dance similar to that which he shared with the brunette, though it finished with the blonde looking hungrily into his eyes while she led him by his tie back to her bed.

As the blonde climbed into the bed and pulled at his tie, the man pulled himself free and recovered his briefcase once more. The music intensified in volume, sounds now crashing throughout the theater, and the pace increased. The briefcase appeared heavier in the man's hand, and it weighed him down as he carried himself back to the brunette's bed on the left side of the stage, once again illuminating in his presence as the blonde's bed disappeared into the darkness behind him.

The brunette's face appeared pained as the man lifted her once again, and they resumed their dance in center stage. Each time she tried to look into his eyes, he would look away in shame. She grabbed his face with both of her hands to force him to look at her, and he turned away from her. She threw herself into his back and hugged him with her arms and legs so that he carried her. The silent tears creeping down her cheeks were visible from the front row, and the man twisted, wrought, and lashed with his body to shake her free.

The brunette was thrown onto the floor, and the man turned to her and lashed at his shirt with his hands, causing it to tear and rip. His balled fist crashed into his chest as he beat his heart with punches, and as the brunette came to him once more, he tried to turn away. He looked over to where the blonde's bed hid in darkness, and the brunette grabbed his tie and forced him to look back at her. As their eyes finally met, his face was twisted into a mask of violent anger, and she stepped back from him in fear. He walked toward her and glared down at her frightened visage. She lowered herself onto the bed, almost cowering, but refused to let go of his tie as he tried to turn away from her. She pulled him toward her and planted a passionate kiss on his lips from her seat on the bed, and he recoiled from her in shock, gesturing at the tears in his shirt.

The male dancer leaped away from her once more, and as he tried to collect his briefcase from the base of the bed, he found himself unable to lift it. He roared in anger, his voice drowned out entirely, rendered impotent by the cresting music. Unable to lift the briefcase, he dragged it by the handle across the floor of the stage. As the brunette was shrouded in descending darkness once more, she lashed about in her bed and reached longingly after the man as he stumbled away from her.

The man, now exhausted, brought his briefcase to the base of the blonde's bed, and as the blonde stepped out of the bed to greet him, the audience let out a collective gasp. The original blonde woman had escaped from the stage when her bed was shrouded in darkness and was replaced by Hannah herself. Now dressed in a flowing white nightgown, she brought herself in front of the man. Kneeling next to the bed, his lowered chin rose only high enough for him to face her pregnant belly. He stroked it gently, and Hannah's hands found both sides of his face and forced him to stand and look at her. She placed a hand on his chest and walked him back to the center of the stage. Each time his face looked back at the briefcase, Hannah would redirect his attention to her eyes.

Once at center stage, the man became free of his anger, and the two danced intimately together, rarely taking their eyes off one another. Despite her size, Hannah sailed beautifully through the air, and her feet deftly supported her as she twirled and leaped around the man. Although his anger was lost to him, there was no joy in the dancing between Hannah and the man. While they looked longingly at one another, their shared sadness brought many in the audience to tears. For no matter how close they came, no matter how much momentum threw their bodies toward one another, they found themselves suddenly unable to touch. They moved as one, next to and around one another, but there was always something keeping them barely an inch from touching.

Suddenly, the dancing and the music stopped. The man stood looking down at Hannah with a single palm raised in front of him at chest level. She stood looking up at him with her palm held in front of his, only a hairsbreadth keeping their touch from meeting. In silence, the man walked toward Hannah, and she was forced to retreat toward her bed to prevent their palms from touching. She looked at their palms, still unable to touch, and with each step back, her features broke into increasing anguish. Her blue eyes glistened with tears, and her palm shook as she willed it not to let it touch his.

Her legs eventually crashed into the bed behind her, and she fell upon its covers. She sat up quickly and watched in mute agony as the man reached once again for his briefcase. Just as with the palms, the man's hand froze a mere inch from the handle of the briefcase as he struggled to make contact. Forcing his face once again into that resolute mask, he forced his hand down upon the handle, and gripped it with all of his strength. His painful cry was muted as the music came crashing back in a crescendo of pain and surrender. The torture and triumph of touching that briefcase and owning its weight were reflected in the symphony that raged around him.

And as he made contact with the briefcase, the light on both of the beds was raised in full, and the light on himself began to fade. Struggling under the weight of the briefcase, the man stumbled back toward the brunette's bed. He was slowly disappearing into the darkness as the spotlight on him faded, and each of the women reached out to him from their beds. As he reached center stage, each of the women leaped out of their beds and ran to him. The brunette grabbed at the briefcase, crying out silently as the handle made contact with her skin. Hannah reached for the man's quickly fading face to have him look at her. He was torn in both directions as he stood fading into the shadows. Finally, overcoming the struggle with her ability to make contact with him, Hannah touched both sides of his face gently and planted a sweet kiss on his lips as he finally faded into darkness, the softness of her touch juxtaposing the ferocity with which the brunette attempted to tear the briefcase from his grasp.

As the man disappeared completely, each of the women flew in the direction that they had been pulling the man and fell to the floor. The music stopped as they hit the ground, and each woman looked down at what they were left with—the brunette with the suitcase, and Hannah with the pregnant belly.

Hannah stood, covered her mouth, and stifled sobs as she made her way to the bed and sat simply rubbing her belly. The brunette rushed back to her bed with the briefcase and hurried with harried hands to unbuckle the clasps holding it shut. She opened the briefcase away from her so that its contents were visible only to her before looking up at the crowd in shock. Slowly, and with shaking hands, she lifted and turned the opened case to show the audience its contents.

It was empty.

The audience froze in captured silence, such that the slow creak of the pulleys lowering the closing curtain were heard throughout the entire venue.

Ashleigh stared at the brunette on stage clutching the empty briefcase. She had watched the final number with a pain in her stomach as her fear, her heartache, her infertility, and her husband's infidelity were imitated on stage to the world. As the curtain lowered and concealed the women on stage from view, the theater erupted into thunderous applause, and one by one the crowd was standing in ovation to the performance. Feeling heartbroken and betrayed by Hannah, Ashleigh stood up from her seat, stormed her way to the aisle, and left the theater.

Desmond, already standing with the rest of the applauding audience turned abruptly and called after her, but the clamor of applause drowned his voice. He had also watched the final number and had seen the arrangement between Hannah, his wife, and himself reflected back at him from the stage. Seeing the women tear him in different directions gave him, for the first time, real clarity as to how his role in all of this was breaking the two women to pieces. Watching from the front row, he had wanted to stand up, to scream about his own internal struggles, about the true weight of that briefcase, and about the losses that had come from the pregnancy. However, the realization that the struggles of Hannah and Ashleigh were bigger than his own had kept him seated.

Now, with Ashleigh storming out of her seat and leaving the darkened theater, he found himself pulled in different directions, just like his caricature on the stage. Should he follow his wife and try to console her? Or should he stay and await the formal conclusion of the performance before commencing his pursuit? Surely, more than one person leaving the front row immediately following the closing curtain would draw attention and cause a stir for the critics he knew would be nearby. Desmond didn't want to be seen as walking out on what was likely Hannah's biggest production yet, especially when this night was the only thing Hannah was getting out of the surrogacy.

His inner conflict was briefly disturbed as the curtain rose once more to reveal the show's cast standing in a line, including Hannah. The applause intensified into a boisterous cheer as the crowd celebrated Hannah, and her achievement. The acclaimed writer and choreographer gestured to her dancers and applauded with the rest of the theater. Despite the turmoil within himself, Desmond couldn't help but the notice the joy and pride beaming from Hannah's smile on the stage—her face looking luminescent in the stage light, her blue eyes sparkling. She turned finally to the cheering crowd and blew kisses to her audience. With her last, she met Desmond's gaze. She held his eyes a little longer after blowing the kiss to him, and he noticed she smiled just a little broader as she looked down at him.

As the curtain began to close between them, he couldn't help but smile back, and all thoughts of his wife left him for a brief moment.

As the stage curtain separated Desmond and Hannah, the lights came back on in the auditorium. Desmond's mind cleared, and he made his way through the crowd in search of Ashleigh, his stomach and head still spinning from the feelings he felt looking up at Hannah.

Behind the closed stage curtain, Hannah turned to her dancers and thanked them emphatically. She made her way to them one by one, hugging them and kissing many of them on the cheek. When she came to Jacqui, she held her longer than the others and whispered, "Merci," in her ear. The dancers laughed together, reveling in the success of their premier. They invited Hannah out for after-party drinks, reminding her that they, of course, wouldn't offer her anything but "mocktails".

Still euphoric from her performance and the minutes-long standing ovation her show had received, Hannah couldn't help but think that she only wanted to celebrate her evening with Desmond. She politely declined her dancers' invitations, but wished them a fun night as she turned to go to her private dressing room.

Hannah made her way to her private quarters on dancing feet. She hummed to herself as thoughts of the night danced through her mind, and she closed the door behind her to her private dressing room, not realizing that somebody was already inside the room, waiting for her.

Ashleigh stood in front of a large vanity mirror, illuminated by the tens of lit bulbs surrounding its reflective surface. She had used her VIP all-access pass to get into the room, and was surrounded by the flowers and congratulatory gifts that flooded the space.

Hannah turned around from the closed door, and let out a startled shriek as Ashleigh's presence surprised her. "Oh gosh, you scared me, Ash," she began, her heart racing in her chest.

Ashleigh didn't turn to face her. She continued to thumb the card attached to a large bouquet of roses as she read the inscription inside. "Did you know," she began, still looking away from Hannah, "that many of these gifts have absolutely nothing to do with your ballet at all?" She turned to face Hannah, and Hannah quickly registered the twisting scowl scarring her expression. "Many of them just congratulate you on the baby—*my* baby."

There was something in Ashleigh's bearing and tone that made Hannah feel scared, and she unconsciously rubbed her belly to comfort her child. The gesture only irritated Ashleigh more.

"What do you want, Ashleigh?" Hannah asked cautiously, making sure to keep close to the exit door.

"When we first met in your apartment, you told me that people often misinterpret your dances. You said that they see what they're unconsciously avoiding, but not your real message. I'm here because I want answers. What I saw on your stage tonight was the three of us—you, me, and Desmond. I saw the story of our arrangement—the agreement, your intimate nights with him, the pregnancy, the burdens it forced him to carry, and the rift it created between us. I watched my husband disappear on stage, just as I've had to watch him disappear from my marriage. Only, in your version, I saw how all of this ends—or at least how you'd like this to end. You get the baby, and I end up with nothing."

"That's one interpretation," answered Hannah.

"And what was with you kissing him at the end while I pulled on the briefcase? Why the hell would I be pulling on a bag full of issues while my husband fades away in front of me?"

"Indeed, why would you?" Hannah answered pointedly.

Ashleigh's scowl turned sinister. "And in the meantime, you're just struggling with the desire to touch and kiss him?" Ashleigh sighed in exasperation. "I came here because I want to know."

"Want to know what?" Hannah asked.

Ashleigh looked squarely at Hannah, and the two women's eyes locked. "I want to know who the 'two' are that you refer to in the name of your show. *I Love You Two.* A cute play on words. But who are the two, Hannah? Is it Desmond and the baby? Or maybe it's what you wish he'd say to you. That he loves you two—you and the baby? Which is it?"

Hannah broke away from Ashleigh's stern gaze as she looked around the room at the flowers and gifts. She had anticipated Ashleigh's reaction to the debut of her show, but had not expected to be alone and trapped when confronted by her. "I came up with the title to this show when the three of us first sat down and discussed the rules of the arrangement. I was second-guessing myself and wondering why I agreed to it at all. I had decided that inspiration for the show wasn't enough of a reason for me to go through with it, and I was going to pull out before we even started. But then I realized that the reason I agreed to all of this was because I loved you two—you and Desmond. I thought that my friend and his wife deserved the child they so desperately wanted, and so this surrogacy would be my gift to you. This show is about you and Desmond, and the experiences I've had because I love you two."

Ashleigh raised her brows, and her eyes widened in surprise. The sternness of her stare broke into something slightly softer as she spoke. "When I met you, everyone knew the effect you had on me, the hope you'd brought back into my life. But what no one ever saw, what I hid from *everyone*, was the fear you brought with it. No one else felt the weight of your steps as you walked back into Desmond's life like I did. No one else felt the effect that you had on my mind as you made me afraid that I would lose my child, my husband, and my happiness to you. And you have no idea what that persistent fear has done to me over these past months. Only I knew it. And I knew it well because I'd spend half of my morning thinking about what you'd be wearing. Wondering if it would have an effect on my marriage. I'd spend whole days thinking about you and trying not to hate the baby *growing* inside of you. And worst of all, I spent weeks wishing that I was you." Angry tears welled in Ashleigh's eyes. "In all of this, I have lost myself, and yet I am the only one who seems to care, or to have noticed all. You have no idea what it's like being alone in a marriage."

"And you have no idea what it's like," Hannah yelled, grabbing her pregnant belly with both hands, "being this full and yet feeling so empty! You want to talk about feeling alone? When the lights go out and this baby is born, will you still be there for me? Will you let Desmond? Will you still ask after me, and bother to see how I'm doing or come to visit? You see, through all of these months you've been preparing to be a mother, and I've been preparing to be alone! When all of this is done, a part of me is going to be missing, and I expect that I will lose my best friend and our baby at the same time."

"*My* baby," Ashleigh correct curtly.

"Your baby," Hannah conceded as she held back tears so that Ashleigh wouldn't see how her words cut through her. "I guess that once you're finished leasing out my uterus, you, your husband, and *your* baby will just leave me be? Do I really make it so easy for people to walk in and out of my life?"

378

Ashleigh's expression gave no remorse. In her eyes, before her stood the wedge that had been driven between her and her husband, the hammer that had been thrown against her marriage day after day since they'd met. "I am not a monster," Ashleigh began. "I know that giving away the baby will be difficult for you, and so I will come to you now and again so that you can see the child. But you will not see Desmond again. He will not be a part of your life. Understood?"

Hannah's sparkling blue eyes brimmed with tears as she whimpered back to Ashleigh, "Ashleigh, please don't take what you don't need from me."

Ashleigh strode angrily toward Hannah, and fearing for her safety, Hannah shied away. Ashleigh paused as she stood alongside a cowering Hannah. "I'm only taking back what's already mine," she spat, and she continued to the door, letting herself out and slamming it behind her.

Hannah stood alone, crying and rubbing her belly, and trying not to remember the way Desmond had looked at her from the front row as the closing curtain fell.

CHAPTER 26

ABSENCE

Several weeks had passed since the resoundingly successful premiere of *I Love You Two*. True to his word, Jack Katan's article, like all others, had been a simple, though well-written feature on Hannah, praising her latest production.

The premier was the only show in which Hannah would dance personally. The other performances simply featured a blonde dancer wearing a prosthetic pregnant belly and careful makeup to create the illusion of pregnancy. However, as the weeks passed, *I Love You Two* gained in popularity, and Hannah's celebrity swelled once more. Along with this celebrity came tabloid gossip. Some publications had erroneously referred to Ashleigh as Desmond's "ex-wife," and at least one tabloid had alleged that Hannah was Desmond's mistress who'd fallen pregnant during their secret escapades.

Every article, however, had featured the same photo of Hannah and Desmond smiling together on the red carpet. Desmond hadn't seen or heard from Hannah since her performance on stage at the premiere. She had mysteriously disappeared from the theater after the show, and no one had heard from her for weeks until fresh photographs emerged of her appearing at various hotspots around the country, the latest being a launch party in New York with an alleged celebrity date.

Desmond had tried to dismiss these articles as nothing more than tabloid gossip, but the accompanying photographs had made this difficult. The latest attention-grabbing headline, "I'm Keeping the Baby" had obviously caught Ashleigh's attention since she left the magazine on their kitchen counter for him to find. Desmond was still sleeping in their guest room, and things had become increasingly strained after he'd failed to timely follow Ashleigh out of the theatre.

At times, Ashleigh would seem affectionate, obviously trying to bring some normalcy to their marriage before the baby joined them. But at other times, she was cold, becoming disaffected again as memories of all the recent hurts came to the fore. That she had left the magazine out for him to find rather than discussing it with him directly showed him that she was once more in the latter mood.

Desmond climbed into his car on the way to another surrogacy support session. He dialed Hannah's number on his cell phone to see if she needed a ride. Just as it had for weeks, his call rang out, and he sat in mute silence as he listened to the robotic voice tell him that her voicemail was still full. The tabloid article sitting on his kitchen counter still resting on his conscience, Desmond tried calling the hotel where he knew Hannah had been staying in Baltimore.

"I'm sorry, sir. There is no one here under the name Lenore," a female staffer told him through the phone. "It's against hotel policy to share check-out dates ... No, I can't give an exact date ... No, not even if you say it's important ... Okay, okay! I can tell you that it's been a few weeks, but I can't say how many."

Desmond had hung up the phone in annoyance and continued driving as worried thoughts plagued him. Why had Hannah suddenly dropped out of communication after the show? Was she planning to keep the baby? Had she simply been using them for her show, and pulled away now that she'd got what she wanted from them? But then, why had she looked at him like that at the end of the show? And why had he been unable to stop thinking about it?

He arrived late to the group, and slipped quietly into the room from the familiar green-tiled hallway; the session was already underway. His arrival was less than subtle as he made his way to one of the two seats that had been conspicuously left vacant for himself and Hannah. Jen had been talking when he stepped into the room, and she continued in a quiet, subdued voice after he'd taken his seat.

"He's so strange now," she said, talking about her boyfriend. "He's possessive, jealous. Just the other week, we were at the mall looking at baby clothes, and he threatened the store clerk because he thought he was flirting with me. The clerk just asked if I needed help! It's gotten even worse since then. He won't let me eat certain things he thinks are bad for the baby; he won't let me go out to see people. I even had to sneak out just to come here tonight! I'm afraid. I'm feeling the way I used to feel with my ex, though now I'm more afraid because I worry what Jason might do to the baby. I told him that he and I could keep the baby and raise it ourselves, but I don't think that's what I want anymore. I want to stick to the original plan, and give the baby to my sister and her husband, but now I'm afraid to tell Jason. What if he flips out? What if he attacks me?"

Shaun leaned forward, a concerned expression on his face. "Jen, if you're afraid for your safety, you should go to the police. Do you have somewhere safe you can go tonight?"

Jen nodded her head slowly. "I could go to my sister's. The baby is due in a couple of weeks, and I could probably stay with her until it comes. But I'd have to grab a few things from his place first," Jen answered to the concerned expressions surrounding her. "He wasn't home when I left. I don't know where he is, but he hasn't been there all day. That's how I was able to come here."

"That's good," Shaun intoned empathetically. "I have to ask, has Jason harmed you in any way?"

Jen shook her head. "No. But I get scared he might. Sometimes he doesn't know what he's doing. He gets in these dark moods. It's like he's drunk, but he doesn't drink. He screams at me at the top of his lungs, and he berates himself for not reenlisting. It can go on for hours. It didn't used to be like this! I swear!"

Shaun got out of his seat and knelt in front of Jen. "Jen, I'd appreciate it if you could let me know when you get safely to your sister's place tonight. You have my cell number. Can you do that for me?"

As Jen finished speaking, each of the now heavily pregnant surrogates took their turn talking. His thoughts occupied, Desmond passed when it was his turn to speak. His eyes turned back and forth between Hannah's empty seat beside him and the empty doorway where he so often saw Todd waiting for him.

Neither Hannah nor Todd showed up that night, and he wondered if both of them were okay.

CHAPTER 27

TIME

Todd woke up in his bed in the early hours of the morning, gasping for air. His desperate need for oxygen made him wonder if his body had stopped breathing while he was asleep. His heart pounded, and each beat rocked his frail body. He rolled over in the darkness and peered through the delicate morning light at Katelynn lying asleep next to him. His lips curved into a small smile as he looked upon her serene, relaxed features. Her arm reached limply toward him upon the bed.

They had welcomed the arrival of their daughter just a week earlier, and Katelynn had instantly taken to her new role as a mother. She had spent every waking moment lavishing love and attention on her daughter and husband, making the most of the brief time that the three of them would share the same world.

He watched as Katelynn's chest rose and relaxed with each slow breath, and he smiled to himself once more as the slightest grin crept across his sleeping wife's lips. His heart still pounded heavily in his chest, and his need to make conscious breaths never left him. The weakness of his body and his dry mouth told him that he should wake her, but how could he disturb her peacefulness only to tell her it was time? He lifted himself from the bed on shaking arms and stood up on legs he wasn't sure would support his meager weight.

As he made his way slowly out of the dimly-lit bedroom, he looked over his shoulder to take one final glimpse of his love. He used the wall to support himself as he unsteadily made his way to his daughter's bedroom. When they had tried to leave the hospital after Katelynn had the baby, the hospital staff had held them up as they attempted to make their way through the front exit. Given his deathly appearance, the hospital had mistaken him for a patient, and stopped them briefly to make sure he wasn't trying to discharge himself.

Todd had answered their furious apologies without looking up from his baby girl, who he carried in his arms. As he stepped out of the hospital, a mechanical voice sounded from the automatic door. "Thank you for visiting the Columbia Gateway Kaiser Center. We hope to see you again soon."

No, Todd had thought to himself as fresh daylight crossed his little girl's face for the first time. *No more hospitals.*

Todd rounded the corner of the hallway and entered his daughter's nursery. His daughter lay awake, fidgeting in her crib. Above her, the name Katrina was stenciled on the pale blue wall, accompanied by a photo of the three of them. Todd moved over to the crib, and Katrina's eyes found his. She stopped fidgeting and settled as his face peered over the wall of her caged confines. She didn't seem to mind his sickly appearance. Maybe it was because she didn't know that wasn't what people were supposed to look like, or maybe it was because she recognized her father, and that was enough.

"Hey, beautiful," he stammered, as much from being overwhelmed by emotion as the sickness of his body. He reached down, and picked up the tiny figure. Holding her warmth against his chest, he moved carefully over to the large, yellow chair they'd placed in the corner so that Katelynn could nurse in comfort. He leaned his tired bones back into the deep chair and held Katrina close to him as he rubbed her back soothingly. Her scent filled his senses, and he wondered if his body smelled of death and decay to her in the same way she smelled of youth and life to him.

"You know," he began, talking to Katrina as she hugged into his chest, "the doctors always told me not to apologize for being sick or for dying. They said it's not my fault, and so I have nothing to apologize for. But I am sorry, sweetheart—not for being sick, but for all the moments I'm not going to be there for you. I won't be there when you scrape your knee, or when you first learn to ride a bike. Your first day of school. I'm not going to be there when you call in the middle of the night, and ask me to pick you up because you've been out drinking with your friends—and make me promise not to tell your mother. I'm sorry for all the moments I'm going to miss. But most of all, I'm sorry that you're going to spend your whole life not feeling the love I have for you."

Katrina let out a gurgling sound and kicked spasmodically against his abdomen, causing him to chuckle.

"You don't have to think about being alive. Even now, when you have no idea how your body works, your body just does it. However, for the past few months, I've had to force mine to keep me alive...to keep the engine running, and force it into overtime. I never had to think about *living* while I was healthy. But my body stopped keeping me alive on its own a long time ago.

"I've kept it running by force of will, just so that I could meet you and hold you like this. But sweetheart, I'm tired. I'm tired of keeping myself alive, of trying not to die in my sleep, and I don't have it in me to keep going anymore. I fought to make sure that I got to meet you, honey, and I did that. Now it's time for daddy to finally go to sleep."

Holding Katrina close, he stood from the chair and made his way back to the crib. She whimpered softly as he lowered her gently back onto the cushioned mattress, and looked up at him with glistening eyes as he spoke to her. "I want you to know that wherever I'm about to go, that I love you, that I'm thinking about you all the time, and that I am so proud of you. From the moment I found out about you, Katrina, yours was the name that was written on my heart, and it always will be."

A few hours later, Katelynn woke to Katrina's pitiful cries from the nursery. She squinted from the lines of bright morning light that filtered in through the bedroom blinds as she slowly came awake. Not finding him next to her, she looked around the room groggily for Todd. Coming more fully awake, she stretched in the bed. *That's weird*, she thought to herself. *Normally Katrina settles when Todd's with her.*

"Todd?" she called out, as she stood up from the bed. She grabbed her robe from the floor and gathered it around her as she stepped barefoot through the house, Katrina's cries getting louder as she approached the nursery.

As she turned into the nursery, her heart sank, and all breath left her body in a single, gut-wrenching gasp. "No!" she wailed as she collapsed to her knees and brought her hands to her face. Her bawling tears hit the carpet as Katrina's cries bounced off the walls around her.

Todd's lifeless body sat slumped in the chair, still clutching the photo of his family he'd taken from the wall.

CHAPTER 28

DUST TO DUST

K atelynn sobbed uncontrollably as Todd's coffin was lowered into the ground. The gentle rain tapped rhythmically on the wooden box, and left brown puddles on the bottom of the grave. The service had been a large and miserable one. Desmond had attended alone, as Ashleigh had never met or spoken with Todd, and he had been unable to get a hold of Hannah to share the news of Todd's passing.

Hannah had also been absent from every surrogacy support session since the premiere of her show weeks earlier. Desmond had been surprised at the number of guests mourning Todd's death, though only because he had never given much thought as to whether Todd had many friendships outside of their own. However, after seeing family and friends gathered in mourning and hearing their stories about his friend, it came as no surprise that so many people would come together to mourn the loss of such a genuine, and good-natured family man.

Desmond had also never given any thought as to what Todd looked like before his sickness had set in. When he had first arrived at the service, he had briefly wondered whether he had come to the wrong funeral. The photograph beside the raised casket depicted a youthful man with dark, curly hair, a short beard, and shining blue eyes. If anything, Todd had looked downright boyish in his good health. When at last Desmond realized that photo belonged to his friend, the tears had set in, and he was grateful for the cover of the light rain.

During the service, Katelynn had handed her newborn daughter to her mother and attempted to address the congregation. At the first mention of her husband's name, however, she was quickly overcome with grief and lost the ability to speak, collapsing into the waiting arms of her similarly grief-stricken father. When the service concluded, the gathered guests had stood and made ready to depart. It was then that Katelynn first spotted Desmond.

"You!" she yelled as she strode angrily toward Desmond's aisle seat. She came to stand in front of him, and her hands lashed out angrily as she pounded on his chest with balled fists. Her voice was hysterical as she screamed and landed blow after blow against his body. "It's because of you! He was always helping you—talking about *your* problems, *your* feelings, *your* family! He should have been spending time making a recording for his daughter...for his baby girl! Do you understand what you've done? My daughter will never know her father's voice! She won't know the way he looked at her! I keep writing down everything I can remember about him—every nuanced detail that comes to my mind before I forget it. But nothing compares to that recording, to her just *knowing* him! You robbed my daughter of that. You *stole* her father from her! Damn you, Desmond! I will never forgive you."

Desmond stood defenseless, willingly receiving the abuse, as Katelynn beat him with her hands and her words. "I promised him," he muttered inaudibly to himself.

His whispered unheard, Katelynn continued to languish in front of him. "Get out of here!" she screamed. The arm she raised to strike Desmond once more was grabbed by her father, and he embraced her tightly and began to lead her back toward the grave. "Get out!" she screamed once more, and a fresh tide of hopeless tears overwhelmed her once more.

Some guests near Desmond moved toward him from their seats and began to usher him to leave. "I promised him!"

Desmond called out to Katelynn as an entourage of family surrounded and consoled her, and he repeated the words once more to himself, inaudibly, as he turned and complied with the multiplying guests readying to escort him away by force.

As Desmond sadly walked away from the black-clad gathering and Katelynn's wailing cries, he noticed another figure watching the service from afar. Once spotted, the figure quickly turned away from him, revealing her long blonde hair and an enormously pregnant belly.

Hannah.

She was already striding rapidly away from him, toward a black vehicle waiting for her on the outskirts of the cemetery. He gave chase to her, calling out her name from afar as he cut a path between the headstones. She heard his calls, but continued to press her way quickly to the waiting car, her golden curls bobbing as she rushed.

Desmond caught her just before she reached the end of the cemetery, and he grabbed her hand to have her turn and face him. "Hannah! Hannah?"

She finally turned around to look at him, but pulled her hand free of his. "What do you want, Des?" she yelled in exasperation.

He stepped back from her, confused. "Han, where have you been? You haven't called. I can't get a hold of you. The hotel tells me you checked out weeks ago, and the papers are telling me you're all over the country, dating and partying. What's going on?"

Hannah scowled at him, angry that he would demand her attention, and that she couldn't bring herself to refuse him.

"Leave me alone, Desmond. Please." She turned away from him once more and took a step toward her waiting car.

Still confused, Desmond shook his head and quickly rounded on her so that he stood in front of her. The intensifying rain continued to fall upon them, matting their hair and giving them both a glistening, but disheveled look. "Hannah, for how long have we been friends? Since when have you not been able to tell me something, to share something with me? For goodness sake, you're carrying our *baby*! Talk to me, please! Just tell me what's going on!" Desmond begged, his voice rising to overcome the lifting breeze.

Hannah looked up at him, and her eyes glistened from welling tears. "Desmond. Please ... don't," she pleaded. He stood looking down at her, waiting. She looked away, a pained expression crossing her face as she fought to find the words. "Why did it never happen between us, Desmond?" she called back, the rainfall masking her tears. "All those feelings you had for me—where did they go?"

Desmond's face creased, a blend of confusion and hurt overcoming his bearing. "You know what happened, Hannah. You never felt the same way."

Hannah threw out an angry hand as she spoke, "How could I? My life was just starting. This person you had feelings for, even I didn't know who she was! I wasn't like you. I didn't know who I was, or what I wanted so early on. I needed to get out. To get away and figure that out for myself. I wasn't ready for the immensity of your affection. I wasn't ready for your feelings. For *this*," she gestured wildly at her belly, "until it was too late."

"What are you saying?" Desmond begged.

Hannah's face tightened. Angry tears escaped from the corners of her eyes and were obvious even amid the pouring rain. She hesitated.

"Tell me!" Desmond shouted.

Hannah looked up at him and into his eyes. "I love you, Desmond!" the words left her lips like a betrayal, and her breath came in heaves. "I know I'm not supposed to, that I found love where it doesn't belong. I *hate* myself for saying it, but I do—I love you, even if I don't want to. And so, I stay on a high. I stay busy, and distract myself to keep you off my mind. I go out. I go to these *awful* celebrity events where everyone is pretending to be happy. Because when the lights go down and the quiet settles in, *that's* when I realize that you're gone, that I've lost you, and there's nothing I can do. And I don't know what's worse…That I could have had you, or that I have a constant reminder of you and what could have been *ours* growing inside of me. I've been trying not to think about you, Des—trying to stay away from you, and ignore the way you make my heart break every day. I didn't even want to tell you this. I promised myself that I wouldn't! Why couldn't you have just let me be? Why couldn't you have just left me alone?"

Desmond stared, wide-eyed, at the woman in front of him. Water beads steadily dropped from the end of her matted curls onto the wet ground beneath her feet. She had told him the words he had spent a decade wishing to hear.

"You don't get to say that to me!" he yelled over the wind and rain. "You had me *praying* that you and I would end up together. I spent *years* longing for you, waiting for you to come back from your adventures. But you never wanted me. Love me? You don't love me, Hannah! You never loved me. All I ever was to you was the ticket to your next adventure—"

"You idiot!" Hannah cried, her arms wrapped around herself as much in comfort as to ward against the freezing cold. "You were never the beginning of my adventures…You were where all of my adventures ended! Every one of my adventures led me back to you! Back to the only place or person that ever felt like home. I'd come to you, hoping that you'd finally realized that you didn't want me to leave, that I was *your* home too. I hoped that you'd finally become the man that says, 'Don't go. Stay with me.' And when you didn't, I went back out to try and find a home somewhere else, but something always led me back to you. The counselor said that the heart only has room for one. *You* were my one, Desmond.

You always have been. You were just too stupid to notice, and so I was never yours."

Angry, painful tears welled up in Desmond's eyes, and his face contorted as he growled over the howl of the wind. "Blame it on hormones, Hannah, blame it on nostalgia. Hell, blame it on regret for all I care. But don't you dare tell me that you love me when you know it's too late. Don't tell me that I'm your 'one' when you know that I'm promised to someone else!" Desmond stormed away without waiting for her response or reaction, leaving Hannah to cry alone in the freezing rain.

Soaking wet, he climbed into his car and beat on the steering wheel with balled fists within frozen gloves. Alone, within the confines of his vehicle, he screamed, unsure whether he had said those rebuking words because he meant them, or because his duty as a husband demanded it. He drove home in silence, unsure of what he was going to say to his wife, and honestly uncertain if he was driving toward the woman he loved, or away from her.

CHAPTER 29

DELIVERY

T he rain had turned to a wintry mix of sleet and snow by the time Desmond arrived home from the cemetery. The drive had not resolved the conflict within himself, and he still had no idea of how to tell Ashleigh what Hannah had confessed to him, or how he would answer the questions he knew would follow.

He stepped into their house and heard rushed footsteps and banging coming from upstairs. Hurrying up to Ashleigh's bedroom with leaden steps, he found her quickly shoving something into a duffle bag, and he wondered if she was already packing a bag to leave him. Ashleigh looked up at him with eyes filled with terror. "Where have you been? I've tried to call you a hundred times!"

"What is it?" Desmond asked, patting himself down and looking for his phone.

"Something's happened," Ashleigh said as she continued stuffing things into her bag. "It's Hannah. She's in the hospital. The baby is coming now!"

Desmond learned on his way to the hospital that Hannah had gone into labor after visiting the cemetery. Her driver had rerouted to Johns Hopkins Hospital, and the hospital had prepped their on-call obstetrician for the unscheduled delivery while she was en route.

Hannah wasn't due for another four weeks.

"It must have been the funeral," Ashleigh offered as she rode alongside Desmond in the car on the way to the hospital. "Extreme emotional distress in the late stages of pregnancy can trigger early labor." Desmond didn't respond. He wondered in silence whether he had caused the early labor by forcing Hannah to confess her feelings for him, only to reject her.

Ashleigh dropped Desmond off at the hospital entrance while she parked their car, and he rushed through the hospital ahead of her. He was prepped to enter the delivery room before she had caught up with him. Hannah looked up at Desmond with concern in her eyes as he pushed his way into the delivery room.

"It's too soon," she said in a weak and quivering voice. "It's too soon." No sooner had the words left her lips when Hannah let out a deep cry as another sudden and intense contraction struck her. Desmond rushed forward to take her hand into his, and she gripped it tightly. Desmond stroked Hannah's face and moved a sweat-soaked strand of hair from her eyes.

"I'm so sorry," he began, but another deep and painful cry from Hannah cut his voice.

"Okay! Who's ready to have a baby?" the obstetrician said cheerfully as he entered the room. Hannah let out another powerful cry in answer as he lowered himself into position between the stirrups.

"Hannah," the obstetrician began after a brief inspection, "You're fully dilated, and so it's time to start pushing. Are you ready to meet your baby?"

Hannah breathed heavily, a mixture of pain and fear causing her breathing to shake. She swallowed hard as she looked up at Desmond.

"Don't let go." She squeezed his hand tightly, and her cries filled the room as she made the first push.

Several excruciating minutes later, Hannah was whimpering from the pain. Tears flowed freely down her red face twisted into a mask of pain and shock. She almost broke into pitiful sobs. With the last push she had given, she had felt something inside of her crack, like her body and soul had simultaneously fractured down the middle.

She could tell that something was wrong.

"One more big push!" the doctor called from between the stirrups.

Hannah shook her head. "Something's wrong," she whimpered. "There's so much pressure. Even between the contractions." She screamed again as pain wracked her body. The pressure inside of her was intensifying, and she feared for the safety of her daughter squeezing between her legs.

The expression on the obstetrician's face shifted, and his cheerful manner broke as he snapped his fingers and muttered something to the lone nurse who rushed to his side. The nurse hurried to the phone on the wall beside the door.

"They're not contractions," Desmond heard her say in a hushed voice. Hannah screamed in anguish as another doctor came rushing into the room.

"Ms. Lenore," the obstetrician began as the second doctor pressed softly on Hannah's abdomen, eliciting another painful cry, "We're going to start prepping you for an emergency C-section. We're concerned that the pressure building in your abdomen may cause a uterine rupture. We need you to stop pushing."

All color drained from Desmond's face at the mention of a uterine rupture. His work in medical negligence had taught him that a uterine tear could cause the baby to slip out of the birthing canal and into Hannah's abdomen, suffocating the baby and causing Hannah to hemorrhage.

Hannah wanted nothing more than to break down into terrified sobs, but she could feel the small body between her legs and knew that she had to stay strong for just a few moments longer. Her face reflected shock and pain, and she looked back at Desmond, terrified.

"Is it bad?" Hannah begged as she tugged on his hand.

He lowered himself so that their faces were level, and inches apart. "It's serious," he offered in a placating tone. "But if they get the baby out quickly and relieve the pressure, then you'll both be fine," he said with tears in his eyes. "You can do this, Hannah. I know you can. There's nothing you can't do."

She squeezed Desmond's hand tightly once more and braced herself against another burst of pain that washed through her body. However, just as the doctors and nurse prepared to move her to the surgery room, she found herself feeling weak and light.

Suddenly lacking the strength even to speak, her head lolled to one side, and she met Desmond's terror-filled eyes. "Hannah!" he screamed, and he dropped to his knees beside her. Hannah's eyes rolled into the back of her head, and her vision went black. As her consciousness slipped away, she barely registered the doctor's frantic words. "The baby's retracting. The uterine wall is breached! We're losing both of them!"

• • •

Hannah's consciousness stirred among the blackness. Far off in the distance, she could hear the metronome of a heart monitor, its beeps weak and far between. A blur of light and color greeted her as her eyes slowly opened. She was in a recovery room. Desmond was sitting beside her. His hand was clutching hers, and he cried freely into the blanket over her lap.

"Des?" she said weakly as her vision came slowly into focus. She felt cold and fragile, even though she couldn't feel the rest of her body. "The baby," she whispered. "What happened to the baby?"

Desmond sat up quickly, his swollen and bloodshot eyes meeting hers. His lip quivered as he readied to speak, but a doctor stepped forward to her other side and answered for him. "Ms. Lenore," he began somberly, "you suffered a complete uterine rupture. The baby slipped into your abdomen and started to suffocate."

Solitary tears began to streak their way from the corners of Hannah's eyes and down her cheeks. The doctor continued, "We performed an emergency laparotomy—it's a large incision through the abdominal wall to gain access to the abdominal cavity."

"What about the baby?" Hannah interrupted in a whisper, each word requiring a great deal of effort.

The doctor sighed heavily and tried to maintain his composure. "She made it. She's alive," he answered, and Desmond's sobs redoubled. Hannah's tears joined Desmond's as relief swept through her numbed body.

"Then, why are you crying?" she asked Desmond through her tears.

The doctor answered once more, his voice low. "The rupture was bad," he answered in a shaky voice. "We got the baby out, but we had to perform a hysterectomy and remove your uterus."

Hannah looked at the ceiling as the realization that she wouldn't ever be able to have another baby hit her. The revelation should have crushed her, but she found herself detached from the news as it crept through her physical and emotional numbness.

"That's not all," the doctor stammered, now clearly struggling to continue. Hannah looked back at Desmond's wet and bloodshot eyes as she listened. "Even with a transfusion, we couldn't stop the bleeding." Desmond's grip on her hand tightened. "We've tried to make you as comfortable as possible, Ms. Lenore, but it's just a matter of time."

"I'm dying?" Hannah asked weakly. Although numb and cold, she felt fine. How could dying feel so painless?

Desmond nodded and wiped at his face with his shoulder.

"Can I see her?" Hannah asked faintly, noting that neither her daughter nor Ashleigh was in the ward with them. She suddenly felt nauseous, and her vision blurred. She struggled to maintain consciousness.

Desmond answered through his tears, "The doctors are with her now in the neonatal intensive care unit. Ashleigh is with them, and they're trying to make sure the baby's stable enough to come here to see you. She's beautiful Hannah, just like you. Just hold on."

"How long do I have?" Hannah whispered to the doctor. Her initial disbelief was quickly receding as she felt her remaining strength slipping away.

"Not long, I'm afraid. It's a miracle you regained consciousness at all." The doctor turned away to join the nurse, adjusting something outside her field of vision.

Turning to Desmond, Hannah bit her lip. Seeing the man she loved so grief-stricken broke her heart. "Speak to me, Desmond. Just ... talk to me until she gets here."

Desmond looked deeply into Hannah's blue eyes. Despite her condition, her sapphire eyes shined brightly. Desmond's breaths shook as his heart searched for the right words. "What can I say?" he offered. "What am I supposed to say to the woman that I love ... to the woman that I have loved every time she slipped away from me, at the moment that she's slipping away forever?"

Hannah's eyes widened slightly at the unexpected confession as he continued. "Being married, I could never admit to myself how I felt about you. But the truth is, each time you came to visit me before you left on your next adventure, I wanted to tell you—to tell you that I loved you, and to beg you to stay with me."

"Why didn't you?" Hannah asked, her voice beginning to fail.

"Because I was afraid you'd stay," Desmond choked. "I was afraid that you would stay, and that a life with me would never be enough of an adventure for you."

"I wish you'd told me," Hannah responded, smiling softly as fresh tears rolled down her pale cheeks.

Desmond could sense her body was failing. He looked to the empty doorway in the hope that the doctors would appear with their daughter in their arms. "Where are they?" he screamed impotently.

No longer constrained by impropriety, Hannah pulled her hand free from Desmond's tight grasp and reached up to touch his face. She turned his face so that he looked at her, and his fresh tears wet the skin of her hand. She stroked his cheek lovingly with her thumb. "Oh, Desmond," she began, "Ever since I came back into your life you've had so many reasons to be sad and broken. Infertility, Poe, Todd. I'm so sorry that I'm going to be another reason for your grief. Promise me that our daughter will know the happy version of you. The boy I knew back in school, and the man with whom I spent that magical night that gave us our girl. She deserves to know that part of you, Desmond."

Still crying, Desmond leaned in past Hannah's hand and kissed her softly on her bluing lips. The sweet succor of his kiss brought a final measure of warmth to her cold body, and she cried as the man she loved was finally hers. She could feel herself fading into the darkness, and she whispered to Desmond as his lips parted from hers, and his face hovered inches above her own.

"Don't go," Desmond whimpered. "Stay with me."

Hannah's lips curved into a weak smile. "Don't cry for me, Desmond. This is just the start of another adventure. I've always loved adventures." Hannah's eyes slowly folded closed, and her final adventure began as she slipped into the darkness.

Overcome with grief, Desmond sobbed into Hannah's chest. "I love you, Hannah. I love you too." He whimpered the words he had been too scared and too unsure to say sooner.

His heartbroken confession was interrupted by a voice behind him. "Did you mean it?" Ashleigh asked from the doorway. She stood, holding his newborn daughter, with tears in her eyes. He turned, still holding Hannah's limp hand in his own.

"Did you mean what you said, or were you just comforting her?" Ashleigh asked again.

Desmond turned back to Hannah and looked longingly at her peaceful face framed by her trademark blonde curls. "Every word," he confessed in a whisper.

Ashleigh's tears broke free as she nodded in understanding. She looked down at the baby cradled in her arms, and made her way over to her husband. "You have a beautiful daughter, Desmond. She looks just like her mother."

Ashleigh relinquished the small infant to Desmond, and he took his daughter into his arms. Standing next to him, she looked at the baby in his arms and Hannah's body on the bed.

"I'm so sorry," she offered as she began to make her way out of the room. "You would have made a beautiful family."

CHAPTER 30

TINY DANCER

Three years later...

D esmond strode through the New York cemetery and
bundled his coat around him to guard against the wind.
He absent-mindedly rubbed the spot on his finger where his
wedding ring used to rest, and the bouquet of orchids he
carried brushed against him. He smiled to himself as blonde
locks appeared and disappeared behind nearby headstones as his
little girl skipped and danced ahead of him.

Ashleigh had left him shortly after Hannah's passing,
having found herself unwilling to compete with the memory of
the woman Desmond had always loved, and unable to raise
Hannah's daughter as her own. They had parted ways amicably
enough, but neither had spoken to the other in the years since
their divorce.

After returning from a sabbatical, Desmond's law firm had
voted unanimously to make him a partner. They had been
impressed with his "victory" in the Poe case. On the same day,
Desmond had tendered his resignation, and he hadn't practiced
law since. Instead, he had assumed the role of executor of
Hannah's estate, managing her affairs since her passing.

I Love You Two had been a huge success from the first
night that Hannah had stepped onto the stage. After news of
her tragic passing spread, people had flocked to the theater to
see what was truly Hannah Lenore's last show. Her New York

production continued its run to this day, and with Jacqui taking on the role as head instructor, other productions of Hannah's shows had begun to tour the world.

Desmond continued walking through the cemetery until he came to Hannah's grave. As he had done countless times before in the years since her passing, he laid her favorite flowers on her grave, and knelt to touch the white granite headstone. He read the inscription: *Here lies Hannah Lenore, who found many ways to love.*

He stood and looked over the headstones to make sure that his daughter was still close by. He had put her in ballet classes from the time that she could walk so that she could be a dancer, just like her mother. His little girl practiced her steps on the grass near him.

"I received a letter from Katan," Desmond said out loud as he talked to Hannah. "Well, not a letter—more of a card. I don't know if you remember, but his cameraman took a photo of us on the night of your premiere. He mailed me a copy of that photo. The card it came with said, 'For your daughter.' Katan is still an ass, but I have to be thankful for that photo. I don't think I ever saw you as happy as you were on that night. You were incredible that night, Hannah. You were always incredible."

He looked over at his daughter and smiled. A butterfly had distracted her from her dancing, and she giggled as she chased and jumped after it. "She's so much like you," he continued. "A dancer, of course, but also in other ways. She has your playfulness and spirit. She's always running around looking for adventure, even in the smallest corners of her world. It's hard to keep an eye on her sometimes. Her hair has started to curl too, and she has your eyes. She reminds me of you more and more every day."

Tears started to well up in his eyes as he remembered the woman he loved, and he choked on his next words to her.

"In a better world, where love might have overcome ambition or chance … or my mistakes, you and I would be together, and she would be our child. At least in her, I get to keep a part of that world…a part of you, and a part of the 'us' that might have been. Until we meet again, I will ache every time I hear your name. I love you, Hannah."

"I love you too, Daddy," his daughter's voice called sweetly from his side. Desmond smiled to himself, and he quickly wiped away his tears with his hand. His daughter slipped her small hand into his.

"Come on, Hannah," he said with a smile as he looked down at his little girl. "Let's go home."

Epilogue

On My Way

The man smiled into his car's rearview mirror as he watched his daughter moving in her child restraint seat in time with the music from the radio. As they continued driving toward Columbia, the music died, and a quick news bulletin cut in. The man changed the station, trying to find some more music for his little girl to dance to.

"Where are we going, Daddy?" the little girl asked from the back seat.

"We're just going to deliver a package for an old friend, sweetie, and then we're going home. Okay?"

"Okay," the girl's voice came back sullenly.

The man pulled into a driveway and parked the car. He walked quickly to the trunk of his car, removed a large cardboard box, and placed it on the porch, in front of the door. He rang the doorbell once and hurried back to his car before anyone could answer.

Katelynn answered the door with Katrina in her arms. She spotted the cardboard box on the ground, and thought nothing of the black sedan driving down her street and away from her. "What's that?" she said playfully to Katrina.

"A box!" her daughter replied excitedly in a high-pitched voice.

"That's right!" Katelynn answered, matching Katrina's enthusiasm.

She crouched down and managed to hug the box without releasing Katrina. Katelynn closed the front door with her foot, and carried the package to her living room. She put Katrina down on the couch, and the little girl climbed over to the armrest to watch her mother open the box. "What's in h—" Katelynn began to ask, but she stopped short as she opened the box and saw her husband's handwriting on a DVD case.

She lifted the plastic case out of the box and examined it more closely. The case read simply: *Dear Katie.* Todd was the only one who ever called her by that name. She opened the case and found a DVD inside, his familiar handwriting once again scrawled onto the disk. *Play me first.*

With shaking hands, she rushed over to the nearby entertainment suite, turned on the television, and put the disk into the DVD player. She walked back to sit on the couch without taking her eyes off the screen. "Oh," she sputtered as a smiling Todd appeared on the screen.

Is it on? He asked of whoever was behind the camera. *It is on? No, it isn't. There's a blinking red light. Oh, that means it's recording? Whoops.* On camera, Todd sat down.

Katie. My beautiful Katie. You kept bugging me for a recording. I was afraid I couldn't condense a lifetime of fatherhood into one recording, and so I kept waiting for the right words to come to me. I realized in the end that it doesn't have to be just one recording. However, I wanted our time together to be as happy as it could be—as happy as it always has been for me—so I couldn't have you helping me with the recordings. Instead, I asked a friend to help me with the recordings, and I made him promise me that he wouldn't tell you about them or deliver them to you for three years, no matter what.

I wanted to give you time to learn to be without me, to focus on our baby, and if need be, to move on with someone else. When I was growing up, I was always told not to idealize or romanticize my expectations of love because no poor human could ever meet the vision that a man built up in his mind when he dreamed of his wife. Katie, I dreamed about marrying a woman like you my whole life, and yet you are so perfect that you exceeded even my wildest expectations of what love could be. Even in our darkest times, your love was always so bright. I will always love you, Katie.

Silent tears slipped down Katelynn's cheeks as she whispered, "I love you," back to her husband.

Now, Todd continued, wiping away his own tears, I have to speak to our little girl—and this should all be that much easier because we finally agreed on a name!

Katelynn's lip quivered uncontrollably as she watched her husband on the screen.

Katrina! Todd continued, his tone brightening. Katrina, sweetheart.

Katelynn grabbed her daughter's attention and pointed at the television screen. "Look, honey, daddy's talking to you!" The little girl's head turned quickly to the screen, her face a mixture of excitement and shock.

Sweetheart, it breaks my heart every time I think of you. Gosh, I hope I made it long enough to get to meet you. Katrina baby, you don't have to go through your life without me. Every time something big happens in your life, I'm on my way. On your first day of school, I'm on my way. When a boy breaks your heart, on your first day of college, on your wedding day, all of it, Daddy's on his way.

Katrina turned to her mom while the video continued to play out on the screen. "What's he mean, Mommy? What's 'on his way'?"

Katelynn dabbed her eyes again with a tissue she'd grabbed from a side table, only to have the wiped away tears quickly replaced with fresh ones. She pulled the open cardboard box onto the couch with the two of them, and peered inside.

Inside were dozens of DVD cases marked with different life events. *Your first day of school*; *When you want me to read you a story*; *When you get your driver's license*; *College graduation*; *Your wedding day*. All of them were scrawled in Todd's handwriting. Katelynn looked back at the screen as her husband talked to her across time.

Katelynn, honey, at the bottom of the box there are a few recordings for you as well, including one for right after this one because I know you well enough to know you'll want more as soon as this video is over.

Todd laughed on the screen, and Katelynn broke down crying as she realized both she and her daughter had the sound of her husband's laugh immortalized on the recording.

I know these recordings don't make up for all the times I won't be there for my girls, but I hope that they help you both get through the toughest times. I love you girls. I always have, and I always will.

Okay, Desmond, you can stop recording this one. No, it's the red button. The other red button. But the light is still blink—

ABOUT THE AUTHOR

Born in Australia, Lynden Renwick is an attorney in his home country, and in the United States. The middle of five children, he was a practicing litigation attorney in Sydney, Australia, when he met Katrina. After six months of dating, Lynden quit his practice, sold his house, and followed her back to the United States. He is now married to Katrina, living in Maryland, and practicing law in Annapolis. 'A PART OF YOU' is his first novel.

www.ingramcontent.com/pod-product-compliance
Lightning Source LLC
Chambersburg PA
CBHW020241110726
47898CB00004B/1343